PRAISE FOR *SACKED*

"Ellie and Knox's bantering was exceptional. From their very first meeting, they were trading barbs and bouncing cheekiness off of each other. This is the kind of sexy/playful combination I'm always searching for and hardly ever find."

—Christie from *SHBB Blogger*

"Sacked is brilliantly written and perfectly titled. Could not put it down!"

— *The Rockstars of Romance*

Sacked is a fun filled, sexy, humorous romance that follows a couple's journey from friendship to love. Facilitated by witty banter, delicious sexual tension, and strong friendships, Frederick's takes an all too common trope, adds a few twists, and infuses it with new life. Fans of Elle Kennedy, Sarina Bowen, and Kristen Callahan are sure to fall in love with Frederick's newest NA offering.

—Tori from ***SmexyBooks***

"...one of Frederick's best releases yet. Prepare to be hit with all of the feels and love every minute of it."

—Rowena from *The BookBinge*

PRAISE FOR *LOSING CONTROL*

"...very fast paced—fantastic main characters..."
—Book Angel Emma

"Frederick weaves a strong tale about love, loss, hope and letting go of the past in order to build a future. She brings two lost souls together who have more in common than either of them realized and it will have your heart in flutters. The sincerity in this book is genuine; your heart will break for these characters; you will cry for them, love them and hope for them."
—JC at *All Is Read*

"*Losing Control* is one HUGE SURPRISE! I absolutely loved it!"
—Lorie Economos at *The To Be Read List*

"*Losing Control* has one of MY favorite things... a nice slow burn. These two didn't just jump into bed together, nope they let that chemistry build and build and build until they came together in flames of glory! The only thing I wish that Losing Control had was... MORE! I need more!!!"
—Nicole from Goodreads

PRAISE FOR
THE CHARLOTTE CHRONICLES

"This was a great start to a new series and is without a doubt going on my favorites list and my re-read shelf…Ican't wait to read the next book in the series because I'm already on edge about it."

—Melissa at *SM Book Obsessions*

"*Last Hit* by Jessica Clare and Jen Frederick will forever hold a special place in my heart because quite honestly, I can't remember the last time I gave a book a perfect 5 star rating. While I was sad to see Daisy and Nikolai's story come to an end, I walked away feeling satisfied."

—Mia at *The Muses Circle*

Titles by Jen Frederick

The Woodlands

UNDECLARED

UNSPOKEN

UNRAVELED

UNREQUITED

THE CHARLOTTE CHRONICLES

Kerr Chronicles

LOSING CONTROL

TAKING CONTROL

REVEALED TO HIM

Hitman Series
(with Jessica Clare)

LAST HIT

LAST BREATH

LAST KISS

LAST HOPE

SACKED

A GRIDIRON NOVEL

JEN FREDERICK

SACKED

This book is a work of fiction. Names, characters, places, and incidents are the product of the author's imagination or are used fictitiously. Any resemblance to actual events, locales, or persons, living or dead, is coincidental.

PEAR TREE LLC
West Des Moines, IA 50266

jen@jenfrederick.com

Cover Photo © ValuaVitaly
Cover Design by Meljean Brook

First Edition: September 2015
CreateSpace Independent Publishing Platform

www.jenfrederick.com

To Elle Kennedy and Kristen Callihan

Thank you for writing such wonderful books. You are both amazing friends and writers.

ACKNOWLEDGEMENTS

WHEN I WAS GROWING UP, I watched football every Sunday with my dad and brothers. I was raised on the Green Bay Packers, the wisdom of Vince Lombardi and the hallowedness of "frozen tundra." (Yes, I know that's redundant but everyone calls it that!) My paternal grand-mother watched the team religiously until her death at the ripe age of 101. Football has been a constant in my family and for all its scandals and problems, it's a game that brings us together every fall. For that reason, I will always love the game and this is my ode to it.

Thank you to my sweet daughter who is growing up too fast and my wonderful husband who is a true life romance hero.

Thank you to my editor who went through this book countless times and pushed me hard to make this story the very best that I could produce.

Thank you to my beta readers: Elle Kennedy (I love your brutal and straight forward critiques. I know I can trust you to tell me that my underwear is showing or that I have toilet paper on my shoe!), Kristen Callihan (You write the best sexual tension!), Elyssa Patrick (Your in-put is incredibly valuable.), Lou (Your emails make me smile.) Meljean

Brook, Jessica Clare (the best and prettiest writing partner in existence), and Michelle Kannan (can you believe we met through someone else's dating story!!), and Lisa Schilling Hintz.

Special thanks to the world's okayest bloggers but best friends: Melissa King and Lea Robinson and the world's okayest friends: Jessica Rupp and Jeannette Mancine. You four made my birthday in 2015 one I will never forget.

Thanks to Robin and Sunita for your endless email support. I would not be able to go from one week to the next without you.

Go Pack Go!

1

KNOX

I DON'T SEE HER UNTIL I'm three quarters of the way up the stands. In my defense, the stadium seats over one hundred thousand people, so it's not until I'm nearing the hundred and fifteenth row that I realize what I thought was a sunspot is actually a person.

Irritation prickles inside my chest. This is *my* time. Before trainers, field crew, coaches, and other players come in, I run these bleachers in blissful solitude. It's selfish, but I've earned the right to be selfish. As the starting defensive end and captain of the Western State Warriors, I've bled on that field, played through immeasurable pain, eaten my share of fake turf. Suffered fucking awful losses. I have a week until the media storm really gears up, and it doesn't seem too much to ask for some privacy.

Now I have to deal with some stalking gridiron groupie and at six in the morning no less. I thought the jersey chasers didn't get up before noon. In the mornings, I'm only interested in seeing the team nutritionist and her breakfast smoothies.

As I draw parallel with the top row, I can see her more clearly and I'm not so annoyed—or blind—that I can't admit the intruder is a hot piece. Nice rack under a fitted sport T-shirt and long legs propped up against the seat in front of her. Dark brown hair caught up in a ponytail. She has an athletic look to her, which I've always liked.

If I did groupies, she'd be on the top of my list, but I haven't dipped my wick in those pots ever. I won't start with her.

Frustrated that my morning ritual is marred, my greeting is rude. "How'd you get in here?"

Before the last word leaves my mouth, I know the answer. I never lock the doors when I come here to run because I'm done in an hour and I don't want to deal with the hassle. Her cool eyes flick over my six foot, six inch frame as if I'm nothing more interesting than a fruit fly.

"The door was open."

This time when my skin prickles, it's not with annoyance at all. More like…interest.

So that's what it feels like to be dismissed.

I don't think I've had that reaction from anyone since I was five, because even as a kid my athletic potential was evident, garnering attention. I dip my head to hide a grin I suspect wouldn't be welcome. So, not a groupie. If she is, she's got better game than anyone I've seen before, because the cold shoulder act apparently works well for me.

I pull my cap off and run a hand through my hair to give myself a moment to regroup. "Sorry. I thought I was alone here. I usually am."

Again her cool eyes measure me—taking in my running shorts, bare chest, stupid trucker hat my brother gave me, aviators—and find me wanting. A thrill shoots through me. Yes, that's definitely interest. *Damn*, didn't realize I had a streak of masochism.

"Do you own the stadium?"

The obvious answer to her question is no, but the fact is I kind of do. In here—and on campus—I'm a god. That sounds like an arrogant sentiment, but I'd be more of an asshole if I didn't acknowledge the truth of it.

This girl, though? She couldn't be less impressed. I glance down at my sweat-drenched chest that has had more than one Western State coed licking her lips and running her hand over my pecs and abs. I don't show off for girls, or at least, I've never felt like I had to before.

There's challenge in the line of her body, in her voice. The competition gene that exists in every cell of my body pings to attention. And that's not all that's rising. So naturally, I drop into the seat next to her.

"I've never sat up here," I confess.

The field looks tiny from this vantage point, and above us are the luxury boxes. People pay a fortune to sit up there. Seems like a giant waste. The only place I want to be in a football stadium is the field.

"Best seats in the house," she murmurs. Her hands cup around her raised knees. The right one has a nasty surgical scar. It looks like a fighter's mark, which makes her about ten times hotter.

I turn my attention to the field to stop the drain of blood into my shorts. "Can you even see the game from up here?" I squint and try to imagine what I look like down there with my pads and helmet, as I ready myself to blast by a blocker and shove the quarterback's face into the dirt.

"Who cares if you can see? I'm here to drink beer and use the cow bell." She mimes ringing the bell.

"This is the church of football, lady." I slap a hand across my chest.

"Oh, is that what they play here? I thought it was soccer." She's playing me and I like it.

"That's sacrilegious. This is clearly where the greatest sport of all time is played." I wave a hand toward the pristine green field and the cavernous bowl that I swear still rings with the cheers of last year's crowd.

"Oh, you're one of those who treats the stadium like it's some kind of church and the players are all Jesus characters designed to lead us to the Promised Land."

"You say that like it's not true."

"You believe in the beauty of the spiral, the fulfillment of dreams, that this is the place where all creeds and religions and walks of life are accepted as long as you have talent." Her words are mocking but her tone doesn't quite get there. She believes half the stuff she's saying.

"It's not the bastion of idealism but you can pursue perfection here." I can't take my eyes off her.

"Then if you believe that, this right here gives you the best seat in the house." Her quiet voice strikes me in the gut. "Up here you aren't distracted by the cheerleaders or the crowd. It's all game and the chase for excellence. You can see the church for what it is—a temple built to revere physical perfection. The spiral looks gorgeous as it cuts through the air and the hits look as hard up here as if you stood on the sideline.

Up here, you can see it all." She bites her lip, as if she'd said too much. "Plus, it's cheap."

I force out a chuckle so she doesn't see how her words have touched me. Not many people feel the game like that. "I guess every place in the stadium has a different view."

"Different maybe, but still bound by the same tension and the same excitement. And the same disappointment." The last word lingers.

I feel her.

I have a lot of bitter regret in me from the way last year's season ended. One win away from the college football champion title game and we couldn't overcome the loss of our quarterback in the fourth quarter of the first playoff game. I force myself to unclench my fist. No point in dwelling on the past. My focus is this year, this time, this championship. I dangle my legs over the seats, nearly touching the row below.

"What position do you play?" she asks.

"What makes you think I play?" I say evasively. Up to this point, she hasn't shown any signs of recognition. There's no fawning that I'm Knox Masters, two time All-American defensive end, winner of every defensive college player award handed out last year. I don't like the way people change when they find out I'm a Warrior. Everything is different then. Calculation sets in. Can I get them tickets? Can I get them access? Am I the path to an easier life?

I just want to kick back and enjoy the quiet with someone who gets it. She does—in every way that's important. This nameless, gorgeous, funny girl who got up at the ass crack of dawn to creep into my stadium is enjoying the sunrise on this hallowed ground as much as I am. I lean back and let the comfortable silence settle between us as the rising sun bathes everything in its pure golden light.

"How about you?" I change the subject and flick a finger toward her knee. "That looks like a surgery scar. "

Her hand moves over it. "It is."

"How'd it happen?" I ask. She arches an eyebrow and levels a look at me says *you've got to be kidding.* Clearly, I'm not getting anything more from her if I don't give a little myself. Does it have to be my name or my position? I grasp the first confession that skips through my meager brain. "I'm hoping I don't ever get injured. Surgery scares the bejesus out of me."

"Bejesus?" Again with the eyebrow, but this time I catch a glimpse of a smile. "We're both adults. You can cuss in front of me unless you're a minor…" She trails off with an impish grin.

"No, I'm *all* adult."

My weak attempt at flirting is met with a snort of amusement. At least I hope it's amusement.

I need to know everything about her. I want to ask her name, find out where she lives, when she'll marry me, but then I'd have to tell her my name. Maybe I can coax the details out of her without giving her much more. "Are you new here at Western?"

She tilts her head to the side. I can see she's considering whether I deserve another answer or whether she's done with me. Short of clamping my big hand down on her leg, I have nothing.

Something flickers in her eyes that I can't read, but when she opens her mouth instead of getting up and leaving, I let out a breath I didn't realize I held. "I'm new. A transfer."

That fits. She looks older than a freshman and she lacks that dazed, confused, overly eager expression most of the incoming class wears for the first few weeks.

"I'm a junior. This may be my last year," I find myself telling her.

Her eyes shoot up. "You…dropping out?"

The surprise in her eyes and the way she said the words *dropping out* makes me think that she does know who I am, but she seems willing to go along with the fiction of pretending I'm a nobody. I appreciate that a hell of a lot.

There's an ease between the two of us. She speaks about this place with the same language and words I understand—a cross between reverence and frustration. Only someone who loves this game talks like that.

"What do you think?" I don't know why I ask, but her answer seems important to me.

She doesn't blurt out an immediate response, but asks me a question instead. "Why are you thinking of moving forward?"

Moving forward. Isn't that the fucking most perfect way to frame it? "The things I'm doing here at Western are things I want to be doing at the next level, and I think I'll be ready at the end of this year."

"You think?" Her eyebrow arches up again.

I grin. "I know."

"Then it doesn't matter what anyone else thinks. If you believe you're ready, then you're ready. Isn't it so much what goes on up here?" She taps her temple with her index finger. "And here." She pats the top of her left breast, a breast that looks delicious even smashed under her sports bra.

I tear my eyes away from her pretty tits. "Yes, you get it exactly." My words are hardly more than a whisper, but out of the corner of my eye, I see her nod in perfect comprehension.

"Thunderstruck" is the song that plays before the Florida Gators and the Alabama Crimson Tide take the field. When future hall of fame pitcher John Smoltz walked out of the bullpen to close out a game for the Braves, the distinctive licks of AC/DC's song hailed down from the sound system and the crowd screamed *thunder* in unison.

It's the soundtrack of the beat down the assholes in *Varsity Blues* receive after their trip to the strip club on Friday night, like none of them had ever seen tits or ass before. Shit, even the Dallas Cowboy Cheerleaders run out to the fucking song. I've kind of hated it, mostly because we don't play the sick grind when we run onto the field.

Right now, as the sun peeks over the top of the stands and lays a solid ray of love on the field of my greatest accomplishments to date, and the girl sitting by me waxes poetic about the greatest game in the world, I get it.

Her.

This one.

The universe is talking to me. I don't need lightning or a torna-do throwing a car at my head. I don't need a running back barreling through the line at top speed to drive home the message. It's in the curve of her cheek, the delicate arch of her neck. It's in her sweet legs and the longing in her face. She loves this place as I love it. She under-stands that winning at this game is about the head and the heart, not just the body.

I'd like to press her down on the concrete risers and show her exactly how well my head, heart, and body work in unison. I breathe deep and try to get a grip on my rampaging emotions.

"And what about you? What are your plans?"

"I want to get a job. Not have to rely on my parents. Their…financial support is like a choker rather than a buoy." She scrapes a hand over her head and down her ponytail. "God, I don't know why I'm telling you this."

Because you know it's me. I'm the one for you, just as you're the one for me. Like recognizes like. However, she's not seeing it as clearly. Already I can see her withdrawing, a little embarrassed by what she found herself sharing.

"It's the seats. The air is too thin up here." I squint down toward the field. "The reason you like these seats up here is because you're light-headed and possibly unconscious during most of the game, making all the shitty plays seem like a bad dream." I stretch out my legs and resettle my hat. "Worse, there's no leg room."

"You're supposed to stand," she chides with gentle mocking. "You can't sit while the mighty Warriors take the field of battle."

I laugh. When she grins back at me in return I feel winded, and not from any exercise I've done this morning.

"I think it's okay to sit during timeouts," I manage to joke. I'm glad I'm sitting down, because if I'd been standing when she threw me that smile, I'd have fallen over.

"I can't see you resting much."

"I may have been a headache for my mom," I admit.

Another smile, only a little one this time, tips the corner of her lips. I guess the idea of me being a hellion amuses her. I fold my hands behind my head. From my vantage point, I appear a little under a foot taller than her.

"You been here long?"

"Long enough to get worn out watching you run the stairs."

My routine is five times around the field, and then up and down the stadium steps for thirty minutes. She must have been here a while. At my raised eyebrow, she merely shrugs, but the light pink that shows up on her cheeks gives her away. Warmth having nothing to do with the early morning sun settles over me. I'm not the only one feeling something here.

"Running these steps is good for my heart. As a bonus it sweats the stupid out of me." I wink but then realize I'm wearing my aviators and trucker hat so that action is for nothing. For the best, really. Winking can be a douchebag move at times.

"Do you have a lot of stupid to sweat out?" She holds back a laugh.

I grin back. "It regenerates every day."

This delights her and she finally allows the stifled laugh to escape. I can only stare at her for a second or two before I have to look away. She's so goddamned beautiful it's getting hard to sit here without looking like a total perv.

"They say admitting the problem is half the solution," she agrees.

"The running is to get rid of the other half."

At six fifteen, the sprinklers come on, spraying the turf. The artificial grass doesn't need the irrigation to grow, but it cools down the field and reduces the turf burn. An idea surfaces and I push to my feet. Leaning down, I hold out my hand. "Race you to the bottom."

She stares at my big paw and then into my aviators. "I can't."

"No one will know." And if they find out, no one will protest. After all, what will the team do? Suspend me? I wiggle my fingers. *Come on.*

She sighs and taps her knee, the one with the scar. "I really can't race you. My knee might give out. I'm fine on flat surfaces, but running down a hundred rows would be asking for something bad to happen."

Aw, fuck. That was stupid of me. "Then walk down with me." She hesitates. "I'm not leaving until you slide on the field with me."

"Gosh, what a wonderful and charming invitation." She rests her hands on her hips. Whether she intends it or not, the action frames her perky tits nicely. I use the cover of my sunglasses to appreciate how generous the good Lord was with her.

"You know you want to," I coax.

She purses her lips. The way that the center plumps out makes me bite my lower lip, to stop myself from leaning forward to see how that ripe bit of pink flesh would feel sucked into my mouth.

In a quick move I don't see coming, she vaults the seat backs in front of us and races down the steps. Bad knee, my ass.

I clamber down behind her, and although I could overtake her, I hover in the background ready to catch her if she falls. Except I get the sense she'd rather have a hot poker up her ass than ask me for help.

"Slowpoke," she says, full of smiles, when we reach the field.

"Did you hustle me?" I ask in mock indignation.

"Yup," she replies without a shred of remorse. "Does that mean the turf contest is off?"

"No way." I pluck the T-shirt out from the waistband of my shorts and tug it on. She makes a sound and I like to think it means disappointment, but since wet grass burn is no laughing matter, I cover up.

"Longest slide wins," I tell her. I swing my arms in warm up.

"What am I winning?" she asks.

I grin at her cockiness. "I'll let you run with me tomorrow."

"I can't wait to lose then." She rolls her eyes.

"Personal pride, babe. That's what we're competing for." I'm not making dumb bets. I don't need a bet to get what I want. After we're done here, I'll take her out to breakfast and find out everything about her. This is for the fun of it, because I want to see the longing in her face satisfied.

"You first then. I don't want you to accuse me of cheating." She nudges her shoulder against my arm, and that small, innocent contact is like a cannon right to my nervous system. I'm on the edge of obliteration but I want more. Now is not the time. The compression shorts under my running gear can only hold so much in.

"Don't be sad when you lose. I'll take you out for breakfast either way," I reassure her and then take off before she can turn me down. At the twenty, I launch myself and slide a good seven yards.

"That's not enough for a first down," she yells from the end zone.

"Let's see what you got!" I holler back. Rolling over onto my side, I prop myself up on an elbow and gesture that it's her turn.

She places one foot in front of the other and swings her arms a few times for momentum. She sprints down, leaping forward and then slides to a stop about a foot past me. Damn. I drag her back by the ankle so that her face is next to mine.

Drops of water cling to her grinning face. I lean forward, ready to lick the moisture from her face but I stop myself when she winces.

"Your knee okay?" I ask, worried that she'd hurt herself.

"It's fine." Her chest rises and falls as she gathers her breath. I have to force myself to look away. Rolling on my back, I listen as her breath evens out.

Apparently the universe's gift requires some work. I'm not afraid of hard work. As the great Vince Lombardi said, only in the dictionary is work preceded by success. Rolling on my back, I stare up at the gorgeous blue sky and revel in the fact that what I'd waited for arrived.

"So you love football, huh?"

She shrugs and turns her face to hide her smile. "It's okay."

Yeah, and I'm not Knox Masters, decorated defensive end, captain of the Western State Warriors, and projected top ten NFL draft pick.

2

ELLIE

I SHOULD GET UP AND leave. Actually, I should get up and sprint the hell out of Union Stadium like we're in *The Dark Knight Rises* and Bane himself is blowing up the field. But I can't. There's a magnet fastening me to the wet turf—a magnet named Knox Masters. It could be that I'm shocked into passivity. I've been around football players my whole life, and not one of them had the gravitational pull of Masters.

"I need to go. Thanks for the run." I push to my feet. I keep the words *I won* to myself. They'd be a red flag to his bull stomping.

"Won't let me have a rematch?" He pushes onto an elbow and I have to force myself to look away from the damp fabric clinging to his chiseled abs. Why couldn't he be a little round around the waist like some linemen? Does he have to be good looking and talented? In the football world, grown men get excited hearing his name. Here at Western, he's the ruler of all he sees.

He doesn't need to have a face that would fit in on a runway, what with being so athletically gifted. I'm surprised someone hasn't broken his nose yet, if not out of jealousy then sheer frustration that one guy has been given so much.

It's unfair, criminally so. Advertisers will love him once he goes pro. That he intends to declare for the draft at the end of his junior year is no surprise. The fact that he told *me*, some nobody he's never laid eyes on before, is a shock. What was that all about up there in the stands?

Can I blame it on the thin air, as he suggested? I feel like he's playing me in some way, but I haven't figured out his angle. Worse, I shouldn't care what his angle is. "I'm quitting while I'm ahead. Besides, it's getting late."

Masters hops to his feet and smirks at my weak excuse. "Because you can get so much done on campus at six in the morning."

I check my running watch. "It's six twenty. The day's almost over."

He tilts his head. "Fair enough, but does that mean skipping breakfast? Because I'm capable of talking about lots of other topics. I'm pretty conversant in basketball, some baseball, and hockey." He flicks up a finger for each sport. "Also, up on *Assassin's Creed*, *Angry Birds*—although I'll admit I haven't played that since high school. I'm more *Clash of Clans* right now." I laugh against my better judgment. His eyes twinkle as he continues. "I'm so-so on topics like fashion, but I'm partial to miniskirts, tube tops, and skinny jeans."

He's running out of fingers. I grab his hand and fold his fingers down to get him to stop. It surprises us both and I start to draw back, but his reflexes are quicker. He flips his hand over and pulls me flush against him.

His long, hard frame against mine causes my electrical system to hiccup, which is the only reason I recklessly say, "I don't know if I own a tube top."

When his bright smile turns hungry, I realize my error. *Oh, Ellie, you are such a dumb girl. Stop flirting with the hot jock and get your ass out of here.*

"If you don't, I wouldn't worry. Running shorts, workout T-shirts, and ponytails are moving to the top of the list of things I'm a fan of."

He leans even closer, and the smell of fresh turf, sunshine, and earthy male fills my lungs and my frame quakes the tiniest bit when I gulp in that dangerous cocktail. This is very bad for me. Yet…I'm not moving.

"So, breakfast?" he prompts with a slightly raised eyebrow. "We can talk about our favorite running shoes and exchange minor details like names and phone numbers."

"I'm a big fan of New Balance," I murmur even though I know I should pull away.

"I'm a big fan of names." He squeezes my hand. "Mine is—"

"Knox! Your smoothie is ready!" A cheery voice calls out from the player tunnel. The sound manages to shake me free from Masters.

"—Knox," he finishes, as if we hadn't gotten interrupted. His lips are inches from my ear. "What's yours?" His hand finds mine again and grips me tight, as if he knows I'll run away at any moment.

Just Knox? It's like he's still hiding. Not giving out his full name, not admitting he's more familiar with the turf we're standing on than 99% of the student body, not taking off those mirrored glasses or covering his hair with his hat. If he's not giving it up, then neither am I. "It's different," is all I say.

My dad named me Eliot Campbell. He wanted a second son. He didn't get one, but I got the name regardless.

"Oh no!" cries the musical voice of the smoothie delivery person. "I'm so sorry, miss, but this facility is closed to the public at all times but game time."

"That's my cue," I murmur, mostly to get my own ass in gear. With a twist, I free my hand. "I'm leaving."

I give a brisk nod to the bouncy blonde in a royal-blue polo. She has the Warriors logo inked above her left breast and she rocks a pair of khaki shorts. Maybe everyone at Western is blessed in the looks department. In her hand, she carries a large Styrofoam cup with a paper-tipped straw.

The blonde nods in approval and shoves the drink into Masters' empty fist. I use the diversion to sprint off the field and down the tunnel. Stymied by the smoothie-bearing girl and my quick feet, I'm gone before he can stop me.

Knox Masters is a beast in person. I've seen him plenty on television, but the screen deceives you on a football player's size. With the pads, the helmet, the motion, and the angle of the camera, you forget that in real life some of the men are huge even without all the gear bulking them up.

He's six-and-a-half feet of hard-bodied, muscled perfection. When he first entered the stadium, he moved so fast I thought it was someone else, a running back or a tight end like my brother, Jack. But as he stormed up the stadium steps like someone had insulted his mother, I'd realized who exactly was providing my early morning entertainment.

Masters is famous in the collegiate ranks to anyone who knows football. Even if you're trying your best to stop caring about the sport, like it's the ex-boyfriend you know is bad for you but can't let go, you'd know who Knox Masters is. Which is why I don't get his coyness. Not once during our conversation did he say a word about the game. Did he honestly think aviators and a trucker hat made an effective disguise? The guy was on the cover of the college edition of *Sports Illustrated* a couple of months ago, for crying out loud.

Not to mention, I asked him outright and he sidestepped my question. But he also admitted that he wanted to declare early—a fact widely talked about by the college analysts, but until it came out of his mouth, only speculation. If I wanted a little bit of fame, I could leak that to someone and ruin it for Masters.

I won't. He knew that somehow.

I'm probably the one person who doesn't want the stranger in the stadium to be a NFL-bound college football player. If he were some normal guy who liked watching football rather than playing, we'd be at breakfast right now, exchanging numbers, arguing about our fantasy football picks, and finding out exactly what colors of tube tops he liked. But football players and I don't mix.

On my way back to the apartment, I stop at the campus coffee shop and pick up a caramel mocha latte with soy milk. My new roommate, Riley Hall, has an unfortunate dairy allergy, which means no ice cream for her. I don't know how she copes with life. I want her to like me because I haven't had a close female friend in a while, and I'm willing to bribe her with soy milk lattes every morning if that's what it takes.

She's up when I get into the apartment, bleary-eyed, leaning against the counter and staring at my tea maker with undisguised frustration.

"Riles, I got you," I call as I kick the door shut.

She nearly squeals with glee when I hand her the coffee. "You are a goddess. I knew you were exactly the right roommate for me when your response to my Craigslist ad was that you made a mean cup of coffee." I open my mouth to confess that the best I know how to do is operate a Keurig, but she waves me off. "I know you lied. It's enough that you understood that coffee is an essential part of the day."

"I thought we were destined roommates because we're two females with male names," I quip. My first name is Eliot; hers, Riley.

"That, too."

"You're up early." I'm glad for the impulse to stop for coffee.

She takes a sip of coffee and blisses out for a few seconds before responding. "Your phone has been ringing off the hook."

"Oh gosh, I'm sorry. I thought I left the ringer off." I grab for the phone I plugged in by the stove before I left for my early morning jog.

"You did. It vibrated so much I thought it might fall off the counter, so I picked it up. I didn't mean to pry, but it's your mom." She makes a sympathetic face. "It showed on your screen."

The phone rings again and Riley waves goodbye as she disappears into her bedroom to savor her coffee. I want to go with her, because I'm sure whatever my mother is calling about at seven in the morning isn't fun.

"Hey, Mom," I answer right before voicemail kicks in.

"Eliot, why didn't you answer?"

"I was running."

She clicks her tongue in disapproval. "I'm sure that's not good for your knee. If you'd watch what you ate, then you wouldn't need to run."

This is the power of motherhood. She's great at criticizing me out of both sides of her mouth. I'm eating too much and engaging in unsafe activities. Boss mother status achieved in two sentences.

I drum my fingers against the cheap laminate counter, regretting I didn't go to breakfast with Masters. It's karmic punishment, I suppose. If I turn down the good things that come my way, why should I be shielded from the bad? "I only run on flat surfaces."

"I hope you're wearing your longer pants. That scar is so visible when you get brown, dear."

She always adds the *dear*, as if the fake term of endearment removes the sting of her words. I look down at my bare legs stretching out from the running shorts I pulled on. The scar looks like a sideways grimace. Most of the time I forget it's there, but trust my mom to bring it up. I drop into a kitchen chair and settle in for the rest of her lecture.

"I have pants," I say, not ready to outright lie to her.

"Good. You want to start out your time at Western on a good note. You don't want to alienate the nice young men by not putting forth a good appearance." Mom is the queen of appearances. In her book, as long as we look good, we *are* good.

Knox Masters didn't seem to care, I want to tell her. In fact, I'm pretty sure he looked at my legs with a hell of a lot of appreciation. I rub my hand over the mark, though, because talking to Mom makes me self-conscious.

"Yes, Mom."

"But I didn't call to talk about that. I have terrible news. Your brother signed up for classes without consulting us!"

Good for him.

"He didn't sign up by himself. He had a student liaison help him," I point out. Mom must know. She, Dad, and Jack all visited Western together.

"That girl did not do a very good job then, because two of Jack's courses are simply too difficult for him to manage himself."

Dread is like a stone. Sometimes it sits in your stomach and makes you want to vomit. Other times it lodges in your throat and chokes you. Either way dread makes you feel terrible. Right now, I feel I *am* stone.

One thing that sold Jack on Western, other than their very real chance of winning the BCS National Championship title, was all the academic resources they have. Every athlete has a student liaison—an upperclassman—assigned to help him or her register. Every class has a tutor available. *I won't lean so much on you*, he'd told me. I was thrilled. No more taking classes I didn't like to make sure I knew Jack's assignments. No more pretending I was interested in Battle Maneuvers of WWII. Most importantly, no more guilty conscience.

I happily registered for classes that interested me, like Creative Nonfiction Writing and Grant Management, the latter being a self-directed course involving writing a real grant proposal, which will look great on my resume.

"Uh huh." If I hang up will this conversation end?

"I've called the Provost's office, and they've informed me that the two courses you need to sign up for are full, but you can audit them. You'll need to go today, however, and sign up."

She rattles them off. One is a political science course, the other a sociology course. Neither sounds interesting to me.

"Mom, the time for registering is over. I did that this summer."

As did Jack. "I can't add two classes to my schedule. I'm taking fifteen credits. That's a full load."

It's not your mom you're turning your back on here. It's Jack.

She continues as if I haven't spoken. "That's nice, dear, but I'm sure two more classes won't be a burden."

What she means is that it doesn't matter if it is a burden.

"What, can't Jack drop those classes?"

"We don't drop classes," she says with an air of impatience. "What would his advisor think? You simply sign up and help as you always have in the past."

"I need all my classes to graduate within two years. Besides, I don't think it works that way."

"It does. Haven't you been listening? I spoke to the Provost's office. They will allow you to add these two classes in addition to the ones you already have, but you need to go today. What time will you go to-day?" Her voice is sharp, losing the genteel quality she likes to put on to pretend that she's a nicer person than she is. Truth is, my mother is a shark, but she has to be to live with my dad. Maybe she was soft at one time, and his constant cheating and absences wore it all away until she was just sharp points that stabbed at you until you bled. It's a little amazing how far her points extend. How they still hurt even though we are miles apart.

My temples begin to throb. I really, really should have accepted that breakfast invitation from Knox Masters. "Western provides all the athletes individualized tutors. They'll do a better job than me. Are you certain that I need to take these classes?"

It's not a question. I know I have to take them. Jack is great at numbers and sucks at reading and writing. I suspect he suffers from a mild form of dyslexia, or maybe that's how his mind works. I've been *helping* Jack out for a long time. That's why I went to junior college with him when he didn't get any D1 offers that made sense to my dad. That's why I'm here at Western, even though I'd have liked to go somewhere else. Anywhere else.

"Do you need to ask that? Aren't we in this together? Do you want your brother to fail? Aren't you already responsible for the fact he wasted two years at that awful two-year school out West? He only has two years of eligibility left. What if he doesn't start this year?"

The list of horribles goes on. I tune her out and pull up the course catalog. The descriptions do sound reading/writing intensive. I bet he'll have to write papers. He can memorize facts and do math problems in his head, but analysis of facts, reasoned conclusions that can't be expressed in digits, are damn hard for him.

Then she pulls out the big guns.

"Need I remind you that your father and I write the checks for your tuition, or did you get a scholarship that we don't know about?"

Masters asked me if I loved football, and the real answer is sometimes. Because while I can't deny the glory of it, the game holds me hostage—or will until Jack graduates.

Frustration and hurt crowd out all the good feelings of this morning. When I ran the campus this morning, I thought about how it would be a new start for me. I found what appears to be an awesome roommate in Riley.

I'd make good friends, work on courses designed to help me get a good job out of college. Maybe I'd find the man I would marry. At the very least, I could find someone to watch movies with and kiss on Valentine's Day.

On impulse, I'd run by Union Stadium to see where Jack would play, and when the gate hung slightly open and no one was around, I crept inside. It was so silent and so beautiful that I climbed to the very top and pretended that I was cheering on my brother and enjoying everything I loved about the game—the feats of physical strength, the excitement of the battle, the romance of it all.

Then Knox Masters came in, running fast like a bolt shot from a crossbow, straight and beautiful in motion. We'd flirted. We'd shared secrets. And after we'd run across the turf, I felt so…joyous in the moment.

Only to come home to this.

"I'm on it, Mom."

"You'll go right now?" It's more a command than a question.

"Right now. I'm leaving as we speak."

She sighs, but it's not relief she's feeling, but regret that she had to spend so much time talking me into something I should have agreed to do the minute I heard about it. Hell, I should have prevented it from happening.

"Thank you, dear. I hope your move went well. Don't tell me about it now. Call me after you enroll in those classes." She hangs up.

I stare at the phone. "Love you, too."

I look up the administrative hours on the website and realize I can't actually talk to anyone for an hour. I have enough time to shower, change, and eat breakfast.

In the kitchen, I find Riley pouring milk over a bowl of cereal.

"Captain Crunch or Fruit Loops?" she asks, glancing over her shoulder at me.

"My mom told me that my scar looked ugly and I should eat less so I didn't show it to the world."

"So Cocoa Puffs with chocolate milk." She sets both boxes back into the cupboard and brings out slow death by sugar.

I shake my head. "I can't. I ate your Fruit Loops yesterday and near-ly went into diabetic shock by noon. I don't know how you do it. You are all of five feet nothing, eat like a horse, and weigh less than a hun-dred soaking wet."

She grins and flexes. "I'm small but mighty and need this nectar of the gods to keep me going. It fuels my metabolism."

"That's not how metabolism works." I grab a bagel and pop it into the toaster. "Sugar slows down your metabolism and—"

Riley holds up a hand. "You can stop right there. I don't want to hear your nutritionist-in-training truths. I've eaten this kind of cereal all my life and I can't stop now. It'd be a cruel shock to my system."

"I thought I told you I was an English major." Technically, I planned to write for a living—grant applications, speeches, reports. After years of writing for Jack, I figured I might as well put my experience to good use.

"Oh, you did, but all the groceries you've bought are healthy stuff." Riley pours herself a giant bowl of cereal and drenches it with her chocolate soy milk. My teeth ache watching her eat, but if eating sugary things for breakfast, lunch, and dinner is her worst trait, she'll be the best roommate ever. "So what are your plans for today? My family is still in town if you want to hang out with us. I apologize in advance for my younger sister, Rachel. She's at that awkward age between knowing it all and knowing nothing. Plus, we can't have her anywhere near your hot brother or she may try to hump him."

"After that convincing invitation, I'll pass. No offense." I'd met Rachel yesterday, and she acted every bit as sullen as Riley describes. "But thanks for the warning regarding Jack. I'm glad you seem to be immune. My roommate at junior college desperately wanted in the pants of a football player. I tried to warn her that so many of the players are one and done. That's how they get the label *player*."

"I'm not saying I'm immune, but I'm not dating my roommate's brother. There lies madness." She stabs her spoon at me to punctuate her point. "Besides, I've had my eye on this guy from my advanced economics class last year. He was adorable and, according to his Facebook status, he's still single."

"Booyah," I say and give her a high five.

"What about you? You into the football players?"

"No. I dated one in high school and that was enough for me." That's a bad memory I don't want to revisit. It's the source of so much guilt, which is why I shouldn't have lingered in the stadium to flirt with Masters, and why I left before I could fall under the spell of his easy charisma. "I don't know what I want, but it's not a jock. I mean, I know football players are all different, but their focus is the same—winning, whether it's on the field or off."

"Yeah," Riley sighs. "It's the same everywhere. Most of the guys I've met just want to hook up."

"I think I'd marry the first guy who hit on me in the bookstore."

We share a commiserating sigh.

"That's not a bad idea," she says between giant bites of chocolate cereal.

My phone rings again. "Jeez. It's like Grand Central in here." But I pick up when I see Jack's face.

"Hey, Jack. We were just talking about you."

"About how awesome I am? That would be my topic of choice, too."

"How about you're not as interesting as an econ major."

Riley winks at me and gives me another high five. "Sorry, Jack," she yells. "You have too much body fat for me."

"What?" he says, instantly outraged. "You tell your roommate my body fat is 8%. In no world is that too much."

"Apparently it is in Riley's world." Riley gulps down the last of her cereal and heads back into her bedroom while I hit my own room to get ready to face administration.

"Your roommate needs a little education, Ellie Bellie."

"First, do not call me that, and second, no dating the roommates." I rifle through my closet to find an outfit that says I'm a serious student. I think that means a skirt and a button down shirt. I find a navy pencil skirt that looks like it belongs in my mother's closet and a white Oxford shirt.

"Yeah, yeah, I hear you. Look, are you having dinner with me tonight? You blew me off last time to have dinner with your roommate, so you kind of owe me."

"I can't. I'm going over to the learning center to meet with the director. She can't make time for me until after six. You should come with." For one of my classes I'm writing a mock grant, and I chose the Agrippa Learning Center, a nonprofit that specializes in helping at risk kids who have learning disabilities.

"No, thanks. Why are you going now? Classes haven't started."

"I wanted to get a jump on things. Are you sure you don't want to come with? It's a cool place."

Maybe you'd get inspired by seeing some kids working through their disabilities. They seemed so bright, interesting, and courageous. I wish Jack could see that, but he refused. As though even going near a center like that would make people think him dumb.

"Ellie, you told me it was painted the color of piss-yellow and smelled about the same."

"I might have exaggerated."

"Yeah, still not interested. You're having dinner with me tomorrow then."

Tomorrow would be Thursday. Did he have a team dinner then? I'd like to avoid the football team as much as possible. "I'll think about it."

"Either you come willingly or I'll send the offensive line to carry you over," he threatens.

"I said I'd think about it."

"Too bad. It's happening," he says cheerfully. "Gotta run. Love you, Ellie Bellie. See you tomorrow at six."

And for the second time before the clock even rolls to nine in the morning, someone in my family hangs up on me.

3

KNOX

I'D CONVINCED MYSELF AT SOME point, maybe senior year of high school or maybe my first year at Western, that going without sex made me a better player. That belief had held me in good stead for years. Whenever I felt like wavering, I reminded myself that the pursuit of my dreams was more important than screwing some girl I wouldn't remember after I'd moved on. So it surprises me a little that while I can't get the brunette from the stadium out of my head, I'm sharper than ever.

This morning's scrimmage feels like I'm playing *Madden* on easy mode. I see everything JR "Ace" Anderson, our quarterback, will do before he does it. I'm reading the shifts in the offensive line as if I was in their huddle. Coach takes me out after the tenth series.

"Save some of that for the game," he orders. "Besides, you're killing Ace's confidence. Go do the ladder. You can work on your footwork and get rid of some of that goddamned energy without demoralizing half your team."

"Yes, Coach." I give him a cocky salute and go off to run through the string ladder set up between the twenty and third yard lines opposite the line of scrimmage. There I do multiple sets of agility exercises—the centipede, the Icky Shuffle, the Riverdance—and the whole time I have brown eyes in my head watching me, clapping for me to go faster and harder.

It's another sign.

I didn't get her name or her phone number, but I'm not worried. A girl who puts on her running shoes before dawn cracks the sky has to know where the gym is. I'll find her. I have zero doubt of that.

After our two-hour morning practice, Coach spends twenty minutes telling us the ways we can get suspended in the weekend before our opening kickoff. Too much boozing, missing curfew. If we want a goddamned lobster tail for dinner, he'd prefer we called him instead of sneaking one out of Kroger's under our workout gear.

"Don't disappoint me, men," he ends, and then waves us off.

Despite the size, the newly laid carpet, and the fresh veneer on the mahogany lockers, the locker room still stinks of sweaty balls and swamp ass. The smell of home. I grin to myself.

"You're in a good mood." Harry "Hammer" Wright drops onto the wooden seat and starts stripping off his gear. Hammer's a good natured southern boy, with a torso covered in ink and a quick smile for everyone.

I lean to the side to avoid being hit with his jersey. He has no sense of personal space. "We had a good workout."

Hammer is a prime example of why I always thought being single while chasing my NFL goals made a whole lot of sense. I'd watched other guys play shitiful games because their personal life was a mess. Their girlfriends cheated on them or maybe he got caught with his pants down.

Hammer is single because his last girlfriend caught him with some out-of-town babe. After a night game, we'd drank with a few of the locals and Hammer decided one of them needed consoling—with his dick. His girlfriend drove up and surprised him at the team hotel. She succeeded with her surprise, but it ended with a lot of screaming, a little hair pulling, and a call to security to get the two girls escorted from the premises.

Hammer got a lecture from Coach and me about keeping it in his pants on away games.

"Easy for you to say, Masters," Hammer whined at the time. "You don't know what the fuck you're missing."

"Get your nutsack under control or your hammer time will be on the bench," I told him.

"You're not human," he called as I walked away. "It ain't right for you to be denying yourself like that."

Hammer's about the only one who gets away with talking to me like that. We roomed together during our freshman year and I spent a hell of a lot of time listening to him lay pipe in his bed. Nothing about Hammer's casual sexual encounters made me believe I missed anything. Sometimes they didn't take more than fifteen minutes before he hustled them out the door so he could play a round of *Madden*.

Then some guys got kicked off the team after they'd videotaped themselves getting a blowjob race. It had all been consensual and the football players weren't the only Western athletes represented in the six-person video, but it'd looked bad. Real bad.

And the guys had seemed more interested in showing off for the camera than the fact that someone sucked their dicks. I've taken more satisfying dumps than the blowjobs those fuckups got.

Nothing had convinced me that my decision to save my athletic skills for the field was wrong…until now.

"Hey, Masters. I know the dinner's supposed to be team only, but my sister just moved in and I haven't seen her in two months since two-a-days started. Do you mind if she comes to dinner?" Jack Campbell stops by my locker. He's a newbie—a transfer from a top tier juco—and by the effort he's put forth this summer, a potential difference maker. As a bonus, he's not an asshole.

"I guess that's okay. She's not a jock chaser, right?"

Hammer snorts. "Yeah, Campbell, we got rules and standards. Only tens at the table. Your sister a ten?"

"Did this become *Deliverance* country and I didn't notice?" Campbell shoots back. He's not an asshole *and* he's got some balls. "Maybe where you come from, you spend long hours deciding whether your sister is fuckable, but I prefer to do that outside my immediate family tree."

"You're good with first cousins, right?" Hammer says in a serious tone, but I know he's still fucking with Campbell. We're not allowed to haze anymore, so we have to get our digs in where we can.

"Yeah, first cousins are fair game." They exchange fist bumps. Sick fuckers, I grin. Sick fuckers, but *my* sick fuckers.

"But, seriously, what's she look like?" Hammer presses.

"You better tell him or he won't stop asking until dinner tonight. You don't want that kind of headache." I throw my sweaty jock and work out gear in the laundry and grab my towel to cover my junk. The locker room got renovated over the off-season and now the showers are on the other side of the building. The team rules require us to cover up with towels because there's a hallway in between. Genius design, boys.

Campbell rolls his eyes. "She's about five foot eight. Long brown hair. Works out, although she needs to be careful, because she blew out her right knee in eighth grade. Uneven surfaces are a bitch for her."

I stop and backtrack. Tall and athletic with a right knee injury? "What happened in eighth grade?"

"She was playing flag football. A douchebag with an inferiority complex and bad technique took her down. He ended up crushing her right knee."

"Man, that sucks." Hammer shudders. "No more talk about that. Bad juju for the locker room."

"I thought you had a brother named Eliot," Jesse calls.

"Nah, my sister's name is Eliot because my dad had naming rights."

Tall and athletic with a right knee injury, and a boy's name? She said it was different. It has to be her.

"Yeah, bring your sister to dinner." The smile I turn on Campbell is so big he stumbles back. "It's good for the team that we get to know your family."

"Since when?" Hammer stands, buck ass naked. "I asked if you wanted to have dinner with me and my sister this summer, and you said no."

"Your sister tried to molest me under the table during the family dinner at the Spring game," I remind him.

"Someone's got to punch your V-card, man. Might as well be my sister."

"You know the rules," Matty, another linebacker, interrupts. He's got dark eyebrows from his mother's Columbian side that always makes him look serious. "No girlfriends. No sisters."

"That's a stupid ass rule. My sister is high quality WAG material," Hammer protests. Hammer's tried to get one of us to take his sister off his hands ever since he found out she was dating a twenty-five-year-old.

"Your sister is also underage." I tighten my grip on the towel. I'd sat across from Hammer's then seventeen-year-old sister, who had rubbed her foot against my dick the entire three-hour dinner. I ended up leaving my seat and standing for the last hour, citing a slight groin pull.

"You're a virgin?"

We all swivel back to Campbell, who appears rooted to the spot.

"Yeah, man, but don't bring that up at any parties." Hammer rushes over and Campbell backs up so Hammer's free-swinging dick doesn't slap Campbell in the balls.

"You're serious."

"As a heart attack." It's not a secret and I'm certainly not ashamed.

Hammer puts his arm around Campbell. "Jack Flash, you were fly out there today, but let me tell you a secret. You will get no pussy at a party this year if you bring up Masters' V-card. All those sweet honeys rubbing against you on the dance floor will get it into their heads that we all want virtuous chicks. We don't. We want to get laid."

I roll my eyes. These guys haven't spent a night without company since they stepped foot on campus.

"Don't forget the line of girls who want to be the one to convince Masters to give it up," Matty chirps.

"Yeah, man, it poisons the well. Don't do it." Hammer makes a gun with his fingers and points it at Jack, who appears dumbfounded by this information. Newbies. What can you do?

Laughing, I leave to take a shower while Campbell deals with the truth laid on him by the team.

When I get out, the reason for the new towel rule is standing in the hallway with her eyes pinned to the floor—Stella, one of the team managers, who happens to be the coach's daughter.

"Coach wants you and Ace in his office now."

"What for?" Ace comes up.

"Don't know." She doesn't look at Ace and he pretends he's not eating her up with his eyes. The whole situation between the two is pretty damn amusing, and as long as it doesn't fuck up the season, that's how it will remain.

I throw on a pair of cargo shorts and a Warriors T-shirt and shove my feet into a pair of flips. Ace leads the way into Coach's office.

"Shut the door and sit down," Coach orders.

As soon as our asses hit the hard plastic, he hands us each a sheet of paper.

"Here's the list of the new guys. Twenty-six of them. Anderson, you're in charge of the offense. Masters, the defense list is yours."

I have ten guys on my list. These are mini leadership tests from Coach. He likes to see what we're made of off the field. We're set on defense, having lost only two senior starters last year.

Ace has the bigger task. Some of his guys, like Campbell, are expected to start and make an immediate impact. However, since they haven't played together before, things like timing and chemistry, knowing what the other player is thinking about before he opens his mouth, will take work.

But they don't have time. In college, we have very little room for error. One loss and we could be out of the national championship hunt before the season is even underway. Last year we lost in the first round of the playoffs because we couldn't score. Ace needs to turn that around, like yesterday.

"Any issues we should know about?" I ask, tucking the list away. I already know my guys. I met them at spring camp and again when they arrived for summer term in June. For the most part they were good guys—young, eager, and hiding their homesickness under a thin sheen of bravado.

"Maurice Kim, Kaleb Shannon, and Jack Campbell all have academic issues. Make sure Campbell stays academically eligible. The other two we are redshirting, so spend less time on them. Andre Getty is already making noise about quitting. He could be a solid backup. If we can keep him, that'd be good for the team."

"There are sixteen players on my list and a quarter of them are already problems?" Ace frowns and shakes his list a little.

Before Coach can tell him to nut up, I snatch a marker off the desk and rip Ace's sheet from his hand. "I'll take this one."

I draw a heavy line through Campbell's name and toss the marker on the table. "We done here?"

Coach nods. "Make sure they know to stay away from my daughter."

"Of course." Ace grabs his list of players and shoves it into his back pocket.

That's when I know Ace is going to be all right during the season, because he doesn't even flinch. If he can stay stone-faced and in control in front of Coach while secretly nailing the most off-limits girl on a campus of twenty-five thousand, then he'll do fine as a starter.

I don't really care who Ace is fucking. There are only a few important things in my life right now, and they start and end with winning the national championship. Ace could fuck a goat if he was into that, so long as he took care of the ball and showed some leadership on the offense.

"What do you think about Campbell?" Ace asks me as we walk toward the Playground, where Ace and I live with the other starters. As one of the team captains, I have a third floor apartment all to myself. Granted, the place is noisy as shit because eight other guys live in the two floors below me, but for the most part, it's decent. When I need to get away, I put on my headphones and zone out. If I need company, I go downstairs and play a couple rounds of *Mudden* or *Call of Duty*. It could be worse.

"Good guy. Hard worker. Has good hands. His routes could be shaper. Timing isn't great with you, but it's early. All you got to do is score three times." I slap Ace on the back.

"That's my objective? Three touchdowns?" he asks in disbelief.

"If we can't hold every team to a couple of touchdowns this year, we don't deserve to be in the playoffs, let alone hoist the trophy." Last year we got lit up by a West Coast team. They scored on us at will and it felt fucking humiliating. I can still feel the sting of that loss today. At the end of that game, I vowed we'd never be caught with our pants down like that again.

"Noted. So what's your interest in Campbell?"

I shrug. "Figured you had your hands full."

He raises his chin slightly in disbelief, but doesn't challenge me. We part ways at the Playground—him to his house and me to mine.

I'm not ready to show my cards yet. The team has a general rule: no sisters because it makes for a messy locker room. Ace screwing Coach's daughter already meant bad news. But if push comes to shove, I'd lay my claim. There are some things you are born knowing: Treat your mother with respect. Family comes first. Bringing down a quarterback is as close to a religious experience as a boy can get. When you meet the girl who'll be sitting on the front porch holding your hand when you're eighty, you don't let a thing like cool dismissive looks, big brothers, or fucking rules stand in your way.

4

ELLIE

THE AGRIPPA LEARNING CENTER IS painted this awful yellow color. Maybe it looked bright when first applied in the prehistoric era, but right now, it's faded, ugly yellow.

The director, Susan Shearer, reminds me of Riley. She's small but full of energy. Her dark hair is cut close to her scalp and patches of it stick straight up as if she's suffered one too many harrowing events.

"Thank you so much for coming back tonight. I'm sorry I wasn't here yesterday when you came. Things are always chaotic here, but the school calendar moved up a week this year, and even though we knew about it we weren't quite prepared."

She motions me to follow her into an office that looks like a paper mill exploded in it. There are reports, drawings, catalogs, and brochures on every surface. "As you can see, we seriously need help, but donors don't like paying salaries. They'll buy supplies or donate equipment, but not for admin staff. So we need a grant."

"I'm just a junior, ma'am. I've never written a grant before." I feel like it's necessary to point this out so she doesn't get her hopes up. I wanted to get experience writing a grant and get an A. "I'm here to write a draft for you as part of my grant writing class at Western."

"I know. Isn't it great?" She points to a stack of papers about five inches thick. "I had Christie, who's our receptionist-slash-secretary you met out front, print out the last five years of budgets, along with our mission statement, program directives, and statistics of usage. The grant we'd like to apply for is an operational one." She motions for me to sit, and when I do she drops down behind her desk. I have to lean to the side so I can see her. "Tell me what you know about Agrippa."

"It's a not-for-profit agency designed to provide assistive learning to students between the ages of four and fourteen. For a nominal fee, students get extracurricular help in math, science, and language." I recite the information I gathered from my internet search.

"Yes, we charge a small fee because that makes sure the student and parent," she bobs her head a little, "or guardian, as the case may be, has skin in the game. They've paid money and they want to get their money's worth—even if the fee doesn't begin to cover the costs." She leans forward, her shoulder brushing an unsteady pile of papers. I reach out to steady it. I don't think she even notices. "Tell me why you chose Agrippa," Susan asks.

"I have a friend from high school who I believe has a learning disability, but she never got tested."

Susan makes a sympathetic noise. "That's terrible. Talk about hamstringing that child for the rest of her life. Early detection and testing really help kids overcome and manage their learning disability. There are so many ways we can help them these days."

I hope this meeting will be over soon. Susan's words make me feel even guiltier than when I talked on the phone with Mom, particularly when I spent all of my morning adding two classes for the express purpose of further "hamstringing" my brother.

"Well, a personal connection is good. It makes you more empathetic. You want to have passion when you write a grant proposal, and a personal appeal makes you really want to get after it." She makes a rocking motion with her fist.

"Is there any chance for adults?"

"Of course. We don't specialize in that, but—" She holds up a finger and digs through a pile of papers on the bookcase near her desk. "Here. This is a great organization for helping adult literacy challenges."

"Thanks. If I see her at break, I'll give it to her." I take the brochure and tuck it into my bag.

"You might want to be careful when you approach her," Susan cautions. "Most people, regardless of age, are quite sensitive about having reading or writing challenges. Adults tend to deny it, particularly if they are functioning well in most other areas."

"I hear you." She's not telling me anything I don't already know. I broached the subject with Jack only once before. We took an SAT prep course as juniors. He'd gotten very frustrated and I suggested extra tutoring. He looked at me with a look of utter betrayal and asked me if I thought he should be riding the short bus. I told him that was offensive. We got in a big fight and didn't talk for about three days. We made up but I never brought it up again. I don't even know if I can now.

"Good," she says briskly. "If you don't need anything further, then we're done. I'll want to see a rough draft by your midterm." She looks down at a sheet of paper. "Is that in October?"

"Yes. I could get it to you by October 1. How's that?"

"Perfect. Rough draft by October 1, and then the final version on December 1." Susan shakes my hand, piles me with paper, and sends me on my way. The brochure burns a hole in my pocket.

JACK SHOWS UP THE NEXT afternoon to check out my apartment and, I suppose, Riley.

"Nice place," he says. "I call dibs on the chair."

He points to a round velvet chair in deep red Riley said she found at a thrift store. It's as comfortable as Jack imagines and I plan to spend a lot of time there in front of the television on Saturdays, watching Jack's games. Despite what I told Masters, I don't sit at the top of the stadium or with the other students. It's too damn stressful.

"You can't call dibs," Riley protests. "This isn't your apartment."

"It's Ellie's, which means it's mine, too." Jack winks at her but Riley is having none of it.

She scowls and shakes a scolding finger at Jack. "You make a mess and you have to clean it up."

"No problem." He smiles again and this time it's deep enough that his dimples appear. Uh oh. I had better separate the two before Riley falls under the spell of Jack's charms.

"Come on." I grab his arm. "I need your help unpacking stuff."

He snaps to immediately and follows me to my room. "What do you need?"

I point to the stack of empty cardboard boxes. "I've unpacked most everything, but I need help getting rid of these boxes."

"Sorry I wasn't here to help you carry this shit up here." Jack makes quick work of the first box, tearing off the tape and punching it flat. "I still can't believe those shitheads didn't drive down with you."

He tosses the now flat box into the hallway and proceeds to efficiently destroy the five other boxes.

"It's fine. The manager had a four-wheel dolly and he helped me bring most of it up."

"Riley wasn't even here?" The nerve in Jack's jaw starts ticking with annoyance. It's not directed at me or Riley. It's directed at our parents. I reach over and pull the laundry basket away from him before he crushes it.

"Her family is in town. Look, I didn't want to stay home any longer and I missed you."

"So what's your roommate like? She seems nice."

"No dating her."

"I wouldn't date her," he protests a shade too vigorously.

"I think she's nice and normal, so you have to stay away."

"Do you see something wrong with this picture?"

Not wanting him to date my roommate, dump her, and make her not want to live with me? No, I didn't see anything wrong with preventing that outcome. "It sounds exactly right to me."

He throws himself onto my bed. "What you're essentially saying is that if your roommate is a great chick, fun to hang out with, totally normal, then she's off limits. If she's burn-the-bunny crazy, though, she's all mine."

I push his feet off. "That's right. Good job on putting together two and two."

"Shouldn't you be encouraging me to date nice girls?"

"First, you don't date anyone. You sleep with girls for anywhere between one night and a month. Maybe two tops. Then I'm left with either the *constant crier* or the *I'm cutting off your brother's dick the next time I see him* roommate." I had both in junior college.

"You're a killjoy, El." He reaches to my desk pushed against the foot of the bed and grabs the miniature Nerf football sitting between my pen cup and Kleenex box. "Besides, I can't help it if the girls you room with turned into bunny boilers."

"Guess what! You don't have to sleep with any of them. Here's an idea; how about you not sleep with the girls who have a tendency to go rabid after you dump them." I grab the football from him and throw it at his face. He snatches it out of the air before it can come within two feet of him. Damn reflexes!

"Next thing you'll say I should stop having sex like Knox Masters."

I stumble on a non-existent fold in my rug and have to steady myself on the edge of the desk. "Knox Masters is celibate?"

Jack rolls over on his side and tosses the football at me. I don't bother to catch it. The ball strikes the back wall and bounces onto the desk, knocking papers onto the floor.

"Not just celibate, but a virgin." Jack bends down and gathers up the papers on the floor. I'm still too stunned to help him.

"No. I don't believe it," I answer flatly. Knox is gorgeous. His abs are so defined that a girl might cut her tongue on his ridged perfection, and based on this morning's interaction, he's got a little charm. Okay, a lot of fucking charm. "Do you really believe he's a virgin? Maybe he tells people he's a virgin and then the girls fight each other to show him the ropes—to be the first."

"Hard to say. I've seen him hook up with girls. One night we went to a club downtown and a girl ate his face off."

Yeah, *so* not a virgin.

"Still, I mean, he could be a virgin." Jack rifles through the papers. Fuck, where is my class schedule? I surreptitiously look around my desk for it. "What's this?" he demands.

I look over at the sheet of paper he's thrust out. Is it…? No, thank God. I grab the intramural informational sheet from his hands and drop it on my desk. The other paper he has is the literacy brochure.

My schedule with *his* classes rests innocently inside a notebook. I stack my papers together and shove them all in the drawer.

"It's the Western intramural schedule."

"What are you playing?" he says with suspicion.

"Softball. Is that okay?"

"Maybe. What position? Not catcher, I hope. Not with your knee."

"This is *intramural* softball, Jack." I emphasize the word in hopes he catches on that I don't want him interfering or riding me about playing. I need to have a life outside of him and football. "And I don't know what position I'm playing. I'm meeting with the team Sunday night."

"You should play left field." He studies the pamphlet in his hands for a second. "What is this? Are you doing some teaching internship? I thought you planned to major in English."

"No, I took a grant writing class this semester and my coursework involves writing a proposed grant for the literacy center." I watch him closely to see if he has any interest at all.

"Glad someone in the family likes writing." He tosses the paper on the desk.

I watch it as it floats down and summon my courage. "Susan, the director of the learning center, gave me this for research. There's a lot of adult learning resources out there. I didn't realize how many, in fact."

Hint. Hint.

Jack's silent and his head dips down. For a moment, I think he's seriously considering my words, but then he kneels on the floor. "Shit, Ellie, I think I got glitter on my shoes. Look."

I look down, and sure enough, there are sparkles on his running shoes. During the move, glitter I used for some high school craft project must have risen to the surface.

"So?"

"So, I'll get hazed over this." He shakes his foot.

"You told me once that glitter was a stripper's calling card. Tell your friends you went to a strip club," I say impatiently. Obviously, he has no interest in learning disabilities, and I'm too chicken to brazenly ask him about it. Jack has always been my best friend, and I'm afraid of saying something that would push him away.

Other people might have resented how their parents focused too much on one kid, but Jack hated that attention and has always gone out of his way to make me feel important and necessary. I repaid him by doing these things, only I'm not sure it's the right way any longer.

I sigh at my own cowardice.

"Good point." He checks his watch. "So you want me to swing by and pick you up in about an hour?"

Oh no. No way I'm going to dinner. "No, sorry. I've got too much stuff here to do."

We both look at my immaculate room with its tidy desk, the clothes all put away, and the once pristinely made bed.

"Rrrrrright," Jack drawls. "I'll be back in an hour."

"No, Jack. Really. I want to stay home tonight. Eat by myself."

"You want to stay home. Alone. Your second night here?" He raises a skeptical eyebrow. "Not to mention, after missing me for the last two months, you drove up early to move in and didn't call me until all your shit had been unpacked."

He stands now, towering over me. He looks pissed off.

"Um, yes?"

"Bullshit. You're coming to dinner with me tonight. And if you keep saying no, I'm calling my entire house to come and carry you out of here." He holds up his phone and shakes it at me. He lives with half of the offensive starters.

Jack doesn't make idle threats, so I give in. "Okay. Fine."

What'll one dinner with members of his team do to me? Besides, in junior college, Jack hung around solely with the offense and Masters plays defense, so I'm not worried I'll see him. Still...

"What's the dress code here?"

"Shorts, flips, T-shirt."

"For me, not you." I throw a pencil at him that he snatches it out of the air. One of these days, I'll learn not to throw things at a guy who wants to catch things for a living.

"It's pretty casual."

"I swear, if I show up and everyone wears a suit and tie, I'll castrate you." I shake my scissors at him before tucking them into the desk drawer.

"Shit. Ties are for away games. I don't know what the girls are wearing these days. This summer it's been mostly nothing. I can tell you that there are a lot of thongs. I remember those." His eyes get dreamy.

"Jesus, Jack. I don't want to hear that stuff."

He laughs and mock throws the football at me. I duck and scowl when he laughs even harder. After a few fakes, he sets the ball down and starts to leave. At the door, he turns back.

"Thanks for coming tonight. I know you told me that you wanted to find a new—what did you call it?" He winds his hand in a circle.

"Tribe?"

He snaps his fingers and points one at me. "Yeah. I thought troop, but I knew that was wrong."

"I want to make sure I broaden my horizons. Find new people to hang around with."

"You know it's okay by me if you hang with us jocks. I'd be okay if you even wanted to date a football player."

"Well, I won't. I went through that horror house and I don't need to revisit it."

Once was enough, thank you very little, Travis F.

"I don't know why you think a guy who plays chess will be better to you than one who plays football." Jack sounds mildly annoyed.

I shrug and pull out my favorite jean skirt. I wore this all summer long. It was the right length between sexy and sporty. I might as well go with something tried and true. Plus it has pockets, which means I can stuff my ID and keys in the skirt and forego a wristlet or purse. "Maybe they aren't, but I haven't ever dated a guy who played chess before."

"I'm all for you exploring new shit, but guys are dicks regardless of whether they wear a jock strap or a pocket protector."

"That's a ringing endorsement of your gender."

He walks toward the front door. "If you decide to take a vow of celibacy that'd be great, but I'm not that naïve."

"Maybe I should hang around with Masters," I joke.

Jack opens the door and steps into the hall. All the traffic stops and stares at him. He smiles and nods to the bangable girls, which it appears encompasses all of the females in the hall. "I thought you didn't believe him."

"Jury's still out."

5

ELLIE

"HI, ELIOT," MASTERS MURMURS AS I wait for the food service employee to spoon a very bland piece of chicken onto a plate.

"Masters." I guess we're skipping over exchanging names. I felt him at my back before he even opened his mouth. He carries a certain crackling energy with him. Tonight he smells freshly showered, which is as dangerous as the slightly sweaty, early morning Masters. I shudder lightly.

"Anything wrong?" There's light amusement in his voice. I'm sure if I turn around he'll be grinning. Since my defenses are weak from the lack of food, I don't even peek at him.

"The food here is lousy." Of course, I say it at the exact moment the server hands me my plate. "But this looks great." I give her a big smile that she doesn't return. Masters muffles a snort while I hurriedly grab my plate before the server tips the tray on my head.

"It's the hall closest to the athlete dorms, so there's a lot of low calorie choices for those in training. But you can ask the grill to make you anything."

I turn then, because I have to, and see Masters has a giant cheeseburger, French fries, and a glass of milk taller than my head.

"Now you tell me."

He plucks the tray from my hands and says, "You should have had breakfast with me. I could've shared all kinds of important Western State secrets with you."

I'm forced to trail after him like a puppy as he makes his way to the back, which has about ten tables shoved together and forty guys. It's a good thing I'm not carrying my tray, because the sight of half the football team sitting together makes my hands sweaty.

I use the only diversion I have available—Masters' butt. It's a work of art and I'm not even into men's asses. It's hard and round, and even though he's wearing cargo shorts, I can still see the flex and release of his glutes. The more I think about Masters flexing and releasing, the tighter my body gets.

No way is Knox Masters, all six-foot-six-inches of prime NFL-bound manhood, a virgin. He's got the wingspan of a god and his hands are big enough that I think they could actually span my waist, which is in no way tiny. When we walked in here, my brother looked almost small at six-four and two ten. I'm not sure what Masters weighs, but he's solid everywhere. His thighs look like tree trunks, and his shoulders are so wide they blotted out the sun when he virtually accused me of creeping on him at six in the morning.

The door to the stadium was open!

Then he spent the whole time pretending he wasn't a football player even after I'd hinted broadly that I knew who he was. I should punch him for that.

Now he's playing another game.

Bodies don't come harder or finer than his. Sure, there are great forms everywhere in college, particularly among the athletes, but Masters is of a different caliber. Already people are whispering *Heisman* and *First Round* in connection with his name. Panties probably decorate the sidewalks as he walks to class. Women all around the campus have to be offering themselves as tribute on the altar of his purported virginity on a nonstop basis.

Jack sits in the middle with his arm around an empty chair. His brows furrow when he spots Masters carrying my tray.

"I'll take that." I tear my eyes off Masters' butt, pluck my tray out of his hands, and settle into the seat Jack has saved for me.

Masters isn't done with me. Jack's eyes get wide as a child's on Christmas when Masters whispers in my ear, "You can run, Eliot Campbell, but this campus is too small for you to hide."

Gulp.

He leaves me without another word and ambles casually down toward the other open seats, as if he didn't—I'm not certain whether it was a threat or a promise.

"What was that all about?" Jack mutters under his breath.

"I thanked him for carrying my tray," I make up.

"And his 'you're welcome' was a secret?"

I dig my fingernails into my palm under the table so I don't blush. "I don't know what's in his head."

That's as truthful as any answer I can give.

"Then you aren't looking hard enough," Jack says wryly.

I look up to see Masters standing—looming really—across the table from us. All the seats are filled, but he sets the tray down anyway in a small sliver of space.

"Move down, Telly, will you?"

"Sure, Masters."

Telly, the Warriors center, shoves his tray down one spot. Soon the entire right side of the table is shifting, one player by one player. Masters calmly takes his seat.

"Thought I'd sit with the offense tonight. See what secrets you all are cooking up."

"Hell, man, you got to ease up during practice," Telly jokes. "I thought you would tear Ace's head off there a couple of times."

Before Masters can say anything in his defense, Ace leans across the table and points his knife in Masters' direction. "Don't you ever ease up on me. You think Ohio will go easy on me, or Wisconsin? How about the teams from Michigan? Think they'll go half speed because this is my first year as a starter? No fucking way. The minute Masters goes soft on me is the minute he's given up on this team, this year."

Telly raises his hands in surrender. "I got you, brother, just joking around with the big man here."

He pounds Masters on the back a couple of times. Masters doesn't even flinch. He calmly lifts his giant hamburger to his mouth, bites off half of it, and winks at me.

That's the last interaction I have with him for about twenty minutes. His teammates unknowingly do all his dirty work to ferret out my information.

Telly asks me where I'm living.

"With a girl named Riley Jensen in the Maplewood Apartments."

"Those are sweet." He nods with approval. "You'll have to have us over."

"I can fit about four of you in the living room."

"As long as one is me. I like chocolate chip cookies, if you're taking baking orders."

I wait for Masters to insert some remark about liking certain cookies, but he's completely silent.

Ahmed Lowe, one of the two main running backs, asks me what my major is.

"It's English Lit. I plan to write technical works for a living, like grants or instructional booklets or anything anyone wants written, but doesn't want to do it themselves."

"Ellie proofs all my work. She does a great job," Jack interjects.

"You can write my papers," Telly says.

I somehow keep smiling as if his innocent—I hope—joke doesn't stab me in the gut. "When you're out of college, I'll write whatever you want, but I wouldn't want to affect your eligibility."

You are an awful person, Eliot. Awful.

Clifton Knowles, the strong side offensive lineman, asks if Jack and I are twins because we're both juniors.

Jack answers for me. "We're ten months apart. I got held back a year and so we ended up being in the same grade."

What Jack doesn't say is that we've been taking care of each other for as long as we both remember, which is why I'm the only female sitting with the football team. There's nearly a hundred guys who dress and seventy who travel, but in the sea of muscle and testosterone, I'm the only girl because this is my third night here and Jack doesn't want me eating alone.

He takes care of me. I take care of him. No matter what.

"That's cool," Masters says. "I have a twin but he plays—"

"—Defensive end for MU," I finish for him. It's common knowledge. Again, they appeared on the same cover of *Sports Illustrated*.

"Ellie probably knows more about football than I do." Jack ruffles my hair affectionately.

My hand goes up reflexively to smooth the errant strands, but a warm look in Masters' eyes—one that gives me those unwanted feelings again—has me dropping my hand to my lap. So what if my hair is messy and looks like a static-y monster? It's not like I want to impress any of these guys. Not at all. I cross my legs and shift in my chair. Masters' green eyes gleam at me. Bastard. No way he doesn't know what affect he has on girls. This whole virgin thing is probably designed to convey he's unattainable for me.

"Hey, boys." A sultry voice interrupts my stupid thoughts. We all look up into a glowingly beautiful face surrounded by a cloud of gorgeous honey blond hair. Her shirt fits tightly and shows off a pair of breasts that rival my generous rack, which I choose to hide under an oversized, baggy T-shirt I stole from Jack in high school.

She places a hand on Masters' shoulder and leans over, her breasts touching the side of his face. "When you're done with your terrible food, I've something special for dessert for you."

The lack of surprise from his tablemates tells me this is a common occurrence.

"Sorry, Bree, you know you'll get a better response from anyone than me."

He squeezes her hand and then gently removes it from his shoulder. She shakes her head in good-humored regret. "If you ever get tired of holding that line, let me know. I figured since this is my last year, I have nothing to lose."

"That's a good policy."

"But it's still a no?"

He gives her a nod, friendly but distant. "Still a no."

She walks off to join her friends, who wait for her at the end of the long row of tables.

"Don't like dessert?" I blurt out.

My brother kicks me under the table and his size fourteens hurt. As I bend over to rub my abused calf, Masters says, "I'm saving myself."

"For what? Marriage?" I joke, because as I told Jack, I don't know if I believe this virgin stuff.

"Not exactly, but close enough," comes the serious but casual reply, and Masters shoves the last bit of hamburger into his mouth as if he didn't just proclaim that the earth was flat.

The chicken breast is as flavorless as I thought, and I'm desperately wishing for sour cream or butter, or hell, I'd even squeeze a mayonnaise packet onto my baked potato if I could find one.

But if I'd been sitting at a five star restaurant and eating the best meal of my life, all the food would have tasted the same—flavored with surprised bullshit.

Which I almost said out loud. Bullshit. There is no way. I've seen this guy on television. Knox has more moves than a dancer in Vegas.

He can swivel out of an offensive lineman's grasp in one step, run down a wide receiver, and introduce a quarterback to the soil of the vaunted Western State's turf.

You can't help but look at his hands, the heavily veined forearms and the bulging biceps, and wonder whether the parts of him that you can't see are as big. You can't watch him move on the field, making fucking magic with his body, and not wonder what it'd be like to feel it flush against your own. Heat chases down my spine and my mouth becomes very dry. I stare at the table in front of him, as if I can see through the tray of nearly eaten food and the wood and metal to see the signs of his virginity.

Which would be what? Do I think there'll be a little wooden plaque that says "newbie?" Shit. I shake my head at my own ridiculousness and then make the mistake of looking upward into Masters' ruggedly handsome face that will no doubt adorn cereal boxes, granola bars, and billboards someday. He's got grass green eyes and a chin chiseled out of granite. In another era, Masters would be the general of an army immortalized in marble for his exploits on the field. Today he's a different kind of warrior—one that crushes his enemies in ten yard increments.

His wide mobile mouth knowingly curves upward and I have an uncomfortable sense he can tell exactly what I'm feeling somehow. I've never felt so exposed. I want to snatch those stupid aviators off the top of his head and plaster them on my own face.

"For religious reasons?" my brother asks.

"For Knox Masters' reasons." Masters' expression doesn't change. He's still smiling, but there's a definite no trespassing tone to his words. Beside me, Jack turns to Ahmed to talk about their single wing formation. That's too much detail for even a fan like me. I tune them out, which leaves me with Masters, who hasn't moved his attention away from me.

I drop my eyes to somewhere around his nose, because his eyes are so green and bright it's like staring into the sun, hypnotic and dangerous.

"I can't tell if you want it to be true," he says in a low voice that I feel as if I'm the only one who can hear.

"I don't know either," I tell him honestly. "But if you are, I think I need to go to church tomorrow, because that means impossible things exist like unicorns and the resurrection."

He laughs then, wide mouthed, white teeth flashing. "Tomorrow's Friday."

I nod. "I know, but it can't ever be too early to repent."

I feel, rather than see, his eyes sweep over me for a long moment as if he's cataloguing my stick straight brown hair, face, and loose T-shirt. "You don't look like you have much to repent for."

"Looks can be deceiving," I say archly with a pointed look.

"They can, can't they?" he murmurs and the deep rumble of his voice does weird things to my insides. Things I shouldn't feel for a new teammate of my brother's. I have two solid gold reasons not to date football players, so no matter how appealing Knox Masters is, he's not for me—even for a one-night stand to alleviate an itch if he wanted that sort of thing, which apparently, he doesn't. I'm still not sure I believe him.

His sexual status or lack thereof is none of my business. Sleeping with football players is not on my agenda, so I yank out of Masters' gravitational pull and turn toward my brother.

"You know some of the guys thought you were a dude because of your name." Masters has finished demolishing his meal, and I feel the full weight of his attention.

I click my tongue in mock sympathy. "It's terrible when you feel misled about someone's identity. What kind of monster does that?"

Masters' mouth twitches. "Everyone has their reasons." He shifts to Jack. "What are you doing tonight?"

"Thought I'd take Ellie out. Maybe go downtown."

"Nah. There's got to be a party around here." He leans toward the quarterback. "Ace, what's the drill for tonight?"

Ace jerks a thumb over his shoulder. "Hammer's throwing a party."

Masters stretches his long arms across the table, circling his tray and reaching across the invisible center line that separates his space from mine.

"We're going to Hammer's party."

The words spread like a wave from one player to the other. Ace might be the quarterback, but Masters is the leader of this squad. I suspect that if he told the squad to strip and run naked in the quad right now, they'd jump up and start ripping off their clothes without a moment's hesitation. He holds them in his large palm. As his smile pulls up at one corner, I feel like I'm there, too. That's far too dangerous a place for me.

I jerk back. Maybe Jack's back isn't big enough for me to hide behind. I think I need to put distance between myself and temptation. "I think I'll stay in tonight. I have a lot of unpacking to do."

Jack, like the good brother he is, doesn't point out that I've already unpacked everything. He tosses his napkin on the table. "Sure. I'll walk you back to your apartment."

Masters stands as we do. "Bring her to Hammer's party. She'll enjoy it."

It's an order, not a request.

6

KNOX

SO THAT'S WHAT SCURRYING LOOKS like I think as Eliot Campbell runs away. I shake my head. Eliot's all wrong for her. Her brother calls her Ellie. Ellie fits better, but it's still not quite right. Maybe *mine?*

"Hard to believe those two came from the same family. Do you think one of them is adopted?" Telly asks as we watch the Campbells exit the dining hall.

"Kind of plain. I barely noticed she sat there." Hammer appears out of nowhere. For a big guy, the lineman moves like a ninja.

"She's got a nice ass." Telly rubs his chin as if seriously considering all of Ellie's well-hidden charms. Tonight she wore what I guess is the baggiest T-shirt she owns. I didn't like seeing her in a guy's shirt, even her brother's. I had to stifle all my instincts when her brother put his arm across the back of her chair.

Seeing her with another male—no matter how little of a threat he is—rouses a very deep response in me.

As for plain…shit, these boys are blind. Ellie has the prettiest brown eyes that spit fire when she argues, and those lips? Holy hell, I'd like them pressed against me and wrapped around my dick. Whenever she pushed them together, I wanted to pry them open with my tongue. Still do.

"How can you tell under the tent she has on?" someone else asks.

"You are men of little imagination," I murmur. I check my watch. It's a little after seven. I should be able to call my brother before I hit Hammer's place. "What time are you opening the doors?" I ask him.

He's staring at me. They all are. I may make out with a random girl here or there at parties, but I've never shown any serious interest. While my sexual status was a joke when I was a freshman, my ability on the field has made it something of a holy artifact. Half the team believes our success is the result of my intestinal fortitude. "I thought sisters were off limits," he stammers out.

"They are to you, Hammer."

MATTY IVERSON, OUR WEAK SIDE linebacker, is in my apartment drinking a beer when I get home. The house we live in is one of eight in a block. A booster bought them and gave them back to the university for subsidized athlete housing, but only the starters live in the Playground, as it's called. I'm not sure who named it, probably some alum four teams ago or something.

I've got my own place on the third floor, but most of the time one of my teammates is up here.

"Why weren't you at dinner tonight?" Eating together every Thursday night is a team tradition. It's not mandated by the program, but you better have a damn good excuse for not showing up. Better to bring your sister, as Jack did, than not come at all.

"The parental units are still in town. They cleared it with Coach at the last minute. I texted you." Matty lifts his phone to show me his text. I pull my own phone out of my pocket.

"So you did." I find the sheet coach gave us of players to watch for and find Jack's number. I punch that into my contacts. If Ellie doesn't give me her number tonight, I'll have to get it from her brother. "You still hungry?"

One dinner a night doesn't really satisfy anyone's appetite, not when you're working out three to four hours a day.

"You know it. What you got?"

I rummage around in the freezer. "Burritos?"

"Hammer having a party tonight?"

We look at each other and then the burrito. I toss it back into the freezer. "Right. Nothing says sexy like ripping one while you're trying to close the deal. Hot Pocket?"

"Yeah, I'll take two."

I throw two in the microwave. "Three minutes, bro. Be right back. I'm calling my brother. You need anything else?"

He throws his feet onto the coffee table. "Nah, I'm good."

I shut the bedroom door and flip open my computer. My brother, Ty, answers the video call on the first ring. He must be watching porn or game film on his laptop.

"When's your bye week?" I minimize the video screen and open a browser window.

"Not until Halloween. Trick or treat, dickhead. Why?"

"Shit, that's nine weeks away. Maybe I can come up there. We've got a bye at the end of September." In the search box, I type Ellie's name. She's on the second page of results. Her header is a picture of her and Jack, and her profile picture is the back of her head. Her profile is locked. It tells me nothing other than she was born in February. She must be twenty with Jack twenty-one.

"Sucks that you have one so early," Ty says. Later in the year, byes are better for our bodies and our teams. We get an extra week to heal, take a mental vacation, and come back ready to fight a major opponent. Instead, we got a fourth week bye. Sucks, but it is what it is. "Why do you want to come up anyway, and what the hell are you looking at?"

"I'm checking out a girl's Facebook profile. It's locked, though." I send him the link.

"Eliot Campbell? Is that a guy?"

"No, her brother is the guy in the picture. She's the one with the ponytail."

"What kind of name is Eliot?"

"She's the one, bro."

"The one what?"

"Dude." I frown. "The *one*."

"Oh, shit. Did she pass the test?" His eyes get comic book wide.

"No, I haven't run it yet. She's new, a transfer student. I was running in the stadium today, doing my early morning routine." Ty winds his hand for me to speed up the story. "Her brother is our new transfer tight end from that juco program out west."

"If she didn't pass the test then she ain't the one."

"I'm telling you the Earth shifted when I met her. I got pissed off that she'd interrupted my workout, and then she started talking about football like it was her religion. She's got a scar on her knee."

"Knox, man, you've got a weird fetish for chicks with scars."

"*One* other girl I thought was hot had a scar." I close the browser. "It's a sign she's athletic. Not scared of getting hurt. Pursuing life with both arms fucking wide open."

"Or it means she's fucking clumsy." He leans back in his chair and folds his arms across his chest.

"This is useful," I gripe.

"Look, the earliest we can get together is your bye week. You think you can keep it in your pants that long?"

"Shit. I don't know. I practically mauled her on the football field this morning. Her T-shirt got a little wet and even though I couldn't see a damn thing—fucking sports bras"—Ty gives me a thumbs up in agreement—"I wanted to take her on the turf in front of God and everyone. At dinner, she sat by her brother, and I had to sit on my hands from reaching across and ripping his fucking arm off when he draped it across her seat. I don't know if I can keep my hands to myself. I know I can't ignore her. She's too fine. Some other guy will swoop in."

"Jesus, Knox, you've kept it together for twenty-one years, and you're throwing it away on a girl you've known for less than a day."

"It sounds crazy, but isn't the whole concept of *the one* crazy? Isn't the test that we Masters have based on metaphysical bullshit that could never be proven? We accept it on faith. You believe it and so do I."

"I don't believe it like you do," Ty grumbles and looks away.

"Bullshit. I know you believe in it or you wouldn't have broken up with Marcie." Marcie and Ty were high school sweethearts everyone expected to marry, until she tried to climb into bed with me one night. She claims she didn't know the difference. It would've been better for her if she confessed she'd done it intentionally. Once Ty heard her say she couldn't tell us apart, he dumped her. He hasn't had a steady girlfriend since.

Ty flips me off but doesn't argue. Someone shouts in the background.

"Hold on." He gets up and slams out of the room. "I'm fucking talking to my brother, you assholes. What is the problem?" More yelling takes place. I can't make it out. Ty returns looking hassled. "Aw, fuck. Gotta run. Someone's hazing the freshmen even though we told them not to. You'll regret it if you don't make her take the test. And pictures don't count."

I don't think I'll regret shit when it comes to Ellie, except not making a move when the gap is open. I'm nothing if not an opportunist. The time between beating the tackle off the snap is a millisecond. You see the opening and go, or you're dropped on your ass and some lesser talent posterizes you, putting you on ESPN for all the wrong reasons.

I'm not sitting on my thumbs waiting for anything, especially not Ellie.

7

ELLIE

THE PARTY AT HAMMER'S HOUSE is exactly how it was back in junior college—lots of beer, scantily clad women, and jocks standing around evaluating the talent. Even though classes haven't officially started, there's a sizable number of students hanging on the porch by the time Jack and I arrive. I don't even want to think about how many there will be once the season gets in full swing. Saturday night after a game? This whole place will get overrun with people.

Inside, though, it's quieter than I expect. Likely, the sultry late summer temperatures are driving people outdoors. The minute we walk inside, Jack gets pulled away by Ahmed.

"Hey, man, come and see this sick play that Hammer pulled off on *Madden*."

"I need to get Ellie a drink," Jack protests.

"The keg's in the back, or if you want a mixed drink, hit the kitchen." Tyrell points vaguely toward the back of the house. "Just tell the guys there that you're Campbell's sister."

And this is yet another reason I don't want to date a football player. It's bad enough being *Jack Campbell's sister*, but to date someone where your entire identity gets subsumed by that? No thanks. Jack hesitates. I give him a push.

"I'll be fine. Really," I insist. "New tribe and all."

The new tribe bit is bullshit because this is a football party. I should have stuck around the apartment and found out what Riley planned to do tonight, but Jack insisted, said that once Masters laid down an edict, he had to follow it for team unity and all that hogwash.

Yet, I bought into it, too, because here I am, at a party full of football players, gridiron groupies, girlfriends, and wannabes. I need to find a nice quiet corner where I can hide for two hours or so until I can convince Jack I should go home.

"She'll be fine," Ahmed repeats, and with another shove from me, Jack allows the running back to lead him off to see whatever amazing exploits are going on in a video game of fake NFL players.

In the kitchen, I find a lanky, acne-pocked guy pouring drinks. I don't recognize him, but given the shit position of playing bartender, he must be a freshman.

"Can I have a Coke?"

"Shit, honey, a Coke? I got all kinds of stuff back here. Don't tell me you plan to pussy out tonight and not get hammered like the rest of us." He pulls out a giant bottle of whiskey and waves it at me.

Pussy out? Nice. I resist the urge to tell him that this pussy isn't impressed with his act. "No thanks. Just the Coke."

He leans over the makeshift counter, a piece of lumber stretched across the space between one end of the opening into the room and the other. "It's not just a Coke, tiger." *Tiger?* "It's a statement piece that says I'm boring as fuck. You don't want to start out on the wrong foot during the first big night of the year. We've got girlie drinks back here for people like you. Now what's your poison?" He tips his head up looking massively satisfied with himself.

"So, you're a wide out?" It's time to put this guy in his place. He's on the skinny side and a hair under six feet. He could be a defensive back, but there's something about the way he leans forward that makes me think he's waiting for the gun to go off or the quarterback to yell *set hut*.

His grin widens. "How'd you guess?"

It's my party trick. Some girls can guess bra sizes. Some guys can do two story beer bongs. Me? I can guess what position you play.

"Your build." I gesture. "They didn't require you to get to a certain weight?"

His grin dies off. "Still working on it," he answers stiffly.

She shoots. She scores. "Okay, I'll take my Coke. Thanks."

"Get her a Coke, bro," a deep voice from behind me orders.

"Oh sure, Knox." The guy's voice nearly cracks with awe that his team captain is standing there talking to him. He digs around in a tub of ice and shoves the red and white can into my hand.

As I leave the line, I tap the top of it, in case he gave it a good shake under the water.

"You crushed that kid. He'll stand in front of his mirror tonight wondering how you didn't see his big guns."

"Maybe he should spend more time in the weight room and less time hassling girls about wanting a soda."

"He's young and suffering from the loss of status. In high school, no doubt, he was the big man on campus." Masters knocks fists with someone, nods to another person, but doesn't stop talking to me. "The transition is tough for some."

A few people give me an appraising look that says *what are* you *doing with Knox Masters.* "Not for you, though."

"I was fucking homesick the first semester. I missed my brother and my family. I had to remind myself why I was here, why I needed to go to practice every day."

The bald honesty surprises me so much I stop walking.

"What?" he asks when he realizes I haven't moved.

"I'm surprised you'd admit to that."

"You think admitting to being homesick makes me weak?" He raises a surprised eyebrow. "Or are you surprised that I have feelings?"

Enough with the tears, you goddamned disgrace! I hear my father yelling at Jack. *There's no place for emotion in this game. Are you a winner or are you a fucking pussy like your sister?*

"I thought stoicism is required to wear the jersey," I say. I try to make it a joke but Masters' knowing eyes tells me he sees right through my thin veneer. I look away.

On the back porch, a long line of people wait to get a beer. No one is getting drunk at this party, because the buzz will have worn off between beers.

Maybe Knox senses I'm about to bolt because he grabs my hand. "Come on."

As he steers me past the crowd, around the keg and toward a dark corner where an overgrown tree appears to eat about half the porch, I start to panic. For a million reasons I don't want to explore, I can't stand with Knox Masters in a secluded corner.

I tug on his wrist. "I think I want to dance."

He levels me with a look that says, *Really? You're pulling that bullshit?* "Then we'll dance."

I sigh. There's no getting away from him.

"Knox! I just got in today!" A bubbly blonde with Hollywood looks saunters over. Her assets are on full display under a tight bandage tank top that plunges low in the front. She's wearing denim panties—shorts so short and cut so high they look like underwear. It's a popular look around here. Most of the girls are wearing a lot of fringe and denim. We could be at Coachella, minus the desert and the bands.

"Hey, Kitty."

She places a hand on his chest, right above his heart and her perfectly manicured nails flex against his navy blue T-shirt. The urge to rip her hand away takes me by surprise. I want to snarl at her, *that chest belongs to me.* I engage in a momentary fantasy of pushing her five feet back and making a slashing motion across my throat.

Fortunately for both of them, Masters steps back.

Kitty's gaze drops to our joined hands. A confused look crosses her face as if she's never seen him hold a girl's hand before. *I know*, I want to say, *it's weird for me, too.* "Is this your…cousin?" she stammers out.

"No, this is my—"

Before he can finish the sentence, Hammer shows up and drapes an arm around both of us. "This is Jack Campbell's sister, KittyKat. Jack's our new tight end transfer. Good hands. She's a friend of the team."

"Oh, that's good." Kitty's smile comes back. She holds out her hand.

"I'm a friend of the team, too." She winks.

That's fine as long as she stays away from Masters. *Ellie, no, this is your way out.* I get my wits together and reach for her. "Actually Kitty, Masters told me he wanted to dance."

"He did?" she says, wide-eyed.

"Masters?" He frowns. "Is that how you think of me?"

I don't have to answer that strange question because Hammer interjects with a look of surprise that matches Kitty's. "You want to dance, man? Since when?"

Masters places his arm around my shoulders. "Ellie is making a joke."

"It's not a very good joke," Kitty says uncertainly.

Masters nods solemnly. "Which is why I'm going to take her to this corner over here and give her some instruction on joke telling. You go dance with Hammer and show him the moves you learned over the summer."

Kitty and Hammer both nod enthusiastically and disappear inside.

"I wasn't making any jokes."

"Trust me. My dancing is a bad joke. You don't want to see it."

He lets me go once we make it past the keg line and I wander to the back corner of the porch—away from the music, the crowd, the Kittys of campus. But I can't seem to shake Masters so I climb up on the top railing and settle in for a night of people watching, which is better than being inside the muggy house watching a bunch of drunk guys play *Madden* on a big screen.

The back of the house juts up against a small green space shared by about six or seven other houses—the infamous Playground where the football team lives. When Jack got the invitation to move into one of the houses, we'd known then that the Western coaching staff had high hopes for him.

Knox leaps, one handed, onto the railing.

"How high can you box jump?" I ask before I can stop myself.

"Like my moves, do you?" He flashes a smug-as-fuck smile and flexes his biceps. My body tightens in an instinctive response. At least I blame it on biology. It's natural for me to be turned on by a big, strong guy. Generations of women have succumbed to the big, brawny male. It's why a specimen like Masters exists. "I can do just shy of five feet. Not as good as JJ Watts, but I'll get there. So, why are we hiding back here?"

"I'm at a party with over a hundred people. I hardly think that qualifies as hiding." Masters hasn't shaved and the scruff around his chin only serves to make him look a hundred times hotter. I remind myself that hairy chins can mean hairy butts and hairy backs, but sadly, that does nothing to quell my biological response to him. I take a sip of my Coke to hide my agitation and hopefully cool myself off.

"It's dark here. There isn't another person within ten feet of you. I think that qualifies as hiding." He leans closer, his muscled forearm resting too close to my ass for comfort. I try to slide over an inch but a tree branch stops me.

"This thing is a hazard." I bat at the branch. It causes a few leaves to fall, but doesn't give me any space to move away. Between his body and this unruly forest, I'm stuck.

"Hammer's too busy to cut it down. Besides, I think people fuck back here. He probably keeps it to provide cover."

I raise an eyebrow. "Is that from personal knowledge?"

"Personal? As in, have I made the mistake of checking out some noises back here, thinking that an animal was rooting around in garbage, only to find one of my teammates getting his pipes cleaned? Then yeah, from personal knowledge."

"Still sticking with that virgin thing, are you?"

"I am." He lifts a bottle of something to his lips and drinks. His big hand nearly engulfs the container filled with clear liquid. Probably vodka. I tear my eyes away from his bobbing Adam's apple because even that is sexy. "You don't believe me, do you?"

"No, I don't." I tilt my head as if a new perspective can reveal the truth. "I don't know why. I look at you and think it can't be true."

He smiles back at me. "I take that as a compliment, but it's true. I mean, I'm glad that you think that I've got some moves. That bodes well for my future girlfriend."

"Is it so important that I believe you?"

He spears me with those brilliant gem green eyes of his. "Yeah, I think it is."

I refuse to explore that sentiment. It's too scary. I ask him another question. "So, you've never made out with anyone or never had a girlfriend?"

"No, I have." His arm has slid over that spare inch and now rests against my ass. I try not to let it affect me. I try to pretend that little contact between his bare forearm and my jean-clad butt isn't spreading into every nerve of my body.

I clear my throat. "So, you're an *everything but* virgin. Newsflash, you're not a virgin."

He chuckles, low and deep. "I've never stuck my dick in a girl. I've never gotten a blowjob. I've never gone down on a girl. But I have got to first and second base."

"I can't believe I'm asking you these things, but I can't help myself. It's partly your fault because you keep answering them. But how about dry humping?"

He takes another swallow from his bottle and then another. Then he drains the whole thing and sets it on the deck floor. "Yeah, I'll admit to that. Do I keep my virgin status?"

"I'll think about it." I'm glad it's dark because I feel hot, and I bet I'm beet red. Why I'm asking these super personal questions of Knox Masters, I do not know. But I'm the one suffering because now all I can think about is what it's like to kiss Knox, to straddle his lap and rub myself against him until we're both crazy with lust. Dry humping? Did I really ask him that? I press my can against my forehead, but it's lukewarm and provides absolutely no relief. I think I need a cold beer. Or some of that rum that the kid offered earlier.

"What are you drinking?" I ask in an effort to remember a tiny bit of manners and hop off my spot on the porch. A few people have drifted over, probably drawn in by Masters' gravitational force.

"Water."

That stops me short. "Water? No beer? No vodka? Season hasn't even started."

"There will be plenty of time to throw down after the season is over," he says mildly, not even remotely offended. "The average time in the NFL is five years. I'll play ten if I'm lucky. Fifteen if the gods smile down at me. That gives me forty plus years to drink myself into a stupor."

The discipline this guy has amazes me. "You're big into delayed gratification."

"Waiting can be worth it."

"How would you know?"

He laughs. He throws his head back, and the deep rumble starts in his body and ends in mine. Fuck me. He's gorgeous, talented, and has a goddamned sense of humor.

Life is so unfair.

8

KNOX

WITH LITTLE EFFORT, I SWALLOW the rest of my laughter. I want to pinch Eliot's cute, frustrated cheeks right now, but I have a feeling that'd go over as well as Hammer's attempt to throw the ball—which means not at all. His arm is shit. If we run a trick play, he'll never be the one to throw the ball down field toward Ace.

She shifts uncomfortably, but I don't make any effort to make that go away. It's a good uncomfortable. She's hyperaware of my existence, which is only fair because I can't stop thinking about her either.

It hasn't been a cakewalk abstaining from plowing every willing girl who's thrown herself at me. It's only gotten worse since I got put on the cover of *SI* with a bunch of other overhyped college players and the caption *Who's Next?* I didn't even want to be on the cover. It's complete bulletin board material. No doubt that stupid picture is up in locker rooms all over the conference full of dart holes.

There is so much willing pussy thrown around that it's hard to dodge. At a big Division I school, all you have to say is you've got a spot on the roster and girls are ready to spread for you. Even the wet-behind-the-ears freshman bartender won't have any problem finding a chick to go home with tonight, even though he struck out hard with Ellie. It's easy to drink water instead of pounding drinks. It's easy to say no to those offers of HGH or money from agents. There are real repercussions to those actions.

But saying no to a hot, dark-haired beauty who wants nothing more than to put her lips around my dick? Or no to the cute redhead who promises me the carpet matches the curtains? Or no to the banging blonde whose barely-there tank top doesn't quite disguise her erect nipples that she apparently has developed from rubbing her ass all over my lap? That takes super human effort. As each month wore on, it felt harder to remember why I'd decided I'd wait.

I'm not religious. Oh, I believe in a higher being. If pressed, I'd say that heaven and hell existed in some form. But my decision to wait didn't stem from some mandate in a thousand-year-old written text or from some guy on top of the mountain. It's a hell of a lot more prosaic and boring. But I've managed to say no because I've waited this long, and it didn't make sense to waste it on a quick and easy fuck in some bar bathroom or frat house bedroom.

But fucking my fist gets real old.

It'd be easier if I was a hermit like Ace, who doesn't like parties and would rather be tied up and whipped publicly than have to sit and make small talk with a bunch of assholes he barely knows, which is why he's hiding in the video game room playing *Madden*. But I enjoy the crowds. It hypes me up to see all these people here at Hammer's house, excited to be with us.

And I'm not at all immune to the easy charm of Ellie Campbell, her obvious love of the sport regardless of her stated bullshit claim that she hated it, and her tight body.

"You ready for Missouri?" she asks.

I avert my face to hide a grin of triumph. Not only is her butt still planted on the railing, but she's asking questions like she can't quit me. I like how the universe lines up perfectly sometimes.

"You bet, but they're a decent opponent."

She snorts. "You don't have to pretend for me. They're terrible and you should win by at least three scores."

Our first game is in less than ten days and we should win it. In fact, our first tough match up doesn't come until week five but you can't enter a game thinking it's won before you even step foot on the field.

"The team you overlook is the team that beats you."

She shakes her Coke can and we both hear how empty it is, but I'm not ready to go inside and get her a new drink. Out here in the dark corner I've staked out, it's almost as if we're alone. I can work with this.

"How fresh is that Ducks loss?" she asks.

"Like yesterday. That loss won't go away until we win the national championship." We laid a turd in that game against the Ducks last year, but this year when we play them, it'll be a different story. "It won't happen this year. I spent the summer watching tape of the spread offense and conditioning like a motherfucker. No one is outrunning me on the field this year. If anyone is gasping for breath during the fourth quarter, it won't be me.

Ellie tilts her head and her hair falls like a curtain, a privacy shield.

I wonder what she'd do if I dug my hand into that hair to hold her steady while I plundered those plump lips with my mouth. Given that one kiss would not be enough, I probably should wonder if she likes public displays of fucking, because once I had my tongue in her mouth, it wouldn't take long before I'd want to have my dick inside her pussy. Said dick now makes my cargo shorts a size too tight.

"How come you and your brother don't play for the same team?" she asks. Her light colored tank top catches the lights, making her look a little fairy like. A sexy fairy. She's wearing a jean skirt, and the tank top is decorated with fish scales—sequins I think. She glitters when she turns. It doesn't show a lot of skin but the hints are there. Like Telly noted, she has a nice ass, but she also has a sizable rack. Her tits might even spill out of my giant hands. I curl my hands into fists to keep from testing that.

"We play the same position and didn't want to compete against each other for playing time like we did in high school."

"That was some *SI* spread." She smiles, remembering something she liked—hopefully me. "Your brother looks a little weak, though. You tease him about that?"

I start breathing lightly because here it is—where the rubber meets the road. Not many people can tell us apart and she's suggesting that she can. "He doesn't get up early enough to lift; doesn't get the reps in," I joke. That's a partial lie. Ty does get up later, but he's a beast. We had competitions all summer, and probably would have ended up tearing something in our efforts to outdo each other if our dad hadn't monitored our progress.

"I'm that way, too. I like to get up early, but Jack's a night person.

He'd rather practice in the afternoon, stay up, watch film, and then sleep until noon. I like getting everything out of the way so I can spend the evening having fun."

"And what constitutes fun for Ellie Campbell?"

"Ellie?" she says with a raised eyebrow.

"Ellie," I reply firmly. Eliot is a weird ass girl's name, although I keep that sentiment to myself. "You look like an Ellie, not an Eliot."

"What does an Eliot look like?"

"Five ten, wears skinny jeans. Maybe has a goatee."

"That's pretty specific."

"You avoiding the question?" It's no casual question. Ellie will be part of my life for a long time. I need to know what she enjoys doing.

She shrugs and flips her hair back, allowing light to come into our small circle. Little spots of golden color hit her forehead and the top of her nose. "I like…football. Watching it, of course. I like orderly things. Opening a new pack of perfectly sharpened pencils. Starting a new notebook. Writing the first goal down in my day planner."

Ellie slaps herself on the forehead. "God, could I have sounded geekier? Let me try again. I like pounding beers every night and smoking a joint before bed."

"I like Geeky Ellie," I tell her and rub the spot on the top of her head that she slapped. The touch surprises her. She stills.

"What are you doing?" she whispers. The words come out almost inaudible, but I'd know what she said if she stood across the room.

"Feeling you." I can't help myself from dropping my hand to her cheek. It feels as soft as it looks. I wonder how soft other parts of her feel.

"I don't think you should do that," she protests, but doesn't move.

"Why?"

Her eyes are like chocolate. I want to eat her up.

"Because it gives a girl ideas." She dips her head and her lips nearly brush the palm of my hand.

Reluctantly, I withdraw. I get the sense I need to slow down for her—that at this point she won't recognize my actions as sincere or genuine. I drop my hand to the rough wood of the porch railing and immediately miss the feel of her skin.

Beside me she makes a small sigh. I choose to interpret it as disappointment.

After a few moments, she breaks the silence and asks, "Why'd you wear your brother's uniform for the magazine shoot? Didn't any of them catch on?"

My heart stops. Literally. It halts for a full second before it hitches back up again. I exhale heavily and put an inch of space between us. She's too potent and I'm feeling weak.

"None of them."

"Really?" The space between her eyes crinkles. I leap down from the railing and back away. But there's not enough space I can put between the two of us. I'm about five seconds from throwing her on the ground.

"Really," I insist. "I wore his MU jersey the entire time and he wore mine. How could you tell?"

"You guys are similar, but it's pretty easy." Her tone is dismissive, as if anyone could tell us apart.

"We're identical."

"If you say so." It's evident she doesn't see it that way.

"I don't say it. That's what reality is." I pull out my phone and flick to the family album. "Here, you see." I show her a picture from this past summer. We're at the lake and we have our arms across each other's shoulders. My brother is wearing the blue trunks and I have the red trunks. We're both wearing matching aviators our mom bought for our birthday. "Look, no one else can tell us apart. Even my dad has issues. Only my mom is able to do so consistently."

"It's not my fault everyone around you has really shitty eyesight." She points to my image. "You're wearing the red shorts."

Holeee Fuck.

"Exactly how can you tell us apart? Seriously now. No jokes. No games. Swear it on a stack of holy bibles."

"I'm an atheist."

"Fine. On a stack of Darwin treatises." I roll my eyes.

"Your jaw is more square and defined." She pinches the photo, zooms, and traces her finger across my jaw. I feel the touch as if her finger actually touched my chin. It sends a shudder down my spine. "And his eyes are weirdly close set. Like horror-show weird. Nothing against your brother. And you're taller and more muscular."

She thinks I'm more muscular. I can't wait to tell Ty these details. Right before we both left for school, in between summer training camp and the start of fall ball, we weighed and measured each other. The diameter of our biceps measured the same. I swipe to another photo. This time we're both wearing suits for my cousin's wedding. Even for my mom had a hard time telling us apart that day. "How about this one?"

"You're the one on the left."

I was the one the left. I tuck my phone away, place my hands on my thighs, and lean over to catch my breath. I wonder if this is how the Hulk feels before he goes green. My heart races, my palms sweat, and I feel like I'm coming out of my skin.

"Is something wrong?" She places a hand on my back and I force myself not to flinch away.

"No. Everything is exactly how it should be." I exhale one more time and straighten to look at my girl's face, which shows equal parts confusion and worry. I grab her hand. We need a buffer and right now the buffer will be people. Lots and lots of people.

9

ELLIE

"YOU LOOK THIRSTY," MASTERS SAYS as he drags me from my corner on the porch toward the keg line and then into the kitchen. I'm blinking from the sudden change in scenery. One minute we were sitting in the near dark, the only lighting from the moon and the tiny Christmas lights, talking about how many bases he's covered, and in the next he's dragging me from one end of the house to the other after the weird photo roll quiz.

He shoulders aside the freshman playing bartender, pulls out a Coke for me, and refills his empty bottle from a pitcher of water in the refrigerator. He really is drinking water.

I find that both charming and strange. My brother is a serious athlete, but he enjoys tying one on. Masters is on another level. I don't doubt for a second that I'll be watching him play on Sundays in the next few years from my living room. As if I needed to find something else more appealing about Masters.

"Thanks," I say when he hands me my drink. I've got to get away from him. Somewhere in this house is my older brother and I should go find him. I head toward a dark hallway I spotted off the living area that's serving as the dance floor for what seems like all thirty thousand students, but I'm stopped by the tether at the end of my hand.

"Going somewhere?" His eyebrow arches slightly and we both know there's nowhere I can go in this house that Masters won't find me. The place is too small. He's too big.

"To find my brother." I tug, but he doesn't release me. I could twist my wrist and stomp off. In fact, that's what I should do. I shouldn't enjoy the feel of his rough fingers around me. I shouldn't tingle in my private places at the thought of that touch elsewhere on my body.

Why is it so hard to do what you should do instead of what you want to do? Maybe the better question is: Why do I want things that are bad for me? Because there's no question that Knox Masters is bad for me. While I may have daddy issues—who wouldn't with my old man—ever since Travis, I've made good decisions when it came to guys. Granted those decisions primarily ended up being avoiding males, but even if Masters didn't play football, he'd be someone to stay away from. I don't like overconfident players and despite—or maybe even because of it—Masters' virginity claim, he's as confident as they come.

He knows he'll be playing on Sundays and he has to know that he's the king of this campus. If he crooked his little finger, 99.9% of the women and maybe half the men would be at his side saying, "*Yes, please*" to any request he may have, no matter how degrading or ridiculous.

This time when I move away, I do the tug and twist, and my hand comes free. The music changes and Silento's "Watch Me" plays. Watch me disappear. I wave to him before I let the crowd swallow me up. He stares at me, a thoughtful expression on his face. I'm afraid of what he's thinking, afraid that his interest might draw me back in, so I turn and dance with the nearest drunken student, hoping that somewhere in this mass of people is that chess player I told Jack I would date this semester.

But my plan is waylaid when a circle opens up in the center of the room, and the football players that aren't hiding in some room playing *Madden* egg each other on to show off their whips, Nae-Naes, and Dougies. You can barely hear the music over the shouts of the crowd. Matty Iverson, the All-American Mid Conference linebacker, starts it off, swinging his hips and grinding low to the ground before jumping back up with one foot in the air. His mop of curly black hair shakes with him.

Another player follows up with his teammates hollering for him to get low. His arms pop and lock, and then he places a hand behind his head and wiggles his elbows as he bounces in a wide circle. I can't help but smile and cheer along with everyone else as one after another gives us a short display of their moves.

The part of me that loves football is the same part of me that responds to this show right here—the pageantry, the athleticism, the energy of the crowd. The beats of the music, the synchronized shouts, all thrum throughout my body.

"You want to dance?"

I didn't even sense him. Masters bends low, his hands finding a perfect resting spot on my waist. His lips are so close to my ear that one could classify it as a kiss. Realistically, though, it's loud in here.

"Not really."

"Yet, here you are. On the dance floor." His mouth curves up by my cheek. He starts to turn me around into his embrace when I'm saved by a shout.

"Masters! Get your white, unrhythmic ass over here!"

Masters shakes his head and laughs, and it's like before, deep and rumbly, as if he does everything with his whole self. My stupid body tightens in response because I know he'd be a beast in the sack. He'd throw every ounce of his energy and enthusiasm, and it'd be dirty, loud, and exhausting. Girls would walk funny for three days.

"We're playing this song on never-ending fucking repeat if you don't come over here and throw down," Hammer calls out. He turns to the crowd, waving his arms up and down, and starts to chant, *Masters, Masters.* The students pick it up and soon Masters—and I—get propelled to the front of the circle.

He rubs a hand down his face and turns back to me. "Don't forget I was an All American pick for both freshman and sophomore years."

Finishing his uncharacteristic bragging, he steps into the empty space and spreads his arms wide, like a ringmaster in a circus big tent. He bellows into the room, "We having fun yet, Warriors!"

Everyone jumps up and screams, "Yes!"

He snaps his fingers, the music spins up, and we watch open mouthed as Knox Masters, soon to be professional football player, the pride of the Warriors national championship hopeful team, begins to dance. He's…terrible.

Knox jerks his arm between his legs followed a half a beat by his second arm. He doesn't look like he's whipping anything so much as attempting to get a hold of an out-of-control jackhammer. His teammates fall into each other laughing. It's obvious they've seen this show before.

Everyone howls and so does Knox. His grin is huge as he dances off beat and tries to grind low as everyone hoots for him to do more. His performance is short, no more than thirty seconds or so, but it's long enough to crack my no-athlete barrier and melt my ovaries.

He ends by falling into the arms of his other defensive linemen, who throw him back and he careens carelessly right to me. I hold out my hands to brace him, only he stops short, expertly back in control of his body once more. The DJ segues into Jason Derulo's "Want to Want Me" and Masters takes advantage of the switch to swing me into his arms, his hips moving in rhythm to the music with much better timing than when he tried to hip flex in the middle of the circle.

"Liked that, did you?" He taps the apple of my cheek that hurts from smiling.

"Maybe." We both know the answer is yes.

"I can make a fool of myself regularly if it makes you smile like this." He grins again and I can't stop my own lips from curling upward. *He's ridiculously irresistible.*

Masters takes this as an invitation to slide one of his big hands around my waist, to rest at the waistband of my jean skirt. His long fingers rest at the top of my ass and he slips his other hand under my hair to palm the back of my head, as if he owns me. Masters tugs my hair back and his green eyes—almost black in the dark light of the dance floor—bore into mine as Derulo sings about needing to be with his woman, about not being able to wait, and getting high by just the thought of her.

Again, there's something in Masters' face—a hunger or desire or need—that scares me. I want to run away from this, but he's fastened me as securely against him as a sailor would lash himself to a mast.

Derulo's falsetto notes seem incongruous against the big, hard body pressed against me and his tones fade away replaced by an even slower, sultrier song. This time it's Ellie Goulding begging to be loved the right way. Masters might be a virgin, but his erection feels huge against my stomach. Rock hard doesn't begin to describe it. Whatever he has in his shorts crushes rocks, decimates them, and turns them into dust. Kind of like all my good intentions.

I can feel them dissolving in the slow grind of our hips. This is a prelude to something, something horizontal and sweaty. I inch back, which is hard to do with a hand at your ass and the other in your hair.

"I'm not having sex with you. Your virgin line won't work on me." I wish I had more conviction in my voice.

"I know," he murmurs into my hair and pulls me back until again there's no space between us.

My God. Every word that comes out of his mouth makes me want to prove him wrong. He presses his face into my hair and I feel his chest move against mine as he inhales deeply. Vainly, I'm happy I showered with my mango-scented shampoo before I came out, even though I swear I had no plans to have Masters sniff me.

His unattainable status works overtime on me. I've become the girl I described to Jack. The one who wants to show Masters how amazing sex is.

"Masters, this won't go anywhere."

He draws back slightly and frowns. "Is that how you think of me? As *Masters?* I'm not your teammate."

"I'm not anything to you."

The side of his mouth quirks up. "That's what you think." His arms go around me again. He leans down. "You're too beautiful for words."

I stumble but his arms hold me upright. I wish I had some resistance left, but my willpower seems to have abandoned me.

He massages my scalp as he uses a muscled thigh to part my legs. I lean into him, drunk off the beat that pulses from the soles of my feet up into my belly. His hands tighten against me, pressing my soft flesh into his harder frame. I feel *everything*—the jut of his hard-on against my stomach, the ridged abdomen barely disguised by his tight T-shirt, the bands of steel that clutch me close. Against my better judgment, I move against him and his thigh slips farther between my legs. The denim of my skirt rides up and the worn cotton of his shorts rubs against the newly exposed skin.

His big hand drops from my ass the tops of my legs and a tremor unmoors me.

"What are you doing to me?" I croak.

"Shh," he murmurs, his lips moving against my temple in a feather-light caress. "We're just dancing."

Only we're not *just* dancing. We're pressed as close as two people can get. His leg is so far between mine that I don't think my feet touch the floor anymore.

"Masters, we can't…We shouldn't…" I can't even finish my sentences because what are we doing? I don't even know anymore.

"I know," he groans. The guttural moan travels through his body, reverberating against me. At least I'm not the only one caught in this strange thrall. He releases me abruptly, swinging me around toward the edge of the dance floor. All around us people do their own versions of upright sex on the dance floor, and no one notices as we sidle down that dark hall. I don't know where we're headed, but I'm going with him.

The deep bass of the common room fades, but as we reach the end of the hall, a new noise greets us. Masters nudges a door open and my eyes blink at the brightness of the room. Inside, a bunch of athletes hunch over controllers attempting to beat the hell out of each other in a video game. Despite practicing all day, they're competing to be the best video game football player. The bright light, the congregating jocks, the removal from the heat and sensation on the dance floor is exactly what I need to snap me back to my senses. This is the last place I want to be, and Masters is the last person I should be fooling around with. So much for my declaration of not doing any football player ever again.

I spin and give Masters a bright smile. "I'm grabbing another Coke."

"There's beverages inside. Plus, your brother is over there." Masters pushes me into the room, and sure enough Jack sits on the wide sectional, tapping furiously on his buttons. "I'll go take a piss and then I'll grab you a Coke. Jack, don't let your sister leave. We're arguing over the best athlete of all time and I'm not done making my case for Bo Jackson."

"Oh, man, she's a Jim Thorpe fan." Jack pats the sofa without taking his eyes off the television screen. "Come sit down, El. Watch me waste this motherfucker."

Gee, can I? I plop down on the sofa. I figure that Masters will leave, Jack will forget I'm here, and I'll be able to make my escape.

"Don't go anywhere." Masters points at me and then jogs away.

I wait for about thirty seconds and then stand, but before I can walk out, other members of the team stop me.

"What'd you need?" one asks me.

"Yeah, Masters said not to go anywhere."

Jack looks up. "You going somewhere, El? You can't leave by yourself. Give me a minute. We've got a quarter left, and I'll walk you home."

"Wait for Masters," someone advises.

I drop back by Jack, because clearly I'm not leaving until the oh-so-great Masters returns. The good thing is that any lingering desire or interest gets entirely eroded by his absence. In fact, the longer he's gone and the more I'm forced to watch Jack have his onscreen Andrew Luck throw downfield, the less I care about ever seeing Masters again. I certainly don't want to dance with him, pressed against his broad frame, or have his rough hands work me over.

Absolutely not.

So I focus on Jack and the fact he's getting his ass handed to him.

"Try an angle route," I tell him. "Don't go long every time."

He glowers, but in the next play runs an angle route for a completion. How long does it take to piss and get me a drink? Not as long as Masters has been gone.

Jack's opponent, a floppy-haired dirty blond who introduces himself as Eric—call me God—Goodwin, scowls. "Man, you can't have a coach in here with you. Not fair."

Jack shoots his middle finger at Goodwin and mutters under his breath to me, "Pass or run?"

It's third and two, and he's got Frank Gore. Duh. "Run."

Jack chooses a trap play, and when the defensive predictably runs toward the opening, Gore shoots through and runs all the way down to the end zone. The room erupts. Jack throws down the controller and starts slapping his hand in the air as if he's spanking someone. His teammates start hugging him and Jack glows. Literally glows, with the broadest, happiest smile on his face. Eric drops his head into his hands in misery.

Jack turns to me. "You ready to go?"

"You have a quarter left." I point to the screen.

"Yeah, no quitting until this game is over. You owe me, man," Eric protests.

"My sister needs an escort home."

"Masters will walk her home." Eric turns back to the screen as if that's the only acceptable answer in the room.

Jack looks uncertainly at me and then at the television. He wants to stay and play. This isn't about the video game; it's a bonding moment, and he's being accepted into a fraternity more difficult to get into than any house on Greek row.

"I can wait."

"You sure?" he asks.

I wink. "Of course, but I need to use the bathroom. Where is it?"

"Upstairs. Third door on the left." Eric waggles a finger in my face. "It's private. No circulating that and no taking a bunch of chicks up with you."

"I swear to keep your little cum domain a secret." I roll my eyes.

The room howls and Jack shakes his head, as if to say that he can't take me anywhere.

I jog up the stairs. I'll potty and then get the hell out of this place.

Third door on the left reveals one bed, a desk, and an old-fashioned Coke machine, its iconic red and white lines visible even in the dimly lit room. I shut the door quietly behind me and walk past the soda dispenser. There's a door slightly ajar and a sliver of light spills out.

I hear a grunt, then a pant, and then a familiar voice let out a frustrated, "Fuuuuck."

I shouldn't look. I tell myself it's because I'm worried or maybe I want to prove to myself that Masters is a lying dog, sexing up some girl after dry humping me on the dance floor. Wouldn't be the first player to do that. Won't be the last. I reach around the frame and push the door open a tiny bit more.

There, in a pool of light, stands Masters, one hand on the sink and one hand gripping the biggest, hardest, longest dick I have ever seen.

10

KNOX

WHEN THE DOOR TO HAMMER'S bedroom opens, I'm so close to shooting my wad that it's criminal I'm interrupted. My free hand darts out to grab the doorknob and slam it shut when I hear a gasp, and then a set of pretty fingers nudge the door open a hair more.

Aw, God. I don't know whether to curse or pray, but this fap job just got a shit ton more exciting, because I know it's Ellie out there, breathing heavy and eating me up with her big brown eyes. I shift slightly, and rest my hand on the counter so my weak knees don't completely give out on me.

"I can hear you."

"Holy mother of God. Maybe you're a virgin because you're too frickin' big for a girl," she blurts out. Her gait is unsteady and she has to grasp the door to stand upright.

A surprised bark of laughter escapes me. "You're not making it any smaller with your big eyes and your compliments," I choke out.

Her audible gasps are like lighter fluid on a campfire. Maybe I should feel embarrassed that I got caught rubbing one out in the middle of a party, but instead I feel myself swelling, hotter under her intense gaze. And she's not going anywhere.

Neither am I.

Before I'd had a nice little fantasy of slipping Ellie's skirt up on the dance floor and pushing my fingers into what I know is the wettest, tightest pussy ever. When she began riding my thigh, I thought I'd burn up right there on the dance floor. Here lies Knox Masters, turned to ash by his unsatisfied lust.

My vaunted self-control slipped, and while I'm sure of her, I know she's not sure of me. Not yet anyway. So I came up here to relieve myself, gain a measure of composure, and go back downstairs loose and ready for round two. Or three.

Only, before I could finish, she appears like my fucking fantasy come to life. Her eyes devour me and her lips part as she struggles to catch her breath. I run my gaze over her gorgeous face and enjoy the sight of her sweet tits doing a little dance inside her sparkly tank top as she pants lightly.

I could come this instant, but I want to prolong this moment. How often do I have a girl as hot as Ellie standing transfixed watching me pleasure myself? I'm milking this moment—pun intended—until I experience the best orgasm of my life. The first of many with Ellie. *The first of many.*

I've done this so many times by myself that the pleasure from it is a little rote, but not now. I feel the blaze torch me from my legs up into my brain. The burn inside me is that pleasure-pain you get when you butt up against the first barrier of your body that says no, but you push on anyway and that endorphin rush floods you as a reward for your persistence.

"Was it the dancing?" she asks huskily, like she's conducting a scientific study.

The cock in my hand grows harder than ever, and I'm leaking so much pre-come I don't even need lube.

"It's you, baby," I tell her. "It's all you. Your tight body rubbing up against mine. The smell of the honey of your hair. Your sweet lips pressing against my chest when you thought I wasn't paying attention. All you."

"I should leave," she says, but makes no move in the direction of the bedroom. If anything, I swear she opens the bathroom door even more.

I slow my strokes down to a snail's pace, squeezing hard at the base so I don't blow. "Only if you want to."

"I-I'm sorry," she stammers out. Her eyes are glued to my dick.

"Are you?" She's not even a little sorry. She's intrigued as all hell. I want to grab her arm and pull her against me, but I know touching her while I'm in this condition is asking for it.

"Kind of, but…obviously I'm not leaving."

I laugh. I can't help it. Her embarrassment at enjoying this is too fucking much, but my laughter doesn't kill off a gram of my arousal. As long as she's standing there enjoying the show, my body is primed for her. "You don't have to leave. This is all for you."

11

ELLIE

HIS VOICE IS A LOW, husky sound that plucks at the already sensitive nerves under my skin. A small sliver of his chiseled abdomen is on display where his T-shirt rucks up. A sparse trail of dark hair arrows down to a shadowed space covered half by his hand and half by his pants. His hand pulls at his dick in hard, swift jerks, and I know in the space a heartbeat two things: I get why it's called jacking it, and I'm not leaving unless the entire Warriors football team comes up and drags me away.

The most illicit, hot porn scene I have ever laid eyes on is taking place in full HD color in front of me. If the house went up in flames at this precise moment, I'd burn down with it because I can't tear my gaze away.

The round, red head of his dick plays peek-a-boo with each twist of his wrist. I notice that he pauses right before he hits the top, almost flicking the ridged area of his circumcised head with a large finger, and that he drags his hand downward with more force that I'd think would feel pleasurable. Not for the first time, I'm struck by how very large he is.

Huge is not at all an overstatement. His fist is big, but it doesn't completely cover his shaft. I clench my legs together, part in fear and part in arousal. Sweet baby Jesus, Tumblr did not prepare me for this.

"How does it feel?" The question slips out before I can stop it.

"Good. Real good. Better since you arrived." His wrist flicks again in steady, even motions. The muscles in his forearms ripple with every down stroke and bunch together at the upstroke. He looks so beautiful and profane at the same time.

I struggled to gulp one breath after the other. There's no air in this bathroom. It's sucked up by Masters' presence. I let out a shaky stream of air.

Masters groans and I *feel* it. The sound is like a touch, winding its way across my body and then under my skin.

"What are you thinking about?" *I'm so screwed.*

He doesn't hesitate. "You. I'm thinking about you. I'm thinking about laying my tongue on your body for the first time. What you'd taste like. I'd want to lick you everywhere. I want to know what every inch of you tastes like."

I must have whimpered because Masters lets out another low, rough noise. "You turned on, baby?"

I press my lips together, but can't stop my head from nodding. If he touches me, he'll know how aroused I am. My skin burns. My panties are wet. I've never felt so turned on and he *hasn't even laid a finger on me.*

"I'm glad." His voice sounds full of aching want. "I'm so close, baby.

Help me. How would you want me to take care of you?"

"I…I don't know," I stutter out because this is completely new territory for me. I've never watched anyone touch themselves, at least not in real life. I've never heard anyone, ever, ask how they could take care of me. The sad truth is I don't have much experience with what feels good either.

The guys I've slept with—all three of them—have been entirely forgettable. I can barely conjure the face of the guy I slept with the summer before I went to college. My junior college hookup was a guy I worked with in Alumni and Development.

"Nothing? You have no requests?" His motion has slowed again, the fierceness in his face lessening, which means he's not as tuned into this moment.

A fierce yearning grips me. I want him to come. I feel ownership over his orgasm, as if I watch *this* then I can own *him*, and in that moment, I'd do anything to stoke his fire. There's an honesty in his voice, the clear way he looks at me with need that I have never seen before, that loosens my lips and words that I have never spoken spill out of me.

"I know what I'd like to do to you," I begin.

A small smile appears at the corners of his mouth. "That's good. Tell me."

"I'm not sure if I could take much in. You're…big." That's an understatement, like saying he's good at football. "I'd have to use my hands. I hear the tip is very sensitive."

He nods. "Yeah. Right under here."

His finger flicks that spot under the ruddy head of his dick. It's so red it almost looks painful. His body quakes as he roughly jerks his hand up and down his shaft. I want to rush over and push his hands aside. *Let me. I can do this really well.*

Some vestige of self-protection exists, because my feet are nailed to the floor. I'm not leaving, but I can't get closer either.

"I'd lay my tongue there then," I say, shocking myself at the brazen words falling out of my mouth. I blame this on Masters, too. His eyes gleam with approval.

"There isn't a spot on your sweet body, Ellie, which I wouldn't want to lay *my* tongue on." His hand goes down. "I'm standing here wondering what you taste like." Up again. "What the skin behind your ear feels like against my tongue." Down. I feel dizzy. His tongue creeps out to rub against the middle of his lower lip. "Whether you are honey or mint or—" He breaks off with a deep guttural moan as if the idea feels too much for him. "I suspect I'll be addicted."

I'll be addicted. As if it's foregone conclusion for him, and those words, full of want and need and determination, are their own kind of aphrodisiac.

"I'd like to taste you, too. You look…weighty. Like, you on my tongue would be substantial."

"That a good thing, baby?" His eyes are almost closed—just mere slits as he stares at me.

"Yeah," I croak. I clear my throat and try again. "Yes. It'd feel like you made a mark."

His eyes flutter shut and he swallows hard. I watch mesmerized as his Adam's apple bobs up and down his throat. "Fuck, yes. I'd like to mark you." He speeds up, his hand moving faster, squeezing harder. "I'd like to mark you with my mouth and with my come until everyone and anyone who came into contact with you would know you were mine."

I gasp in shock at the same moment that he begins to come. He throws his head back as the long, ropey seed jets from his body into his waiting hand. He looks amazing, and I've never wanted anything so badly in my short life.

My body trembles from the aftershock of *his* orgasm. His eyes drop to mine—a laser beam holding me as captive as any rope.

"How was it?" I manage to eke out, despite having witnessed the most erotic scene of my entire life. The hoarseness of my voice, the genuine interest, takes away any flippancy I try to inject.

"Better than I've ever felt before," he says again with his disarming honesty. "But not as good as it will be with you."

12

ELLIE

I'D LIKE TO SAY THAT I stand there boldly and have a rational discussion with Masters about what happened. I don't. Oh, I stand there and gawk while he flushes some tissue down the toilet and washes his hands. I get a little lightheaded when he reaches down, calmly tucks his still sizeable shaft inside his shorts, and zips up. But the moment he takes a step in my direction, my hypnosis breaks and I flee like a chicken chased by a whole den of foxes. I hear him call my name, but I ignore it and sprint out of the bedroom. At the bottom of the stairs, my heart swells with relief when I see Jack leaning against the wall outside the room where he'd been playing the video game.

I grab his arm. "I'm ready to go."

I don't look behind me, afraid that I might see Masters and I'll be caught up in his tractor beam of a personality. Jack, the prize brother that he is, doesn't ask me a single question, but slips his phone into his front pocket and follows me out of the house.

"You didn't even want to see where I'm living?"

It's not a sincere question. He wants to know why the hell I'm trotting down Carpenter Avenue like the house behind us caught on fire.

"Yes, tomorrow. Or the day after." Or whenever Masters isn't around.

It's as if he reads my mind, because he asks, "What's going on with you and Masters?"

"Me and Masters? There's nothing going on between the two of us. I barely know him," I squeak. Truth is, I actually know a lot about him. He's a good—no great—college football player. He's got a sly sense of humor. He's a good sport. He claims to be a virgin. He told me the hottest sexual experience of his life was me watching him masturbate. That lightheaded feeling comes over me again and I trip.

Jack catches me and sets me upright. With his hands around my shoulders like iron, I can't do anything but stand there while he looks at me searchingly. "It didn't seem like nothing when he whispered in your ear before dinner. He made half the table move so he could sit across from you. You disappeared for a very long time and Ahmed said he saw Masters practically lose his virginity on the dance floor to a brunette."

"Why does that brunette have to be me?" I pretend to be hurt by the accusation, but it doesn't play with Jack.

"Ellie," he says in gentle consternation, "I may be a terrible writer, and it might take me a couple hours to get through thirty pages in a textbook, but I can still add two and two together. I'm not dumb."

"I know you're not dumb."

Jack hates it when his intelligence gets insulted. In middle school, he got flagged as slow, which infuriated our dad. He threw a fit, both at school and at home, which embarrassed and humiliated Jack. I started helping Jack then, slowly and silently. Anything to keep him from getting yelled at by Dad, anything to keep that destroyed look off Jack's face.

It started innocently by proofing a paper, inserting commas, correcting homonyms, stuff like that. My mother caught me, and I thought I would get into big trouble. Instead she came in later and told me that I needed to do it for every paper. Then every open book test. Thank goodness I didn't have to take the SAT for him. I'm not sure how we would have pulled that one off.

Jack doesn't know. When I finished "proofing," I'd put all the papers in a pretty binding and Jack would turn those in.

If he found out, he would kill me. He would absolutely murder me and leave my body out for the crows. I hate my parents, and worse, I hate myself for agreeing to the masquerade. *Please let him have a break-out season.*

"You know I don't care. I want to know. I'd prefer to hear it from you than from someone in the locker room."

"I thought you guys had a no girlfriends, wives, or sisters rule in the locker room?"

Jack scoffs. "That rule is fucked constantly. Back at Wyoming, one girl dated three of the players. If the players go there, then they have to chill out about the repercussions, and they did. It's not ideal, but shit like that happens. If you were interested in Masters, I'd be okay."

"How can you be?" I explode. "Don't you remember what happened?"

"I remember that Travis Farrington was an asshole who threw away a chance at a state championship because he couldn't get in your pants.

That's on him, not you."

"Jack, you had to go to junior college for two years before you got your D1 scholarship!"

"So?"

"So!"

"Yeah, so? I went to the best juco in the nation. I played a shit ton of pro-style, spread offense football. I racked up god-like numbers and got an offer from the best college program in the nation. Now, I'm a starting tight end for a team favored to at least make the playoffs, if not win it all outright. By my calculations, I should send Farrington a fucking gift basket. I won't because he's a douchebag. Look, if you want to be with Masters, be with him. Don't let this stupid football thing stop you. Shit, he plays on defense. He's not in charge of who throws me the ball and when. Plus that guy wants to win more than anything. As long as I'm valuable on the field, I could fuck goats in the locker room."

"Is that a quote? Because it sounds like something Masters would say."

Jack smirks. "There's nothing going on, but you know the types of things he'd say?"

My shoulders slump. "I don't know what's going on. It's complicated. I didn't mean to dance with him or anything. He came out of nowhere and wouldn't take no for an answer." Jack's face tightens, so I hurry and add, "Not like that. He didn't force me. I just…" I spread my hands. "I have no explanation for it."

"I do." He squeezes my shoulders and his quiet support seeps into me. "You wanted to, and that's enough. You don't have to have a reason. I already told you the past doesn't mean shit to me." He releases me and then slings an arm around my shoulder, propelling me down the sidewalk toward my apartment. "You and me got a new start at junior college, and we can keep it going here. Only two more years, and Mom and Dad won't have any say in our lives." Jack toes the line for me, too. "Enjoy yourself here. If Masters is the guy you want, if he wants you to be his *first*," Jack chuckles at this, "then you should go for it. Just don't tell me any details."

Oh, Jack. His kindness kills me. Every giving, unselfish word that comes out of his mouth drives the stake deeper into my guilty heart. It does exactly the opposite of what his motivational speech intends to. If anything, I need to stay away from Masters even more. "It's more than Farrington."

"Then what is it?"

Because you always look at everything in a positive light. Because it's naïve to think that Farrington did something unusual. If Masters decided your team should turn against you, then the entire team would shut you out and it would get a hundred times worse. Because I'm cheating for you and I'm scared that if I get close to someone on the team, my secret will slip out and that can't happen.

Those are all the reasons I can't give voice to. So I settle for a response that I'm not sure that Jack will even buy but it's the only one I have right now.

"I just want someone who's not an athlete."

Jack sighs. "If that's how you want to play it. We drew the short end of the stick when it comes to parents, but I've always had the team. You've only had me. It wouldn't be a bad thing to have another person on your side, Ellie. Besides, you could do a lot worse than Masters. He's a good leader. Very chill in the locker room. Easy to talk to. He knows everyone's names, even the redshirt freshmen."

"You date him if he's so wonderful," I retort. I want to talk myself out of my stupid attraction to Masters, not develop it.

"He doesn't swing that way," Jack grins. "Plus, I don't do virgins. Too clingy."

"You're a jerk, Jack."

He laughs and ruffles my hair. I wish I could lean into him, but Jack is right. I've relied on him far too long. It's time for me to make my own way.

13

KNOX

I SLEPT LIKE A BABY. After Ellie left, I went straight to bed. I wasn't lying when I told her it was the best orgasm I'd ever had. In fact, I'm a little concerned that I won't be able to come without her around, now that I know what it *could* feel like.

I suspect that jacking off is all I'll be doing in the foreseeable future. She's skittish, and if I rush too fast I might be on the ass end of a hit it and quit it if she ever did give in.

About two seconds after my orgasm ran through me like a freight train, her eager, captive expression turned to embarrassment and then apprehension. I'm not sure if she is more afraid of me or what she's feeling but we've got plenty of time to work that through.

In the morning, I get up and run five miles like it's nothing, and then meet Matty at the weight room.

"That smoothie this morning tasted fucking awesome. What d'you think she put in it?" he asks.

I think back. "Spinach, because it looked green. Banana. Maybe strawberries?"

"Papaya," Hammer grunts between blows of the sledgehammer on the tire. "Got to be because it tasted sweet."

"Papaya? Where the fuck did that come from?" Matty scoffs. "It was pineapple."

"We had pineapple three days ago, and this tasted sweeter, so it was something else." Hammer jabs twenty pounds of iron in Matty's direction. "Papaya is a sweeter fruit."

"Where the fuck are they getting papaya?" Matty sits up and places his hands on his hips.

"Same place they're getting the pineapple and bananas, dumbshit."

I don't know whether to laugh or ask Matty to hit me in the head with a fifty-pound weight. The conversation is ridiculous, but if Matty and Hammer weren't arguing about something then it wouldn't be a day ending in Y.

"Hey, Masters, got a minute?" Campbell steps up by the weight bench. I nod but don't stop because I'm nearing the end of my second set of seated dumbbell front raise lifts with the twenty-pound weights.

"What's up, Campbell?" I set the weights down on either side of the bench and reach for my water jug. Campbell doesn't answer but looks pointedly at Matty and Hammer, who are still arguing.

"How do you even know if papaya is sweeter than pineapple?" Matty scowls.

Hammer lifts the sledgehammer over his head and brings it down on the tire. "Papaya has a higher fructose level."

Jack and I exchange looks because neither of us can believe these two are still arguing about the fucking fruit.

"Matty, Hammer, I think Jesse needs some help." Jesse didn't need a damn thing, but it's obvious Jack wants to talk privately, or as privately as you can in a weight room where fifty guys are lifting, throwing ropes, and doing chin ups.

Campbell lifts his chin in thanks as the guys wander off to see if Jesse can mediate their dispute. "What's with the shrug before you do the dumbbell front raise?"

"Isolates the rotator cuff muscle."

His eyebrows shoot up. "Nice. Didn't learn that at juco."

"Small weights, more reps are my recommendation but I suspect that you didn't come to talk to me about that."

"Yeah." He drags a hand through his pretty boy hair—about the same shade as his sister's. The other guys on the team are blind. Ellie and her brother have many similarities—the color of their hair, the deep brown of their eyes. Ellie's a lot shorter, but she's got the same kind of internal strength that Campbell has. "I don't know what's going on with you and my sister. She's an adult, so I can't prevent her from dating anyone, but if you hurt her, I'll come after you. I'm psyched to be playing here, but I'd give up my place on the team if that's what it came to."

If Campbell meant to scare me off, he's not doing a good job of it. Knowing she's got a brother who cares about her? That her brother is the kind of unselfish guy who'd put his family first? I rub a hand across my chin while I think of a good way to respond. I won't lie and say I'm not interested, but I also don't need to tell him that I intend to bone his sister into next year, or that I spend most of my down time thinking about her naked, spread, and ready.

"I watched your tapes when I heard we made you an offer and hoped you would be a solid fit here. When you showed up and worked your ass off without complaining once, I knew that Coach had made the right choice."

"That's real nice of you, Masters, but that's got shit all to do with my sister. She's…a sweet kid. She might talk a good game, but she's pretty soft under that outer shell."

"I hear you. And you absolutely should kick my ass if I hurt your sister, but I have no intention of hurting her. I'm dead serious about her."

He looks confused. "You barely know her."

"I know enough. Sometimes it happens in an instant and sometimes it grows. Like you said, she's an adult and can make her own decisions, but I appreciate that you have her back and that she has yours. Reminds me of the relationship I have with my brother."

I pick up my dumbbells and start my third and final set. Campbell stands there watching me.

"You need anything else?" I ask.

He looks suspicious but shakes his head no. Matty and Hammer must have been watching us like hawks, because they reappear almost immediately.

"It's papaya," Jack says before he goes back to the offensive squad. "Saw her put it in this morning."

"I knew it," Hammer crows. He shoves his hand toward Matty. "You owe me two beers tonight."

Of course they bet over what fruit got put in the smoothie. I wonder what bets they've made over me and Ellie. Then I think it's better I don't know, because I'd have to kick their asses and that wouldn't do a hell of a lot for team unity.

ELLIE

I DON'T SLEEP WELL…AT ALL. The whole night I keep replaying the bathroom scene in my head and it often morphs into something dirtier. Like Knox gesturing with his free hand to come closer. When I do, he points to the ground, and I fall to my knees and open my mouth.

Fortunately, Jack and his team stay busy for the next couple of days, and even better, he makes time for me away from the team after I turn down every single one of his dinner invitations.

I start my work on the Agrippa grant even though classes haven't officially started. I'm fascinated by all the accommodations the law requires schools to give anyone deemed to have a learning disability. If my parents had tested Jack when he was younger, or if they had paid attention to how he did in school rather than on the field, his circumstances today could be so different. I can't dwell on the past, but I can learn—in case Jack has a sudden change of heart.

While I can push the Jack thing to the back of my mind due to many years of practice, Masters is a different story. It takes until Sunday to convince myself that the Thursday night bathroom porn show was an aberration. We, despite having nothing to drink, got intoxicated on shit like the moonlight and the excitement of a new year. Those are weak justifications, but a girl has to have something to hold on to. Like Masters' dick. A girl could really hold onto—

"You should try this on," Riley says, interrupting my dirty thoughts. Thank goodness for that, because I need to get him out of my head.

Riley holds up a red strapless dress with a skirt that looks short enough to be a belt.

"I'd worry I'd 'Lindsey Lohan' everyone every time I moved."

"It'd look good on you. You've got great legs."

"And you look like a delicate fairy. I think you could pull that off. I need something longer, with more coverage. Why are we buying dresses anyway? Did we join a sorority and I missed it?"

"We're not buying anything. We're enjoying the scenery. How about this one?"

This one happens to be a one-armed body con dress that looks as wide as a stocking. I lift the price tag. "Two hundred dollars for a dress? I think not."

"I could make something like this for about $20."

"Make it like how?"

She shrugs and places the dress back onto the rack. "I sew a little."

That's what she does in her room when the door is closed? I smother a giggle. "Is that what you've got going on in there? I wondered what that humming noise was."

"What did you think it was?"

"I don't know. A really high-powered vibrator?"

"Seriously?" Her mouth falls open.

"No, God, I don't know. It was a passing thought." I grin. "There's nothing wrong with a little mechanical assist. Helps you miss guys a lot less."

"Well, this is good roommate information. When I hear a humming noise from your bedroom, I'll make sure to leave a cigarette outside your door."

I crack up. "And when I hear humming from your room, I'll come in and watch." Because I'm good at that, apparently. Soon Riley and I have both folded in half, laughing ridiculously loud between the Lycra and chiffon in the dress section. "Come on," I gasp. "We need to get out of here before they kick us out."

In the food court, over a diet soda and shared pretzel, I ask Riley how she got started sewing.

"We're not very well off. I learned to make my own clothes."

"That's very *Pretty in Pink* of you," I say admiringly.

She makes a disgusted face. "Molly Ringwald made a really ugly dress."

"It netted her Andrew McCarthy, though."

"True." Riley drowns her pretzel bite in the cheese. "Anyway, I'm here on scholarship and I've got a work study job at the student center. This is a splurge for me."

"A job and a full load? I'm impressed."

She shrugs as if it isn't a big deal. "What about you?"

"What about me? I don't think my intramural softball team will demand too much from me."

An uncertain look passes over her face but then it resolves into something like determination and she leans closer. "I saw your class schedule on the counter."

Oh crap. I need to stop leaving stuff out. I'm not used to living with anyone. At junior college, we had dorm suites, which meant I had my own room. I need to treat my apartment like that—and keep my private stuff private. "Seven classes is a huge responsibility. Did your classes from your other school not transfer?"

I stare at my torn pretzel piece. "Some of those classes looked interesting and relevant to my major, so I asked around and found out I could audit them."

"Ellie, I'm your roommate, which means whatever goes on in the apartment stays in the apartment."

I don't like perceptive people, I decide. Masters is like that, too. He can read every emotion that I have. I try to make a joke of it. "So if I'm Dexter, you're okay?"

"If you're eliminating terrible people and cleaning up after yourself, then yes, I'm on board."

I glance into Riley's warm hazel eyes and see nothing but acceptance. But I'm not ready to confess to a secret I've kept for nearly a decade. I don't even know if Dad knows the full extent of the work I've done to keep Jack eligible, even in high school. It's something that only my mom and I communicate about. "I'll keep that in mind."

"Good. How about we go to the bookstore? Wasn't there a book you wanted to get?"

THERE IS, BUT I CAN'T find it on the shelf when we arrive at the store. Riley excuses herself to go look at the craft books while I hit the information desk.

"Do you have the latest book by M. Kannan? It's a fantasy."

"Sorry, that young man over there picked up the last copy." The gray-haired lady points down the aisle toward a tall, imposing frame propped up in one of the chairs by the in-store cafe. A tall, imposing, *familiar* figure.

I march over before my warning system has time to power up and urge me to run for my life. "What are you doing here?"

"I'm gathering reading material. I asked this hot girl out to breakfast, but she turned me down. I think my potential topics of conversation were too limited." Masters holds up a biography of our current president in one hand and the fantasy novel I've been waiting for an entire year to read. "Help me out here. If you had breakfast with a stud like me, which book would you rather discuss?"

"Masters, seriously, what are you doing here?" I refuse to let him charm me. He's wearing his standard uniform of cargo shorts and dark T-shirt. This time the knit is a deep green that makes his eyes pop. I'll pretend his mother bought him the shirt and not a former girlfriend, because it's totally a color a woman would purchase.

"I'm buying a book." He looks at his full hands. "Maybe two since you can't make up your mind either. What are you doing here, Ellie? You aren't following me, are you?"

"What?" I say a little too loud and heads turn our direction. "No, I am *not* following you," I hiss in a much quieter voice.

He lowers his own voice and I have to lean in to hear him. "It's okay if you followed me. I approve of your stalking."

"I'm not stalking you," I bite out, but then because I want to buy the book in his left hand, I paste a smile on. "I think the biography. Why don't I go put that other book back for you? This book has sex in it." I point to the novel.

"Good thing I'm over eighteen. It's frustrating to want things that people hold out of your reach." He shakes his head in mock dismay.

"Don't you have practice?"

"Not today. It's Sunday. Even football players get a day of rest." He smiles but it dies off when I continue to glare at him. He sets both books down on the table. "I want you to go out with me."

"I don't date football players," I answer automatically.

This concept is apparently so foreign to Masters he literally scratches his head. "So you had a bad past experience. We're not all the same person."

"It has nothing to do with a bad breakup and I know better than to say all football players are like one asshole."

"So, you did date one." He nods as if this is the answer to everything.

"Yes, but he didn't break my heart. Or at least not in the way you think he did."

I felt hurt when I found out Travis had cheated on me, but I also felt glad to see the ass end of him. What made me angry was the way he treated Jack. That's what pissed me off. That's the warning I take with me.

The problem with Masters is that I'm very attracted to him, more so than a normal girl is attracted to a normal guy, which is why I can't just walk away from him. I know that standing here having this conversation gives all the wrong signals. If I really didn't want Masters, I'd walk away. We both know it.

"Okay. We have this *thing*," I wave my finger between our bodies, "going on. I think the best thing we do is have sex, burn it out, and go on our own way. I won't even tell a soul that we did it and you can continue with your virgin cover story."

His face tightens. I don't know if it's because I accused him of lying or because I want to have sex without any emotional attachment, which is weird because most guys would jump up and down for joy at this offer. "If all I wanted was a quick lay, you and I both know I could get that without any effort. I want something more than that from you."

"Welcome to disappointment. It's character building."

I force myself to turn around and walk away. The chair scrapes behind me, and then his big hand turns my shoulder and backs me up against the bookcase holding stories about dead girls hacked up by serial killers and other true crimes. Seems apt.

He leans down, so close I can smell him—a mix of warm male and citrus—and it's so good my knees get a little weak. "I'm not experienced, but I know when a girl is into me, and you're into me. You want to play it casual, then that's how we play it…for now. But fair warning, I'm bringing everything I've got to tear down your resistance. My specialty is reading plays and then overcoming the barriers."

I lock my legs to keep from falling over and pull out the biggest barrel I have. "Masters, there are things about me that if you knew, you wouldn't want to spend another minute in my presence."

He considers my words, the silence taking on heaviness, and part of me already aches for what I could have if I was any other girl at Western. "Have you killed anyone?" I can feel his eyes assessing me and I keep my gaze averted, afraid of what I'll see in his moss green gaze.

"No."

"Have you slept with my brother?"

"What?" I can't prevent myself from gawking at Masters, who's smiling as he asks the question. "No! God, I've never even met him!"

"Are you catfishing poor athletes from Auburn? Wait, don't answer that, because I don't think I'd find that objectionable. Oh, I have it—" He snaps his fingers.

"This isn't a joke, Masters."

He tucks a stray piece of hair behind my ear. "Until you tell me what it is, it's not a reason to stay apart either."

I suck in my lower lip to prevent throwing myself at him and telling him to take me.

"Why?" I ask helplessly.

"Because I like you."

He grips me by the chin and lays down the gentlest, sweetest kiss. In that kiss, he tells me everything. That he wants me. That he's willing to take it slow. That he's not giving up. He kisses me as if this is the only thing he wants to do for the next ten hours.

His lips barely move but I can feel everything in me surge toward him. The short wedges I shoved on this morning feel precarious. I grip his shoulders to steady myself and then find myself rising up on my tiptoes to press deeper against him. He hauls me flush against him until I can no longer touch the floor.

His one hand palms nearly my entire back while the other angles my head for better access. He may be a virgin, but the guy knows how to kiss. His tongue finds places inside my mouth that I didn't even know could feel good.

All the pent up desire boiling in me for days comes pouring out. I attack him with my kiss, biting his lower lip, sucking on his tongue. Against my belly, I can feel the hard ridge of his very large erection. The image of him standing in that dim light, stroking himself until he comes, flits through my mind in a series of graphic, 3-D images.

"God," I breathe as he abandons my mouth to trace the line of my jaw with his lips. He growls in response and pushes me back against the bookcases, but I don't even mind that the shelves bite into my back. I just want more.

He gives it to me. We cling to each other, feeding off each other's seemingly endless need, until I hear a gasp and then a muted giggle. Those two faint sounds somehow manage to break through the haze of lust, and bring with it the realization that I am in a very public place. I wriggle against him and he sets me down reluctantly.

"We're in the bookstore," I say in a scandalized voice.

"You've never kissed a guy in the bookstore before?" He grins, the wicked mischievous grin I'm beginning to associate with something tremendously naughty. "There's a first time for everything."

He steps away, breathing heavily. His untucked T-shirt—the one I apparently ripped out of his shorts—hangs long enough to cover part, but not all, of his bulge. After he's done adjusting himself so as not to scare any children in the store, he strides over to his abandoned books.

Riley's face pokes itself around the end of the bookcase. "Is it safe to come into the True Crime section? Because I saw some mauling going on and ran for safety."

"Har, har." I push back my hair with a weak, shaking hand.

"Who's this?" Masters says, returning with his two books. Make that one of his books and the book that belongs to me if he would let me buy it.

"Riley Hart. Knox Masters. Masters, this is my roommate, Riley."

"We're back to Masters, huh? Disappointing." He shakes Riley's hand. "Nice to meet you."

"You guys look like you had an intense conversation." She smirks.

"Ellie and I are discussing where she's taking me on our first date. I hope it's not to that dog movie. I swear he'll die at the end and then I'll sob like a fucking baby. Nearly had to walk out of *Bridge to Terabithia*. That shit is not good for my image."

Just like that, Riley's pants get charmed off.

"You could go to one of her intramural softball games," she offers helpfully. "They play on Wednesdays."

I glare at Riley for revealing that tidbit, but she avoids my eyes.

"Intramural softball? I like the way you think." He smiles at Riley and she smiles right back. "Tell you what, I'll buy that fantasy book, but you can read it first. Then when you're done you can bring it back to me, and we'll go out and discuss it. Hold on while I pay for these books."

"No," I protest but neither pay attention to me. Masters leaves, and this time both Riley and I watch that fine ass, covered in cotton, as it disappears from sight.

"Stop panting. It's embarrassing," I grouse and pull myself away from the bookshelves.

"Holy shit. I take that back. Did I say I wasn't into athletes? Because I've changed my mind. Football players are totally my type."

They're everyone's type, I think sourly.

"And Christ on a cracker, he *devoured you.*" She laughs semi-hysterically. "I once heard this ridiculous rumor that he's a virgin. Can you believe it?"

"No, I can't."

"Yeah, I thought it sounded off when I heard it. Probably some— what do you call them?" She winds her hand.

"Jersey chaser? Gridiron groupie?"

"Yeah those. Probably one of those got turned down and started the rumor because, honey, he wants to do you so bad I thought for a minute he'd take you right here and now, and we'd get kicked out by mall security."

"Let's go," I tell her. I don't want to talk about the spectacle I made of myself. I want to escape before he comes back, even though he does have my book, dammit.

"I thought you wanted that book?" Riley peeks around the corner. "Besides, he's coming back, so it's too late."

"Fine." I straighten my own T-shirt and try to inject steel into my spine. "Thanks." I hold out my hand for the book. I might as well take it if he's so willing to let me borrow it.

Instead of laying the book in my hand, he holds up his phone. "I'll need your digits so me and my book can stay in touch."

"I'll give the book to Jack and he can give it to you."

Masters raises an eyebrow. "Is that the direction you want to take this?"

Dammit. No. I rattle off my cell phone number in a sour tone, which has zero effect on Masters' good humor.

"Here you go." He puts the book in my hand. "Think about where you'd like me to take you for dinner when you're finished with it."

"Why so interested in eating with me?" God, that sounded filthy.

By his smirk, he thinks so, too. Locker room talk has taken all the innocence out of this virgin. "I'm interested in all of it."

Riley makes a choking sound and I know I've turned bright red.

"I've got to get back to campus," he says. "Can I give you two a ride?"

"No. I've got some stuff to buy. Girl stuff." I glare at Riley.

"No problem. See you back at school." And then he's gone.

Thankfully Riley doesn't say another word…until we exit the bookstore. "So when is the wedding?"

"What are you talking about?"

"You said you would marry the first guy who hit on you at the bookstore."

"Riley, you are not funny. Not at all."

"Really? I'm feeling pretty hilarious."

15

KNOX

MATTY IS IN MY APARTMENT again when I get home from the bookstore. The encounter with Ellie has left me in a good enough mood that it doesn't bother me that he has half my cupboard spread out on the coffee table and his big ass perched on my preferred side of the sofa. I give him the business anyway.

"Matty, don't you have a home?" I kick the door shut and throw my purchases on the table.

"Yeah, but you have better snacks up here." He reaches for the bag and rifles through the contents. "No comics? Your taste in books is questionable. Please tell me this book is for class."

"I did have a book that had guns, machines, and sex in it, but I saw Ellie Campbell in the bookstore and had to give it to her or else." I grab the half-empty Doritos bag and shove a handful of the fake cheese wonders into my mouth.

I pull my phone out from my pocket and pull up Ellie's entry. I wonder how long it will take her to read the book. "Are there rules for when you should text a girl?" I vaguely remember the guys arguing about this in the locker room.

"Three days unless it's a booty call, then any time after ten," Matty says and flips the channel from the NFC preseason game to the AFC preseason game. It's week three and the undrafted rookies, practice squad guys, and late pre-season signs are getting their chance to play their way onto the fifty man roster. It looks like the Seattle second and third string is beating the pants off the Kansas City team. Not looking good for KC.

"They need a good pass rusher," I murmur between bites.

"And a decent quarterback, offensive line, and secondary."

"That, too."

"Wait. Did you ask me when to text a girl?" Matty rouses from his football induced stupor. "Is this a Western coed?"

I nod.

He looks at me in disbelief. "You're Knox Masters. Didn't you just say your name?"

If only that's what it took. Actually that's all it did take most of the time. Having a jersey hanging in the closet was all some girls needed. Ellie is not one of those girls. Just my luck.

"I did, but she's not jumping at the chance to go out with me."

"Dude, wait, does this mean you're going to have sex?"

I don't answer, but I can't help the shit grin that spreads.

"Holy fuck," he shouts and starts to high five me. Then he stops abruptly, hand hanging in mid-air. "You can't. I'm sorry to be a cock-blocking son of a bitch, but you can't. We got the national championship on the line. You gotta keep that locked down."

"Matty, you don't get a say in when I have sex." I pick up the remote and switch to the NFC preseason game.

"It's a team issue," he insists. He starts punching stuff into his phone.

"What the fuck are you doing?" I grab for the phone but he holds out one hand and presses send with the other. The damage is already done by the time I wrestle the phone from him. Sure enough, I see a group message for the entire defensive line to get the hell up to my apartment for an emergency meeting. The rush of shoes on the stairs thunders into the apartment before half the team bursts through.

"What's the emergency?"

"Did Masters get hurt?"

"I was watching Adult Swim. This better be good." The last comment comes from Hammer.

Matty stands up. "Masters here thinks he wants to mess with a good thing."

Eight men, all weighing over two hundred pounds, crowd into my small apartment. If I was prone to claustrophobia, I would freak out. Once the shit show gets started, though, it's impossible to stop. I fold my hands behind my head and stare at the ceiling while the guys gear up.

They all want to stick their noses in because I've spent the last year harping on the importance of team. We win as a team and we lose as a team. Now we're discussing my non-existent sex life as a team.

"What good thing?" Hammer grabs the Dorito bag and pours the remainder of the chips in his mouth. The other guys raid the fridge.

"Masters wants to lose the big V."

"He wants to lose our game?" Jesse, a new starter on the line, asks. He's ordinarily quiet, hanging out with his longtime girlfriend.

Hammer slaps him across the back of the head. "Not V for Victory, numbskull. Virginity." Hammer tosses the empty chip bag onto the coffee table. "Masters, my man, if you're looking for tips you've come to the right place." He muscles Matty aside and takes a seat. "First, to prevent a false start, jack off at home before you go out. If you're out for more than a couple of hours, excuse yourself and pump another one out in the bathroom. That way you won't get a reputation for being quick on the trigger. These chicks will spread that shit faster than crabs at a frat house. Second—"

"Shut up, Hammer. You're supposed to be telling him to keep his pants zipped," Matty snarls. "Not giving him tips on playing hide the salami." At Hammer's blank look, Matty throws up his hands. "Don't you want to win? Masters here is the monster on field because he doesn't play off the field. Haven't you made that connection yet?"

"Ohhhh." Hammer gets it.

I figure now is the time to step in. "Guys. We lost last year. That shellacking we took at the hands of the Ducks? That had nothing to do with what I did off the field and everything to do with the fact that we didn't make the plays and they did. We didn't get enough pressure on the quarterback. We allowed them to light up the backfield. They had us chasing players all over the field that didn't even have the fucking ball. We lost because we played shitty ball. This year, we won't play shitty ball. Not next week, not right before the bye, not in November."

Matty's wavering and Hammer looks troubled. Looks like I'll have to talk in the terms Matty used. "Look, we haven't won the championship in the last two years and I've kept to myself. Now's the time to take chances."

Hammer turns back to Matty. "Should we get Ace over here?"

"No way." Matty shakes his head emphatically. "This is a defensive unit issue."

I drop my head into my hands. It's hard to believe my pursuit of Ellie has turned into this.

"Have you cleared this with Kintyre?" Hammer is the only one that calls my brother by his full name. Everyone else, including my mom, who named him Kintyre for reasons we can never confess to anyone, calls him Ty.

"Ty knows," I say shortly.

"If he said yes, I bet he's spiking our guns," Matty declares. He crosses his arms and glares at me.

"No way," Hammer disagrees. "Kintyre's not like that. Plus he has no chance. Not with the kindergarteners on his offensive line."

Matty considers this and concludes Hammer's correct. "Truth." They exchange fist bumps.

"Let's call him." Hammer's suggestion receives a chorus of approval.

Jesus, these guys act as if I take an unanticipated shit I should check in. I rub an agitated hand through my hair. I guess I need to let them work it out of their systems, because it seems if I don't, they won't focus on anything else. If they think it affects our team unity, it will affect their on-field play.

I kind of wish we could go back to arguing where fruits land on the fructose scale.

"Kintyre, my man, what's happening?" Hammer places his phone on speaker and sets it on the coffee table in between the Doritos dust and the empty bottles of Gatorade.

My brother's voice slides out of the speaker. "Not much, Hammer. You living up to your name?"

"You know it. Well, not right this second," he replies. "You talk to your brother lately?"

"Not today," Ty responds cautiously.

"Your bro is threatening to mess with our team mojo."

"Ahhh," Ty drawls. The light has dawned. He coughs, likely to cover up to howling laughter he wants to release, but won't. "Hammer, you trust Knox? You ever see him give less than a hundred percent on the field?"

"No."

"You know you're like the brother from another mother to me, but you got to trust your teammate. Think of it this way. He's reaching max potential. Like maybe his virginity placed an artificial cap on his play, and now, with this girl, he's going to the next level."

Matty and Hammer nod slowly, evaluating this new piece of information.

"That it?" Ty asks.

"Yeah, man. Thanks. Good luck to you this weekend."

"You, too."

A text buzzes on my phone. It's Ty.

You're welcome.

Thanks for nothing, dill hole, I type back.

I'm laughing so hard I can't text anymore. Good luck.

Jesus. I'm surrounded by assholes everywhere. Is it any wonder I'd want to spend time with Ellie?

Hammer slaps his hands together. "Okay, we're in agreement. Masters should bang this chick."

They look at me expectantly as if I'm supposed to produce her right that minute and take her in front of them.

"If I was a chick, I'd date you, Masters. I've seen your dick. It's good," Hammer assures me.

"Fuck that. It's not the size of the wand. It's the wizard using it," Daryl Nunn, our nose tackle, pipes up. He, like Potter, wears a pair of black glasses when not on the field.

"Not according to Voldemort."

Hammer's retort generates a sharp bark of laughter from me, but poor Jesse looks confused. Hammer sighs. "Voldemort wanted this certain wand, but only Harry could use it."

"Men. Can we get on subject here?" Matty waves his hand toward my bent head. "Masters asked me for texting advice. The girl is turning him down."

The amount of disbelief in Matty's voice is heavier than the sledgehammer in the weight room. Memo to self: do not bring up women around the team again. Have I hassled these guys when they had chick problems?

I squeeze the back of my neck. Maybe.

Oh shit, probably.

"Maybe she's got a boyfriend already," Jesse offers.

"We can take him out," Matty replies immediately.

"Like how? Kill him?" I say sarcastically.

"Nah. But maybe maim." Matty shrugs. I can't tell if he's serious or not.

"We aren't maiming anyone." I rub my temple.

"What if she's a lesbian?" Hammer asks.

"She's not. If it's the girl Masters danced with at Hammer's party, she's at least bi. I had to leave because I got worried my girlfriend would get pregnant off the hormone high the two of them generated," Jesse says.

"Hey, wasn't that Campbell's sister?" someone asks.

I pretend I can't hear.

Matty whistles and I hear a quiet "damn, son" from Daryl.

"Okay, she's single and not a lesbian." Hammer's criminal justice degree kicks in. "Is it her brother? Man, we need him. He's got good blocking technique and good hands. Runs a tight route. Do we have to take him out?" Hammer's worried.

"No, it's not her brother." The last thing I need is these guys turning on Campbell. That'd be good for team unity. Not.

"Masters wants to know when he should text her," Matty informs everyone.

"I think he should text her now." Daryl straightens his massive shoulders as if the answer is so obvious the question should never been put up for debate.

"No. Three days or she'll think you're panting after her. Got to play hard to get." Hammer picks his phone up from the table and shakes it at me.

"I am panting after her," I interject. I want them to know that not only do I want her, I don't care who knows it.

"You can't tell her that," Hammer objects.

"Why?" I ask impatiently. I'm ready for this conversation to end. I was ready about ten minutes ago.

"Because you lose all the hand in the relationship. She'll have you by the balls," he says earnestly.

"That's what he wants," Jesse interjects, but then turns to me. "How do you know this is the chick to do the deed with? You've waited all this time, and you've known this girl for what, a day?"

The guys fall silent again and it's clear this question is important to them. When you're a recruit, the coach takes you around the school, showing you the facilities, promising you that you'll not only play, but you'll also compete on one of the best teams in the best conference. He promises your parents that he and his staff will be your family away from home. Then when the sun goes down, the players take you out. They tell you about the easy classes and the easier women.

When you sign, the song changes. They've got you now, and they want to whip you into shape. That includes speeches about wrapping it up, avoiding the girls who believe you're their ticket out of the life they don't currently enjoy or to the life they want. There's this strange dichotomy as an athlete—here's as many women as you want, but be careful because 99% of them have a trap in their vagina.

I glance at Jesse, thoughtful. "When did you first realize you wanted to play football?"

"Don't know the first time. It seems like I knew all my life."

Now I turn to Hammer. "Hammer, you played three sports. Excelled in all of them. Got drafted for baseball. Turned it down to play football. Why?"

"Felt right." Hammer tosses his phone between his hands, thinking about my question. "I loved it more than the other sports. It was the only one that all the sacrifice felt worth giving up everything for. It… felt right," he repeats.

"It felt right," I echo meaningfully.

"So she's your football?" Matty asks, quick to understand where I'm going with this. And people accuse jocks of not being perceptive. "What about actual football?"

"I want to have it all," I say simply. "Don't you?"

They nod slowly.

Matty speaks up again, wrinkling his forehead. "Okay, so if it feels right, what do you need us for? Text her whenever you want, dude."

I shift awkwardly, and then release a choppy breath. "But…" Now I hesitate, because the thing about being a team leader? You need to convince your teammates that you're capable of leading. You know, that you actually know what the hell you're doing one hundred percent of the time.

"I guess…" I exhale again. "I know I want her, but that doesn't mean I know how to get her."

Hammer snorts. "You're saying you don't have moves?"

I narrow my eyes. "I have moves." Then I give a sheepish look. "But for the sake of argument, let's say I need to win over a chick, how do I go about it? How'd you get your last girlfriend, Hammer?"

He shrugs. "She was some jock chaser who hung around all the time, and it got easier to say she was my girlfriend than argue about it."

"Lovely." No wonder he cheated on her. I quickly turn to the rest of the group, hoping at least one of them isn't a total moron in the boyfriend department. "Who here has a serious girlfriend? None of you?"

"Jesse does." Hammer points his phone at Jesse, who ducks his head sheepishly.

"I don't know. I've dated the same girl, Caitlyn, since ninth grade. We had the same advisory class, and sort of started dating. I didn't have to win her over or anything."

Awesome. We're a bunch of clueless men. We might know how to execute a blitz, stop the run, read a route, but with women, unless they are offering themselves on a silver platter, apparently our collective knowledge couldn't fill a shoe. "We need some expert advice."

"My sister reads *Cosmo* a lot," Hammer offers.

"Isn't that the site that said girls should give donut blowjobs?" Jesse asks.

"A donut blowjob?" Matty pipes up.

"Yeah, like it goes over your dick, she sucks your dick, and eats the donut."

"But teeth?" Matty looks intrigued but scared.

"But blowjobs," Jesse replies. "And donuts," he adds as an after-thought.

"Sounds like the best goddamn site on the Internet. Fire it up," Hammer orders.

ELLIE

WEEK 1: WARRIORS 0-0

I WAKE UP THIRTY MINUTES late with grit in my eyes. At least I don't need to look good this morning. I have Jack's two classes today, and I need to appear as inconspicuous as possible. I pull on a light gray hoodie, jam a hat over my head, and pull on a pair of ragged jean shorts. After brushing my teeth, I'm out the door.

Riley is still sleeping when I run to class. She told me she was a night owl and tried to schedule her classes after lunch. Mine are scattershot, particularly after my schedule had to expand to include Jack's classes. The sociology class takes place at eight in the morning, which is where I'm headed right now.

It's still hot, but I have my hood up, because the last thing I need is for Jack to spot me in the room and subject me to a number of uncomfortable questions. I thought about telling him that I'm taking the classes, but he'd get suspicious. As he should be. I'm working on a good excuse such as "looked interesting" or "are you in this class, too?"

None of my reasons sounds very good so I hope to avoid him. Unlike junior college, where most classes had under fifty students, nothing at Western is particularly small. Riley told me that unless it was an obscure major, most of the classes had at least a hundred people in them, sometimes more, which means I could easily hide in a back corner.

I'm right on time and breathe a sigh of relief when I spot Jack halfway down the auditorium-style seating, chatting with a pretty blonde.

The professor walks in, introduces her teacher's assistant, and begins lecturing on whether movies reflect societal norms or challenge them. From the online course syllabus, I'll be able to write the year-end paper in my sleep. Frankly, I think Jack will be able to do it as well since one of the movies we'll be discussing is *The Lord of the Rings* trilogy. Jack has seen it about twenty times.

I reach inside my backpack to pull out a notebook so it looks like I'm paying attention and my hand brushes against Masters' book. I pull it out. The reason I'm so late this morning is because I stayed up all night reading. It was every bit as good as I'd anticipated and I couldn't put it down. I told myself one more page and then the clock flashed three in the morning.

I finished, but the whole time I read, it occurred to me that Masters had made a big gesture. Had it been me first in the bookstore and Masters had shown up panting for it, I'd have told him to wait. I might have even demanded to see a book from his personal collection to see if he was even worthy of lending a book to. You never knew with people. Like Jack? I could never share books with him. He dog-ears pages, sticks shit inside his books. I once found a sock in one. It was clean, and he claimed it was the only thing available to use as a bookmark, but *come on.*

Masters blithely handed the book over. Granted, I had to give him my phone number, but he hadn't used it. I waited all afternoon and into the evening, and the stupid phone stayed silent.

I run a finger over the raised lettering on the cover. I haven't given him many reasons to text or call me despite the fact he's been nothing but good to me from the start. Yes, he didn't come forward and tell me his name the first time we'd met, but looking back I see where he came from. Guys like him must be inundated with people wanting things and it will only get worse for him when he gets to the NFL. So he's gun-shy, which is perfectly reasonable.

I haven't been reasonable or completely honest. If I'm honest, I'll admit that Knox Masters is exactly the type of guy I want to date. He dominates a sport I love. He's confident but not arrogant. He's funny, able to laugh at himself, and…shit, hot as the fires of Mordor. I mean, the One Ring could be forged in his hotness.

I want him.

Watching him in the bathroom with his hand wrapped around his dick—that was the sexiest thing I'd ever seen. And when he said it was his best sexual experience, I nearly came on the spot.

Knowing that he hasn't had anyone else is nearly impossible to ignore. I could be the first one to have his tongue between my legs. I could be the first to watch his eyes roll back in his head as I swallow him as deeply as possible. I could be the first one to take him inside my body. Being the first is more potent a drug than I'd realized.

My phone vibrates. I know who it is before I pick it up.

Knox: *How's my book?*

My thumb hovers over the screen wanting to enter *When can I see you?* Jack's given me the go-ahead. And he's right. I could use another person on my team. It's not like I have dozens of friends here at Western. There's Riley, of course, but I can't plan every social activity around her. In the end, though, I chicken out and type out a different response.

Me: *She's good. I have her in my backpack.*

Knox: *You already done?!*

Me: *Couldn't stop. Plus, I wanted to get it back to you before you left for the Missouri game.*

Knox: *Did you like it?*

Me: *Yes. I stayed up all night and will be a mess today but it's totally worth it.*

Knox: *You in class?*

Me: *Haven't you got a copy of my schedule yet? I'm so disappointed.*

Knox: *I figure you'll give it to me eventually. Besides I do know your softball schedule. Did you pick your team based on the name?*

Me: *The Horny Toads? That's a real animal. And no. I was randomly assigned because I didn't have a team last year.*

Knox: *Google tells me there is no such animal named the horny toad. A horned toad, yes. Horny no.*

Me: *Are you a biologist? I could have sworn your SI profile said International Relations major.*

Knox: *I like that you have my bio memorized.*

If I meant to deter him I'm not doing a good job of it. At this point,

I don't know what I should do. I know what I want. That's to jump into Knox's brawny arms and let him carry me away. I'm not convinced that's what I *should* do.

Me: *Maybe I'm hot for your brother.*

Knox: *Nah. You already told me he's weak with weird eyes. I shared that with him and he's upset so you've got no chance. You're stuck with me.*

Me: *So you're saying if I insult you, you'll go away.*

Knox: *Nope. Now I know it's your strange way of flirting with me. I think that's called negging.*

Me: *You think I'm negging you?!*

Knox: *Negging—insulting someone to gain their attention. If the shoe fits…*

Me: *The shoe does not fit! I am not negging you.*

Knox: *Don't worry, baby. I know I'm irresistible but you don't want to appear overeager. I'll see you at your softball game on Wednesday.*

Me: *What? No!*

But he doesn't respond.

The rest of the morning passes in a blur until I hit my last class of the day—the second of Jack's classes I'm auditing. Politics and Games turns out nothing like I expect. It's not really about games, but game theory, which I don't understand. From the moment that the professor opens her mouth to the minute that the TA hands out the assignments at the end of class, I'm worried. Jack sits rigidly in his chair, his pen poised, but no notes hit paper. Three girls managed to position themselves around him, but their chairs could be empty for all the attention he gives them.

Five minutes before class is over, I start to pack up. I need to get out of there before Jack turns around. If the theoretical class is difficult for me to get, it's a hundred times harder for Jack. He should drop it, but I don't even know how I'd bring that up. *Oh by the way, Jack, I passed by your political science class and it seems like a mind fuck. Maybe you should drop.*

After the way he responded to my mere suggestion of visiting the learning center, I'm sure that this proposal would be met with the same disinterest.

"LEFT FIELD OKAY WITH YOU, Eliot?" Ryan Schneider asks. Ryan's the team captain. About an inch under six feet, he's trim, attractive almost to the point of prettiness, and a damn good pitcher.

"No problem." I slap my hand into my new glove. It feels stiff and weird. I've never played softball before, but Ryan assured me that the Horny Toads only care about having fun, unlike some of the other teams.

Megan Billings, a biology major who's tamed her wild hair into two bushy ponytails, points to the bleachers behind home plate. "Wow, look who showed up to watch the game today!"

I don't even have to look. I feel Masters' eyes boring into my back. Ryan's head pops up and his eyes widen. "Is that Knox Masters?"

"Yeah, and I think the other guys must be on the team, too. Look at the guns on those guys."

"You're drooling, Megs." Ryan points a finger at her face.

Her dark eyes sparkle. "I wouldn't be human if I wasn't drooling a little. Right, Eliot?"

"Call me Ellie," I respond automatically. As to whether she should be drooling over Masters? I have no comment on that.

"Good thing we're fielding first," Megan gloats as she grabs my wrist and leads me to the outfield. She's playing center. "That way we can ogle the manflesh."

I figure I better confess to her that I know the team, or at least part of them. "The guy with the brown hair sitting on the left side is my brother Jack. He's a tight end for the Warriors."

"Ohhh." She slaps a hand over her mouth. "Is it okay that I'm objectifying your brother?"

"Sure, have at it." I laugh.

"So they're here to support a teammate's sister. Cool. I wonder if we should try to win now."

"Let's not ruin a good thing because some football players have nothing better to do with their Wednesday night," I reason, and then move away to left field.

As the night wears on, we wind up winning despite Ryan's assertion that the Horny Toads aren't interested in keeping score.

"Nice fielding tonight, Campbell," Ryan gives me a high five and then slaps his glove against my butt in what I guess is a victory slap. He gives it to the rest of the eight players. "Any one up for the Gas Station?"

Half the team raises their hands. The other half shakes their head.

"How about you, Eliot?" Ryan asks.

"Think I could get that book back from you, Ellie?" Masters' voice interrupts before I can answer Ryan's invitation. "I'd like to read it on the plane ride to Missouri this weekend."

Only an asshole would say no, I tell myself. Otherwise, I would turn Masters down in a heartbeat. "Sure."

Masters turns to Ryan. "Nice team you have there."

"I didn't realize we added a gunner to the team," he jokes and points to me. "She said she hasn't ever played before."

Masters gives me an appraising look. "She's got good hand/eye co-ordination. I think it runs in her family."

A faint smile dances around the edges of his mouth. I shake my head.

"Let's go, Masters." I grab him and half pull/half push him away from the dugout.

"Nice to meet you, Knox," Ryan calls out. "Good luck this week-end!"

"Thanks, man," Masters calls. He places a hand on the low of my back. "See how your friend called me Knox."

"Because it's your name," I answer.

"Yet you call me Masters."

"Also your name." I quicken the pace to put some daylight between his tempting hand and my weak back.

"Hmmm," he murmurs. He lets his hand drop between us and I allow two seconds to throw myself a pity party over him not touching me anymore before I march forward to the apartment.

Somewhere along the way, though, I find my gait synchs with his. Our arms move in unison and there's a heavy tension that builds with each step. I can hear his even breaths, smell his spicy skin.

My skin prickles and I almost feel him touching me even though there's at least a hand span between us. His field of magnetism is that large. I can't stand this close to him without wanting to feel him against me.

I'm a basketful of nerves by the time we get to the apartment complex.

"It's the third floor," I inform him when we stop at the front door. "Do you want to wait here?"

He looks at me incredulously. "I think I can walk three floors, Ellie."

I try to shrug nonchalantly as if it doesn't matter at all if he's inside my apartment, when in reality I'm wondering how long it takes before I attack him.

We climb the steps side by side, and this time, our arms brush. Even that slight sensation sends a tingle throughout my body. I'm practically dizzy with sensation. At the top of the third floor, he grabs me and pushes me into an alcove.

He bends forward and kisses me, sweetly and softly. Apparently my grungy attire or slightly sweaty skin don't matter to him. He keeps his hands on either side of the doorframe of the alcove, holding himself slightly away. I don't like that space between us so I twine my arms around his neck and tug him closer. He makes a noise—not quite a grunt, not quite a moan, but more of a sigh of happiness. It fills pockets in my heart I didn't know were empty. As he draws back, I follow him because I'm not done with that kiss.

"What was that for?" I ask hoarsely. His fingers are the tiniest bit shaky as they smooth a few strands of hair away from my forehead.

"I hadn't kissed you since the bookstore. That's a long time."

My lips part at the sincerity of his words. They aren't a line—at least not to him.

He captures those parted lips between his again. This time his tongue delves deep into my mouth, finding places that have me moaning in longing. He lifts me with ease, using his football player strength, and pushes me against the wall. I wend my fingers into his short straw-colored hair and wrap my legs around his waist.

All sense of preservation lies somewhere between the softball field and the apartment. He's wrecking me, in long licks and tiny bites, one tender and scorching hot kiss at a time.

I want to suspend time and remain in this moment forever with his big frame blotting out the light and his mouth memorizing every curve and plane of my face. I feel weightless, protected, and cherished.

Under my fingers, his shoulder muscles bunch as he reaches down to stroke a firm palm along the outside of my thigh. His kisses are making me wet and hungry. He makes low sounds of appreciation and I rock against him in growing desperation.

After what seems like both an eternity and not long enough, he allows my legs to slide to the ground. His head drops on my shoulder and I can feel his entire body heave as he tries to regain his breath and his control.

After three shuddering breaths, he pushes away from me.

"I need to wear longer T-shirts when you're around." He tugs out his shirt and tries to pull it down over the erection tenting his shorts. We exit the alcove and walk past four doors to stop at my apartment.

"Do you want to come in?"

He gives me a rueful smile. "I better not. I need to get home, get some beauty sleep, and prepare for the game."

I try not to let my disappointment show. "You worried about the game this weekend?"

He shakes his head. "Not worried. Eager. I've waited since last December to get back on the field. I want to make grown-ass men cry. I want to imprint the paint from the yard markers and grind it into their skin. I want them to go home and have nightmares about meeting me on the turf." He looks down at me. "But I'm not taking it for granted. They're a weaker team but it's their home field. Anything could happen."

Right. The odds in Vegas are probably fifty to one that the Warriors lose.

"Do you really believe that?"

He pauses for a moment. "Yeah. Anything could happen. Ace could go down. He could throw a half dozen interceptions. We could fumble on every kickoff and punt return. We could forget how to tackle. Do I think those things will happen? No, but I can't go into the game thinking it's won before the last whistle blows."

"When's your charter bus leave for the airport?"

"Around eleven." He leans an arm against the door and it takes real effort not to swoon at the sight of the bulging muscle in my periphery vision. "How's Jack doing?"

"What do you mean?"

Masters cocks his head. "He's on my list."

"What list?" I straighten and push his arm away from my head.

"Ace and I watch over the newbies, make sure they don't get into trouble, know the unspoken team rules."

He looks at me curiously, as if wondering why I'm making a big deal of this. I shouldn't but I can't seem to stop myself.

"Why is Jack on your list?" I snap.

"Because his grades are on the border of eligibility. I'm checking in to make sure he's got all the help he needs to pass his classes." He narrows his eyes. "Is that a problem?"

I paste on a fake smile. "Of course not, but don't tell him."

"Why not?"

"He's sensitive about that." I jut my chin out. Why can't Masters do as I ask?

He rubs the back of his neck. "Jack's a smart guy. I'm sure he knows that he's on the bubble. He could be an important part of our team this year. Last year we struggled with scoring. With Ace, Jack, and Ahmed, we have decent scoring options."

"So you'll stalk him?" My voice starts to get high.

"Nooo," Masters draws out slowly. "I try to save that for girls I like."

"I think you should go." I cross my arms over my chest. Dating Masters would be like holding my hand over a flame. At some point, I'll get burned. I don't need that in my life.

17

ELLIE

GAME DAY: WARRIORS 0-0

"I HAVEN'T SEEN JACK AROUND," Riley comments as we settle in for Saturday's game.

"He's getting ready for the game."

"Is it like this all year? They disappear for the weekend?"

I hide a smile at Riley's disgruntled tone. Jack has become a regular fixture at the apartment. Sometimes it's just him but oftentimes he brings a teammate with him. Riley and I would have dinner with him or hang out, but on Friday the team left for the game and it's gotten eerily quiet.

I haven't seen Masters since I gave him the book back. I wish I didn't regret that I pushed him away. Telling yourself that you're doing the right thing and feeling good about it are two totally separate things. Eating broccoli is good for you, but it tastes like shit, and that's pretty much how I feel not getting one flirty text from Masters or seeing him pop up around campus.

"From September through November they're pretty busy, but Jack says he has the most trouble in the spring when there's no rigid schedule. They have a thirteen week schedule with twelve games," I explain. "One week is a bye where they don't have any game and then the thirteenth game is the conference championship. If they win, and they should, then they go into a four team playoff for a shot at the national title."

"Student athlete seems so glamorous. Full tuition scholarship, free tutors, first pick of classes, but it does seem like they work hard."

"Very."

We'd last seen Jack on Thursday, and he'd been hurting. Riley made him put his foot up and I got ice for his knee. The nonstop pampering probably made up half the reason he enjoyed coming over.

"How come you aren't at the student center?" Riley shoves a handful of popcorn into her mouth.

"I don't like watching the games in public. If you go to a game, you have to sit with a bunch of people who don't know the game, but think they know it. They're yelling about the bad refs, or if your brother misses a catch, you have to listen to them talk about how terrible he is." I shake my head. "It's better at home."

"I don't know anything about the game," she points out.

"Will you yell nonstop about how bad the refs are?"

She shakes her head. "No, but I'll ask a lot of questions."

"Fair enough. What do you know?"

"That there's a quarterback, Tom Brady's balls deflated, and there's a Super Bowl."

I stifle a laugh. "It's a start."

"Why do they hold hands when they walk to the middle of the field? Are they afraid they'll lose each other? Do they play a game of Red Rover, Red Rover to send one of the Hawkeyes right over? And then if we win, we get the ball?" she jokes as Ace, the running back and three others walk toward the fifty yard line.

"It's team unity. They'll also slap each other on the butt all the time."

We share a smirk.

"Where's Jack?"

"Right there. Number 88." I press pause and point to the screen. "He'll be on the line of scrimmage where the center will hike the ball to the quarterback."

"He looks big."

"It's the pads."

"And I'm sorry to say this in front of you, but holy Christ, his ass is tight. They all have tight asses." She shifts forward. "Why haven't I watched this before?"

"You didn't know." I pat her back. "But now you do."

"What does Jack do?"

"He's a tight end. He's responsible for blocking and catching the ball—usually he'll run across the middle. The guys at the end are the wide receivers. They are usually the fastest on the field. The running back is the one behind the quarterback."

"They named a position after his *ass*?"

I grin. "All sports are like that. Like MMA? It's the most homoerotic sport on the planet. Half naked guys rolling around with their faces in each other's crotch."

"I'm becoming a fan already. And where's your fiancé?"

I roll my eyes but scan the sidelines when the camera pans to number 55. "Right there."

I freeze the screen. Masters has his helmet up, with the ear pads resting against his temple. His mouth piece is half inside of mouth, half out of it as he intently watches the action unfold. He looks…magnificent. The sleeves of his uniform are tucked up under his pads, and underneath the fabric, his muscles bulge.

The Warriors start off slowly in the first quarter. The Missouri quarterback isn't very good, but he manages to get lucky and run for about twenty yards. Three more plays and they're in kicking distance. I curse when the forty-three yard try splits the uprights perfectly. On offense, the Warriors can't seem to move the ball more than five yards. The team is scoreless before the first quarter ends.

During the commercial break, I rummage around our cupboards looking for something to drink with my Coke. I'll need to anesthetize myself if the game continues like this.

"I'm guessing that was a bad period."

"Quarter," I correct her. "They play four quarters. And yeah, it was bad."

Masters was right. They can't take one game for granted. I watch as he walks up and down the sideline, taking the time to talk to his teammates. He slaps a couple of them on the helmet and squeezes the neck of another guy. The other players nod and smile at him. He's not chastising them but encouraging them. *Keep your heads up. We got this,* I imagine him telling the guys.

"But it's just one quarter, right?"

"This is college ball. Strength of schedule is really important, and if you play a weak opponent, you have to play really well. Dominate. And you can't lose."

"Not even one game?" She's shocked.

"Pretty much. If you lose one game, there's a real good chance you won't make it to the playoffs, and that's the only thing that matters in college ball."

"Wow." Her eyes go wide as she takes this new information in.

During the second quarter, the defense picks up. Masters opens with a sack, throwing the offensive lineman aside like he's a piece of trash. Masters is on the quarterback before the guy can get his shoulders straight down field and just like that it's second and twenty-three.

"What do the players say to each other out there?" Riley asks as we watch Knox jaw at the opposing side as he returns to the line of scrimmage.

"Probably something disgusting about their mothers."

"Really?"

Maybe not Masters, though. He didn't seem like the type of person to insult a player's mom; insult the player yes, but not someone attached to the player. "Some guys do. Masters is probably telling the O-lineman that he's soft and that he'll spend a lot of time on his ass. Jack would tell the safety who covers him that he's too slow and ask if he needs roller skates to keep up."

Riley grins. "I wish we could hear them. That'd be fun."

"Too much cursing." I smile back. It's fun watching with Riley. All last year, I sat in my dorm room and watched the games by myself. My roommate liked to sleep with the players but she sure as hell didn't enjoy watching the game. I forgot what it felt like to have company, and how much nicer it is to share an experience with someone, even a bad one.

The first quarter field goal is the only score that Missouri manages to eke out. The Warriors defense, led by Masters, is stifling. If they aren't sacking the quarterback, they attacked him as soon as the ball leaves his hands.

The team struggles on offense, but Jack makes a great catch in the third and runs it for another thirty yards before he's stopped. They manage to punch the ball across the goal line three more times, and the game ends twenty-one to three.

Riley and I jump out of our seats and cheer as loudly as any of the fans at the game. It's the most fun I've had watching one of Jack's games in years.

We drew the short end of the stick when it comes to parents, but I've always had the team. You've only had me. It wouldn't be a bad thing to have another person on your side, Ellie. Besides, you could do a lot worse than Masters.

My eyes follow Masters around the field as he slaps helmets and gives one-armed hugs to his fellow teammates. He stops in front of Jack, whose face is lit up like a spotlight. He's so happy. The two exchange a few words and something Jack says makes Masters laugh. Then the camera cuts away.

"Will they come home today?" Riley asks as we clean up the living room.

"They should."

And maybe Jack will come over along with his teammates. Or maybe he'll text me, say that there's a party somewhere, and we should come. I'll go and find Masters, we'll get a little drunk, he'll forgive me for my cold shoulder, and we can pick up where we left off.

My phone buzzes and my heart skips hoping its Masters.

Not getting out today. Apparently there's bad weather coming in and we're not flying.

No, just Jack. I try not to be disappointed at his words.

"I guess not." I show Riley the text message.

Sweet catch in the third. And nice YAC stats. I type back.

"What's YAC?" Riley asks peering over my shoulder.

"Yards after catch. The number of yards that a player gets after he catches the ball."

Just in the third? I was killer all day! JK. Not gonna lie. It felt great. This will be a good year.

Jack and I exchange a few more texts and then I tuck the phone away. I can almost taste his happiness. Even if they did come home and had some raging party, I wouldn't go, because I can't trust myself around Masters.

"Hey, you okay? Is Jack okay?"

Riley touches my shoulder. I look down at her concerned face and the urge to confide in her nearly overwhelms me. I don't tell her the whole truth but the burden of it is weighing me down. "Jack is on the bubble academically. He has problems with some of his classes and it brings his grades down. He'll never win awards, but he's not dumb."

"And?

"And Masters apparently has to check up on him."

She nibbles on her lip. "Why don't you tell him that you'll check up on Jack? That way Knox gets taken out of the loop."

I stare at her.

"What?" She rubs her forehead. "Do I have ice cream on my face?"

"No. That's a genius idea, and I don't know why I didn't think of it."

"See?" she nudges me with her shoulder. "This is why it's okay to share things. Two are better than one."

The tension that set in on Monday eases. Maybe this is the way for me to have it all—secure Jack's eligibility and give Masters a chance. So I take a deep breath and text him.

Great game. You guys played fantastic.

There is no response.

I only have myself to blame.

18

KNOX

POST GAME: WARRIORS 1-0

MY PHONE IS DEAD. GIVEN how crappy the day has been going, I'm unsurprised. Game one is in the books with eleven to go. If we play like we did today in any of those upcoming games, we can kiss our national title hopes goodbye.

"You got a charge?" I nudge Matty. I don't think I've gotten a text from Ellie, but that doesn't stop me from obsessively checking my phone.

"No. Sorry, man. Mine's on life support, too." He shows me his phone face. The battery indicator is red. "I'm working on a local meet up, and if my phone dies before I can get all the details locked down, I'll be pissed." He flips to Instagram where some busty brunette has posted a thousand selfies. "Like her?"

I shrug. She's pretty, but she also looks like everyone else Matty has screwed in the last twelve months.

"How about her?" With a flick of his fingers, he brings up another profile.

"They look the same to me." Lots of long hair, big boobs and tiny waists. They look kind of breakable. One thing I like about Ellie is that she's solid. I don't have to worry about holding back with her.

That is, when I get her. I haven't heard from her since she gave me the book back. My guess is that she's offended I'm keeping track of Jack. It's not like I'm reading his answers or pre-grading his papers. Who's got time for that shit? I've got my own classes and don't need to add that burden.

But maybe she thought I insulted Jack, called him dumb. He's obviously not. Our playbook is complicated and he's had zero problems catching on. She's mad about something. When my parents argue, my dad says that you have to give mom time to cool off.

So that's what I'm doing. I figure it's worked for my dad for nearly twenty-five years. Why not me?

The bus stops in front of the hotel, but before we get off, Coach stands at the front.

"No curfew tonight, but you guys screw this up and you'll be required to be in your beds every night at seven for four months," Coach threatens. "The team bus leaves for the airport at four in the morning. Anyone not on the bus will be suspended for the next game."

Everyone promises to be angels as we file out and then mill around in the lobby while Stella gets everyone's room keys.

"We're meeting some locals at the bar next door." Hammer jerks his head toward the lobby door.

I look at my dead phone.

"I'll hang out for a bit," I concede. It's good for the team, I figure.

When Hammer raises his fist and yells, "Masters is in," I know it's the right call. Stella hands out the room keys but before I can head up, Coach grabs me. "Watch out for your guys."

"I got it." I nod.

Upstairs, I plug in my phone and exchange the suit for a gray workout T-shirt, jeans, and a pair of flips. Matty and Hammer have their Warriors T-shirt on. I make them change. No sense in advertising our team allegiance given that we spanked the hometown team.

While they switch out their shirts, I call Ty on Hammer's phone since he's the only one who had the good sense to charge it before the game.

"Good game, man," he says upon answering.

"Thanks." I throw myself on the bed. Ty had a game on Thursday night that they won. "We're stuck here because there's some bad weather in Chicago."

He groans. "Fuck, that sucks." You don't want to spend more nights away from home than you have to. It messes with your schedule. But teams are cautious about flying in bad weather given that if the whole charter goes down, you've lost the entire program. "You going out?"

"Yeah, with Matty and Hammer." I rub a hand over my hair—the short cut ensures that it doesn't totally look like ass since I don't like to even brush it. Matty, on the other hand, uses more product than some girls do. In fact, some of the girls he's slept with give him tips on how to take care of his long hair.

"What's going on? You sound uneasy. Was it the first quarter? You guys just shook out the dust of the off season."

Ty's attempt at encouragement hits off the mark. I'm not uneasy. I'm tense. The post-game high has worn off, but I'm still edgy because I can't stop thinking about Ellie.

Tonight the guys will come back with out-of-town strangers, and given the location of our hotel, it won't be college coeds either. Matty's told me more than once he likes his women older. They know what they want and aren't afraid to vocalize it.

"It's the girl." He sounds concerned.

"Yeah, the girl."

"What happened?"

"I think I offended her." I explain the Jack situation. "So I thought I'd give her some time to cool off, like Dad does."

"You sure she's the one?" he asks cautiously.

"Fuck, man, I'm not sure about anything right now. We played like shit in the first quarter. Against a better team, we might have been sunk. We can barely score and if our defense isn't playing lights out then our chances of a title are gone." I take a couple calming breaths. "And I'm definitely not sure about her."

Then I think of the sharp set of her chin every time she says something that she thinks I'll disagree with. The sparkle in her eyes when she talks about football—the sport she says is just okay. Right, and I'm a ballerina. The way her brother and she get along. They're a unit like Ty and I are a unit. I'm not uncertain anymore.

I've always known what I want. From the minute I could walk, I wanted to play ball. From the moment I realized I could have dreams and make those dreams a reality, I vowed I'd play on Sundays.

Now? Now I want one prickly Eliot Campbell and not even her barricades will keep me out.

"Actually, I *am* sure about her." I hear a pounding on the door. Clearly my teammates are tired of waiting for me. "Hammer and Matty are back. I'll call you later."

"Okay, bro."

Downstairs, Jack Campbell shows up along with Ace and a couple of the other offensive players.

"Good game." We exchange chin nods. The offense and the defense have different mindsets. They want to score. We want to destroy them. It makes for uneasy times even when we're on the same team.

"Thanks. Felt good to play again."

That's a sentiment I can get behind. About twenty of us head out. The rest of the guys are underage or calling their girlfriends.

The bar down the street has plenty of action. Half dance club, half sports bar, we settle in to watch the night games. I find myself a table in front of the Wisconsin/Alabama game. Right off the bat someone's BCS hopes will get bruised. Hammer and Matty join me. We order a round of beers and a couple of appetizers and settle in.

The Crimson Tide's defense is a ball-busting, soul-crushing machine. I simultaneously admire the hell out of them while wanting to beat them into the turf. They're one of the teams I wouldn't be surprised to play in the playoffs.

During halftime, the score is tied at ten all, and Matty and Hammer leave to meet up with the local talent.

"Hey," a soft voice greets me.

My head swivels to find a sweet thing standing at my side, one hip jutting out and long red fingernails tapping away at that round shape. If she meant to draw my attention there, it's a success. I flick my eyes upward. She's pretty. Real pretty. Dark tight curls, skin that reminds me of the fall leaves, and a top so low that I wonder if I'm seeing nips or that's a shadow from the big screen. "You Knox Masters?"

I nod.

"You play for the Warriors, right?"

"Right." I scratch the side of my neck as I search for a nice way to tell her to get lost.

"I saw you on the field today. You looked amazing." Her lips look red and very shiny, and she deserves some kind of response. I'm not sure what it is.

She leans forward and presses a kiss against my cheek. "That guy gave me $100 to deliver this to you."

Two tables down, I see Jack's eyes narrow. I shift backward.

"Okay, thanks." I take the card. She doesn't leave. I look up and see an older guy tip his head toward me. He must think I'm stupid. Agent contact at any time before the season ends could ruin my eligibility. I pick up the card, rip it into tiny pieces, and dump it into the ashtray in the middle. Nothing will affect our chances of winning title this year.

"The card was his idea. The kiss was mine."

"Need something, sweetheart?" Hammer comes to my rescue.

"Oh no, I was telling Knox here how much I like his game."

Hammer puts an arm around her shoulder and gently turns her away from the table. "I play for the Warriors, too. You know much about football?" She shakes her head as Hammer leads her toward the dance floor. "I play on the quarterback's blind side. That's his weak side. Only the best defensive players get that position." He looks back over his shoulder and winks.

I give him a salute and slide off the chair. Time to go home. When I arrive, Matty's got the Do Not Disturb on the door. I ignore it and walk in. A woman is bouncing, reverse cowgirl style, her brown curls springing in rhythm.

"Don't mind me," I say easily. "Just getting my book."

"You can join us," Matty offers. "Lana won't mind."

"It's Laura." She scowls. But then stops bouncing and turns to me. "You're Knox Masters, right? I saw you on the cover of *Sports Illustrated*."

"Yeah? Which one was I?"

She looks confused. "The one in the Warriors uniform."

That's another reason I'm sure about Ellie. She can tell me and Ty apart. All the fucking time.

Matty sits up and rubs his hands along the side of the lady's thin frame, and then up to cup a very large, very perky pair of tits. Not gonna lie. My body reacts. I'm twenty-one. There's a hot naked chick offering herself to me.

"Thanks for the offer. I'll read my book."

"Your loss." She shrugs and returns her attention to Matty.

I grab my phone and book, and head up to the tenth floor's concierge lounge. Coach gets us access so we don't have to sit downstairs and answer questions from the press.

I open the book and…it smells. Not bad but girlish. I lift it to my nose and inhale. It smells like her. And I can't let another minute go by without contacting her.

I power up the phone, and as soon as it comes online, the message I've waited for appears. *Got you.* I grin to myself.

I shoot her a reply. *Phone was dead. You up?*

When the text message alert dings, all the tension of the day drains out of me. I slump down lower in the chair to get comfortable.

Ellie: *Yes. Sorry about the other day. The thing with Jack caught me off guard. He doesn't want people he respects to think he's dumb.*

I don't want to text her. I press dial and wait for her to answer.

"Masters?"

I close my eyes in irritation at hearing my last name.

"You there?"

"Yeah. I'm here."

"I'm sorry," she repeats.

"We're on the same team, you know. We all want the same thing— for Jack to play."

She sighs. "I know. But Jack is…sensitive about his grades. He doesn't want people he admires to think he's dumb or slow."

"I don't."

"Then how about I check up on him?"

"That works for me." I don't care about Jack. I mean, I do in the sense that I want him to succeed, because that means our offense succeeds. But in a contest between caring about his classes and wanting Ellie, she wins.

The next sigh she lets out sounds like relief. "When will you be back?"

I smile at the slightly anxious note in her voice. She wants to see me. My whole body perks up at this.

"We'll be back at nine. I plan to crash for a few hours. I'll call you when I get up."

I hang up, because I'm not giving her an opportunity say no.

19

ELLIE

WEEK 2: WARRIORS 1-0

"FUCK," JACK SAYS, THROWING HIMSELF down on the sofa.

"What's wrong?"

The team got home this morning, and Jack had a meeting with his tutor over lunch. Apparently it didn't go well.

"My tutor sucks. She spends more time trying to climb into my jock. I tell her I need her help and she hands me this paper." He thrusts it at me. "What is this?"

I scan the paper. It's a list of different models and a brief description of each. "An outline of sorts."

"I signed up for this specific course because I thought game theory would be something I'd understand, but I don't get even one of the concepts." Jack looks anguished. "All these fucking models. I'm supposed to regurgitate this in a mid-term and final?" His bleak eyes meet mine.

"Ellie, if I fail the class, my eligibility will disappear. I need to at least pass the midterm. I should have dropped the fucking class."

The time for that has passed, unfortunately. "What about the play-offs?"

"Not to go all Denny Green on you, Ellie, but what playoffs? I won't even be around for those games if I can't pass this class. What was I thinking?" He drops his head into his hands and groans.

"It's Jim Mora."

"What?"

"Jim Mora had the postgame rant about the playoffs. Denny Green did the 'They are who we thought they were' bit."

Jack stares at me as if I've lost my mind. Jim Mora was a coach for the Indianapolis Colts whose postgame rant in response to a reporter's question about making the playoffs went viral. *Playoffs? What playoffs?* he's seen spitting out from the podium. Green, the coach of the Cardinals, played an undefeated Bears and almost beat them, until the fourth quarter where the wheels came off and they lost the game. Green lost his shit during the post-game press conference. The reporter had to feel grateful for that barrier, because Green looked one step away from introducing his fist to the reporter's face. Kind of how Jack looks right now. He'd like to take physical action against something—the class, the course syllabus, his tutor.

I need to watch my words carefully so that it doesn't look like I've been sitting in the same class for the last two weeks. I put the tutor's worksheet aside.

"Okay. Let's look at game theory from a football standpoint. Take Seattle's last play in the Super Bowl. Both run plays and pass plays from the one yard line had a close to 60% chance of success. But any play can be defended if the defense knows what to expect. If the run game is more powerful, then the rational decision is to run the ball because their physical resources are geared toward running. But the Patriots knew that Seattle had a more powerful run team, so their expectations play a role. Seattle decides that the expectation has a higher value than the powerful running game and calls a pass play.

"You have the statistical average of success of any given play impacted by the physical resources—your players—measured against the opponents players and the players expectations."

"The political parties are opponents and the election is their Super Bowl, with the primaries and all of the stuff that comes before it acting as the season." He's starting to get it. Maybe I won't have to do anything for him. He makes a few notes. "How do I find out the statistical chance of success?"

"Demographics. I guess that's why polling is so popular. The parties try to analyze the likelihood of success of a position before moving to the bargaining table. Individual actors, such as the president, can increase or decrease bargaining power based on the position of power."

"Size up the strengths and weaknesses of a certain political structure, the general mood of the electorate, and then predict?"

"I think that's a fair analysis."

"But there are like a dozen different models." The space between his eyes gets tight.

"It looks by the syllabus, you're only studying four of them."

That cheers him up considerably. "Thanks, Ellie. That helps a lot. I don't feel as helpless as I did before."

"So your grade is based on a midterm?" I ask, pretending I don't know.

"An ungraded one, a few assignments we can do outside of class by logging into our student account, and then a final paper. Five thousand words on one of these models applied to the passage of a National Marriage Act."

"I'll proof whatever you need me to proof." I'm dreading the paper myself. I don't fully grasp game theory, and I foresee a lot of outside-of-class reading in order to manage two extra papers—one for Jack and one for me.

"Thanks." He leans back and looks at the ceiling. "Maybe Dad is right, and I am a dumb fuck."

"You're not." I squeeze his arm. "This sort of thing is tough for everyone. You should see these kids at my grant center—"

"Oh fuck, what time is it?" He glances at his phone. "Sorry. I have to go. I'm going to miss a team meeting." Jack jumps to his feet and throws his book into his gym bag. He refuses to meet my eyes. I hate that he's down on himself because of this class. Jack has always hated dumb jock jokes because they hit too close to home. But he's not dumb. On the field and with his team he doesn't feel that way. It's only in the classroom.

"Dinner later?" I ask hesitantly.

"Maybe." But by the despondent tones in his voice, I'm guessing that's a no.

20

ELLIE

"YOU WERE RIGHT. THE BOOK was good." Masters' eyes are heavy lidded, but it probably has more to do with tiredness than any sexiness on my part. We're eating ribs, for crying out loud. When I okayed this place, I forgot that eating ribs are the messiest meal around. Right up there with slurping spaghetti noodles.

Like everything Masters does, he manages to consume a full rack with ease and physical grace. One rib goes in his mouth and the bone comes out clean.

I struggle for about five minutes to cut the meat off, and then think *fuck it*, because I'm hungry, and start gnawing on it like the rest of the patrons. Masters smiles at me so I guess I don't look too disgusting.

"Did you stay up all night reading it?" I shove the basket of mostly eaten ribs aside and start wiping up. It takes three paper towels and a wet wipe before I feel human again. I pop two peppermints in my mouth and watch as Masters does the same.

"Most of it. I read a lot on the plane to the game. Fell asleep on the way home." He stretches, and I try not to pant too much as the worn blue of his T-shirt stretches across his defined pectorals.

"Your roommate didn't mind, or do you, Knox Masters, get your own room?" I tease.

"I don't think Johnny Football got his own room on the road." He grins and I swear I hear panties drop three tables over. "Matty was, ah, occupied and I sat in the executive lounge. They have food up there. Free." The smile on his face turns conspiratorial. "I ate a shit ton of olives."

His confessional tone makes me laugh. A silence settles between us—the kind that happens right before someone ends a call—but I don't want to hang up. So I ask him something that's bothered me since we met in the stadium. "Why didn't you ever tell me to keep your draft plans a secret?"

"I knew you wouldn't tell," he replies. The surety in his voice sounds obvious.

"How?" I shake my head.

"I just knew and you haven't, so I'm right." He leans forward and pins me with those turf green eyes of his. "Sometimes I know things in my gut immediately. Like in the game against Wisconsin my freshman year. I knew that they would run a trick play when I saw the tight end drop back off the line of scrimmage. I watched the tight end the whole time, and when he got the ball and flicked it back to the quarterback—"

"You were there. You intercepted the ball and ran it in for a touchdown. Your first one as defensive end for the Warriors."

"That's right." This time his voice is a tiny bit smug. He has every right to be. I'm here, rattling off his game plays like he's a rock star, and I'm a groupie who knows every lyric to every song, even the ones on the B-side of the album.

"Anyone else up there?" I ask, changing the subject.

"Ace. He looked over at me a lot, hoping I'd leave."

"Why?" I know the defense and offense like to hang separately, but that seems extreme.

"He's banging the coach's daughter, but thinks we don't know. Everyone but Coach knows."

I blanch. "I'm guessing that this is a problem for Coach?"

"Yeah." Masters shrugs as if this is no big deal.

"He could cause problems for Ace."

"No."

"He could," I insist. Why can't he see this? It's like Jack and high school all over again. "Ace could get benched or worse."

Masters is so smart about the game. I can tell the way he acts on the sidelines, constantly in communication, that he's clued into his teammates. There's not a moment I've been with him in public that someone hasn't stopped to say hi to him, and he's always greeted those people with an easy smile and a word of gratitude. *Thanks for watching the game. Thanks for cheering for us. We need your support. Sixth man!* High five.

But about a potentially season-wrecking affair between his starting quarterback and the coach's daughter, he's blind. Can I chalk this up to his sexual inexperience?

A big warm hand reaches across the table and tugs. "You done?"

I look down and see I've shredded a paper towel. "Yeah."

With a concerted effort, I loosen my grip and let Masters pull the towel out of my hands. He stands up, throws a few bills on the table, and hustles me out of the restaurant.

The September night is warm, but I feel chilled inside. Jack's poli-sci class and the trouble with the team quarterback make me uneasy.

"I wondered why Jack went to juco. He's too good of a player not to get a D1 scholarship."

I lick my very dry lips. Maybe if I tell Masters it will put him on notice—at least alert him to potential trouble.

"I once dated the quarterback for Ward High School—the 'punk ass bitch' as Jack likes to refer to him. Travis was pressuring me into having sex and I refused. He told me it was fine and that he wanted to wait, too, but went off and slept with as many girls as possible behind my back. Someone finally told me and I dumped him. I was humiliated and angry that he'd cheated so obviously on me, but I wasn't sorry to see the ass end of him." As I tell him the rest of it, Masters face grows dark. "Jack found him the next day and roughed him up."

"Good for Jack." Masters nods with approval.

I sigh. That was Jack's response, too. I didn't agree. "Jack got a one game suspension. Next year rolls around and Travis decides that Jack doesn't need to be thrown the ball. Ever. Maybe in another school Travis would be yelled at or even benched, but Travis' father was the coach. So Jack got about ten passes his junior year and less than that his senior year. Jack didn't have the game film to convince a quality school to give him a scholarship," I finish.

"I'm sorry that happened," he says gruffly.

I peek at him under my lashes and his jaw looks tight.

"Jack says it worked out for the best because he's with the Warriors now."

"He's right. Still doesn't mean it didn't suck." We exchange grim smiles. "What happened to the QB?"

"He flunked out of his first semester at USC because he drank too much."

"Sounds like it couldn't have happened to a better person." Masters stops outside my apartment building and pulls me around to face him. "Jack'll be fine here. The team will be fine. Coach wants to win more than anything, and he won't crater his own chances because one of his players is sleeping with his daughter. Trust me on this." He strokes a bit of my hair behind my face and tips my head up. "Everything is will be fine here. For both of you."

"Just let you take care of everything?" I ask wryly.

"Nah, I'm not saying that. I'm saying worry about the things in your control." His hand keeps sweeping across my forehead and his face lowers until it is only inches away from mine.

"Are you saying I have other things to worry about?" I ask hoarsely.

"Yes. Right now you should worry about getting me inside your apartment before we shock everyone in the building." He smiles, but it's a dark one full of promise.

I gulp but grab his hand and pull him inside. We don't talk. There's nothing to say, or at least nothing I want to give voice to. Masters must feel the same way. He grips my hand tightly, but stays slightly behind me as if he's willing to let me lead.

The apartment is quiet and dark. A slight hum can be heard from Riley's bedroom. I note the sound and give myself a little reminder to be quiet. These walls are paper thin.

Masters shuts the front door behind him with one hand and jerks me against him with the other. His mouth is on mine in an instant. It's wetter and hotter than the bookstore kiss. I fist my hands in his T-shirt, pulling it up and over his head. Our lips separate for a second and then we're back, fused together with our tongues doing battle. My hands rub themselves all over the ridges and valleys of his tightly defined chest and abs. Holy Jesus, he is ripped. My knees go weak.

His hands feel just as hungry. They cup my breasts, squeezing them, molding them together, and then releasing them to roam across my back and down to cup my buttocks. He lifts me upward and I jump on him, wrapping my legs around his waist until I'm flush against his hard erection. It feels bigger than it did when he jerked off in the bathroom—and back then, it looked like a monster. God gave with two hands when it came to Masters. His arms are as big as my thighs and they hold me up effortlessly.

He swings me around and presses me against the door, grinding that big body against mine.

"My room," I croak out. I need to be horizontal. I need to have him driving that large powerful frame into mine. I have never felt so alive and full of need as I have in this moment. I'm wet between my legs and feverishly hot. I rub against him and repeat my plea. "My room. The bed."

We stumble toward the room still fused together, not wanting to separate for even a second. The door latches shut, but once inside the dark, small space, lit only by a low light on my desk and patches of moonlight streaming between the cheap mini blinds, he doesn't immediately fling me to the bed.

Instead, he drops his head to my neck and then my shoulder. He drags his mouth down my shirt and then lowers to his knees. He's so tall that even in that position, he still seems massive. I rest my hands on his shoulders because I don't have the strength to stand on my own.

He tilts his head up and an impish grin appears on his face. "You tell me if you don't like something. It's my first time, you know."

He lowers himself even more to kiss my thigh. I lock my knees and pray for some strength. His first time? Holy mother, those words *are* an incredible aphrodisiac. His tongue licks its way up toward my sex and then feathers down the opposite leg. There's nothing tentative in his touch. No lack of surety when he pulls down my panties and pushes my short knit skirt up to my waist.

There's a heavy groan. I look down to see him biting hard on his bottom lip.

"Sweet Jesus, baby, you are so gorgeous." He places a big palm over my trimmed hair and rubs. The heel of his hand places exquisite pressure on my clit. I start to shake. "You like this?" He glances up for approval.

I nod and then nod some more, feeling like a bobble head. I'm only capable of one motion right now.

"Can you get off with just this?"

I'm so close I could get off with him holding me.

"Then how about this?" He replaces his hand with his mouth and the moment his hot breath and wet tongue makes contact with my skin, I go off. I shove my fist into my mouth as he lashes me with his hard tongue. My knees completely give out but his right hand shoots up to brace my butt while the left reaches up to squeeze my breasts. If this is how good he is his first time, I might not survive the second one.

My heart pounds against the thin wall of my chest and I fear it will burst out. Every surface of my skin feels like it's on fire, and I'm a hot, needy thing filled with incoherent sounds and pleas for more. He doesn't relent. He doesn't ease off as my body trembles from one high into another. He keeps feasting on me as if he's never had anything better touch his tongue.

"You taste so fucking good," he groans. "So wet and tart. I could stay down here all week."

I've given up stifling my own sounds. I push my hands in his hair, tugging on his short strands while he still holds me up, exposing me to his ravenous mouth. I feel greedy but I want more.

"Masters," I whisper. "I need you."

He pauses, mid lick, mid suck, and draws back.

"What'd you say?" His voice is gravelly and rough and rubs across my sensitized skin as surely as his hand.

"Let's go to the bed," I beg. He lets me sink to the ground in front of him. I kiss the side of his neck, salty with his sweat. When his still body doesn't move, I sense something is wrong.

"What is it?" I ask.

He frowns. His face glistens from the moisture of my body and I feel both embarrassed and aroused.

"Did you just call me Masters?"

I shake my head, but we both know I did.

"Shit." He pushes to his feet.

I reach for him and reflexively he helps me up, but as soon as my feet are flat on the floor, he turns away. Searching a moment, he finds his T-shirt and rubs it across his face.

I grab for him again.

"I'm sorry. It slipped out," I babble.

"Why is this so hard for you?" He pulls on his shirt and shoves his big feet into his flips I hadn't realized he'd even kicked off.

"I don't know," I say miserably. "Why can't we just sleep together?" I sound like a whiny five-year-old and I kind of feel that way, too—like my favorite toy has been snatched from me.

"You know why." He's irritated. He places his hands on his hips and stares down.

I run my hand on his biceps and am perversely pleased when he trembles almost imperceptibly under my touch. He's so, so fine. "You just had your tongue between my legs. I've watched you jerk off. Yet this one little thing you can't let go?"

Masters rubs the side of his neck, the action shaking off my hand. "If it's one little thing then it shouldn't matter if we don't have sex."

"What do you want from me?

He hauls me up against his body and his unabated need nearly burns a brand against my stomach. "I want you to admit that this is something more than a casual fling. That it means something. I'm not giving it up for a one-night stand or even a one-semester stand. I could've done that the minute I walked onto campus. Hell, there were girls available during my recruiting trip. I had a girl ready to ride my jock after the game."

My mouth drops open. I don't like the thought of that at all.

He smiles grimly at my displeasure. "And not just one. Two, three.

Whatever I wanted. And I could have that right now. I could walk out into the hallway of your apartment building and there's someone out there who will take me up on an offer to fuck me silly. If that's all I wanted, I wouldn't need you."

His brutal honesty is killing me.

"I do care about you."

He shakes his head and sets me aside. I follow him out of my bedroom and down the hall to the door like a puppy in desperate need of affection. I can still feel him between my legs, his hard jaw working against my thighs, the suck of his mouth. The sounds, oh God, the sounds he made.

At the door he stops. "I didn't wait for religious reasons," he informs me. "I waited because if I wanted a physical release, I had my hand. I waited for the right girl."

And I'm…the right girl? I'm too scared to ask the question out loud because I'm afraid of the answer. I know what I want it to be but I'm too chicken to reach out for it. But I want to. Holy hell, do I want to.

"So are we done?" I ask in a tiny voice.

"No." He sighs and then releases a self-deprecating laugh. "I'm not done. Are you?"

"No."

His eyes close in what looks like relief.

"Okay, then." He pulls open the door and I still follow him because I'm not prepared for him to go. "I'm not into games between us. I want you. Badly. I know you want me too but it's more than sex for me. When you work that out, it'll be amazing. I'm willing to wait. I'm really good at waiting."

I shiver at the thought of what all he's good at. He starts walking away and I hate that he's leaving without me giving him something.

"Wait," I call. He turns back. "Thank you. It was…incredible."

The side of his mouth curls up in a half smile. "Yeah?"

I give him a little more encouragement. "The best ever."

He stalks back and presses me against the wall by to the open apartment door.

"Me, too, baby." He grips me behind my neck and I'm lost the moment his lips meet mine.

I hear sounds around us, people coming and going, but neither of us pay any attention to that. There's only him and me and the vortex of feeling he creates between us with the mere press of his mouth. Okay, and his big body muscling me up against the wall. There's that, too. I sneak a hand between us and grip him tightly. He freezes and groans into my mouth, and the sound makes me vibrate from the inside out.

But he doesn't fall back into the apartment. He collects himself, inch by inch, and then steps away from me.

"Come inside?" I whisper.

"Not tonight." He shakes his head and the sting of rejection is slightly offset by his obvious regret.

Because I can't help myself, I ask, "Why not tonight?"

"You're not ready."

"And when do you think I'll be ready?" I put my hands on my hips in exasperation.

He palms my cheek. I swear I can I still feel his mouth between my legs.

"You can start by calling me Knox."

21

ELLIE

"SO THAT'S KNOX MASTERS." RILEY watches as I slam the door shut.

"Yes."

"Wow. He was all over you. I thought he would unhinge his jaw and swallow you whole in the hall. Half the floor raced to get their cameras to make amateur porn."

"I know." I stomp into my bedroom and throw myself face first on the mattress. I feel like banging my feet and hands against the surface. I keep seeing him and his big hand and his dick. I feel his rough jaw between my legs and the glorious orgasms he drew out of me. I then hear him say I'm not ready. Where does he get off saying I'm not ready? I'm totally ready. I don't think I have ever been more ready. My body aches in places I didn't know could ache.

I feel empty. Like there is a Knox-shaped void inside of me.

"Is Masters really a virgin?" Riley asks curiously.

"He says he is."

"He looked like he wanted to lose it to you. What happened?"

I press a finger against my temple. "I called him by the wrong name."

"Like another guy's name?" she gasps.

"No, his last name."

"Oh."

She doesn't get it. I roll over.

"He thinks it's my way of saying that sex between us would be meaningless."

"Is he right? Are you using his last name to create emotional distance?"

"I don't know. Maybe. Yes. He accused me of just wanting sex, as if that's a bad thing," I try to joke.

Riley doesn't laugh. "He obviously thinks you're special if he wants to sleep with you."

I swallow. "Yeah."

"Is all you feel for him physical? Like you want to nail him and be done. Or I guess be nailed by him."

"No." My gut clenches at the thought of him taking up any number of the offers available to him. I'm not stupid. I know what it's like for these players. Even at the junior college, when it became apparent that Jack would move to a bigger, better program, the girls flocked to him. Masters could have anyone on campus by snapping his fingers. I don't want him with anyone else. "I like him," I admit. "He's a terrific person and—" I choke. "I don't want to get hurt."

"No one does," she says softly.

"Riley, I can't replay this with you right now, because I'm so damned confused. Could we possibly table this discussion until tomorrow when

I'm cogent and not completely flustered from what happened outside our apartment door?"

"We can. We absolutely can."

"Bless you."

The rest of the night is terrible. I don't spend even one solid minute sleeping. Every time close my eyes I see him, dick in hand. I hear the thud as his knees hit the floor and then the cool air followed by his hot breath when he pulls down my panties. My entire body is one big throbbing ache.

The three guys I've had sex with have been okay, but I have never, ever been so turned on. And what does Masters do? He walks away.

I don't even care that I'm witnessing some extraordinary discipline and what it could mean in the sack. I'm wired and pissed off.

I rub myself, but the relief I get is fleeting. My only solace—and it's a small one—is that he has to be in as much pain as I am.

"Didn't sleep well," Riley notes in the morning. I'm eating her chocolate-covered cereal. It seemed like the right thing to do when I got up frustrated, horny, and upset.

"No. I wish you actually had a high-powered vibrator in your room instead of the sewing machine. I can't hump that, can I?"

She stares at me wide-eyed and a little fearful. "Um, no. Please don't do that to my sewing machine."

I close my eyes and try to gather a little patience. "I'm not, but God, I'd like to punch him in the nuts."

"I thought you wanted those nuts to do something to you."

I wave my hand. "I can't even with him."

"Or odd?" she jokes.

"This is how terrible he is," I huff. "He's driven me to using Tumblr words in real life."

"You should seduce him. He's clearly interested. Put on a sexy dress and make sure he can't say no."

I set down my fork. "Riley, you are a fucking genius. I'll do it after the game on Sunday."

"Why wait?"

"He'll be more susceptible after the game. They have so much adrenaline from a win and they need to expend it somewhere." I grin wickedly at her.

She laughs. "And that somewhere is all over you?"

"Exactly."

Masters wants me. That much I do know. I need to convince him to let go. And remember to call him Knox.

Masters—I mean Knox—texts me during the sociology class.

Knox: *You mad at me?*

Me: *Why would I be mad?*

Knox: *So, really mad.*

Me: *No idea what you're talking about. Good luck with the game this weekend.*

Knox: *Is this your way of saying I'm not seeing you this week?*

Me: *You're so bright.*

Knox: *I do have your schedule now…*

Me: *I can report you to campus police.*

Knox: *I'll see you next week.*

Me: *Or after the game.*

Knox: *Keep talking.*

Me: *After you win this week. Maybe I'll see you around.*
Knox: *All right.*

22

KNOX

POST GAME: WARRIORS 2-0

IT'S STANDING ROOM ONLY AT the Gas Station by the time Matty, Hammer, and I roll in. Two games down and ten to go. We cheerfully accept the back slaps and high fives as we navigate our way to the bar. This time we deserve the congratulations. The team fired on all cylinders. We played fantastic defense, getting four sacks, generating two fumbles. Campbell caught two touchdown passes. Ace threw the ball like Peyton Manning.

More importantly, we played with intensity. Today everyone was hungry—and not just Ace and I showed it on the field. After the game, when game balls got handed out to the players, Coach talked about building off this win and making sure that our best games were ahead of us. This second game was just the start. Then he told us that we had no curfew, but he didn't want to read about our names in the papers tomorrow unless it had something to do with scoring on the field or saving a busload of old ladies on their way to bingo. Then we were excused.

Now we're here, basking in the praise and adulation of our classmates.

Or some of us are. Hammer heads straight for the bar to do shots. His nickname doesn't solely exist because of the hits on the field. Matty already has some Alpha Phi hooked to his hip. She has half her body pressed against his arm while he gestures for the bartender for another drink. I think she's either trying to assimilate into Matty's body or absorb him. Later tonight I'll find some half man, half sorority sister passed out on my living room floor.

Someone presses a bottle into my hands. What the hell? But I might need to get lit tonight if Ellie doesn't show up. I find a place off the edge of the bar where I can see the door.

I'm not certain she'll be here. According to Jack, she doesn't go to the games. The starting whistle blew before I had time to question him further. Post-game, I asked again. He gave me a look that said I was being obvious, but what did I care? The punk. If I wasn't so fucking happy at his play, I might have punched him in the mouth.

But if she didn't show up to the post game celebration, it wouldn't be because she hated football. Just one player. Me.

I fucked it up, making too big of a deal about her slip of the tongue. Girl's got a few barriers. Someone hurt her—someone she cared about—hard, and she's worried. Not just for herself, but for her brother. I can get behind that, and even better, I understand it. If Ty had gotten the ass end of a stick, I'd be wary, too. And wasn't that about half the reason I haven't been laying pipe the whole time I've been here?

I blame my asshole attitude on the fact that most of my thinking power went into my pants last week. Jesus, the first taste of her was enough for me to shoot my wad. I already hovered on the razor's edge just by kissing her thigh. Who knew that particular part of the body felt so soft?

All week I couldn't get the taste and feel out of my mind. I'd fucked my fist so hard and so often it's a miracle my dick isn't so much raw meat right now.

I exchange high fives, receive back slaps and more than a few invitations, but my gaze doesn't waver. There's only one girl for me, and if she doesn't show up, then I'll go to her.

So what if her head wasn't in the same place mine is? Maybe the universe doesn't move at the same rate for her. In the meantime, I need more of her. I've only had a sample, but I wasn't lying when I told her I could have stayed between her shaking legs all week. Nothing on this fine earth tastes as good as she does.

Early on, after I'd decided I would wait, I'd marked below the waist as a no go zone. I pride myself on my personal self-control and self-discipline, but even I knew that a hand below the waist meant clothes would come off and the virginity thing would be in the past. It's also why I didn't move to the bed even though Ellie panted that word like it was the only one in her vocabulary.

A bed and Ellie made too much temptation for a poor boy like me to resist. But I'm done resisting. I'm done making demands. I'll lay myself at her pretty little toes and smile if she decides to walk all over me. Because eventually, eventually, I'll wear her down. Eventually I'll get her. Like I've read every offense. The first time it might take me by surprise, but after a little film, a helluva lot of practice, there's no O-line that can stop me. No barrier I can't overcome. No defense I can't wear down. Eventually.

I glance at my phone. Its blank screen mocks me, as does the door that opens but never seems to spit out the one person I want to see. Time to take the mountain to Mohammed then. I look around the room to check on my guys. Matty, Hammer, and Jesse take up one side of the bar. Matty nods at me. He's in charge and will make sure our side of the field gets home. Ace sits in the corner staring hungrily across the room at Stella, who's talking to some basketball player. Ace looks like he's about to throw the beer bottle into the guy's head, and the way he tossed the ball around today like a dart and not some awkward oblong piece of leather meant he'd make good contact.

I stride over. "You're not fooling anyone. Keep your head in the game. Play like that next week, and we'll wear the crown."

Ace rolls the bottle in his hand and then glances over my shoulder. "We're not all made like you, Masters. Some of us have a life outside the game. Some of us want a life outside the game." He tips his head back and drains his bottle.

I set the drink someone shoved into my hand in front of him. "Then go get that game. Don't sit on your ass waiting for it to come to you."

"Is that what you're doing?" Ace mocks. "Pursuing your objective? Because I haven't seen Campbell's sister tonight anywhere."

It stings a little, but not so much that I can't provide an even response. "That's why I'm leaving."

"Or maybe she doesn't want to be with you." He tips his head toward the front of the bar, where Ellie stands wearing a shirt that must be too big for her, because the shoulder keeps slipping down to expose a golden circle of skin. A circle of skin that some dickhead is staring at.

Ace grabs me as I start to stalk toward them. "Be gentle. We need that dickhead."

I must've said something out loud. I shrug him off. "We never reach that far into the wideout depth chart anyway."

Hopefully he only needs one hand to catch the ball, because the one he laid on Ellie's shoulder is getting ripped off.

"Mother o' God, who's the smokeshow?" Matty whistles near my ear.

"Ellie Campbell," I say abruptly.

"No shit?" he asks, following close behind as I cut a swath through the bar patrons. "I don't remember her being so, ah, fit. The whole makeup thing and big hair really looks good on her."

"Go away, Matty."

"Gone."

The freshman leans close to her, his eyes bright with excitement as he uses his height to leer down the front of Ellie's shirt.

"Hey, Emma, right?"

"Close…I'm Eliot." She dips her shoulder down until the dillweed's hand falls away. But that motion only serves to drop her shirt farther down her arm. The fabric of the top clings to the tops of her breasts and the big hoop earrings she wears flash in the light. She's wearing a lot of smoky eye makeup and red lipstick and all it says to me is fuck me, fuck me hard. "This is my roommate, Riley."

She tugs her tiny roommate's arm forward.

"Riley? Eliot? Are you two…guys?" Asshole frowns.

"That's right. We're two guys." She looks at Riley, who smothers a laugh behind her hand.

"Hey, Knox." Riley waves. "Enjoy your book?"

"I did, thanks for asking. Need something to drink?"

"Sure. I'll have whatever is light on tap."

I tip my chin toward the bartender to get his attention and then turn toward Ellie, but before I can take her order, the dipshit starts talking again.

"Ah, right. We met at Hammer's party. The Coke drinker."

I can almost hear her eyes roll in her head but she gives him a courtesy smile.

"You planning to have some fun tonight or drink your Coke?"

Somehow, despite being a few inches shorter than the idiot, she manages to look down her nose at him. "I plan to have zero fun tonight and you're doing a good job of making that happen for me."

He scratches his nose in confusion because he apparently can't make out whether she insulted him or complimented him. "Did you watch the game today? I play the slot receiver. Number 87. Maybe you saw me on the field?"

If you looked at the sidelines.

"I don't go to the games," Ellie tells him.

He doesn't give up because she's the hottest, brightest thing in this room. "So you wanna dance?"

"Not with you."

Because she's with me, you chode. I keep that to myself.

"Ellie, you want something?" I step in between them, tired of watching the exchange like a bystander.

"Sure, *Knox*. I'll take what Riley's having."

I don't miss the emphasis she puts on my first name. I hold up two fingers and the bartender gets to work.

"I didn't know if you would come."

She shrugs. "Riley wanted to see what a postgame celebration looked like. I tried to tell her she'd have as much fun as getting magic marker drawn on your face at a slumber party, but she didn't believe me."

"I haven't had this experience at Western before." Riley grins widely at me. I find myself smiling back.

The bartender delivers two beers and a water. I hand them out.

"Then you need to have a full Western experience." I look around for Matty, who would be more than happy to introduce Ellie's roommate to all the benefits of being with a Warrior player—at least for tonight.

Before I can hail anyone, Riley gasps. "Oh, there's my Facebook crush! I'll be back." And she slips through the crowd before Ellie or I can say anything.

A cough at my back reminds me that the dick koozie must still be here. "Hey, Knox. Great game, huh? I was telling Emma here about how she should come watch the Warriors."

"Yeah…" I pause as if I can't remember the name of the wideout. I know he runs fast, but runs a sloppy route and catches the ball too close to his body despite having baseball-sized mitts. He scowls as I leave him hanging but since he can't even bother to get her name right, I don't care. "Greer giving you a bad time?" I say to Ellie.

She does a subtle eye roll that Greer misses. "Took you long enough."

I'm not sure if she's talking about how long it took me to get to her side or how long it took me to pretend to remember Greer's name.

"I'm saving my energy for later."

Her mouth drops open into a perfect circle that gives me plenty of filthy ideas. And then, because I don't want to deal with any more Greers in the world not understanding how the teams are currently set up, with Ellie and me on the one side and the rest of the peckerheads on the other, I grab her around the nape of the neck and plant a deep, wet kiss on her perfect lips. Her mouth opens and I take full advantage of this by sliding my tongue inside. I lick her hot tongue, the roof of her mouth, and then the sensitive spot behind her teeth. She trembles beneath my hand and blood rushes to my dick.

Greer gets shoved aside, but I'm not sure if me or Ellie did the pushing. She backs away, lips swollen and red as cherries.

I turn to Greer. "Go away."

He shows his remarkable speed and disappears into the crowd.

"Want to sit down somewhere?" I ask her. Every time the door opens, more people come in, and while I'm grateful to be pressed close to Ellie's hot-ass body, I'd like to be able to apologize to her without screaming.

She arches an eyebrow because there isn't any seating evident in the room.

"I forget this is your first time." I plaster her to my side and make my way toward the back. Down at the end of the bar I see Jack watching us with narrowed eyes. *Brother, I'm sorry you had to watch me maul your sister*, I apologize silently, *but it was either kiss her in front of ev-*

eryone or piss on her leg.

I lead her down a short dark hallway and out into the back that opens onto a tiny patio the size of a postage stamp. There's a couple of people out here. Telly Green sits with his longtime girlfriend, along with Clifton Knowles, another offensive lineman. Their girlfriends are sorority sisters. I give them a nod of acknowledgement and go to the opposite side of the patio, where there's a cropping of uncomfortable looking rocks.

"Just think, Ellie, once you graduate you'll never go to a place this classy again," I joke and brush my hand over one rock until it's as clean as I can get it.

She sits. "Rocks are hard to find in other establishments."

"Right?" I crouch down in front of her. She looks shy, which is not how she's appeared before. I clear my throat. "I'm glad you're here. Thought you might not come."

"I debated. Not really my scene." We both turn to stare at the back door. The music is loud, but the din of the crowd inside is even louder. It's a party scene, but I get what she's talking about. She prefers to stay away from the football players and the baggage they bring. For the hundredth time since last weekend, I curse myself for not being more sensitive about her past.

Picking up her hand, I turn it over and trace a crease from one side of the palm to the other. She trembles at the simple touch.

"I'm sorry about last week. I put some pressure on you that you didn't deserve," I say slowly. "I guess when I said that you weren't ready I really meant that I wasn't."

She curls her fingers up around my finger and tugs. "I know you're not the guy I dated in high school. I wanted to believe I didn't have any baggage from dating, but I guess I do." She gives a rueful laugh.

"You're not. We all have stuff going on in our heads. Abstaining hasn't been easy for me. When I first got here, I didn't announce my status, but to some of the guys my going home every night alone, not taking the offers handed to me, marked me as strange. Some thought I was in the closet. Others didn't know what to make of me. They got it out of me after homecoming. The booze flowed pretty heavily. It started a joke. Then it became a contest. Who would get Masters to break? I wasn't kidding before about the number of girls available at any time—from the recruiting trip forward."

She grimaces and I skip the details of how they tried to break me. Of how they'd parade girls through the Playground as though shooting RedTube videos. They'd have girls perform in front of me. For guys who share a locker room, having sex in front of each other is nothing. There'd be full-on orgies. Contests on who could hold out on a blow job the longest. They'd run train on a girl—willing—but sex was a contest.

"Is that why you waited? Because women were—or are—a distraction?"

"At first, yes. All the time. You know we're walking hormones from about age ten and forward." She covers her face to hide a smile. "And college is worse because there are no parents. Everyone has access to a bed. There's no rules. The diner is open 24/7."

She muses, "But the food didn't appeal to you."

"It did…until it didn't. It seemed soulless." I hesitate and rub her hand a little harder than necessary. *Strap on your balls, man,* I chide myself. If Ellie can share something painful from her past, she deserves some honesty from me. "My brother and I are identical twins. You seem to be able to tell us apart, but on the cover of *SI*, not even my mom knew until we confessed. People in high school always got us mixed up."

"People like girl people?" Her gaze is knowing.

I nod. "Girl people. You don't really want to be with someone who's ready and willing to sleep with your brother. Who sees the two of you as interchangeable. One of Ty's girlfriends told me that we looked the same and she wanted to know if we felt the same."

I let out a sigh. "Worse thing is that it wasn't the first time it'd happened in our family either. My cousins are twins. Let's just say that the divorce lasted longer than the marriage."

She winces. "That's pretty awful."

"Right." I press her hand to my lips. "So, I get how what happened to us in the past affects how we act now. What decisions we make and shit like that. I'm sorry."

"Me, too. I'm really, really sorry." She looks dejected.

"Look." I shift on the balls of my feet. "I don't care what you call me, Ellie. I want you. I've wanted you from the minute I saw you at Union Stadium and I haven't stopped wanting you. I don't think you're a distraction or a soulless fuck. We're meant to be."

She gives me a tight and uncomfortable smile. Oh, fuck. This isn't going to end the way that I hoped. A slight ache develops in my chest. The kind of feeling that creeps up after a bad loss.

"What is it?"

She leans forward with a grimace. "It's that time of the month."

I give her a blank look. What time of the month? It's September.

Two weeks into the season. We're two-and-oh and—the lightbulb turns on. "I am not a smart man."

She shakes her head. "Timing sucks."

I stand up and pull her with me. Leaning down, I hide a relieved smile in her hair. "It's okay. I'm a pro at waiting."

23

ELLIE

IT'S HIS PATIENT EXPRESSION THAT gets to me. He shouldn't have to wait. Not for another single minute. I might be unable to have sex with him, but there are plenty of things I can do to him and for him that he's never experienced before.

The twinge below my skirt isn't from arousal, sadly, even though my heart's beating faster and I'm hot despite the coolness of the night air. It's really starting to feel like fall. The leaves are golden and red, the air is crisp, and football is on television what seems like Wednesday through Monday. I donned a pair of tights, a short skirt, sexy top, and then detoured to the bathroom to find that my period had started. Which meant tomorrow I'd be down. But I had tonight. And I want to give something back to Knox. An apology? A promise? A preview of what's in store for us? I'm not sure, but I'm not letting Knox go tonight without blowing his mind. Literally.

I grin at him. "Come with me."

"I don't know if I should be afraid or turned on by that smile," he murmurs, but follows behind me readily.

Inside the dark hallway, I start trying the doors I spotted on my way out. The third one gives way and I pull Knox in quickly before anyone stops us.

"I thought you said that it was your *time*."

There's almost no light in here. I reach into my pocket and pull my phone out. Flicking on the flashlight app, I wave it around the room. "It is that time, but that doesn't mean that we can't have a little fun."

The room isn't very large, and there are storage shelves all around which look rickety and uncomfortable. We'll have to use the door. I set my phone to the side and push Knox up against the door.

"If you wanted to make out, I think we could have done that on the rocks outside. I'm not real shy," Knox says.

I ignore him and slide down to my knees. Bracing my hands on his thighs, I look up. "I hear this is your first time. Tell me if you don't like something."

He chokes on a laugh when I throw his own words back at him. He's already thick and hard under his jeans. I rub a palm up the length of his shaft. He shudders and leans against the door.

"In all your spank bank material, did you imagine having sex at a club?" I ask, still rubbing and still staring at him. I wish I could see him better.

He nods slowly, a wary look in his eye. "I might have."

"And what were you doing?" I undo his belt buckle. He sucks in a deep breath and then pushes his torso away from the door so he can pull off his blue Warriors T-shirt. He does it with the one hand. I've never figured out quite how guys do that maneuver, but it'll always look sexy to me, especially when Knox does it. I scrape my fingertips over his ridged abs, reveling in how his body shakes under my hand.

"Usually they faced away from me and I nailed them from behind." He gathers my hair into a ponytail and holds it aloft so he can see better.

"Them?" I ask with a raised eyebrow

"Well, it *is* a fantasy." He grins. The grin fades away as I lower his zipper. His eyes shutter shut and he starts muttering to himself.

"What are you doing?"

"I'm reciting all Reggie White's stats so I can pretend that I'm not on the verge of coming before you even pull my dick out of my pants."

The hand in my hair tightens. His other hand lands on the nape of my neck. I can feel his fingers flex against my skin as if he's got a thin leash on his excitement.

"Just wait. It gets better." He's so large and so rigid that it's almost a struggle to pull him out of his jeans and the confines of his boxer briefs.

"I'm trying to tell myself it's going to be awful so that I can last longer than six seconds," he groans.

His cock is velvet soft, like a rod of steel wrapped in the finest silk. I lean in and run my nose along the edge of it. The musk of his sex invades my lungs. I have never been so turned on. I want to drop a hand between my legs, because now the ache down there isn't from pain, it's from need.

I lap at the tip, licking away the salty evidence of his arousal.

"Ellie, baby," he hisses through clenched teeth. "You're killing me."

Beneath my hands, his legs tremble with the effort to stay still and not ram his hips forward. Have I ever felt this powerful? This machine of a man shakes with desire, and I haven't even gotten to the best part. My heart swells at his response. I open my mouth and take him in.

"Fuck. *Fuck*." It's a curse, or maybe a prayer, and his control snaps.

His hand winds into my hair to pull me closer, to hold me still while he helplessly jacks his dick into my mouth. The shaft seems to thicken, getting larger and harder. His grip is tight. With another guy, I might have jerked back, but this one? I want him to remember this—remember *me*. I suck with more force, twisting my wrist in tight quick movements.

I'm kneeling on the floor of a tiny closet in a dingy college bar. My tights are likely ruined, but I don't care. I don't feel dirty. I feel great. Amazing.

The musk of his groin, the heated scent of his body and his arousal smells intoxicating. The heavy weight of his cock on my tongue, filling my mouth, pushing all the way back in jerky out-of-control motions has me so turned on that I'm drenching my panties. If I didn't need both hands to do this right, I'd have one between my legs.

"Jesus, Ellie, baby," he pants. "I'm going to come."

He tries to pull away, but I follow him, sucking and licking. I refuse to let him go. He releases one long groan and gives up. He jerks against my mouth, his seed jetting down my throat and coating my tongue. As I swallow him down, he tells me how good this is, how good I am, how he can't believe *how fucking good this feels*.

When he's stopped coming, he reaches down to pull me against him. Uncaring that he's come into my mouth, he kisses me. No, he ravages me. His hands tangle in my hair as he licks inside my mouth, tasting himself, tasting us.

"I can't believe I'm the only one who has ever done that for you," I murmur when he lifts his head from mine and tucks me against his chest. His heart thunders in my ear. It may be wrong to be with him, but there's no possible way for me to stay away. I'm an addict and he's my fix.

"Believe it." He continues to pet me, smoothing my hair down the back of my neck and over my shoulders. His chin rubs against the crown of my head. "Are you sure we can't have sex, because I don't care that it's a particular time of month."

"No. I mean, yes, I'm sure. No sex while I'm—you know."

"Sadly, I do." He sighs. "Why?"

"Because it's messy."

"So, we do it in the shower," he pleads.

I shake my head. "No, your first time should not be in the shower."

"I'm a guy," Knox reminds me. "I don't need candles and shit. I just need you."

The evidence of his need grows between us. "I thought you were good at waiting."

He grunts. "I never had your mouth around me before. Eat a lot of protein this week. You'll need your energy next Saturday."

This time it's my turn to groan. "You sound like you have big plans."

"You have no idea," he whispers.

ELLIE

WEEK 3: WARRIORS 2-0

THE POUNDING ON THE DOOR won't stop. I try to shove my head under the covers, but the asshole outside our apartment doesn't have a quit button. Hopefully Riley will crush the persistent intruder with her sewing machine.

"Ellie, I know you're in there." The deep voice sounds vaguely familiar, but who can tell through the layers of blankets I have thrown over my head.

"Go away!" I yell and throw the pillow at the door. It slumps to the floor before it even reaches the door. Sad. I didn't even get the ability to throw a pillow. I slide further down under the covers as another cramp hits me. Gah. I'm not sure why it's more painful this month than in past months, but even swallowing four Advil has done nothing for me.

I spent Sunday in a daze. Knox and I sat in his apartment watching the pro games, holding each other's hands, and kissing until we were so turned on, I felt like we could have lit the entire campus. But Monday I'm too ill to get out of bed.

The banging mercifully stops and the door latch to my bedroom clicks.

Must be Riley.

"I'm dying, Riley. I think my body wants to kill me. Would you mind picking up my pillow, putting it over my face, and ending my misery?"

I hear the faint sound of the cotton getting swept off the floor and then the soft plop of my pillow at the head of my bed.

"I never realized you could be this dramatic. If you get tired of your English classes, I think the theatre department has missed out on a talent like yours."

The deep rumble of Knox's voice startles me. I kick at the blankets, but they seem determined to entangle me. I end up tossing and turning until I'm a pretzel-shaped mound of covers. He chuckles, then reaches out and slowly frees me from my prison.

"How did you get in?" I scowl and try to ignore the cartwheels my heart turns.

"Riley let me in. I explained to her that I'd left my playbook in your backpack."

"That's a lie." I push up on one arm and notice that he's undressing. His shoes are toed off and he's pulling his T-shirt over his head. His entire wardrobe must be Warriors workout gear, cargo shorts, and flip flops. "Why are you taking your clothes off?"

"Because it's more comfortable." His hands are at his buckle when alarm bells start going off.

"Not your shorts!" I fling my hand out. "I draw the line at your shorts."

He grins, and I realize I just invited him into bed with me. Falling back onto the pillow, I give in. The pain in my abdomen has sapped all my energy. "Fine. Undress. You'll do what you want anyway."

The metal of his heavy buckle hits the floor, and I try to suppress the shivers of glee at the sound.

"Shit, your bed is small," he says as he climbs under the covers.

"Maybe you're too big," I toss back.

His body rumbles as he laughs. "No such thing."

Then he starts rearranging me. He turns me so I face the wall and slides a big muscular arm under mine. His hard biceps turns out to be a surprisingly comfortable pillow. At my back, his body curls around mine, his knees bending to fit into the crook of my bent legs, the top of my head under his chin. His other big hand settles on my stomach, his pinkie rubbing against the lace waistband of my panties. And just like that, the heat of his body starts to invade mine, easing my aches, soothing away the cramps.

His breath is steady and even, and I find myself matching him. There's absolutely nothing erotic about his touch. It's meant to be comforting—and it is. He's like a giant heating pad. His hand makes broad, slow circles around my stomach.

"Why are you here?" I ask.

"Jack mentioned during film that you weren't feeling well."

"So, you came over here and pounded on my door?"

"Someone's got to take care of you. Your brother thinks you're strong, but even the strongest people need someone to lean on. Besides, this is my job. Not your brother's."

"What's your job?" My words start to slur together as he strokes me into a stupor.

"Taking care of you is my job. Has been since I first laid eyes on you."

His certainty in the way everything is supposed to be starts to rub off, because I don't question him. Or it's possible that with each sweep of his hand, I lose brain cells to his comfort. "Speaking of Jack, how is he?"

Frustrated, I think. To Knox, I say, "Fine. He's not happy with the poli-sci course, but I don't know who in that class is." It's hard for me, too. It's even harder to write two papers for that darn thing. "There's no attendance policy, because if you don't show up for even one class, you're lost."

"Is that what Jack says?" Knox murmurs against the back of my neck.

My brain feels scrambled by his nearness, but I manage to eke out a half-truth. "That's what everyone says."

The post class complaining is enormous. One girl I sit near writes about a book's worth of notes, but at the end of class she looks defeated. Jack hasn't taken a single note. He sits about twenty rows below me, his hands folded together, staring straight at the teacher. I can't see his eyes, but my guess is that defeat is too mild of an emotion for what he feels, as the teacher drones on about Bayesian and Nash equilibrium and Pareto efficiencies.

I used Jack's password to login to his account this week, and had to change at least half of his answers to a worksheet. The worksheets are designed to help us formulate our end of the semester papers and aren't graded, but I didn't want the professor to look back and wonder why there's such a disparity between Jack's paper and his semester coursework.

"What about his tutor?"

"He says she's too busy trying to sleep with him, and since he turned her down, she's not been very helpful."

"Hmm." His chest rumbles against my back. "He should bring that up to Brian Newsome. He's the associate director for football student services. Brian would find Jack a different tutor."

"No," I twist in his arms. Jack would not want anyone in the program to know he's struggling. "And don't you say anything either." He's silent too long. "Please, Knox."

"All right, baby. I won't, but just because he's having problems with class doesn't mean he's getting kicked off the team."

"He's new. Let him get this one semester under his belt."

Knox turns me back over, tucking his large knees behind mine and resting his chin on the top of my head. "I won't say anything. Now, why don't you get some sleep?"

That sounds like the best suggestion ever.

I WAKE UP WITH HIS dick nestled against my ass and his big hand around my waist. One jerk of his thumb and he'd be touching my breast. His hand is so freaking large and there's a tree trunk shoving its way into my panties. I wouldn't have been human if I hadn't pushed back against the rod of steel or exhaled extra hard to see if I could move his fingers closer to my aching nipple.

"You need to get out of this bed within five minutes, or you'll be breaking the seal," he growls in my ear. "That time of the month or not."

It takes all my will, but I manage to scramble out of the bed. Somewhere in the middle of the night, we moved so that he leaned against the wall and I faced the door.

"Where's Riley? What time is it?" I scoop my wayward hair out of my face and grope around for my phone to check the time.

"Riley is in her room, and it's about ten."

"Ten!" I yelp. "We've slept for like five hours."

"Yup," he says with a complete lack of concern.

"I'm hungry." I try to smooth down my hair. Knox's smile tells me I'm not doing a very good job of it. He rolls out of bed, a lithe mountain lion. His muscles flex and extend as he stalks toward me.

"You look beautiful." He pulls me against him and nuzzles his face into the side of my neck. Predictably, I want to melt.

I shove away from him. "I need to use the bathroom." I need some distance.

"Me, too." There's a naughty look in his eyes.

"Alone."

He puts on a fake pout as I push away.

"I'll order some food. What are you interested in?"

I rub my empty stomach. "Anything," I say truthfully. "As long as there's a lot of it."

On my way to the bathroom, I knock on Riley's door. The humming stops. I still think it sounds like a big old vibrator. I wonder if she needs one given that she hasn't hooked up with anyone since we've lived together, not even cute Facebook boy, who apparently doesn't understand that Riley is the best thing he could ever hope to have.

"Knox is ordering food. Do you want any?"

She doesn't say anything.

"His treat," I add.

"Um, okay, yeah, I could use something."

Sometimes I forget that Riley's a scholarship student, and truth be told, it's not like I have a lot of extra cash lying around, either. My mom sends me money monthly, but it's just enough for food and laundry. I should get a job, but between my course load and Jack's extra classes, I'm not sure where I'd find the time.

After I'm done taking care of my business in the bathroom, I set out plates and glasses while Knox goes down to the front of the apartment to pay the delivery guy.

"Food's here." He sets two large plastic bags on the table and unpacks about ten boxes. At my raised eyebrows, he shrugs. "I was hungry. You're hungry. You can't ever have too much Chinese."

"God, late night egg rolls. You are the bomb dot com." Riley comes streaking out of the bedroom. Her hair is tied up on the top of her head like a kewpie doll, but I don't look much better with my five-hour bedhead, my comfy pajama bottoms, and Jack's old T-shirt from high school.

"You need a new shirt." Knox hooks his finger into my collar and pulls me to him.

"A Warriors shirt?" I press my lips together to suppress a smile.

"A specific Warriors shirt."

"Why don't you take yours off right now and give it to her," Riley suggests and waggles her eyebrows.

"Good idea." He whips it off and hands it to me. Riley gives a wolf whistle. Knox sits at the table and starts shoveling food onto his plate.

It takes me a while to stop drooling, and I have to kick Riley under the table to get her to tear her eyes away from Knox's perfectly sculpted chest.

Sorry she mouths at me, but I can't really be mad. His body is a work of art.

"You're right about never having too much Chinese," Riley says between bites of Kung Pao chicken. "Once, my mom made this huge dish of Singapore noodles, and my dad teased her that we had enough to feed the entire city of Singapore. But she had the last laugh when the next day we had a terrible storm and it knocked out our power. We still had enough Singapore noodles to last us the entire day."

"There's no such thing as too much food," Knox agrees. "My brother and I ate enough that my mom had to go to the grocery store twice a week to buy milk. We'd drink a gallon every couple of days."

"You have a brother?" Riley asks.

"Twin," I interject. "Knox says they're identical."

"Everyone says we're identical because we are." Knox pulls out his phone and flips open his photo album. "See."

Riley's mouth drops open a little. "God, there are two of you? How is that at all fair? And which one is you?"

"He's the one in the red board shorts." I point to Knox in the picture. "His brother is the one with the soft chin."

"Soft chin? They have the same chin. They're i-den-ti-cal," Riley scoffs.

Knox shakes his head and turns to me. "It's freaky how you can tell."

I don't get how it's so weird. They're clearly two different people. Riley scrolls through more photos. There are dozens of shots with Knox and his brother—smiling, goofing around, play fighting. Several with their parents. It's clear their family is a loving one. At Knox's urging, Riley pulls out her phone and shows us pictures of her two younger brothers and her parents, who look almost young enough to be her siblings.

"They were teenagers when they had me," Riley explains. "They're only thirty-eight now. Mom says it's weird because most of her peers just now have kids, and they're almost empty nesters."

"You have a gorgeous family, Riles." I don't even bother to hide my envy.

"Thanks. We don't have a lot, but we've got each other." She shrugs, a little embarrassed. "Trite but true."

They both look at me as if I'm going to whip out my phone and show off my little family album, but there wouldn't be any pictures of me and my parents in them. The only ones I keep are those of Jack and me.

I wipe my mouth. "I'm done for the night. Thanks for the food, Knox."

"No problem," he says easily. Rising, he helps me clear the plates. Riley tidies up what few leftovers we have and then disappears into her bedroom. Knox dries while I wash.

"Didn't want to share any pictures of your own?" Knox asks quietly.

I hesitate because my family isn't like Riley or Knox's. My first inclination is to shut him down, but I know he doesn't deserve that. "My dad is the type that if Jack won the Heisman, he'd wonder why Jack didn't get more votes."

Knox keeps drying. "And you? What would he think of you?"

"He doesn't." I brace my hands on the edge of the kitchen sink, not enjoying the feelings that Knox's questions dredge up. "My dad was this great college player. He had these dreams of going pro, but he literally could never make the cut. With Jack, he gets to live out his dream again. With me?"

I push away from the sink and turn to face Knox. He gazes at me with steady compassion, but no pity. I'm grateful for that because I think I would have kicked him out if he felt sorry for me. "When he had Jack, he thought he'd get to mold him into this awesome player, but Jack didn't grow until like the tenth grade. He looked short and skinny. I wanted my dad to be proud of me so I played, too."

"Did that win his approval?"

I make a face. "Of course not. I was still a girl. We both knew I'd never play on a real football team. But I played flag football with the boys until eighth grade." My scar itches as I remember the hit. "A guy rammed into me and shattered my knee cap. It was an accident, but that was it for me and sports." Until I started playing softball which is why Jack worries.

Knox makes a sound in the back of his throat. "What'd your parents do?"

I swallow to get rid of the bitterness so I don't sound like a shrew. "They weren't there. Another parent called the ambulance. Jack held my hand on the way to the hospital and helped take care of me after." I stop abruptly because the pain of the remembered rejection feels raw. I don't want to cry. Not over my parents and definitely not in front of Knox.

Without any more questions, he empties the water, and drapes the towel over the side of the sink. He picks up the shirt he took off and then wraps his hand around mine. Silently, he leads me into the bedroom.

In the dark of the room, he pulls off the T-shirt I'm wearing and tugs his own over my head. The shirt smells of Knox—like fresh dirt, energy, and warmth. He kicks off his shorts and climbs into the bed, scooting all the way to the wall.

"Come in here. I'm cold," he says.

I move like a robot. When he's done tucking himself around me, he kisses the side of my throat, my ear, and then my temple—a trail of sweet affection that begins to thaw the cold that had settled in when I think of my parents.

"We don't get to pick the family we're born into," he says into the quiet night. "But we do get to choose the family we live with. I choose you. You're all that I'll ever want."

My throat closes up. The words I'd love to say back get choked by my fear.

"Shh," he whispers. He lays his broad hand over my left chest. "You don't need to say anything, baby. I can hear your heart."

That's enough for him.

I fall asleep wrapped in the embrace of someone I couldn't even dream of having—not in a million years. I never imagined someone like Knox Masters existed. Or that he might love me. But if he knew what I did for Jack? How it could jeopardize their whole season and the pursuit of the championship?

He wouldn't want to hold me at all.

KNOX

GAME DAY: WARRIORS 2-0

THE FLIGHT TO MICHIGAN TAKES an interminable three and a half hours, which I pass staring at the last text from Ellie.

Ellie: *I'm wearing your jersey.*

She sends a picture with the message. Her head is cut off, but she's kneeling on her bed and her ripe tits are pushing at the top of my number as she pulls at the bottom of the jersey. Her legs are bare, and I swear I see a shadow of my favorite spot beneath the mesh. My number looks really good on her. Really good. As Matty said when he saw her in the bar, a holy mother of God smokeshow.

I lied when I said I was good at waiting. This week has felt unending. Worse? We had an away game, which meant by the time that Ellie felt better, I sat on a chartered plane to Michigan. I saw her a couple of times this past week, and each of those times left me with a hard-on the size of a log and balls bluer than a Smurf's.

On Tuesday after dinner, I stopped over to her apartment and found her pulling out winter gear. Apparently girls have seasonal clothes. Late fall meant boots and sweaters.

"Wear this one. I like you in red." I pulled a soft, furry red sweater from the pile.

"Since when do you like me in red?"

"Two days ago you wore a red shirt. Flowy." I shoved over a bunch of soft stuff and sat down on her bed. Her shirt was black and had a nice V that hinted at her equally nice cleavage.

"It's Bohemian Chic."

"Whatever. The color looked good, but it seemed too loose. I couldn't see your pretty tits. Plus, I like V-necks because you can do this." I hooked a finger along her neckline and drew it down low enough to expose one lace-covered breast.

"You'll stretch it out," she protested.

"I'll get you a new one." I could see one really good use of my future NFL money—buying clothes for Ellie. Sexy ones. Ones that show off her tits and ass and legs.

"I bought this a year ago on vacation and—" Her breath caught when I latched on to one large, juicy nipple, built for sucking on. "What are you doing?" Since I had my mouth full of tit, I didn't answer. I had better things to do than form words for a question with an obvious answer.

She leaned into me, her hands dug into my scalp. Mmmm, that felt good. "I thought you were a virgin."

"I have a good imagination," I mumbled as I moved to the other side. Didn't want the left breast to feel abandoned now, did I? Hell no. The T-shirt got in my way so I tugged it up and over her head. The bra clasp confounded me so I settled for pulling down the lacy cups, which actually had the added benefit of pushing the boobs together.

I shift in my seat thinking about it.

That led to more making out and Ellie rubbing herself against my leg until she came. She wouldn't let me touch her under her clothes. But I forgot to complain when she whipped open my jeans and introduced me to ball sucking.

I take a deep breath and try to regain some self-control. I tug the bottom of my shirt down, but it doesn't do a hell of a lot to hide my hard-on. I should probably think about something other than Ellie's hot mouth around my dick and balls.

I didn't go home with her after the softball game on Wednesday because I wasn't sure I could take another bout of teasing and dry humping with her. But by Thursday, my already thin willpower whittled away when she showed up for dinner wearing a short blue skirt and a tight Warriors T-shirt under a button down sweater. After dinner, I took her to my apartment where I spent a good hour becoming familiar with every patch of skin above her waist.

Her tits and I are close friends now. Best buds, really. And she's very sensitive at the nape of her neck. I can place my hand there, and a second later, she'll shiver. I enjoy doing that in public knowing that she's getting turned on. That her panties are getting wet. When I took her home, I gave her my home jersey and instructed her to wear it during the game. I took all her brother's T-shirts out of her drawer and replaced them with five of mine. I had to ask Stella to order a few replacements.

Me: *If we lose this weekend, it will be because my hard-on killed me.*

Ellie: *I'm sorry. Whatever happened to your hand?*

Me: *The hand doesn't do it for me anymore. My dick rejected the hand. It says that it's had your mouth, your hand, and nothing else will do.*

Ellie: *I'm sorry (not really).*

Me: *I'll be back around 11. Please say you'll be awake.*

Ellie: *I'll be awake. It's not like it's easy for me either. At least you got off last week.*

Me: *Baby, I would have done anything for you.*

Ellie: *We need to stop. These texts aren't making it easier for me.*

Me: *Wear the red sweater.*

Ellie: *Not the jersey?*

Me: *If you wear the jersey, I'll shoot my wad before I step across the threshold. Have a little mercy.*

Ellie: *Mercy isn't what you want from me.*

Me: *Okay, going to the head now. I'm either going to jack off or drown myself.*

Ellie: *Think of me either way.*

Me: *You're a cruel woman. But don't change. I like you that way. I'll see you tomorrow. 11. Be ready.*

Ellie: *I have the rose petals, flowers, and champagne you ordered.*

Me: *Is that for Riley? Because she's not seeing you for three days.*

Ellie: *I have class on Monday.*

Me: *Be prepared to skip.*

Matty grabs for my phone. "What are you smirking about? Is Ellie sexting you?"

"Fuck off, Iverson." I plant my hand in his face and push.

The charter plane isn't all that big and Matty crashes into Hammer who shoves him back.

"Fucking sit in your own seat," Hammer growls.

We're all getting chippy. Seventy players, many of whom are in excess of two hundred pounds and taller than six feet, means a full, stinky flight.

"I'm tired of sitting. When's this tin can landing anyway?" Matty whines. He turns to Hammer. "Masters hasn't said a word to me all flight. All he does is stare at his phone. He's sexting with Campbell's sister."

Hammer leans over. "She sending you pictures? I could use a little inspiration for the game tomorrow."

I stare at him. Does he really think I'd share a picture of my hot-as-fuck girlfriend with him? That picture's mine. She's mine. No one will look at Ellie half dressed, sexed up, or otherwise but me. "Hammer, if you plan on a pro career, you best shut your mouth or your face will be too broken to play."

"Sheesh." Hammer sits back and folds his arm like a five-year-old. "I liked you better when you weren't giving Campbell's sister the D."

I flick him off but force myself to put the phone away. No point in torturing myself like this.

POST GAME: WARRIORS 3-0

WHETHER IT'S JUST OUR YEAR or we're anxious to get back to Western, we smother the Michigan offense. They only score in the fourth quarter after we're up by four scores, one of them a fumble off a sack that Matty picked up and ran in for a touchdown. Ace and company punch it in for another touchdown, and just like that, we're a quarter of the way through the season undefeated.

The plane ride back feels twice as long as the trip to Michigan.

Hammer and Matty spend the entire trip debating whether Godzilla would beat a T-Rex.

"T-Rex has the tiny arms. There's no way he can get in there and land a body blow." Hammer slaps his fist into his palm.

"He hits Godzilla with his head. He always uses the head. The arms are just for balance." Matty glues his elbows to his side and swings his head around. The rest of the team around them starts to laugh because it's hilarious seeing Matty pretend to be a short-armed T-Rex. But Hammer? Oh no, Hammer is completely into this argument.

"No way. Look, I can punch you out with one fist to your puny head." Hammer swings at Matty. The two start wrestling and the D-Line coach comes back before the two can have an all-out fist fight.

I guess this is better than the last argument Matty and Hammer had, which was whether road head was better than the mile high club. I didn't understand why you couldn't have both. I want to have Ellie everywhere and anywhere.

I pull up the picture again.

By the time the bus from the airport arrives at Western's campus,

I'm pretty much a walking erection. I try to move as normally as possible but I'm grateful that Coach gives his "Good game, don't do anything stupid" speech on the bus so I can get out of there as soon as possible.

"Going to hit the Gas Station?" Matty asks.

"No."

"But—"

"No." I don't even look at him. I jog to my SUV, texting Ellie along the way.

Me: *Your place or mine?*

Ellie: *Mine. Riley is gone for the night. She's at a friend's.*

Me: *I'll be there in ten minutes.*

I spent the time this past week researching. I've read a hundred blog posts and online articles about women's sexuality. How it's hard for them to come just from penetration and that foreplay—lots and lots of foreplay—is the key to success. I know Ellie can come for me. I got her off before with my tongue. And I'll lick and suck and rub her to as many as her body will take.

I make it to her place in five minutes. Sure, I ran two red lights—disobeying Coach's instructions—but if I ever had an emergency, I'm sure this qualifies.

Luckily someone is leaving as I arrive. The girl holds the door for me and I run upstairs to Ellie's third floor apartment. My dick gets abused in my dress pants as I move, but getting to Ellie fast is my only imperative.

"You're early." Ellie beckons me inside. She must have sensed I had gotten here, because the door to her apartment opens before I can get my fist against the wood to knock.

"Really? Because it felt like forever." I eat her up with my eyes. Against my explicit instructions, she's wearing my jersey and nothing else. Even her feet are bare except for a tiny pink bit of shininess. It's hard to stand here and not attack her. She backs up as I stalk inside and kick the door shut.

"Is this what you wear to your away games?" She flicks my tie, and I flinch at that small touch.

"Yeah. Coach's rules. Suit coat and tie for away games. Dress pants and button down for home. Tie's optional then." I recite the rules but my attention focuses on one thing and one thing only. Taking the jersey off Ellie.

"You look hot in a suit."

"You look hot in my jersey. You'd look better with it off."

I reach down and whip it over her head. I'm staggered by her gorgeousness. Tipping my head back, I pinch the bridge of my nose. "Shit, Ellie, I won't last."

"I think that's the whole point." She giggles—a girlish, strange sound coming from her. At my look, she sighs. "I'm nervous, like this is *my* first time."

Thank Christ.

"It is." I reach for her, allowing myself to only touch her hair. "It's your first time with me. You aren't ever sleeping with another guy. Okay?"

I say it lightly, but it's not a joke to me. No way can I imagine Ellie with another guy or me with another girl.

"So, you plan to ruin me for all other men?"

"That's the plan." I'm dead serious. I'm also done talking.

I reach for her and we go at each other: mouth, hands, legs. She rips at my shirt, and I feel the buttons give way. It's fucking hot how she's attacking me as if she can't wait for me to be inside her. I help her as much as I can while still holding her against me. Somehow, we get my clothes off and I sweep my hands under her ass until she hooks her legs around my waist. I nearly break a leg sprinting to the bedroom.

"Since I've got almost no self-control, baby, we'll see to you first."

"Oh, Knox." She pulls me down on top of her and starts sprinkling kisses on my face. "I missed you and I'm desperately horny. Please don't make me wait another minute."

"You are not helping," I admonish sternly. I take her wandering, magical hands and shackle them under one of mine. There are benefits to being bigger than her. I reach between us and slide my fingers down the front of her pussy. "Does it feel good?"

Because Christ, it feels good to me. I think of Hammer's grotesque feet. Try to conjure up the smell of old socks and jock sweat. Anything to keep me from spewing onto her sheets. She is so soft. Must not think about how soft she is or how wet my fingers are.

I whimper silently.

"Yes. Yes, it feels so good."

"Tell me how to make it better." I'm determined that she has one orgasm before me because I know it will be over for me within about five seconds of getting inside of her. Hell, five seconds might be optimistic.

She dips her hand between her legs and rubs in circles. I watch her, memorizing her touch and then take over. I must do something right because she arches up, thrusting against my hand.

I lick my lips, remembering how it felt to have her on my tongue, and I dive between her legs. "You smell amazing." I let the scent of her fill my nose, my head, my lungs. I inhale until every intake of air is scented with her musk. She quivers beneath me. Her parts are shiny and slick and the taste of her is everything against my tongue. I want to eat her up before and after every meal. I test my tongue against her body. How she likes the flat part. How she likes it arrowed and hard and lashing against that tiny piece of flesh that begs to get sucked and bit and soothed.

Her hands dig into my scalp and pull hard.

"What is it? Am I doing something wrong?" I jerk up, my lips coated with her.

"Don't stop!" she cries.

Ah gotcha. She'd tugged me closer, not away. I duck down to hide my smug smile. I must have done something right.

"I know that shoving your face between my legs is not cool but, holy hell, Knox, what you're doing to me…"

She sounds amazed. I love that. She's having her own first. Both of my heads swell bigger.

"No, baby. This is awesome. Fuck my face," I order her.

"Are you sure?"

"I've never been more sure of anything."

I don't need to tell her twice. Her thighs clamps round my ears and she grinds down on my tongue.

"Oh, Knox, your fingers…use your fingers."

"Where, baby?" I like her telling me how to make her feel good. She's coaching me to do my best and I've never wanted to perform so well my entire life.

"Inside of me." She pulls on my hair and thrashes her head from side to side. "My clit. Everywhere. I need you everywhere!" The last word comes out a thin, reedy cry.

When I slide my first finger inside of her, I nearly come all over her nice rug.

God.

Fuck.

Christ.

The wet heat of her against my hand has me nearly coming. Sex with Ellie requires more discipline than anything in my entire life.

She's so tight. I have a moment of panic. Will I fit inside her? Peering up, I check in with her. She's grimacing but it doesn't appear like it's in pain because she's pushing against me.

"Knox, yes," she says and thrashes her head from side to side. "More."

"Anything you want." I lean down, still clutching her two hands in one of mine, and suck her clit into my mouth. She screams and the snug channel around my fingers spasms, giving me tiny hugs. I swallow hard. To feel that around my cock? My brain nearly short circuits.

I feast on her, flicking her little swollen sex with my stiffened tongue. Against my thrusting fingers, her blood pounds out a swift, relentless rhythm.

"Knox, Knox," she chants.

I pull my fingers out abruptly. It's too much. I rear up and grab the packet of condoms I've been carrying around since the blow job.

Her eyebrows shoot into her forehead. "A whole strip?"

"I didn't want to run out." I grin.

She huffs out a small laugh. "You're such an overachiever, but…" She reaches for my hand. "I'm on the pill, and I know you're clean."

"I am." It's an obvious statement.

She licks her lips. "I'm clean, too. I went to the health center for a test this week."

"Are you saying—" I can't even finish the question. All amusement is wiped away as I think about sliding into her raw.

Nodding, she plucks the condoms out of my hand and tosses them aside.

"I'm ready, Knox."

So am I.

I spread her thighs and take myself in one hand. We both watch as the blunt head of my cock pierces her. She cries out and I freeze. "Fuck, am I hurting you?"

"Oh, Knox, no. But you're so big. Give me a minute," she pants.

I start counting backward from a thousand. She wriggles a bit and then taps me on the wrist to let me know I can move.

I slowly sink into her inch by excruciating inch. Her legs widen even more, and my wire thin control snaps. Her velvet embrace burns me up. I push all the way in until my balls rest against her ass.

I'm not sure if I'm in heaven or hell.

No, I know exactly where I am. I'm home. Where I belong. Where I've always belonged.

The rightness of it all clicks into place. I was right to have waited. I was right that Ellie was the one.

I'd fantasized about this moment a million times, but the real thing is indescribable. None of those things I'd read prepared me for what it would feel like for her walls to cling to my shaft. I couldn't have ever conjured up what kind of rush it feels like to get sucked into her body. Or how I'd feel like a fucking conqueror when she writhes beneath me.

The sensations roll over me. Nerves that I didn't know existed come alive and tell me that I'm two seconds away from coming in her so long and so hard her ancestors will feel it. Her nipples are tight, fat buds begging for my mouth. Grabbing a hip in one hand and bracing myself with my other, I lean over and capture one bouncing beauty between my lips.

"Ellie. I—" I break off when the walls of her pussy tighten around me. Is she doing that on purpose? "I can't…hold…off."

She slaps her palms against the wall as the force of my body drives her across the bed. "Harder, Knox. Let go. I won't break."

I dig a knee into the mattress for leverage and go at it. My hips jackhammer into hers. My balls slap against her ass, and her fingers dig deep into my shoulders, marking me. I completely lose it. I don't know my name, where I live, what position I play. I only know that I'm balls deep in the sweetest, tightest grip in the world, and I'll die happy here between Ellie's legs.

Underneath my frame, Ellie's body writhes and bucks in rhythm with mine. Her mouth opens, gasping out pleas for me to fuck her faster and harder. My body responds as if she owns it.

Blood pounds in my ears, an ocean of sensation floods my nervous system, and the loudest, fiercest roar that has ever left my mouth pours forth. Her mouth finds my neck while I shudder and jerk as my come jets into her welcome pussy. I collapse on top of her, a heavy spent *thing.*

"Oh, Knox." Her breath sounds unsteady, and her heart thuds against my chest.

"Is this heaven?" I mumble into her damp skin.

Her arms tighten around me. "No, it's Iowa."

My breath catches and then roars out. I can't stop laughing. I'm shaking her tiny mattress and she's laughing with me. Of course Ellie quotes a famous line from a classic sports movie to me right after we have sex. Right after I lose my virginity to her. Of course.

Of course.

Because she knows sports. Loves it like I do. She's so perfect for me. I mouth my thanks to the man upstairs for sending Ellie down to earth and letting me find her. I knew she was the right one.

Knew it.

"Sorry," I say, apologizing for crushing her but unable to move. "Please tell me you enjoyed that even a little. Lie if you have to."

She's still laughing, her smaller frame vibrating under mine. "I came, Knox. Didn't you feel it?"

"I don't know what I felt," I admit. "I think I saw that light all those people who have a near death experience claim to have seen. I'm okay if this is how I go out." I find some small reserve of strength and roll off her, pulling her with me so my still-hard dick gets to stay inside that warm, tight embrace. I wonder if I can wear her. Whether there's some campus provision that would prevent me from walking around with her attached to my dick. I should get my student liaison to look into that for me. "Christ Almighty, I've never felt so good."

"Not even when you got the offer from Western?" Her lips move against my chest, inches away from my nipple.

I tip her head up so I can look into those big brown eyes of hers. I shake my head in dismay over her sad comparison. "Not even close. This is the best thing ever."

"Better than winning the championship?" She grins.

I think for a minute. "That would be a close second."

She tucks her head under my chin again. I rearrange her legs so that I don't slip out. Although given how hard I still am, I don't think there's any danger in that.

"Are you sorry you waited?" she asks softly.

"No way. This was perfect." I kiss the crown of her head. "You were perfect."

"Are you sorry I didn't wait?"

Ah, is that where her uncertainty came from?

"Why should I be? You had different circumstances. Besides, I tell myself that all your previous experiences were terrible. Don't correct me if I'm wrong. I'm happy to be wrong and ignorant in this matter."

I stroke her back, running my fingers along the sharp edges of her shoulder blades and tracing the bumps of her spine. I circle her waist with my hands.

"Your fantasies aren't that far off the mark," she admits. Her fingernails scratch over my nipple, my pec, and down my side. My dick perks up even more.

"Really?"

"Yes. Watching you touch yourself in that bathroom was hotter than anything I've personally experienced. It's why I couldn't stay away even though I knew I should."

"I'm glad you didn't."

"I'm glad you didn't give up on me."

"Never." I tilt her head up and capture her mouth. "You ready for round two?"

"Only if I get to be on top this time."

The sacrifices I have to make…

AFTER SUNDAY, IT'S LIKE I can't get enough. I stalk her around campus. I drag her down four flights of stairs after one of her creative writing courses, shove up her skirt, and take her in the corner of a stairwell.

Her heel digs into my ass as I pound into her as if the entire universe's rotation depends on how fast I can make her come. When she does come, it's usually with this tiny gasp. It's a sound that I hear in my dreams. I replay it when I'm on the road, along with all the other noises of our sex: the sweaty slap of our bodies as I jam against her; the sweet suck of her pussy as it hugs me tight; the feral grunts from my own throat as the orgasm overtakes me and I lose all control.

I sneak her into the athletic center because I want to christen my locker. She rides me, rubbing her body all over mine while she comes on my dick. That may be a mistake, because every time I sit in my locker, I think of her, us, and I get hard. Getting hard in the locker room is not a good idea. But she has her own problems. She's taken to wearing skirts and thigh high tights because I've ripped the crotch of so many of her regular tights, and because, she admitted, she's tired of her tights having a wet crotch after an encounter with me.

The new obsession I have with her doesn't affect my play on the field. If anything, my focus is sharper there. Things happen in slow motion. It's like I know the play before the ball even gets hiked. I start racking up ridiculous numbers. Two sacks in one game. Three in another. I get an interception and run it in for a touchdown in three different games. It's unheard of. ESPN's *College Game Day* becomes a Knox Masters highlight reel.

Life is fucking good.

26

ELLIE

WEEK 8: WARRIORS 6-0

"YOU LOOK EXHAUSTED," RILEY OBSERVES as I drop onto the sofa by her. She's studying some kind of ethics and law, based on the paperwork strewn about. "Is it all the sex you're getting? Because I swear if I was getting it as much as you do, I'd have trouble walking."

"I wish." Although truthfully some days I am sore. It's been five weeks of non-stop sex whenever Knox can find a spare minute from football and classes. The team is still undefeated and there are only five weeks left in the regular season with a conference title game in December.

Knox had suggested we visit his brother over the bye week—the week that the team has no game, but I had softball practice. Knox took my rejection with ease and we spent that entire weekend in his apartment, trying out as many positions as he could dream up. I did not like the one where my head was lower than my hips but all others were a go.

He has the stamina of Secretariat, not to mention that he's hung like a horse, too. Apparently my sex has muscles in it that can get bruised and worn out. Complaining about this to Knox results in more oral. He loves giving head. It's kind of amazing. Sometimes he acts like he enjoys going down on me more than anything else, which can't possibly be—

"Earth to Ellie. Come in, Ellie. The little people who don't have sex are pretending not to be jealous of your nonstop action, but your horny face isn't helping." Riley waves a hand in front of my face.

"Sorry." I try to look repentant. "It's the game theory class. I barely understand it myself."

"Which makes it difficult to help Jack," Riley finishes.

I swing around in surprise. "You know?"

She grimaces. "I've suspected for a while, but since you didn't want to say anything, I didn't bring it up."

Panicked, I grab her wrist. "You can't say anything, Riley. If it got out…Jack's eligibility would be gone. He might get kicked off the team, lose his scholarship." I swallow. "I could get kicked out, too. If you saw him in class, Riles." I scrub both hands down the sides of my face. "It'd break your heart."

Riley turns her hand over and grips mine. "I'm not saying anything. Why'd he take it anyway? Isn't it supposed to be hard? Every time I mention it to someone they get this haunted look in their eye. It's like the class causes PTSD."

I lean my head back against the rolled edge of the sofa. "It's the name. Politics and Games? People sign up thinking that it's this fun class that will give them something semi-coherent to talk about at net-working parties when we graduate. Instead, it's this soul-sucking combination of applied mathematics and theoretical behavioral studies. Jack took it because his stupid liaison told him it was math heavy, but it's not. It's not about numbers and equations at all, or at least not in a way that he understands it."

"What are you doing? How much trouble could you get into?"

"I'm changing some of his answers. Not all of them, but he plans to write a paper about the Super Bowl, and the decision that the coach had to make at the end of it whether to run or pass during a short yardage play. I wanted to make sure that his worksheet answers match up with the paper he'll turn in at the end of the year."

"How are you substituting your paper for Jack's?" She nibbles on the side of her thumb. How ironic that she's studying ethics, and I'm detailing the way I'm cheating for Jack.

"I suggested the topic to him. He'll write it and I'll proof it."

"So, you aren't really cheating."

"I am." I hang my head. "He's got all the concepts down, but he doesn't articulate them well. So I rewrite sentences or sometimes whole paragraphs…or whole pages."

"Oh." She wrinkles her nose. It's the perfect summary of my terrible situation.

"What do your ethics books say about this?" I try to make a joke of it but it comes out bitter. I regret it immediately but Riley doesn't take offense.

"How long have you done it?"

"When haven't I? My parents are not the warmest people. Dad has very high expectations of Jack. In eighth grade, Jack came home with two Ds on his report card. One in English and one in history. Dad lit into him. Called him every name in the book. Said he was so dumb that it'd be a shock if he could even get a job pumping gas at the local convenience store. I couldn't sleep that night. Jack's face, the terrible expression on his face, like he was worthless, kept me up. I couldn't let him be a target for Dad again, not if I could do something about it." My face is wet from tears I didn't even realize I shed. I dash them away. "My mom found out and suggested"—more like demanded—"I keep it up."

"So you've covered for him for years."

I nod.

"I suppose he never got tested because of your father?"

I nod again.

Riley whistles. "Wow. I guess my ethics class would say to look to the harm. Is it affecting the curve of the class? Probably not. Is his getting a passing grade diminishing opportunities for someone else? No, he's not taking away any academic scholarships. The only person who could be hurt would be…" She pauses, not wanting to say the obvious so I finish for her.

"Jack. Jack's the one who gets hurt by my doing his work for him. But the entire team would get harmed if it got out." The hard lump that lives in my stomach travels up to my throat. Hoarsely, I continue, "Not only does the cheating endanger his right to play, but the entire season could be affected. The Warriors could be excluded from bowl contention."

"This sucks," Riley sympathizes.

I spend two seconds internally debating the rest of it, but figure if I can talk to anyone, it's Riley.

"Riley, I've been writing this mock grant for the learning center, remember?"

She bobs her head. "You're writing a proposal for your grade?"

"Yes, that's the one. So I've been doing all this research, and did you know that colleges have to offer accommodations for people who have learning disabilities?"

"I suppose that would make sense." Her eyes grow wide as she gets exactly where I'm going with this.

"I want to tell Jack, Riley. At Western—or heck at any school—if he's determined to have any kind of disability, they have to make special arrangements. It's the law! He could do an oral exam, instead of a written one. Instead of a paper, he does a presentation. We haven't done anything wrong…yet. I've changed some worksheet answers, but nothing's graded. He gets one grade based on a final paper."

"But you're afraid," she guesses.

I nod slowly. Each time I've approached it with Jack he's shut me down. I don't want the only real member of my family to turn his back on me, but like Riley said. The only person who I'm hurting right now is Jack. "I am scared. He's the iron at my back. He's supported me and cared for me. I don't want to lose his love or respect. And I don't know what Knox would say either."

"Oh, honey." She places an arm around my shoulders. "This is tough. If you keep quiet, you're hurting Jack. If you tell, you're hurting him. Any way you slice it, someone is going to be unhappy, including you."

But that's no reason to stay silent.

WEEK 9: WARRIORS 7-0

"YOU LOOK STRESSED, BABY," KNOX declares over dinner. I tug my sweater down. The late October weather is chilly. "You worried about meeting my brother?"

That's absolutely the last thing on my mind. Knox's brother, Ty, is coming to visit him this weekend for the game and he's staying over for a Halloween costume party that night. Really, I think it's a test to see whether I can tell the two apart in person. I'm certain I'll pass, although part of me wants to pretend, for a moment, that I'm confused. So Knox won't bring it up again. But I won't because that's probably over-the-top mean.

"No," I answer tersely. I wanted to talk to Jack tonight but he said he had a study group for his stats class. I felt immediately relieved and then guilty for feeling relieved. It's a vicious circle of awful. The sooner I confront the issue, the better for all of us.

"The game?" he presses.

"Should I be?" I counter.

He shakes his head and leans forward. "Nah, we'll crush them."

"They're the number four team in the country."

Knox's unshakeable confidence would probably be irritating if he didn't back it up every Saturday.

"What is the Warriors' ranking?" He cups his ear.

"Number one."

He winks. "That's right." A mischievous look crosses his face as he leans forward. "Why don't we go back to my room and I'll give you a nice rub down to help get rid of all that stress."

"The last rub down lasted all of five minutes before you had me plastered against the wall." I brush a hand over the back of my sweater—the tight red one that Knox likes so much. "I think I still have drywall in my shirt from that."

His eyes gleam. "I like standing up. Good leverage."

I should explain how it's also nice to have a soft mattress at your back, but as long as I have Knox here, I might as well ask him a question that's burned at the back of my mind all day.

"Knox, if something happened on the team. Like a guy got caught cheating or he got arrested for drunk driving, what would happen?"

"He'd be kicked off," Knox replies immediately.

"No questions. No second chances?"

"No. Coach Lowe doesn't tolerate that kind of stuff. If there's a distraction, the distraction gets eliminated."

God.

"What about if he had problems making grades?"

Knox leans forward and his face takes on a concerned expression. "You got something to tell me, Ellie?"

"No. I'm just, um, thinking about topics for a creative writing class on team unity."

The side of his mouth curls up in slight disbelief.

"Really," I insist.

I don't think he believes me, but he doesn't press. "A guy with academic problems would probably get suspended until he could get his grades up."

"What would happen with the team?"

"It's hard to say." Knox drums his fingers lightly against the table top as he studies me. I try to look as innocent as possible. "It could mess with the team dynamic. If it was a player on *my* list, Coach Lowe would be pissed at me because I'm supposed to be on top of that. If there's anything I should know about Jack…"

Inwardly I wince. I don't want to lie to him, but I need to tell Jack first. He deserves that from me.

"If I had something I could tell you, I would," I end up saying.

Knox cocks his head and then reaches across the table to grab my hand. "Okay. I trust you."

Talk about a knife to the heart. There's almost nothing he could have said that would make me feel worse. I struggle to put a smile on my face. Briskly, I change the subject. "How are your classes going?"

"Good. It's interesting, because I thought I'd get completely bored this year, knowing I wasn't planning on graduating. Instead, the classes got more entertaining."

"Are you rethinking your plan to declare early?" Knox had told me a week ago that Coach Lowe agreed that he should enter the draft after his junior year. The hype around his play is very high right now and there's always the risk of playing another year of college ball. Knox can always go back and finish his last year of college. He might not ever have another chance at being drafted in the top ten, which is where he is currently projected.

"No. I want to play with the best and the best play at the next level," he says simply. "It's good that Coach supports me. If he didn't, I guess I wouldn't get to go early. Scouts rely on his assessment. He's told them I'm mature enough to go early and that I can handle the extra responsibilities."

The Warriors have sent several players to the NFL ever since Coach Lowe took over the program, so it's not surprising that pro scouts rely on his word.

"I can't believe his endorsement matters so much." I wonder what Coach Lowe would say if he knew that Knox allowed me to shield Jack's progress from him. Nothing good. I scowl into my basket of untouched food.

"It's not just Coach. These scouts investigate everything about you, down to how many times you go see a trainer during the week, what you write on social media, which is why I don't have any accounts, how many protein supplements you take. I heard that they even rate your girlfriends."

I gawk at him as he nods in rueful agreement. "I know. It's wrong. It's part of their confidence calculation. If you have a hot girlfriend that means you've got the swagger you need to play pro ball." He winks at me. "Don't worry. You're a ten."

I can't even muster up a smile at his compliment. "I guess when you're looking at spending seventeen million plus, you want to make sure you're getting your money's worth."

"That's right. I'm not worried about it. I don't have any character issues or skeletons in my closet. It's all good."

He holds his arms out wide in careless, happy abandon. I'm going to end up hurting everyone I care about.

27

KNOX

SOMETHING IS UP WITH ELLIE. I suspect it's her brother and that he's struggling with classes. But Coach gets everyone's transcripts at midterms, so Campbell must still be eligible or he'd be on the bench. I'll have to talk to Jack tomorrow, which will likely piss Ellie off, but it's got to be done. I shouldn't have let her take on that burden anyway. Coach put that on me, and I should have kept up with it like I did the other players.

But there's no point in getting into it with her tonight. She's pretending not to be upset, and given that she's trying hard to put up a happy front, I don't press her.

I do know one way to cheer her up for real though. "You want to stay over tonight?"

"I don't know." She bites her lower lip, the juicy one I like to suck on while I'm dragging my dick in slow motion in and out of her tight body.

"I'll do all the work." I wink at her, and when she rewards me with a slight smile, I figure I'm headed in the right direction.

She leans into me as we walk out of the rib joint; not a very Ellie thing to do. She likes to walk on her own two feet. On the one hand I'm thrilled she's leaning on me. On the other? I'm a little worried. But I'll take good care of her tonight.

Matty's in my apartment when we get back. "Oh, hey, thought you were eating?" He rises to greet us.

"We were, but we're back." I jerk my head toward the door. *Time to go, Matty Iverson.*

"Hi, Matty." Ellie gives him a weak finger wave but doesn't move from the doorway until I give her a push.

"Bring anything for me?" he says hopefully.

Above Ellie's head, I glare. *Get out or the next time I see you, I'll shove that bag of Doritos down your throat and you'll be shitting Mylar for a week.*

Matty's self-preservation instincts kick in and he hops up. "Gotta go. Have a honey coming over tonight. Any recommendations on what I should wear, Ellie?"

He smooths his hand over his unruly black hair.

Ellie stares at him.

Awkwardly, he drops his hand. "Okay, I'm going now."

What's wrong? He mouths as he passes by.

I give a half shrug. I don't know.

"Good luck," he mutters under his breath as he closes the door.

"Tired, baby?" I ask when we're alone. She lets me tug off her jacket and somehow remembers to toe off her own boots before collapsing on the sofa.

She shakes her head. "No, I'm fine."

Right. You look about as fine as a beach after a hurricane.

"How about a shower? You're shivering."

She shrugs again. I could have said, *Let's eat babies; they're full of protein,* and she would respond with a nonchalant lift of her shoulders.

I tug her into the bathroom. It's plain—white tub, white tiles, small cabinet with a sink. I suck at cleaning, but fortunately for us, the Playground houses get cleaned once a week. Even though its technically student housing, the cleaning is an unspoken perk of being a starter on the football team because as far as I know, we're the only ones who receive this service. Supposedly it's part of the rent, room, and board that we're allotted.

I ripped the shower curtain down a long time ago because I got tired of rubbing up against that plastic piece of shit. I throw a towel on the floor, which soaks up most of the excess water, and call it a day. Tonight I flip the knobs on and wait for the old heaters to kick in and send the hot water up three floors. In the meantime, I start undressing Ellie.

It's not as fun when she's standing still as a ghost. Most of the time we're undressing each other like it's one big race to see who can rip the other person's clothes off faster. Sometimes it does result in an actual rip. But I'd sacrifice any number of buttons or shirts or clothes if she would stop acting and looking like a wax museum figure.

My body and my head aren't on the same page. When I get Ellie down to her undies, I start thinking about comforting her in other ways. My dick tells me he can make her feel better, and since I'm not sure, maybe I should test it out. For science. It doesn't get better when

I pull her panties down her long lean legs and unhook her bra strap.

I bite down on the inside of my cheek, but the exploding pain doesn't make my erection lessen even a little. Still, I ignore it because that seems like the right thing to do. My dick apparently hates doing the right thing and stubbornly points at her.

"Knox." Ellie places her slender fingers on my forearm as I lift her into the tub.

"Yeah, baby?"

"I don't want to be alone." She looks down and crosses one bare foot over the other.

"Oh, sweetheart, you aren't." It takes me no time to strip off my clothes. I hop into the shower and nudge her under the heated stream of water. I squeeze some shampoo into my hand and then go to work on her hair. She leans into me, resting her forehead on my chest while I massage the soap into her skull. She moans, a soft, pleasurable sound that races down my spine and settles somewhere in the vicinity of my dick.

Her hands come up and press against the sides of my waist. I swallow a groan but my dick bobs happily between us. Who knew that part of my body was erogenous? I try to ignore how turned on I'm getting as she kneads my sides.

It gets impossible when she runs her fingers down my obliques.

"This might be the sexiest part of your body," she mumbles against my chest.

"Might be?" I slather shampoo down her back, mapping her with my hands. I feel the bony edges of her shoulder blades, the strength in her rib cage. Lower sit the gentle curves of her ass and the hidden crease between them.

"I'm a fan of your happy trail." Her hand dips between us. "And where the trail ends."

I don't respond immediately because I'm busy savoring the feel of her hand on my dick. I pump helplessly against her palm. Her tongue darts out to lick the water off my pec. I flex it for her and she giggles.

"You're making it hard for me to stand upright, baby."

"Hmm?" She licks me again. And then again.

"Shit, baby, that feels so good." With a growl, I delve between her legs. I run my fingers along the outer edges of her sex, squeezing and rubbing as I go. Her body strains against my hand.

I know what she wants because I want the same thing. I want my dick inside of her, driving into her hard. But I've also learned that the longer we hold out, the longer we tease each other, the better the feeling.

Like I told her a long time ago on Hammer's back porch, I'm a pro at delayed gratification.

She's gotten to know me. That night in the bathroom, she watched me with fevered intent. It was so hard not to grab her, throw her against the cabinets, and fuck her right there. She learned something that night and she's applying all her knowledge right now. She slides her palm up and down. I jerk out of her grasp because I'm too close to blowing my lid.

"Not yet," I order.

I drop to my knees and push her legs open even wider until she's completely exposed to my gaze. Her clit practically screams for me to suck her. I flick it with my tongue and feel my chest swell with pride when she cries out my name.

"Knox, please."

I cover her with my mouth, sucking in that sweet pearl, lashing it with my tongue until her fingernails dig into my skull. This is our first time in the shower, and it'll be memorable. All of our first times will get burned into her brain, like she's burned into my heart.

I spread her legs wide apart and pin her to the tiles of the shower wall. As promised, I'll do all of the work. Although this isn't work. This is…hell, it's more than play or fun. I feast on her because I can't get enough. I don't know if I'll ever get enough of her.

There isn't a moment of the day that I don't want my face buried between her legs or to be balls deep in her pussy. I want my name to be the last word on her lips when she falls asleep and the first thought in her mind when she wakes.

Right now, she's chanting my name and whatever caused her to feel upset earlier doesn't bother her now. Her head presses against the wall and her back arches as she grinds against my mouth and face.

The blood in my dick pounds like a beast clawing its way out. I can't wait another minute. I surge to my feet and line up my cock at her entrance. Her heat scorches me and I'm not even inside her yet. She wraps her arms and legs around me as I surge forward.

We share a groan when I'm fully seated. She starts squeezing immediately with those goddamn muscles of hers.

I gasp. "Give me a minute, baby. I need to catch my breath."

Her body quakes against mine as she laughs. "I thought you were this big strong athlete with loads of stamina and discipline."

"I practice football, not sexual Olympics," I retort. She squeezes me again.

This girl. I shake my head. She's challenged me from the moment I laid eyes on her.

"I guess I'll have to teach you a lesson." I swing her around, cupping her ass tightly in my hands and carefully step out of the tub. "Squeeze me again and we're both going down."

She yelps and clings tighter to me. The situation gets worse because her slippery tits rub against my chest, and her hot little cunt slides up and down my shaft as I hobble my way to the bedroom and onto the bed.

I throw her down and climb on top of her. Caging her between my arms, I bend down and nip her lip. "You're asking for it. Hope you don't have too much going on tomorrow because you'll feel really sore."

"Bring it." Her lips curl into an almost feral grin, but underneath I still see the hurt from earlier. Part of her wants me to fuck away her pain and another part of her wants to be held and soothed. I can give her both.

I claim her mouth at the same time I thrust inside of her. Her channel is wet and ready, and I slide in with no resistance. She's still tight as fuck and I have to pause for a minute before withdrawing.

We find a rhythm, slower than normal, as if we both want to get lost in this physical world where it's only her and me and all the pleasure we can wring from each other.

I rear back, almost coming out of her completely, and then drive forward with bruising force. Her body welcomes me. Her legs fall open, her arms wrap around my neck, her mouth eats away at mine. I bury my nose in the sweat-dampened skin of her neck so that every breath I take fills my lungs with *her.*

Ellie bucks against me, telling me with her body that she wants more. Christ, the knot of pleasure that's built in me since I first started taking her clothes off is close to bursting.

Please come, baby. Please come, I plead silently.

"I'm so close," I grind out.

"Me, too." Her legs tighten around my hips. "I'm close, too."

I feel it. Her body's a taut string ready to go off. I reach between us and find her engorged clit. She gasps at my first touch and tries to scoot away.

"Oh no, you don't," I tell her roughly. I pinch and roll that small spot of flesh between my fingers. She gives a keening cry as the climax grips her and then reaches up to bite my shoulder.

Stars go off in front of my eyes and I fracture. I reach under her legs, practically folding her in half, and hold her there while I pound into her like a frantic animal.

"Knox. *Knox.*" Her nails dig into my biceps as the orgasm I've held off for so long shoots out of me. I buck and pump wildly as she milks me with her tight pussy. I come for a century and then collapse next to her, chest heaving like I've chased a wide receiver from his ten yard line to the end zone.

Even though we're totally spent, we can't stop touching each other. I methodically rub her from shoulder to wrist. She runs her toes against my calf. We place kisses on the bare flesh we can reach without moving too far.

"Bathroom sex. Was that on your list?" she jokes after catching her breath. She's not quite back to her old self, but it's closer. I breathe a mental sigh of relief.

"What's not on my list?" I say lightly.

She props herself up, and my eyes fall to her still rosy tits. A few bruises form on the tops where I may have sucked a little too long and hard. I don't feel even remotely sorry about it. I shove one hand underneath my head and try not to look too pleased.

"Do you have an actual list?"

"Not written down," I admit. "But I have a mental one. Shower sex was up there. The locker room definitely."

"Where else?"

"Bus ride, plane ride, road head. Maybe on the back of a motorcycle. Your ass would look real nice bent over a bike seat."

She tweaks my nipple. "You don't even have a bike."

"Not yet, but who knows."

She scoffs. "Your NFL contract would prevent you from buying one. Isn't there some dangerous activities ban?"

"So, I buy one, and it sits in the garage with the Bugatti and Aston Martin—and I bend you over all of those."

"How about I do the bending?" she teases.

"I thought we were talking about *my* fantasies." I roll her over before she can pinch me again because holy crap that hurt. Nipples get really sensitive when all your blood has risen to the skin. I plan to use that new knowledge to my advantage. Bracing myself over her, I bend down and nip at her mouth, and then her neck.

"When does Ty get here?" she asks.

"He's coming straight from the airport to the game. We'll meet him afterward. You sure you want to make dinner? Because we can go out."

"No, I want to." She makes a face. "I guess I want to impress him and show him how sweet and domesticated I am."

We both laugh at that. She's not sweet and she's not super domesticated. She's tart, a little mouthy, and just right for me.

"He'll love you."

"Really? How do you know?" Her finger writes a five repeatedly on my chest. I tell myself it's because she's as obsessed with me as I am with her.

"Because I do."

She continues her finger tracing silently. I bite back my frustration. It doesn't feel real good to have my declaration hanging out there. Maybe she didn't get it. I rub my tongue against the roof of my mouth until I feel like I can say the words.

"I said I love you."

It comes out as almost an accusation.

Her breath catches and she turns her face to hide it against my chest. I hear something, or more accurately, feel a mumbling against me. When she raises her face to mine, it's wet with tears.

With a trembling voice, her own words tumble forth. "Oh, Knox, I love you, too. I'm pretty sure I don't deserve you."

The real anguish in her voice kills me. I clutch her closer to me. I wish I could squeeze her uneasiness out into the open where I could bash it with my fists. But emotions don't work like objects.

All I can do is be there for her.

28

ELLIE

TUESDAY

"YOU CAN STAY HERE, YOU know?" Knox says as he tugs on his running shoes in the morning.

"No, you have a lot of team stuff to do and I need to work on a midterm paper for my creative writing class." None of which I got done yesterday. He grabs my neck and pulls me in for a swift, hard kiss. I want to call him back, extend it longer because I don't know if it's the last one I'll ever get from him.

"Okay. I'll text you later." And then he's off.

I wait for Jack. It's not the best time to approach him given that he has a game in a few days, but he'll always have something going on. Today's Tuesday. He has four days to get his head on straight. And I'm done making excuses for myself.

"What's up, Ellie Bellie?" Jack asks as he lets himself out of his house. "Don't tell me that you were at Masters' until this morning. I think we work best on a 'Don't Ask, Don't Tell' basis," he jokes.

"Do you have a little time?"

He checks his phone. "Sure. I planned on going over to the weight room and getting in a little cardio, but I can do that later."

"I thought we'd go down to the park on Court and Seventh." It's a tiny abandoned playground with four swings and a tattered slide. I've never seen anyone there.

He raises his eyebrows but gestures toward his Jeep. "Sure, let's go."

The drive to the park on the south side of campus doesn't take more than ten minutes. My hands shake the entire way, and I have to press them between my legs to keep from alerting Jack to how upset I am.

"Do you want to get out?" he asks when he pulls onto the broken pavement.

It's close in here. If there's an explosion, we should probably be out-side. "Yeah."

We climb out in silence but once the doors close, Jack turns to me. "Want to tell me what is going on?"

I take a deep breath and the chill air sends a bracing shock to my lungs. "I love you, Jack."

"Love you too, El." His face is heavy with suspicion but he doesn't hesitate in his reply.

Grief stings the back of my throat, making my voice hoarse and scratchy. "Do you remember when you got those two Ds in eighth grade and I offered to proof your schoolwork?"

"Yeah."

"I've never stopped." I inhale again, searching for the courage to say the rest of it. "I've helped you for years, changing answers here and there. Rewriting your papers. Just enough that I hoped no one would notice but you'd never get another D." I force myself to watch him as the expression on his face moves from confusion to comprehension to out-right horror. "I'm auditing your sociology and game theory classes so I know exactly what you have to do to maintain your GPA. I've changed answers on your worksheet questions and on your ungraded midterm."

At first, he doesn't respond. He merely stares at me like I'm an alien bug that he's never seen before—an awful ugly one that he'd like to stomp.

"You're cheating."

I nod.

"And you've been cheating for me since the eighth grade?" There's a vicious, ugly tone in his voice. Disgust, disappointment, full-on anger. It's all there. "Fucking middle school?"

I start crying, not because of my pain, but because of the anguish in Jack's voice. It hits me in the solar plexus like a blow. He turns and slams his hands on the top of the hood of the Jeep. "Since fucking middle school?" he repeats with a shout. "I must be the dumbest fuck in the entire world. I couldn't even pass out of fucking middle school without your help?"

"No!" I cry and reach for him. He jerks away.

"Why are you telling me?"

Here it is. Jack's perception of himself is demolished and my next suggestion will crush him even more. "I think you should get tested. I think you have a learning disability. If you're tested," I rush on even though he starts protesting, "if you're tested and the results confirm it then you can do alternate things, like take an oral examination or do a presentation of your findings instead of writing a paper. You could have more time to do your assignments. Have take-home exams instead of timed classroom ones."

"You want me to go and get some test that says I'm retarded? Who needs that when I have you?" he sneers.

It's my turn to jerk back. "Don't say that. There's nothing wrong with you. Nothing's wrong with anyone like you. If you could see these kids at the center—"

He cuts me off. "Is that why you are doing that grant work? To make you feel better about yourself? About *your* cheating? I never fucking asked you do to this!"

He jerks his hands through his hair, pulling on the ends. As if he can't stand to look at me, he turns away and stalks over to the slide. I wrap my arms around my middle, trying to keep all my inside parts from falling out through the big gaping holes created by this whole damn mess.

"I know you didn't ask," I say to myself. "I know." I wait for the rest of it to sink in for him. The minute that it does, he comes charging back, stopping only a few inches from me.

"I could lose my scholarship over this. I could lose my team. Fuck, I could ruin the team's chances for a National Championship."

His litany of all the negative repercussions flays me open but he isn't saying anything I haven't already thought about.

"Look, I know I should have told you before. I wanted to stop. I did, but I didn't want you to lose your eligibility. That's why I did it."

He makes a disgusted noise in his throat. "So you've wanted to stop cheating for me, but I'm so fucking dumb that you couldn't."

The injustice of it makes me want to scream but mostly I am tired. Tired of doing the dirty work. Tired of feeling guilty. Tired of everyone not acknowledging the real problem of Jack's disability. Tired of myself for enabling him.

"You're right. I was wrong to do this. I thought it was the right thing—" I cut myself off. Did I ever think it was the right thing? Yes, probably years ago before I knew better, but not now. It hasn't been right for a long time, but I still did it.

I try to search for another answer, but keep coming up blank. The only answer was to not start in the first place. But when you're twelve, and your mom comes to you saying that the one thing you can do that will make her proud is to help your brother? No problem, you think, because your brother hung the stars, and you're happy to do these seemingly small things. Because you love your family and you want their approval. You want your mom to look at you with the same glow of pride that she gives your brother.

And you don't think about the consequences until it's far, far too late.

Jack is tired, too. His shoulders slump in defeat and that's what breaks me.

"Do you and Riley sit around and talk about how it's a good thing that I play ball well, because I'm not smart enough to do anything else?"

"No!" I nearly shout. "I never think that."

His cruel words saw at the bond I didn't think could ever be severed.

"Jesus, I got to tell Coach." He drags a rough hand through his disheveled hair.

I hug myself tighter. "What about Knox?"

"What about him?" He scowls. "You chat him up about this, too?"

I shake my head miserably. "You're on his list."

"What list?"

Oh shit. He doesn't know. Knox didn't say anything to him? I close my eyes briefly, gather up what little composure I have left. "He's got a list of players to check up on. You were on it and I said I'd do it for him."

"I'm on a fucking watch list?" He starts pacing. "Oh hell, Ellie. You have to break up with him."

"Why?" I shouldn't be surprised. I knew it was coming, but it's still not a blow I'm ready to take.

"Coach Lowe finds out Masters let you do the checking up and he'll be on Knox's ass so hard."

It's good that Coach Lowe supports me. If he didn't, I guess I wouldn't get to go early. I think the scouts rely on his assessment. He's said I'm mature enough to go early and that I can handle the extra responsibilities.

Jack nods grimly at my moan. "Coach could even think Masters was in on it with you."

My breath halts at Jack's words. Because Knox and I are sleeping together, because we're a couple, Knox could be tainted by my actions. Coach could take away Knox's captaincy. Scouts will start whispering about his lack of character and he could drop down the draft ranks faster than a concrete block in the pool.

"Oh God." I cover my mouth. "I'm sorry, Jack. I'm sorry for everything."

"Let's go. I need to tell Coach. I might need to start sitting out games immediately. Get in the Jeep."

"You're going now?" I don't feel prepared for this. I was only ready to talk to Jack, not tell the world, but I climb into the passenger seat anyway.

"Better get it done with. If I play a game and I'm not eligible, then that win might get taken away." He guns the engine. There's so much bitterness in his voice. I wonder if he'll ever forgive me.

"I'm going with you."

29

ELLIE

WE ARGUE ABOUT IT THE entire way over to the athletic center, but I tell Jack if he doesn't let me come with him, I'll show up anyway. In the end, he gives in. He tries to lecture me on how it'll all unfold, with him taking the blame and me standing there like an extra piece lettuce on the side that no one wants to eat.

"Hey, Coach," Jack calls out tentatively as we approach the open door to Coach Lowe's office. It's a spacious one, with a desk bigger than my bed back at the dorm room. Lowe himself isn't much taller than me, and as fit as any one of his players. He has a full head of gray hair and a solemn look on his lined face.

"Come in, Jack." He gestures for us to have a seat. The two chairs in front of his desk are Spartan—all wood and not a speck of cushion. That's saved for the brown leather tufted sofa, with its back against a wall decorated with plaques, and the big chair behind his desk.

I take one seat, but Jack remains standing, his fingers hooked around the back of the wooden chair. So I stand back up, too.

"Coach, this is my sister, Eliot Campbell."

Coach Lowe's hand feels dry as dust and I try hard not to give him a limp-wristed shake in return. "Nice to meet you, sir."

"What's this all about?" Coach Lowe rounds the desk and takes a seat, gesturing for us once again to sit down. His voice is laden with suspicion, which it should be because a player doesn't show up on Sunday afternoon introducing his sister for shits and giggles. Jack remains standing and so I do, too.

Before Jack can open his mouth, I answer Coach Lowe. "I asked Jack to bring me here to tell you that I've helped him, unofficially and without him knowing, for years. And by helped, I mean, I've done some of his work for him."

Jack tries to interrupt me. "No. This is not all on Ellie. I should have known what was going on, and I was too happy passing classes that I probably shouldn't have passed, so I didn't question it."

"No. Jack didn't know anything about it." I protest. "It was all my idea."

"Oh, Mom had nothing to do with it?" Jack raises a furious eyebrow.

Coach Lowe whistles, and Jack and I shut our mouths quick.

"The both of you sit down," Coach Lowe snaps. The authority in his voice acts like a whip and we both race to take a seat.

"Now I want you to start from the beginning and go slow." He points at Jack. "Your sister first."

"Where's the beginning?" I ask. "From when Jack and I started here at Western or before?"

"How long have you been *helping*?" His emphasis on the word indicates he knows exactly the type of help I'm talking about.

I lick my dry lips. "Eighth grade."

Jack makes an uncomfortable sound. This has to be terrible for him, and I hate that I'm here, talking about his troubles in front of someone he respects a great deal. Out of the corner of my eye, I see his head dip forward as if his shame weighs him down.

Coach Lowe steeples his fingers together and looks thoughtfully at the both of us.

"You been tested, Jack?" he asks after silent consideration.

"No, sir," Jack replies, his voice almost inaudible.

"Our dad is a…" I struggle to find the right word so I don't say something too offensive. "He has high ideals and having a son who isn't perfect in any way doesn't fit his world view."

"This isn't anyone's fault but my own," Jack replies bitterly. His head swings up and there's fire in his eyes. "Nothing has happened that would put the program in jeopardy, but I'll have problems passing one particular class this semester."

"If nothing has happened, why are you here?" Coach Lowe challenges. Jack's mouth snaps shut. Lowe's sharp eyes swivel back toward me and it takes a concerted effort to hold his gaze.

"Because I probably won't be eligible after finals." Jack's regained his composure, too.

"All right. Let's hear from—Eliot, is it?" At my nod, he continues, "What exactly have you done here at Western?"

I detail exactly how I've used Jack's access codes to check his homework, correct worksheets, and help frame an outline for his paper for him in the game theory class. The sociology one Jack didn't need help with. Like I suspected, he chose to write a paper similar to one he'd produced in junior college.

Coach Lowe takes notes while I talk and Jack stares woodenly at something behind Coach Lowe's head. When I finish, Coach Lowe presses a button. A girlish voice answers, but I can't make out exactly what she says.

"Stella, is Ace in the treatment room? When he's done, tell him to come in here." He cuts off the connection before Stella responds. His next call is to Brian Newsome, a name I recall Knox brought up before. He's the associate director for football student services, but I didn't know exactly what he did. "Brian, I need you to come down and talk to me about a student issue."

Brian responds that he'll be there in five minutes.

Once done making calls, Coach Lowe addresses Jack again. "What happened to your tutor for the class?"

Jack's cheeks turn a dull red. "She wasn't real helpful."

He doesn't want to get the tutor in trouble.

Coach Lowe harrumphs. He's fairly insightful and can probably guess the problem from Jack's lack of response. We don't exchange any more words until there's a knock at the door.

"If that's you, Ace or Newsome, come in. Anyone else, get your ass out of here."

The door opens and Ace's face appears. Following him a trim, eyeglass-wearing man in his mid-forties enters the room and closes the door behind him. He must be Brian Newsome. In one hand he has a coffee cup and the other a notepad. He takes a seat on the sofa. Ace leans against the door, a worried look on his face.

Coach Lowe sketches out the issues without any preliminaries. "Campbell here is in academic trouble. His sister has done work for him, none of it graded, but inappropriate anyway. Campbell feels like he won't pass a class—what's it called?"

"Politics and Games," Jack answers.

Brian lets out a low whistle. "That's a very difficult class. How'd you end up in it if you aren't a political science major?"

"I needed an elective and the student liaison assigned to me said it was math heavy and fun."

Coach Lowe points a finger at Brian. "Get the name of that person and find out if he or she is gaslighting my players. Also get a list of our tutors for that class. Seems we have a jersey chaser on the list."

Jack shifts uncomfortably in his chair. He doesn't like for anyone to get in trouble over his issues. I only want to protect Jack and Knox.

Coach Lowe turns his attention to Ace. "Jack Campbell was on your list. What happened?"

Ace and I exchange a look because we both know that Jack somehow got on Knox's list. I don't know what Knox and Ace's relationship is. The offense and defense don't mix a lot. Different mindsets and personalities.

"I said that I would check up on Jack." I don't say whom I told that to. Jack scowls at being treated like a child. God, this is so awful. I want this to be over five minutes ago. "Obviously I did that because I didn't want anyone to know about my behavior and how it would adversely affect the team. I pretty much threw a fit about it." The words are as much for Ace as any one. I don't want Knox suffering repercussions for my actions, I silently tell Ace, but I can't tell by his expressionless face whether he's getting it.

"That true?" Coach Lowe asks.

Ace pokes his tongue into the side of his cheek but nods. "Yeah, that about sums it up."

None of us are lying, exactly, but we aren't telling the whole truth either. For his own reasons—none of which I know—Ace will back me up here. Jack raises his eyebrows slightly in surprise but keeps his own mouth shut.

Coach Lowe heaves a big sigh. "Here's what'll happen. Brian will take you, Jack, to student services or whatever it's called, and get you tested. Brian, how long will it take?"

"A couple of days, maybe a week at the most."

"Have it take a couple of days." He points the tip of his pen at Jack. "We're putting you on academic probation until the results of those tests come out. If they show you have a learning disability, then we can do stuff for you. Right, Brian?"

"That's right. If you have a reading or writing disability, Western allows for reasonable accommodations. Those can include oral examinations instead of written ones. Take home tests instead of in-class tests and any other services deemed reasonable and necessary by the administration." He rattles off a few more ways that Jack can get help, none of which make him feel any better.

"Will I be able to work out with the team?"

"Work out, yes. Play, no." Coach Lowe levels a hard look at Jack. "If you had come to me sooner, we might not have had to suspend you, but this late in the year it's safer for the program."

Meaning any wins that they have won't get jeopardized by Jack's academic standing.

"It's my f—" I start to say again but Coach Lowe cuts me off with a swift slash of the pen.

"And for you, Miss Campbell, starting tomorrow morning you are hereby banned from the Western State football team. I don't want to see you within fifty feet of anyone wearing a football jersey. If one of them is in your class, you sit as far away as possible. You don't talk to them. You don't smile at them. You don't even breathe the same air as them. You got that?"

I nod. My own cheeks flush red hot with shame as if I'd gotten caught by Coach Lowe having sex with Knox in the locker room.

"If I see you near any player, I'll kick that player and your brother off the team. I don't care if it's Knox Masters or Ace here. Their continuing ability to play depends on you, Ms. Campbell."

I gasp when the full impact of the ban hits me. I'm supposed to cook dinner for Knox's brother this Friday.

"What about Jack? He is her brother," Ace points out.

"Obviously I can't prevent you from spending time with your family, but on campus, keep it as minimal as possible."

"So the ban is all players but her family," Ace presses. I glare at him to shut up before he gets himself in trouble.

Coach Lowe narrows his eyes at Ace but says tersely, "Family is exempt." He turns away from Ace, done with him.

Jack opens his mouth to protest but Coach Lowe doesn't want to hear from him either. "You want to stay on this team, you play by my rules. Your sister is a problem and you need to excise problems from your life if they affect your play."

"With all due respect, sir, my sister has only ever wanted to help me. She's not the problem. I am for not facing up to my issues before. I never wanted to admit I might have a learning disability. I don't like it much now either. But it's there and I'll do that testing, but Ellie has only ever wanted to help."

"That's a nice speech," Coach Lowe replies coldly. "But this is my team and my rules. You want to play, you'll have to abide by the punishment I send down." He points his pen at me again. "I don't want either of you telling the players about this. I'm not the bad guy here."

I can see it's on Jack's tongue to protest. I catch his arm. "Please," I beg softly. "If you get kicked off the team, I'll be sick with guilt for the rest of my life. Please let's take our lumps. Otherwise I'll never look at myself again without utter loathing."

Jack's face hardens from regret to resolve. With a short nod, he turns to Coach Lowe. "Okay. I want to play."

Coach Lowe waves his hand. "Get out of here. You've all got stuff to do. Ace, how's the arm?"

"Good, sir. Feels good."

"Keep icing it."

"Plan to."

30

ELLIE

I WAIT UNTIL WE'RE OUT of earshot of Coach Lowe's office before spinning on Ace. "Do you think he'll kick Masters off the team?"

"Maybe not. But he'd probably pull his support for Masters going pro after this season. I wouldn't test Coach." Ace walks off, presumably to continue icing his arm.

"What will you do?" Jack asks. "Text him?

I rear back. "No. I won't break up with him via text. Is Coach Lowe bugging the phones? I'm calling him." No way I would do it so cold-heartedly.

"He'll talk you out of it," Jack warns.

I wish.

When I get back to my apartment after classes, I check the time. Knox will be going to film class. I rub a hand over my eyes, wanting this to all go away.

He picks up on the first ring.

"Hey, baby, what's up? You excited for the softball game tonight? Undefeated Horny Toads!" He lets out a low whistle. Oh shit. I forgot. We're playing last year's intramural softball champs—the Gilded Lilies—the team with Champs in gold foil on their pullovers and matching hats. He continues, "I also picked up our costumes for the Halloween party. I'm warning you right now. I look damn good in pink. You won't keep your hands off me."

Knox and I planned to go to a Sigma Chi Halloween party as Power Rangers. Red for me; pink for him. He thought it ironic.

"We're breaking up," I blurt out.

"No, I can hear you fine."

"Not the phone line. Us. We can't see each other anymore."

"What are you taking about?"

"I don't want to see you again. I'm sorry to say this, but when I learned you were a virgin, I wanted to be your first. Make my mark on you. I figured after I had you, I'd have my pick of any guy at Western."

He laughs at first, but then sputters when I don't join in.

"Are you fucking serious?" There's finally a hint of anger in his voice.

"Yes." I'm so glad we are not face to face.

"Did you hit your head or something? I'm coming over. You sound like you suffered a concussion."

"No, don't come over. I-I—" I look around wildly for an excuse and seize on a random one. "I'm seeing someone else and he's here."

"Since when?" he demands.

"He's on my softball team. The shortstop. Ryan Schneider." *Oh, Ryan, I am so sorry I'm throwing you under the bus.*

Silence hangs between us.

"Put him on," Knox growls.

"No."

"Let me talk to him."

"No. I'm sorry. We're done." In a rush I hang up, afraid of what Knox will say or do. He calls back immediately and I put my phone on do not disturb. Then I block him because Jack is right. I'm weak when it comes to Knox. Very weak.

WEDNESDAY

MY GOOD INTENTIONS EVAPORATE WHEN he shows up at the softball game. He looks gorgeous. Big, brawny, and all mine. Except he's not anymore, and if Coach Lowe gets word that he's here with me, we're both in trouble. Knox doesn't even pretend he's here to do anything but hassle me. He leans against the edge of the wall that serves as the home run marker.

"You have to leave," I hiss without turning around. "We've broken up. You can't be here."

"Why, because your new boyfriend will see us together?" he asks, a hint of mockery in his voice.

"Who?"

"Schneider," he reminds me impatiently. "The guy who's taken my place between this morning when I ate you out and sometime after your last class of the day."

I flush a dull red—both at his crude words and my obviously bad lie. I need to think of better excuses.

"Hey, Schneider," he calls out.

The rangy shortstop raises his head and looks around. Knox whistles and Schneider trots over, completely abandoning his position. The power of Knox Masters.

"Hey, Masters," Schneider greets him like a long lost brother. They do a complicated thing with their hands and a half hug. "What's up? Seven-and-oh with only five games left. That's pretty damn exciting."

"We've got nothing on the Horny Toads." Masters nods toward the field. "Although Ellie says that the Gilded Lilies are tough competitors."

"Those girls know how to use the bat," Schneider replies.

Then why aren't you minding the field? I cry in my head. Outwardly, I try to signal Schneider in on the fact that I've used him as a beard. My wriggling eyebrows and furtive hand gestures are greeted with a puzzled look.

"Ellie tells me that you two are seeing each other now," Masters says casually. He turns and spits about an inch from Schneider's toes.

"What?" Schneider yelps. He jumps away from me. "Gosh, Ellie. I think you're a good left fielder, but I thought you knew I played for the other team. Oh, look, the Lilies are up to bat." He quickly scampers off.

"Schneider's gay?" I gape.

Knox looks at me with a pointed stare. "Your gaydar needs work. Also your lying."

My gaze drops to my sneakers. "We shouldn't see each other anymore."

His large hand cups the back of my neck. I don't look up even at that, afraid of what I'll see there. Of what I'll do. "Are you worried about Ty coming? I told you he'll love you."

Oh, Knox.

"We still on for tomorrow?" The uncertainty in his voice kills me.

I nod because I know what I have to do.

He retreats to the stands and watches my Horny Toads get shellacked by the Gilded Lilies. They do know how to use their bats *and* their gloves.

"What was that all about?" Schneider mutters in the dugout as we're gathering up our equipment.

"I want to break up with Knox and I used you as an excuse. Sorry." I make an apologetic face.

"Use someone else next time," Schneider hisses. He pats his nicely gelled blond hair. "I'm breakable."

How did I miss that Schneider was gay? I guess because I only have eyes for Knox. No one really exists for me but him.

Knox waits for me, but I see with a sigh of relief that Jack is there, too. "Sorry, I can't go out tonight. Lots of homework. My rough draft for the grant is due."

I hurry in the opposite direction while Jack distracts Knox.

There's one thing that will make Knox believe we are over. It's the place I didn't want to go, but I have to.

FRIDAY

"HI, MATTY." I DROP MY two grocery bags on the kitchen counters.

Matty waves his hand from the sofa. I think there's a permanent indentation from his butt on the cushion. His dark hair gleams wet from his shower.

"Do you have your sexy costume picked out?"

"Knox picked them up yesterday." I need Matty to get out of here.

"How come this dinner is a secret?"

Jack had Knox issue a team wide omertà—no one speaks of the fact that I came here tonight—or I wouldn't come.

"Coach Lowe doesn't want any distractions," I answer. It's true enough.

"Huh. He never said anything to us."

"He told Jack. I don't want to cause any trouble." Also true.

I don't want to be here cooking dinner for Knox and Ty. I'm not in the partying mood, but I have to see this dinner through. I have to act as if nothing out of the ordinary happened, which means I'm excited to see Ty, excited for the stupid Halloween party, excited to cook this meal.

And I have to banter with Matty even though my mouth is coated with acid and self-loathing. "I think the question is: do you have your sexy costume picked out?"

"I can't go as sexy, Ellie. If I did, none of the other guys would get laid. All the honeys would be flocked around me and that's damn unfair."

I laugh, but he's probably not far off the mark. Matty has zero problems with the ladies.

"Where is everyone?"

"Everyone or Masters?"

"Everyone. Knox will show up. After all, this is his place."

Matty and I share a smile because we all know that Matty treats it like his place. Jack was probably right making me come here and go through all these planned events as if nothing has changed. It's impossible not to be around the team and not laugh. They are a great group of guys.

"Knox had to do a couple of interviews. He's famous now." Matty wiggles his eyebrows. "Besides, I heard you were cooking dinner."

"For *Knox*." I emphasize his name.

"And his brother."

"Is your last name Masters?"

"It might as well be. Plus, I can help you. I know how to cook." Matty gets off the sofa and waltzes into the kitchen.

"You do?"

"Yeah. What did you bring?" He starts to dig through the sacks.

"Steak and potatoes." I grimace. "Not very original."

"If you don't mind, I've got a good way to cook steaks. I like to baste them in butter."

"Baste? That word sounds professional to me."

"My dad's a chef," Matty admits. "I might have picked up a few things from him."

I slide the steaks over. "Have at it, but I'm still pretending I cooked tonight."

"No problem." Matty knows this kitchen better than I do. He pulls out a cast iron pan and sets it on the burner. "Salt and pepper are in the cabinet by the sink." He points to the cabinet and I trot over to pull out the spices. "You salt and pepper the steaks while I get the rest of this ready. What do you think for potatoes? Scalloped or regular baked?"

"I planned to put them in the microwave," I confess.

Matty looks at me like I'm a heathen. "Yeah, I'm making scalloped."

He instructs me on peeling and then slicing them while he adds more salt to the steaks.

"If your fan club could see you now, they'd be standing outside the door in a line like teens waiting for 1D."

"What makes you think they aren't already? I had to beat them off with a stick on the walk from Union to here." He flashes a grin and I realize that Matty Iverson is gorgeous. His blue eyes are a shocking contrast to his jet black locks, and he has a wide, infectious smile. It doesn't hurt that he's ripped underneath his V-neck sweater. I never noticed Matty's looks before, because when Knox is around all I can do is look at him.

"The defense played great last week," I tell Matty. The team won twenty-four to fourteen. The offense still struggles but the defense was stifling. They are still undefeated and with only five games left, their national championship hopes are running high which is why I need to do the right thing with Knox now even though the only more painful thing would be to take the kitchen knife to my chest.

"Jack had a great game. We really need him on offense. I swear he's the only one who can catch sometimes." Matty bends over and throws the potato, cheese, milk, and bread mixture into the oven.

"Excited about tomorrow?"

"Yeah, the Badgers are a good team but we're better." He picks up a towel to wipe off his hands and looks at me with chagrin. "I worried about you and Masters at first. I thought he might get distracted and not as sharp on the field, but he's elevated his play."

I didn't doubt that for a minute. Once Knox steps on the field, you can tell the only thing on his mind is eating the quarterback for lunch. There's nothing but steely determination in his eyes. "He's hungry for it."

"No kidding. He watched every post-game interview, every minute of the championship celebration last year because it made him angry." Matty winks at me. "We like an angry Masters. Besides he wants to win it this year."

"I know. He's declaring." Ace knew it so I figured most of the team did as well.

"He'd be a fool not to." His lips quirk up in a rueful smile. "I'm happy for him. It makes sense because if he stays another year, he risks injury. His draft stock is high this year so there's no reason to wait, but shit, I'll miss playing with him. So yeah, this year, we've got to win it. If we don't win the title, our careers here will be a bust. All the potential and nothing to show for it."

He shakes his head and the dread I managed to shelve the other night slides into my stomach.

"You'll win." I try to project as much confidence as I can.

"Knock on wood." Matty bangs the cabinet above his head.

My phone buzzes. I pull it out and read the message from Knox. "They're on their way."

"Great. Let's get these steaks seared." He throws a stick of butter into the pan followed by the steaks. The smell of deliciously cooked meat fills the kitchen and I try not to gag as my guilt churns in my stomach. I busy myself with cleaning up and avoiding Matty's gaze. I don't need him seeing how upset I am and then grilling me on what's wrong until Knox shows up with his brother.

"We need biscuits," Matty declares. He grabs my arm and pulls me over to the stove. "Keep spooning the butter over the steaks. I'll be right back."

He disappears down the stairs. Alone, I can only think of Jack's words and how stupidly I've jeopardized everyone's future. Not just Jack's. Not just Masters'. But Matty's and Hammer's and the future of every other guy on this team who has sacrificed so much to have their perfect season.

I shouldn't have come here. I should have called Knox and said it was over. Lingering over the corpse of our relationship is bad for everyone. I press my hand against my abdomen, but the knot won't go away.

By the time Matty returns from wherever he disappeared to, the lump in my stomach has grown to the size of an elephant.

He's got something clutched in his big fist.

"You're making biscuits from scratch?"

He slaps a roll of refrigerated biscuit dough onto my palm. "Ta da!"

"Thank God." I smile weakly.

"Why's that?"

"Well, finding out you made biscuits from scratch would have totally demoralized me, so I'm glad to find out that you are merely mortal when it comes to this."

"No one makes them better than the little puffy dough man."

"Hey, there you are." I turn to find Knox and his brother standing at the door. Both of them are staring at me.

I know what this is. This is "The Test." Knox wants me to show him I can tell them apart, like I do from the pictures. It's the one chance I have. The one action I have never wanted to take. Already the hollowness of losing Knox sets in, but I love him too much to kill his dreams with my selfishness.

I glide to both of them and then place my hands on the first brother's shoulders. His arms close around me and when I lift my face for a kiss, he dips down to press his foreign lips against mine. Over his shoulder, I can see Knox's eyes—the confusion, disappointment, the hurt.

I close my own because I can't see that pain. I close them and keep kissing Ty until his tongue slicks against my mouth.

I pull away because I can't go that far.

"Hey." I point to Knox. "This is the infamous Kintyre?"

Ty's grip around my frame tightens—probably in frustration and disappointment.

Behind me, Matty is silent. He's curious about the test, but he doesn't know I've failed.

I wait for Knox, but it's Ty that responds. "Yeah, honey, this is my brother."

Knox stares at me, willing me to pick up on the mistake. He's never called me honey. Baby, sweetheart, but never honey.

I smile blindly back at both of them and wait for Ty—acting as Knox—to introduce me to my boyfriend. As he drags Knox forward, I wonder how long they'll play the twin switch and how many times they have done it before. Would Knox actually let Ty sleep with me?

The thought disgusts me. I want to swipe my hand across my mouth to erase the kiss. Doing anything more intimate with Ty would be soul sucking.

I don't know how anyone can't tell the difference. I'd know blindfolded which was Knox and which was Ty. Ty's hands feel different around my waist. His fingers are thinner and shorter. His body is more bulky. His smell is different. I can't let this stranger touch me for one more second or I'll get sick, so I pull away.

I clear my throat. "I failed, didn't I?"

Knox steps forward, his expression wavers between confusion and unhappiness. "You kissed my brother."

I give a half laugh and choke back my tears as I grab my purse. "At least it wasn't with tongue. I'm going now."

"Wait," he calls, but I push by both of them, grab my coat, and leap out of there.

Knox grabs me halfway down the stairs.

As I turn back, I see Ty leaning against the open door. He's judging me. "Let her go."

"Shut up. Did you really not know?" Knox doesn't believe me, or he doesn't want to.

I give the best acting job I can. "I don't know." I wave a flustered hand between the two of them. "I don't even know who's standing in front of me right now. Is it the brother, or is it Knox?"

Knox looks like I've slapped him.

"Sorry, I know you wanted me to be the one. Sorry I ruined it for you." I'm surprised at the calmness of my tone. I knew this would happen all along. I'd expected it. Knox is too decent of a person for someone like me. I knew I never deserved him. All this time I'd fooled myself more than anyone else. Jack isn't the dumb one in the family. It's me. It's always been me. Somewhere I find the ability to give Knox a half smile. It strikes him like a physical blow and he jerks back. "Think of it this way. Your seal is broken and you can take advantage of all the girls available to you."

Knox hisses and drops my arm.

"Let her go," Ty says again.

And this time…

This time Knox does.

31

KNOX

SHE DOESN'T LOOK BACK. NOT even once. Behind me, Matty shuffles awkwardly in the kitchen. Nothing about this seems right to me. Not Ellie leaving. Not her completely defeated. Not her walking off without another look.

None of it.

Matty breaks the silence. "Take a page from the Matty Manual. Fuck the girls you *don't* care about. It's a lot less painful when you both move on."

He gives me a half-hearted pat on the shoulder and disappears down the stairs. I go inside.

There's an ache that develops at the core when you have a bad loss. It seeps into your bloodstream and it takes days for that regret and sorrow to work its way out. In the pros, when you're injured, sometimes they take your blood and send it into a centrifuge to spin out all the bad shit. It's called a PRP—a platelet rich plasma injection—and supposedly it works like a miracle drug to ease your pain, promote healing, even reduce swelling and ligamentous injury.

That's what I need right now. A PRP to my heart—*Pulp Fiction* style. One needle jabbed into my left pec repeatedly until this hideous fucking pain disappears.

"Bro, I am so sorry." Ty sits, hunched over on the sofa. His hands hang between his legs, tossing the remote back and forth. I stare at the sidewalk Ellie walked down. A few of the guys mill around on the porch.

Snow starts to fall onto the common area of the Playground. At some point, the guys downstairs will throw on their gear and start tossing the ball around, messing up the pure white blanket.

"I messed up back there," I conclude.

"Yeah, by not waiting. Why didn't you come up for the bye?"

"She had a softball game." I grab the remote from Ty to force him to look at me. "No, I messed up by going through with the test. I know she worried about it. She acted weird all week, asking me questions about the draft and then breaking up with me in a fake way. It must be because of the test. You don't do that sort of shit to people you care about. You don't put them through a fucking obstacle course and withhold your affection at the end of it if they trip up. That's what Ellie's parents have done all her life."

"I could have taken her into the bedroom right there," Ty snaps angrily.

No, she had already drawn away. The contact between them was slight. It made me sick to see it, but she barely touched him.

"She's not Marcie," I tell him.

"She's not the one," he shoots back. "You got it wrong. But like she said, you don't have to hold back now. You can do anyone you want."

The idea of being with another girl makes me sick. I can actually taste the bile in the back of my throat. "No."

"Forget about her. She's nothing. Besides, you can't let this affect you." Ty states the obvious. I don't bite his head off for it though. He only wants to help, but he doesn't know Ellie like I know her.

I stand up.

"Where are you going?" he demands.

"Out." If I tell him, he'll try to stop me.

I've got nearly a foot on Ellie, so it's easy to catch up with her. I grab her shoulder, and when she turns, she has tears on her face and her nose is Rudolph red. My heart squeezes.

"I'm sorry." I try to pull her against me but she resists.

"For what? Me not able to tell you two apart?"

"No, for making you go through with it. It doesn't matter." I reach for her again but she backs away. "I don't care."

Her lips twist in a bitter line. "I kissed your brother. There's absolutely no difference between the two of you in real life. It even felt the same."

I ignore the stabbing pain, the image she's conjuring. "Why are you lying to me?"

She presses her lips together. They're trembling. *She's* trembling. I can't take it anymore and I pull her rigid frame against mine.

"I can't be with you, Knox. I told you I wanted to sleep with a virgin and now…now you deserve someone better than me."

"Don't say that shit, Ellie. You don't believe it."

"You don't want to believe it. I don't know how many times I have to tell you that I'm not the one. I'm not. Go home, Masters. Please."

It's the use of my last name that breaks through my thick skull. My hand drops to my side. This time when she whirls around and runs, I don't chase her.

Ty is still sitting on the sofa where I left him. ESPN is on. They're talking about the matchups tomorrow but none of it registers.

"You want to talk?" he asks quietly as I toe off my boots.

"No." What's there to say? I fucked up. "Let's eat."

The food is cold but Ty and I eat it anyway. We talk about the Cougars' offense and the inability of their offensive line to get their pads low enough to stop a hard charging pass rush like ours. It should be an easy win for us. The Cougars are the second-worst team in our conference.

After dinner, Matty comes up to tell us some of the guys are going to watch *Any Given Sunday*. I beg off citing tiredness as an excuse and they let me go without calling me on my bullshit. Knowing I need some privacy, Ty accepts the invitation and leaves.

In the quiet of my bedroom, I take myself in hand and close my eyes. There I see Ellie as she looked that night at Hammer's party. Her eyes went wide as saucers and she licked her lips as if parched as a sinner in the desert.

In every line of her body, I read she wanted her hand around my dick. She wanted me in that moment more than I've wanted most things in my life, until I met her.

She started panting. I don't know if she even realized it. Her breath came short and her chest heaved, pushing those pretty tits against her sparkly top, making my vision blur.

I tighten my grip around my dick, using all the pre-come to lube my shaft. I cup my balls with my free hand and let my head fall back onto the pillows. The images in my head shift from that night to the one where I took her for the first time…or maybe it's more appropriate to think of her taking me. Whatever. That night I knew a God existed. That heaven existed.

The hot suck of her body on my dick gave more pleasure than I thought I had in me. I move my hand more rapidly and my hips jack into the air.

I love you.

I don't know who's saying it in my head—me or her or us together, but the memory of it makes me come in one long shuddering motion. The orgasm rips through me, tears open the scar tissue over my heart, and renders me a gasping, pained mess.

The lonely night stretches endlessly in front of me.

GAME DAY: WARRIORS 7-0

AT THE START OF THE game the next day, I don't feel different. When I stand on the sideline, I'm as eager to get on the field as ever. At least I understand what goes on during a football game. My goal is to stop the ball from advancing down the field. There's no uncertainty here.

But today I'm sluggish off the snap. My feet feel heavy and everyone speeds by me like I'm standing still.

"What's going on in your head, Masters?" Coach shouts at me when I come off the field, after Wisconsin scored the second touchdown.

"Nothing, Coach."

"Well, start thinking about some plays."

Our defensive coordinator is less generous. He grabs me by the facemask and screams, "Get your head in the game!"

The other guys huddle around me on the bench as Coach Johnson draws up the plays that Wisconsin is running. They aren't surprise plays. But they're getting off the ball faster. Their cuts are sharper. The left outside linebacker whose ass I've owned for two years is pushing me backward.

"She's in your head, man," Matty hisses when Johnson moves down to talk to the backfield.

I shake my head. "No. We're just off today."

That much is true. Everyone on the field is slow today. Ace seems to throw everything a yard too short. Campbell isn't playing. I don't know if he's injured, but he's standing on the sidelines, dressed in a suit and tie.

Our corners get wasted in the backfield. Matty, Hammer, me, and the D-line move like our cleats stick to the turf.

At halftime, we have managed to move the ball a total of thirty yards on offense, and above our heads a big fat zero hangs on the giant scoreboard. The home crowd jeers us as we run down the tunnel.

Coach tears us a new asshole in the locker room, telling us we're playing like quitters. We get time to piss and hydrate before we're given the heads up that we need to be on the field. I straighten my pads and head for the door when Coach grabs me.

"You're playing like this is some unranked, non-scholarship team we've put on our schedule to pad the wins instead of the fucking Big Ten champions," Coach hisses. "This is the real deal, Masters. You want to win the championship?"

"Yes, sir." I ignore the fact that my fingers are numb from the cold and pain, and that there's a throbbing in my ankle that developed sometime in the middle of the second quarter after I tried to sidearm the right side offensive lineman.

"That doesn't sound real convincing to me. If you're thinking about Sunday, stop. If you're thinking about the title, stop. The only thing that should be in your head is eating those Badgers for lunch." Coach's voice raises at the end.

When the guys in front of me pause, the D-line coach yells: "What the fuck are you ladies gawking at? Get your asses onto the field."

"Yes, sir. I want to win."

Coach swings me around. He's five inches shorter and probably a hundred pounds less, but I let him toss me around like a fish on a sailing boat.

"This might be the closest thing you have to being God, Masters. Ninety-five percent of the pro players don't get a whiff of a championship. They chase it all their lives. You have it in your fucking hand. What will you do? Will you piss it away? Or will you grab that opportunity by the fucking balls and claim it as yours? If you want it, nothing stands in your way. Nothing." He slaps his clipboard against his thigh and stalks out.

"Come on, Masters. The team relies on you," the D-coach chides.

The image of Ellie rises to my mind.

If you want it…nothing stands in your way.

"Yes, sir." I pull down my helmet.

It's not Ellie that cost me this game. It's me. My inability to see the damn forest for the trees.

"Next possession is ours." I stand and walk down the line of seated defensive ends and linebackers. "No more first downs. Hammer, you stuff that motherfucker at the line. He's creeping to the left every time they run. Jesse, go inside. Forty-five is way weaker on the left. He'll try to hold you every time." Down I go, talking to each one until the whistle blows and it's time for the defense to take the field.

For three downs, we stuff their offense and the defense leaves the field excited. We don't even mind when we have to strap on our helmets three minutes later because Ace and company can't get a first down. We slap each other's shoulder pads and helmets, go out there, and drive the opponents deep into their own territory.

This time, with better field position, Ace and Ahmed, our running back, hook up for a short pass play which Ahmed turns into a sweet run down to the twenty. We settle for a field goal, but it's a score. We don't have the donut hanging over our heads.

We score again and close the gap. At ten to fourteen, we're down by one score. In a miraculous turn of events, with only a minute left, I knock the ball out of the quarterback's hands in the end zone, and when their running back recovers it, Jesse is on him.

Safety! Twelve to fourteen!

We're still in this goddamn game. We run around, bumping each other's chests, slapping asses, and knocking our helmets together like it's the motherfucking Super Bowl.

I run down the sidelines, yelling encouragement in everyone's ear. Heads are up and eyes are hungry but the clock is against us.

In the end, we run out of time. We started our comeback too late, and when the clock flips to all zeros, we are short by a field goal.

We've lost.

32

ELLIE

POST GAME: WARRIORS 7-1

"OH NO. OH NO." I press my palms to my face. I stare at the television as if I can will more time on the clock. The game can't be over. It can't. There has to be a few more seconds left.

I pick up the remote and try to fast forward it, but it's at the end of the game. I rewind it only to have to watch the end again, and the outcome remains the same. It's a loss. Their perfect season is done. If Knox hadn't hated me before, he does now. Same with Jack. It's one thing to forgive when the one thing in your life you really cared about goes well.

When Jack got his D1 scholarship, Dad was elated. He treated everyone with his certain brand of kindness, which ranged from effusive praise for Jack to offhanded compliments to Mom and me all spring and then into the summer. The demon came out when Jack struggled. The year before junior college was a nightmare.

"Is it bad?" Riley's on the edge of the sofa, a foot curled under her. She's folded over a pillow that she's alternatingly bitten and squeezed.

"Yeah, it's bad." I reach up and feel sweat across my forehead. It's part from shame and part from agony.

The team started off terribly. Fumbles, turnovers, missed opportunities. Knox allowed a weaker, slower offensive line to manhandle his defense for two quarters. Their days at the top of the polls are over. The question is how far they'll fall.

I blow out a shaky breath.

With this loss? Any chance I had at getting back together with him after the season ends is done. Nail in the coffin, the vampire's exposed to sun, done.

I force myself to watch ESPN on which the commentators talk about the Warriors laying a big fat egg on the field.

"Masters played himself out of the Heisman with that game," one smug bastard says to another on the set.

"They don't give them to defensive players in the first place, and secondly, if they gave it to him, it would have been the result of an exceptional season. This game showed him and the Warriors as average."

"God, did you fuckers even watch the fourth quarter?" I yell at the television. "A sack, five hurries, three tackles, and a safety, and that's average?"

Riley peeks her head out of her bedroom. "I have Xanax. Do you want me to slip one into your Coke?"

I throw a pillow at her, and it nearly knocks a picture off the wall.

"Seriously, these assholes say Knox played an ordinary game. Did that look ordinary to you?" I gesture toward the television.

"Um, no?"

"Exactly." I flip the picture off. "Fuck."

"Why's this so bad?" she asks from the safety of her doorway. She's afraid of me. She probably should be. I'm a destroyer of things. "It's one loss. I understand they'd be upset that they aren't perfect, but is it that bad?"

"In college football, yes, one loss can devastate you. Only four teams get to play in the BCS title game. It's a four team playoff for the national title. They call it the BCS National Championship or Bowl Championship Series," I explain at her puzzled look. "With Auburn and Oregon having perfect records, a bunch of one loss teams will have to battle it out for those last two slots."

"But there are four more games," she points out.

"Right, four more times they can lose. Then the conference championship. Plus, it's a late in the season loss. The team they lost to was ranked, but lower than them. It could mean that they dropped out of contention for the national title." I throw myself onto the sofa. "It will depend on the polls Tuesday. If they fall too far…" I can't even bring myself to contemplate what that will mean.

"Tuesday, when?"

"8:15 p.m. EST. They are announced on ESPN."

"Okay, I'll prepare the Xanax cocktail for 8:16 p.m. then."

"Thanks," I say sourly. I stomp to my bedroom and crawl under the covers, wishing I could go to sleep and wake up with a redo of this day. Of this whole week.

Jack calls me a couple hours later. His voice sounds so heavy and sad that it's hard for me to keep from breaking down.

"How are you doing?"

"Shitty," he admits. "I hate that I wasn't out there." He'd gotten his results back on Friday, but his professors didn't get notified soon enough, so he's out at least another week. His weary inhale goes so long and loud, I can feel the wind sucking through the phone. "The team is demoralized. Half of them have gone out to drink themselves into a stupor and the other half is trying to castrate themselves in their rooms."

I don't need to guess which half Knox falls in. The loss no doubt kills him. He probably thinks it's all his fault and is mentally going over every play, examining where he could have played better and how he let his team down.

"I'm sorry."

"Coach reamed us a new one. We're not going to be able to sit down for a few days. Said he saw pee wee football squads execute better than us." Jack cracks his neck to relieve tension. The awful sound makes me wince. "We have to win next week and hope everyone ahead of us slaughter each other."

"Is…Knox doing okay?"

"Haven't seen him. After the game he disappeared. I don't know where he is." I try to keep it in, but a small moan of pain escapes me. Jack tries to reassure me. "It's not your fault. Masters needs to learn to compartmentalize better, but everyone's emotions are riding high."

"Which means they blame me, or will once they find out."

He hesitates. "No."

"Don't lie to me!" My voice comes out shrill and shaky.

"Okay. Okay," he quickly concedes. "Some of them will blame you, but it's not your fault. If this is the worst that Masters ever experienced, then he's lived a pretty fucking charmed life. He's got to strap on his balls and man up. Everyone has shit in their life they have to shut out. Girlfriends. Home life. Bad grades. Or maybe coming home and hearing your dad tell your sister that she's a worthless cunt. That can fuck with your mind. And you have to keep reminding yourself that you aren't your dad."

I cover my mouth to hold in a gasp. "I didn't know you heard that."

Usually when Dad yelled at me, Jack wasn't around.

Jack gives a humorless laugh. "I came home early because I'd tweaked my knee. Coach let me go without argument. I think I knew I was finished with the team at that time. I should have transferred to another high school, but I didn't. Other people's dickhead actions aren't your responsibility. So you broke up with him. It's still his responsibility to get his head together on the field. If he was in his right mind, he'd be the first to tell you that shit."

Jack's tone will tolerate no argument. The matter is done for him. I'm his sister. He'll always side with me. I guess that's the difference between true love and infatuation. True love takes up for you—no matter what. It always sees your side of the story. It listens for the truths.

I take a few deep breaths and gather my composure. "It's only one loss." I tell him, offering him my own sort of support. "Last year no teams in the playoff were undefeated. The most you'll drop is to three, maybe four tops."

Jack makes a sound. It could be interpreted as agreement or disgust. A bit of both I decide.

"Try to put it out of your head, Ellie," he says wearily.

A beeping interrupts us. I look at the phone and see it's my mom. "Hey, Jack. It's Mom. No doubt she wonders why you stood on the sidelines."

"Don't take it."

"I have to. If I don't she'll keep calling me."

"Don't let her push you around then." He pauses. "I know she made you do this. I know she's probably blackmailing you. That's her style. Don't want anyone to think her kids are flawed or her old man cheats on her like it's an Olympic event."

The phone beeps again.

"I could have stopped."

"You did," he points up. "You stood up to me. Now it's time to stand up to her."

He hangs up.

My right knee aches around the scar. I rub it, but the pain doesn't go away. I don't think it ever will. The agony I felt when that kid—whose face I can't even conjure—slammed into my knee is nothing like what I'm feeling now. There's a chill in my blood and a pain in my bones that I'll have to live with each day.

During the last week, I still held on to some hope that I'd be able to go to Knox and apologize and convince him to take me back after this semester ended. Foolishly I kept this stupid little dream that Jack would successfully pass all his classes by himself, and next semester, after they'd won, I'd go to Knox and apologize. But I know after the loss, there's no hope left.

I've lost him.

33

ELLIE

MY MOM'S RING TONE STARTS up again. On the scale of one to negative one thousand, the desire to answer the phone lies somewhere below hell. I brace myself. "Hey, Mom."

"Eliot, is it such an onerous task for you to answer your phone when I call you?"

Actually, yes, your calls are some of the least desirable experiences in my life.

"Sorry, I was in the bathroom."

"I'm your mother," she continues, "and I pay for this phone. And your apartment. And your tuition. And likely the clothes you're wearing and the food you eat, so perhaps you can muster a tad more enthusiasm when my identification appears on your phone."

I pull out a pad and paper. Under *Find a job*, I write, *Get disposable cell phone.*

Chastened, I mumble, "I'm sorry."

"Well, I didn't call to argue with you." Her impatience is evident. She's probably sitting at the kitchen table, drinking tea, and drafting comments on all the websites about how the commenters are ignoramuses for blaming the loss on Jack. "I'm very concerned about Jack. We watched the game today, and as you can imagine your father is beside himself that Jack wasn't playing."

That's code for he spent the entire game shouting curses at the team, Jack specifically. I bet Jack could hear those screams and rants inside his helmet. Dad is in Jack's head.

"Jack's not feeling good about that either." The one good thing about talking on the phone is that I can make all the faces I can't when we're in the same room. Right now I'm making a *screw you* face.

Doesn't matter because Mom continues as if I didn't even say a word. I'm not sure why she hates voicemail messages so much, because our entire conversation consists of her talking *at* me. No response but agreement required. "Your father and I wondered why Jack wasn't on the field. I called Coach Lowe and he instructed me to talk to my son. Since Jack isn't answering his phone, you will tell me."

A direct command. I might as well tell her.

"Jack's on probation until it can be determined that he needs special accommodations for his classes."

"Special?" She says that word as if it contains a disease, and by passing through her lips, she's exposed herself to a terminal illness.

"I told him what I've been doing and he wanted to stop. Immediately."

On the other end of the line, there's a swift intake of breath. "You what?"

I could have said I killed children and animals, and she would have responded with less horror. I drop my head into my hand. "Jack has a learning disability. You and I both know it. He needs real help, not me fixing his answers and writing his papers. He needs to learn how to do this on his own, and Western has great programs designed to help students with learning disabilities."

"There is absolutely nothing wrong with Jack." Her tone comes sharp and angry.

I take a page out of her playbook and power forward as if I'm the one in charge. "Of course not. He's very smart, but he struggles with reading and writing, and that will adversely affect him for the rest of his life unless at some point we stop enabling him. I won't continue to hurt him."

"Are you an education major now? I thought I paid for an English literature degree." Disdain drips from her words.

I try again. "If Jack is tested, the school would have to make certain accommodations for him. Instead of writing papers, he could do an oral exam. He would be allowed more time to finish a final or he might be allowed to take it home."

"Eliot, my dear, if you're tired of helping your brother, I can certainly see if there's someone else interested in taking your place." Her voice is anything but loving. The term of endearment is poisonous. "But of course, that means I will no longer provide for you in the way that I currently have. Since you're no longer doing your job."

I grip the phone tighter in my hand. "He needs our help."

My words are met with stony silence. When she speaks, her tone is ice cold. "You should be glad that tuition is nonrefundable. If I could, I would cancel the check and you would forfeit this semester. Don't expect another cent from your father or myself. Your father never wanted to pay for your college anyway. I had to do it out of my own funds. I sacrificed for you."

My eyes sting. When I rub my cheek, I'm almost surprised there's moisture there. I would've thought by now I had grown immune to this. After all, I knew it would come. Knowing, though, doesn't seem to prevent pain.

I'll get over this pain. It's the loss of Knox—someone who genuinely cared about me and thought I was special—that I won't ever get past. The words flung about by Mom? Those are surface arrows. They hurt, but they heal over.

Knox is a soul deep wound. A self-inflicted ruination of my heart. I pushed my heart through a cheese grater and now I have to deal with the fact that all I have left are tiny fragments.

"I'm sorry," I whisper but those words aren't for my mother. They're for Knox.

"You are an ungrateful child. You have always been ungrateful. Spoiled and rebellious."

I laugh at that charge. I've always toed the line for her. After all it had been *she* who told a twelve-year-old to cheat for her brother. But there's no point. I don't need her acceptance anymore. I'm done.

"Did you hear me?" she demands. "You'll not get another cent from me. In fact, when I get off the phone, I'm cancelling your cell phone and removing your name from the charge account."

"You do that, Mom. You do that." I hang up the phone then. There's nothing more to be said between the two of us.

At my desk, I reach inside the second drawer and push aside the tape dispenser, brightly colored paper note flags, and pull out the *Sports Illustrated* magazine. Knox's brother—wearing Knox's blue and gold uniform—stands at the forefront flanked by two college players on either side. Knox is one of those players. He's wearing a silly grin and the red and white of his brother's team.

I trace my finger around his large frame. Out of all the girls he could have chosen, he waited for *me*. He'd said I was special. He treated me like I mattered. He *cared* about me. He...*loved* me. And I threw that back in his face.

I did it to protect him. I believed at the time, and still do, that staying as far away from him as possible until Jack completes this semester successfully—without my help—is the best course of action. Doesn't mean it doesn't hurt like the motherfucking devil.

I hug my arms to my sides. My skin feels clammy and goose pimples dot every exposed surface. Idly, I wonder if I'm in shock. I could use that Xanax cocktail right now.

KNOX

WEEK 10: WARRIORS 7-1

LOOKING AT MYSELF IN THE mirror had never been a problem be-fore. I had pretty simple goals—play hard enough to win games and influence scouts. I cared about my family and my team, and we were almost always on the same page.

This morning, I have a hard time meeting my own gaze in the bath-room mirror.

I don't like what I see.

It's not just the sour taste of losing, but the way I had lost. I should have cleared this thing with Ellie before the game. It's my own damn guilt weighing on my head.

I splash cold water on my face as the door to my apartment opens and closes.

It's not Ty. I drove him to the airport at four in the morning so he could make his six o'clock flight. "It's only one loss," Ty told me before he exited the car.

"It was a bad loss to a bad team," I replied curtly.

"Then you need to dominate in your last four games. Don't let all this other bullshit affect you." He gave me a hard squeeze.

Easy to say; less easy to do. But Ty's right. I have to put this game behind me. One thing that separates the greats from the wannabes is the ability to shake off a loss. To forget how bad you played and show up in the next game like you're the motherfucking champion.

I waited twenty-one years to have sex because I had this ideal in my head, but I'd waited as long for a title. Ty and I never won one in high school. Ironically, our high school team suffered much of the same problems the Warriors had—a weak offense. Ty chose to go to a school that featured a premiere quarterback. I came to Western. Ty's fancy pants quarterback suffered a career ending injury last year, and his chances for a title went out the window.

This year looked like my year. Ace threw the ball well enough to provide a decent cushion on the scoreboard. The defense clicked like a machine with one brain and one heart.

And Ellie showed up. Long legs, hot body, loved football, sarcastic sense of humor, and fucking knew the difference between my brother and me in every picture I showed her.

It was my year…until it wasn't. And the minute things didn't go my way, I folded like a cheap lawn chair.

I don't like that. I've got to make things right with my team and with Ellie. She's scared about something. Last night I replayed every conversation I had with her and the one we'd had right before the dinner with Ty struck me as weird. All that talk about affecting my draft status? It didn't add up for me.

I wipe a hand down my jaw and go out to see what the commotion is.

I find Matty in the kitchen. "Who was that at the door?"

"Jack," he says. "He brought this over."

He tosses my away jersey over the back of a chair. So that's how it'll be? She doesn't even want to talk to me?

I don't like that. Not a bit. I stomp back into the bedroom and pull the phone away from the charging cord. I pull up Ellie's number and stab the call button.

A mechanical voice answers telling me Ellie's number has been disconnected. I check the number and dial again, like the recording instructs. Same thing.

Disconnected.

The hell? She sends Jack over with my jersey. Disconnects her phone so I can't fucking call her?

I squeeze the phone tightly in my hand.

"Why don't you let me take the jersey to the trainers? I'll get it cleaned up before the game next week," Matty offers.

"Good idea, bro," I pick up the jersey and almost throw it to Matty until I catch a whiff of it. It smells like Ellie. Smells like citrus and *girl*, and fuck if my fist doesn't clench around the material and refuse to let go. "On second thought, I'll send it over with the rest of my shit tomorrow."

I have no idea if that's a lie. I just know that right now I'm not ready to get rid of it.

Matty's eyes show a measure of concern that I'll need to address. I force my fingers to loosen around the polyester and toss it over the back of the sofa.

Apparently I'm not ready to eliminate Ellie from my life even though it's easy for her to erase me from hers. What I can do is go about repairing my relationship with my team—starting with Matty.

"I'm sorry about yesterday's game. My head wasn't all there for the first couple quarters and that's not right."

Matty gives me a half smile and small shake of his head. "Masters, you played like a demon and I'll always be proud that you were my teammate." He slaps me on the back. "I'm making pancakes downstairs with the rest of the team. Let's go down before they're all gone."

I make my way down to the first floor where most of the defensive starters have gathered around Hammer's table eating breakfast. I stop near the foot of the table where an empty place waits for me.

"You okay, man?" Hammer asks.

"Other than the fact that I feel like shit for letting you guys down on the field yesterday, I'm okay." The look of relief that passes across each and every one of their faces tells me I'm doing the right thing. I wait for Matty to come tromping down the stairs. He joins us at the table.

Once he takes his seat, I give all the guys an apology. "I'm sorry for last week."

"No, man. That wasn't you." Jessie shakes his head vigorously, making his tight corn rows bounce. "You had that chick in your head. If it's any one's fault it's—"

I cut him off before he says anything too stupid, because Jessie's a good linebacker and his replacement…not so good.

"Was Ellie—" Fuck, it hurts to even say her name. "Was she on the field yesterday? Did she wear number fifty-five while my ass sat on a bench?" Jessie mouths no as I say it. "No. I stunk it up in the first quarter. I stumbled over my own feet like a newborn colt. That was me. I didn't shed blocks. I let a weaker guy push me off the line. And I'm sorry for my play." It's important for my team to see me take responsibility, so when we go back to practice on Monday, they are as focused as ever.

"When we go out on the football field, everyone there has practiced as much as we have. We win because we want it more than they do. We care less about the pain in our shins, our swollen fingers, and our bruised bones than we do about victory. Yesterday I let the vision of our success slip away and the win went with it. So I'm sorry, and I'm here to tell you it won't happen again. From now on, from the first whistle to the last, I will not take a play off. I'll focus on nothing but winning. I make that pledge to you now."

Hammer thuds his hand on the table, slowly, like a war drum.

"Nothing but football from here on out," he concurs.

One by one each player makes their own pledges, and with each word and passing moment, we begin to reknit the spirit of the team. The heaviness that wore me down all last night and this morning begins to subside a little.

"Now you guys need to accept my apology so I don't have to keep running down all the shit things I did yesterday. There's no reason to blame the girl I—" Love. I clear my throat, but the word I can't say hangs out there like my fly is open and my dick's flopping in the wind.

Matty jumps in like a fucking superhero.

"How early is too early for a dick pic?" He waves his phone.

"No dick pics before ten." Hammer scowls.

"Is that what the donut blowjob site says?" I ask, a reluctant smile curving across my face. I sense another epic Hammer and Matty disagreement coming on, and damn if we don't need it.

Hammer nods. "I think I should write for that site. I read other articles and some of them are written by *dudes*." He spits out the last word with disgust.

"Why's that bad?"

"Because these guys aren't using their power for good. They're passing out advice to a bunch of horny women, but it's all about sappy movies and what kind of noises girls should make in bed."

"What's your suggested topics?"

Hammer's face lights up. "I'm thinking things like 'Top ten reasons why swallowing is good for your health' and 'It's okay to watch ESPN and have sex at the same time' and 'A threesome makes for better roommate relationships.' Shit like that."

Heads nod in agreement around the table. "You got scientific proof of that?" I ask with a full-fledged grin. We all know he doesn't.

"Fuck, man, this site talks about using fruit and baked goods during oral. They don't need scientific proof."

I stifle a laugh.

"You're not the hero we asked for, but the one we deserve," Matty pronounces and the two exchange high fives.

The team will be all right. Now I have to fix Ellie and me.

ACE COMES UP TO THE apartment after I take a short run to work off the carbs and fat from breakfast.

"Hey, man. I'm glad you're here. I wanted to apologize for busting your chops earlier in the season. Obviously I have no place to talk." I get him a beer which he takes gratefully. Matty's watching television in the living room.

"It's no big deal. I shouldn't sleep with Stella anyway." He takes a couple long gulps of the beer.

"Hey, if she's the one for you, then I've got no quarrel." If anyone told me that Ellie and I were a bad fit, I'd punch them in the mouth.

He tilts his head back and I wait for him to spill whatever he's here to talk about. We don't mingle a lot—Ace and I—but he's a decent guy, and I think he'll make a good locker room leader when I'm gone. Matty will helm the defense and Ace the offense.

"I'm here about Ellie."

His bald statement catches me off guard. I pause in the middle of reaching for a bottle of Gatorade. "What about her?"

The door of the refrigerator swings shut. Ace rubs the back of his neck. "I'm not supposed to talk about this, but we both know I do a hell of a lot of shit I'm not supposed to do. Coach put a ban on her. Said if he saw her with any member of the Warriors team, her brother would get kicked off. He made some noise about kicking us off too, but I doubt he's serious about that."

We're five games away from possibly getting to the playoffs. No, he's not benching either Ace or me. I rub my chin. "This is about Jack, isn't it?"

Jack didn't play yesterday. Coach said he was inactive at the beginning of the game, and nothing more.

"You know?" Ace leans against the sink. The sounds of the game come from the living room, punctuated by cheers or groans from Matty.

"I suspected he had problems academically. I should've talked to him about it. I meant to, but Ellie asked me not to. So what happened, and how do you know about it, but I don't?" I ask impatiently.

"Jack and Ellie showed up on Tuesday. I was getting my arm iced." Ace had taken a hard hit a week ago. "Ellie cheated for him. Using his access code to sign in and do some worksheets and midterm answers. The only good thing about it is that none of the work was graded."

"For that goddamn poli-sci class," I curse. Ellie always acted evasive about Jack's progress, but I chalked it up to protectiveness. She didn't want me to know he struggled. As if I cared about that. But why freeze me out? "Why did Coach question you? He saw me put Jack on my list."

"Maybe he didn't see what name we'd traded. He only knew we had traded a name. Or, I think he wanted to see if I'd take responsibility for the team."

Ace had stepped up big time.

"Holy shit." I let loose a bitter laugh and squeeze my neck tight in one hand, hoping to relieve the tension that took root there. "Ellie and I talked last week about me declaring early. I fucking bragged to her that I didn't have anything to worry about because I didn't have any skeletons in my closet."

He presses his lips together. "She broke up with you so your statement would stay accurate."

"And I wouldn't let it go. I hounded her, so she had to prove it to me. That's what the business with Ty meant." It's a good thing the glass bottle is in Ace's hand and not mine, because I would've have thrown it at the wall in frustration. Getting angry won't solve anything. Information will. "What else did Coach say?" I demand. "I want to know everything."

Ace outlines Coach's ban, word for word.

"He said immediate family is outside the ban?"

"Yes."

"In front of you and Brian Newsome?"

"What are you thinking?" he asks suspiciously.

I tell him exactly what I'm thinking.

His eyes go wide in shock. "That's crazy, man."

I jut my chin out. "If someone said you could play ten years as an elite NFL quarterback if you would only jump across a cliff as wide as your wing span, would you take that chance even if you could fall and get broken from the attempt?"

"Of course." He scowls.

"Then what I propose to do is the least crazy thing in the world."

He leaves, shaking his head in skepticism. He must not love Stella, because if he did, he'd get it. Completely.

MONDAY

MY FIRST TARGET IS MATTY. If I get him on board, the rest of the defense will follow. Ace will work on the offense. He doesn't understand, but he wants to win.

Matty shoves away from the brick wall of Carter Hall. We've watched Ellie walk to all her classes today in between practice and our own classes. She's got a lighter load now that she's not taking two extra courses for her brother. How'd I miss that before?

Matty digs his hands deeper into the pockets of his winter coat. I can tell by the tenseness of his shoulders he's unhappy. "I don't like seeing you like this, man. You're like a fucking boomerang. She tosses you away, but you keep running back to her."

A captain's relationship with his teammates is an emotional bond. I sawed a notch in it by letting my emotions affect my mental sharpness. We repaired it, but I have to step lightly or run the risk of damaging it again. Like Ellie said the day we first met, winning is about the head and the heart. Not so much the body.

So I'm careful with my response. "When have I ever gotten discouraged by a setback? If you don't sack the quarterback the first time, do you give up?" He shakes his head slowly. "Right, you keep going. It doesn't matter if the guy on the line weighs a hundred pounds more than you and plays like the second coming of Gene Upshaw, that quarterback is yours. You dictate the play at the line of scrimmage even if it takes you the entire game. The whistle hasn't blown for me. This thing between Ellie and me isn't over."

"When will it be over?"

"We will never be over." I don't raise my voice. I don't say the words with any force, but there's nothing I've ever said with more conviction. Matty recognizes that.

He blows out a stream of air that turns white in the November chill. "I don't want to fall for any chick then, if that's what it's like."

It's my turn to look astonished. "You'll endure non-stop training and excruciating post game pain. You don't mind cracked ribs, joint pain, or the bone deep bruises you have to treat with a motherfucking ice bath that's so cold your balls try to climb inside your asshole. You're okay with all of that for one moment of triumph, but you won't suffer a few weeks of heartache to gain a lifetime of real happiness?"

He looks uncertain. "I don't feel that way about anything but football."

I clap him on the shoulder. "That's because you haven't found the right one." I shove his beanie over his eyes and walk toward my own class. Behind me I hear Matty's footsteps.

"You think there is a right one? For me?" His voice sounds halfway between hope and fear.

I grin evilly. "Yeah, and I bet she wrings your balls, Iverson."

He drops his hand to cover his groin, but his face still shows interest. He's on board, which means the rest of the guys will fall in line...except for possibly Jack.

I nab him after film on Tuesday.

"Hey, Campbell. Got a minute?"

He pauses in the hallway outside the film room. The other offensive players brush by us. "Sure." He doesn't sound enthused.

I get straight to the point. "Your sister's number is disconnected. I need her new one."

"No, you don't." He turns to leave.

I grab his arm and lower my voice. "Ace told me about your meeting. I don't want to jeopardize your playing time. I just want to talk to her."

He jerks out of my grasp. "You think I fucking care about playing football more than I care about my sister's wellbeing? Fuck you, Masters."

As he stomps away, I rub a hand through my hair. That didn't go as I had planned. Jack might be someone I need to address later, after all the pieces are in place.

I stake out the apartment and follow Riley to class on Wednesday morning instead of Ellie. "Riles, Ellie's phone is disconnected."

"Are you following me? Because stalking is deemed a violation of the honor code. An honor code violation would mean you can't play on Saturday, and gosh, wouldn't that be terrible?" The expression on her face says that me being suspended would make her day.

"I just want to talk to Ellie," I coax.

"Has your number changed?" she asks.

Confused, I reply, "No."

"Then if she wants to talk to you, she can call you, can't she?"

Perhaps Riley doesn't know about the ban, but before I can clarify things for her, she slips into her class.

What did I say to Matty about not getting down in the face of defeat? Once again my words come back to slap me in the face. On Thursday I go back to Jack who ignores me as much as possible. Given that we play on opposite sides of the ball, watch different film, have different specialty coaches, it's actually pretty easy for him to pretend I don't exist.

That is, it would be easy if I wasn't constantly up in his business.

"What do you want, Masters?" he finally relents on Friday when I sit on the porch of his house and refuse to leave. Ace probably made him come out.

"I want you to give me a chance to explain."

"Fine," he says curtly. He jerks his chin upright to indicate I should start talking.

"I screwed up, both on the field and off of it. I love her. I want to make this right with her." Even after I confess this, he remains grim-faced and unforgiving. I don't need his forgiveness, only his cooperation. I continue, "Ellie's an adult. She needs to be given the chance to make her own decisions. You know she'd be pissed as hell if she thought you were making them for her."

Annoyance flickers in his face when I register that hit. "If she wanted to call you, she would." He repeats the same excuse he gave me earlier that week.

"We both know she isn't going to do anything that jeopardizes your position or mine. She's making a sacrifice for all of us, but she doesn't have to do it alone. Give me a chance," I plead.

He looks in the direction of Ellie's apartment and then back at me, weighing my words against her response. "I'll give you one chance."

I jump up and pound him on the back. "Thanks, man. You won't regret it."

"Don't fuck it up."

"Can I do worse than I already have?" I half joke.

This admission tugs a grin from him. "Probably not."

With Jack on board, Riley follows. We win on Saturday and then the next week and the week after, giving us a record of ten and one. Despite creeping up the polls, the wins don't give me the same high.

I spend the rest of my time skulking around campus, watching Ellie as covertly as possible, between lifting, practice, and games. I stay as careful as possible, because if I get her brother kicked off the team, she'd never forgive me.

Watching her is painful and not the good kind of pain that precedes a wave of endorphins as you break into the next level. It's a sharp, constant pain as if someone took a cleat and peeled back the skin over my chest. Now the wind keeps whipping past all my exposed nerves.

Every time I see her it's a reminder of everything I'm missing. Yes, I missed fucking her crazy in her tiny bed. Or making out with her in all the stairwells and hollows on campus. I missed the warm feeling of her body next to mine. The little gasps she makes when I slide my dick in just the right spot. I was getting good at it, too. But more than that I just miss *her.*

I miss the sight of her bent head as she studies. The way she so precisely copies her notes from her notebook into her computer. How all of her teeth show when she laughs. How her eyes light up when we argue over players and teams. I miss her sharp insight into the game.

It's not easy to watch her without someone noticing me. Even with my winter coat and beanie, there's always another student who calls out my name and wants to congratulate me on how well the Warriors are doing.

But I can't stay away from her. If I see her, I think, then she's still mine. What I told Matty has become the anthem of my life now. Ellie and I will never be done. Our story is a forever one.

I just need to get everyone on that same page with me, including her.

35

ELLIE

WEEK 13: WARRIORS 10-1

"BROOMBALL, ELLIE?" JACK ASKS WITH disapproval when he picks me up from the ice rink where I practice with my new intramural squad. It's mostly the Horny Toad softball team with a few others.

"I played eight weeks of softball and came away with only a skinned knee," I remind him. He's still worried I'll get hurt, but nothing could be more painful than losing Knox. I didn't realize I'd feel this way, like a hollowed out tube of a person. I'm skin and bones, but underneath it's one big tumbleweed blowing around an empty wasteland.

He grunts his disagreement, but doesn't say another word about it. Smart, because I'm not changing my mind.

It's been three weeks since the loss. Three more games and three more wins. Their record stands now at ten and one, with one regular season game left. As long as they win on Saturday, they'll play for the conference championship. The Warriors have moved up the charts to number six. Is it bad to hope for the other teams to lose? Maybe, but I cheer for it anyway.

Things worked out okay. Jack is back playing. I've barely seen him because he's spent so much time re-doing the worksheet answers. The professor let him do an oral presentation, but the university is making him take a course over winter break and then during the summer. He's not thrilled about it.

I got a job waiting tables at Buster's, and they all love me because I volunteered to work double shifts over Thanksgiving. I have no plans to go home. I'm not even sure I'm welcome at home.

I'm not making much money beyond rent, and I can see that if I want to finish my degree, I will need a second job. But having money of my own makes me feel independent in a way I hadn't realized I needed.

I miss Knox every day. Sometimes I imagine I see him out of the corner of my eye, but when I turn it's another student. It's hard to watch the Warriors, but I can't keep away. Riley refuses to watch with me. She uses her business as an excuse, but I think she's mad at Knox and Jack.

I don't blame Knox at all. But Riley said that Knox's test was stupid, and he either loves me or he doesn't. I try to tell her it wasn't only the fact I had intentionally mistaken Ty for Knox, but the things I'd said to him afterward and how I'd almost ruined their season.

She steadfastly disagrees, which makes me love her all the more. She's wrong, but she's on my side. I found a teammate in the person I least expected.

I miss the guys. Even the Horny Toads all looked at me with sad eyes during the last game, when the stands were nearly empty. No more Warriors to cheer us on. A figure stood two fields away. I pretended it was Knox, but we still lost.

A number of players on the softball team play broomball during the winter, so I signed up for the Horny Toads broomball team. Ryan tells me the Horny Toads play worse broomball than softball. Our team doesn't win a lot, but we have fun playing the game. I need a little fun in my life.

I'm existing. Some days it's hard to get up in the morning, but at some point, the piercing pain will fade. It's got to, because I can't live my entire life feeling like I'm only half a person.

"Why are you wearing your suit, by the way? Is there a team event I don't know about?" I straighten the collar on his tailored suit.

"Yeah, special team event. How'd your meeting with Financial Aid go? You okay next semester?" He maneuvers the Jeep out of the parking lot and onto the road.

I try to keep my eyes away from Union Stadium, two blocks from the ice rink. Not that Knox is there, but it reminds me of him and that hurts.

"It's not great news." I look down at my cheap disposable phone. "I talked to Financial Aid and they said without Mom or Dad co-signing a loan, I probably won't get enough to cover the full cost of tuition. And since Western is out of state for us and I have to pay the full ride, waiting tables won't cut it."

"Can I co-sign for you?"

"No. You have the same sketchy credit situation I have."

He squeezes the steering wheel tight in frustration. "When I'm out of school, I'll help you pay for college."

"Jack, I can take care of myself. I've got an associate's degree. I can get a job somewhere, and I'm three semesters from getting a bachelor's degree. I can still write. The Agrippa Learning Center plans to submit my grant almost unchanged, and if they get it, I'll have a great resume builder. I just need you to be my brother." I reach over and squeeze his hand.

"Do you love Masters? Like forever love him?"

I choke on my saliva. "Where did that come from?"

"I just need to know."

Well, this is awkward. "What does it matter?"

"It just does," he insists.

"Fine. Yes, I do." There's no point in lying about. I'm not exactly Miss Happy Pants every time Jack sees me. "But it doesn't matter, because in a few months he'll be drafted, and he'll meet some beautiful actress or model, and he'll forget he ever met me."

Jack ignores my whiny comments. "No doubts about him. You okay with the way he treated you?"

"What way did he treat me? I had to pretty much assault his brother to get Knox to believe I didn't want to see him." I glower at Jack for his unfair accusations.

"The ban by Coach was shitty. Completely unnecessary." Jack pulls the vehicle into the athletic center parking lot.

"Did you forget something?" I peer out of the tinted windows.

"Sort of. Sit tight." He climbs out, but instead of running inside, he rounds the front bumper to my side. "Come on."

"I don't think I should be here. I'm under a ban, remember?" I look around for signs of Coach Lowe. I'm with Jack, but there could be random Warrior players around. I don't want to get anyone in trouble.

"I know, but we'll be quick. I promise."

"I don't know, Jack."

But Jack won't be denied. He reaches in, unbuckles my seat belt, and lifts me out. "Hold your horses! I'm coming," I grumble and zip up my jacket.

My boots make a crunching noise in the snow as we hurry indoors. We walk down one hallway and then another until we reach the door labeled "Practice Facility." I jerk out of his grasp. "Jack, I can't go in there."

He turns and grips my shoulder. "Do you trust me?"

"Yes." But now that he asks me, I'm wondering if I should.

"Then come on."

It's because of the urgency of his voice that I allow him to pull me inside. I gasp because it isn't empty. A bunch of his teammates are there, all dressed up in their away suits. Riley is there with a big garbage bag in her hands.

Knox stands with two older people, who look suspiciously like his parents from the photos I've seen.

And…a woman wearing a judge's robe.

"What's going on?" I must have said that out loud. "Is someone from the team getting married?"

I try to remember who was dating seriously enough to get married, and why I would even get invited to the wedding.

Knox breaks away from his parents and comes over to grip my hands. "You, if you'll have me."

"What?" I nearly shout.

"Come on, let's go out in the hall." He drags me back to the doorway where Jack and I entered. I feel a million curious stares at my back, and am intensely grateful when the door slams shut.

Under the bright fluorescent lights, I see darkness under his eyes. A slight bruising, as if someone slapped him or he hasn't slept well. Perhaps he's partied late. He certainly has good reason to. My throat begins to ache. Why has he come here? It's tortuous to see him in person. It's one thing to watch him on the television. There's something about the pads, helmet, and uniform that provides a distance. I can see him as just Knox Masters, the really great football player, instead of Knox Masters, someone who whispered he loved me and took me to heaven every night we stayed together.

Here, in the flesh, with his beautiful face looking at me intently, all I can remember is that at one time I could lay my hands on his shoulders, crawl into his lap, and tug his head down to kiss him. It's both painful and glorious to stand this close to him, but not touch him as if he's mine.

"Ellie, I know about Jack, the ban, all of it."

My heart stops and then stutters to life again with a roar of adrenaline as his fingers curl around my cheek. The calluses scratch against my skin in that rough, familiar way of his.

"Then why am I here?"

"The ban is for anyone but family members. We get married and the ban is solved. I mean, yes, you can't go to the games, but you never did anyway. There are only two games left before the playoffs: the last regular season game and then the conference title game. After we win the national championship, I'm announcing my eligibility, and once that's done I won't be a student athlete anymore. You can come to my pro games."

He says they're going to win like it's a foregone conclusion. The rest of his words don't make any sense, at least not to me. "Wh-what?"

"She doesn't believe you." Jack pokes his head out the door. "Our parents have spent her whole life convincing her that she's second class. That she's not valuable because she doesn't wear pads and she doesn't have a penis. She's never had anyone want her that way. She's waiting for the other shoe to drop."

I gape at Jack. He gives me a sad smile.

Knox takes my shoulders. "The only other shoe I've got has a hell of a lot of love. Some horniness, too. I love you, Eliot, and I want you to be my wife."

My eyes start to blur, but it looks like he's unbuttoning his coat and getting down on one knee.

"I feel like I was born knowing I should be a football player. The moment I touched the pigskin, the universe shifted into its rightful place. I felt that very same way when I saw you sitting on the top of Union Stadium all those months ago. It's why you were my first."

He thumps his hand against his heart. "I love football, but I love you more. None of this the wins, the glory, the triumphs—will taste as sweet without you. Will you, Eliot Anne Campbell, be my wife?"

He picks up my limp hand and slides a beautiful diamond on my finger. It's an antique setting with a gorgeous center stone, surrounded by filigree in white gold and diamonds. The whole thing is blindingly beautiful.

I can't believe this is happening to me. Nothing this good has ever happened in my life. I don't have any proper response in my head. It's a whirling, confused muddle. This gorgeous man is proposing to me. He wants to pledge in front of all of his friends and family that he wants me, the most imperfect of beings, as his forever.

I have only one answer I can give him. The only answer he deserves.

My hand goes to my throat as I whisper a shaky, watery, "Yes."

Knox jumps to his feet. "All right, then. Let's get you dressed."

Not the response I thought I'd get. Maybe a kiss? A hug? But instead, Riley rushes through the door, and from the garbage bag she pulls out a beautiful ivory gown—no, it's a skirt. Made with a mountain of tulle.

"What is this?" I cover my mouth. The tears that I'd fought back start to fall. Jack gets flustered, but Riley grins. Knox laughs outright.

"Do you love it?" Riley asks with a tinge of apprehension.

"Of course, I do." I pull her into my arms and hug her tight. "You are my best friend, aren't you, Riley?"

"Yup. We're sisters of the heart." She gets teary, too.

I hug her, dwarfing her tiny body in my embrace. She rushes me down the hallway into a training room where I shed my jeans for her frothy creation. Her bag produces a tight white cashmere sweater with a scoop neck banded in pearls and tiny cap sleeves.

"The waistband is satin," she explains, and in the back she ties it into a huge bow.

It looks like a dream. She even produces a veil. Together we fix my makeup. Riley brought everything I'd need, even a pair of white heels.

"How did you do this?" I ask, fingering the white netting.

"It didn't take that long. And since it's just a skirt, I could make it somewhat adjustable." She pulls at the skirt and veil to get it just right.

"What about a marriage certificate?" I fret. "Is this even legal?"

"You'll sign that in front of the lady with judge's robes. She's apparently a real judge that Hammer's mom knows." Riley grabs me by the shoulders. "Are you sure about this? Because I'm sure that there are other ways for you to pay for college. And the football season is almost over. Knox and you can be together when it's over."

This is why Jack asked me all those questions in the car. He thinks that marrying Knox will get me back into school, but I'd never marry anyone just for that reason.

"I love him, Riles. My heart beats for him, and when he's not with me, I'm not complete. It's reckless, but if he wants me, then I'd be a fool not to take this chance with him."

It's not even a chance. The way he looks at me with all that love and certainty, it's about the least risky act I'll take my entire life.

A hallway door bangs open and we both jump. Riley and I exchange nervous looks. Is that the coach? Someone else who could get us all in trouble? We peer out of the glass in the door and I see my father.

At first, my heart flutters with excitement. He's here to give me away. But then as he gets closer I realize he's not wearing a suit, but instead slacks and a sweater. My dad's a businessman. He knows what to wear to every occasion. Plus, there's the pissed off look on his face that doesn't match a *I'm happy you're getting married* expression.

I pull open the door and step out. He stops a few feet away from me, his brown shoes nearly brushing the edge of my voluminous skirt.

"Hi, Dad." I hate that my voice trembles as if I'm a scared little five-year-old.

"I heard about this nonsense from your mother and have come to put a stop to it. I know the full details of your punishment. You are to stay away from the team. If you do not, your brother could suffer severe consequences."

He grabs my arm to drag me away.

I jerk out of his grasp. "No, you're wrong. The exact terms—"

He throws up a hand. "I don't need to hear your bullshit. You're coming with me."

The door to the practice facility opens and closes. "Sir, please shut up and sit down, or get the hell out."

"Knox Masters." My father looks the dark-suited figure up and down with disdain. "You're welcome to fuck my daughter when it doesn't jeopardize my son's play on the field."

"It's not Knox. It's his brother, Kintyre," I say.

Ty smiles at me and straightens his black tie. "It's the tie, isn't it?"

Knox has a blue one on—Warrior colors.

"I just know, Ty. You can't pull those tricks on me."

"You don't know how happy I am that I can't." He leans in and gives me a soft kiss, then offers his arm to Riley. "May I walk you down the aisle?"

She grabs his arm, but turns back to give me a worried glance. When Jack appears, she gives a sigh of relief.

Jack takes one look at our dad and charges out. "What the hell are you doing here? You told me you wouldn't come if the commissioner himself showed up."

I notice for the first time that Jack stands three inches taller than Dad, and that Dad looks…small and weak.

"I thought you'd stop this farce, but I got a phone call from Masters' parents begging me to attend, and that I would regret not seeing my only daughter get married. What I'll regret is not saving you from your sister and her idiocy." He straightens the bottom of his sweater. "I came to put an end to this disaster."

"It's not a disaster." Jack shakes his head in disgust. "You're the disaster. Get out. Neither of us wants anything to do with you." Jack turns to me and puts his arm around my shoulders. "Come on, Ellie. Let's finalize the new team. I think you made a good decision with your draft pick."

I let him draw me away, because in front of me waits my new life. Behind us, I hear our dad sputtering, but when we get through the practice facility door, a line of broad shoulders blocks the doors. No one else will come in.

Knox's mother comes forward. Jack stops in front of her and steps to the side. Mrs. Masters lifts a strand of pearls and hooks them around my bare neck. "Something borrowed."

I have to swallow rapidly to keep from crying. "Thank you, Mrs. Masters."

"Nicole, my dear. It's Nicole." She pats my cheek. "Or Mom."

Then she steps away and Jack takes her place again. He draws me forward to stand next to Knox at the fifty yard line. His teammates draw close.

"I'm not supposed to have contact with the football team," I hiss.

"There's no one here but your family. And your family-to-be. Amirite?" Knox asks.

"I don't see anyone else," Jack answers. The two of them look into the crowd of navy and black suits who all turn and look behind them.

Jack turns back and shrugs. "No one here but family."

The judge marries us. It's all a blur for me. I say the words "I do" when prompted, but I mostly remember Knox's strong hands holding me up the entire time.

36

ELLIE

AFTER THE VOWS, THE HUGGING, the backslapping, Knox hustles me outside and half carries, half drags me toward his SUV. He nearly shoves me into the passenger seat and then races around to his side of the vehicle. Climbing in, he locks the doors, starts the engine and then turns to me.

His hand comes up to cradle my skull, tilting my head toward his. "I've missed you, baby."

"I missed you, too." There's no point in pretending I don't still love him.

He inhales deeply, his eyes shuttering closed for a second before popping open again. A half smile appears on his lips. "Three weeks seems like three years, doesn't it?"

"It's been endless," I admit.

"Baby, I am so sorry."

"What are you sorry for?" I jerk back in surprise, but Knox pulls me toward him, only to have my progress stopped by the console between us.

He curses and turns to put the SUV in reverse. "I need to get you out of this car. These victories, the past weeks…" He takes his eyes off the road for a minute to glance at me, and I see real anguish there. "None of it will be right until you've forgiven me and I get to hold you again."

A sob lodges in my throat. I swallow heavily to drive it away, but it makes my voice hoarse when I reply. "I'm so sorry I lied to you about Jack. I'm sorry I kissed your brother. I'm sorry that I placed your team in jeopardy with my actions." I cover my eyes. "If anyone needs forgiveness, it's me."

Knox barks out an abrupt laugh. "And I didn't put you through the wringer with my stupid fucking test?"

"It wasn't stupid," I cry.

He curses again. "I wish we weren't in this fucking car, because I need to hold you right now."

"Where are we going?" I use the veil to wipe my tears. I hope mascara comes off tulle.

"Hotel." He grins. "Gift from my parents."

"I can't believe they let you get married."

He drapes an arm across the back of my seat and tangles his fingers in my hair. "We're adults. I've always known what I wanted since I came out of the womb. They knew better than to argue."

I suppose that's right. He's a bulldozer, forging forward to take what he wants. And somehow he wants me. "I love you, too," I whisper.

His hand tightens in my hair and he makes a sharp right into a parking lot of a strip mall that's apparently closed for business on Sundays, because the lot is empty. In one swift movement, he has the parking brake on and my seatbelt is off. He hauls me over the console and into his lap. It's a tight, uncomfortable fit. The steering wheel digs into my side. My legs dangle awkwardly over the console. Knox's seat belt hadn't fully retracted in his haste, and it pokes into my right butt cheek.

But I've never felt better.

I allow my hands to roam over his gorgeous face and into his hair. It's getting long enough to brush the collar of his suit coat. I take one deep breath after the other, filling my lungs with his scent.

My tears start falling.

"No, no, please stop," Knox says in a panic. "What can I do?"

His hands try to brush away my tears and the sweetness of the gesture only turns up the waterworks higher. I don't make any effort to stop them or him.

"These are happy tears," I inform him gladly. "I didn't think I'd ever have the chance to touch you again." I take his hands, placing them over my sweater covered breasts. Instinctively, his palms curl around the round flesh. His thumbs graze my sensitive tips. "You feel so good," I moan. "Never stop touching me.

"I won't," he swears. "I won't ever stop."

He curls forward, closing the small distance between us. His mouth meets mine with so much tender love I explode in bliss. He tastes minty and male and so wonderfully familiar. His tongue snakes inside to rub against the roof of my mouth, along the ridges, setting off a riot within my taste buds. He's the best thing on the menu, the only flavor that will ever appease my growing hunger.

I run my hands freely underneath his suit coat. We have a mountain of clothes between us and I'm desperate to get them off. I want that the hair-roughened skin against my more delicate frame. I want to run my tongue over those hard muscles and take the hardest, velvety part of him into my mouth, into my body, into me.

"We need a bed," I whisper throatily against his mouth.

He groans and tightens his hands around my breasts one more time before lifting me back onto my side of the vehicle. With exquisite care, he reaches over and buckles me in. Satisfied that I'm secured, he reaches a hand up to my face and brushes my hair back. "I love you, Eliot Masters. I still love you."

Water drips down my face. "If you want me to stop crying, you can't say those things to me." I clutch at his hand and presses waterlogged kisses into his palm.

He releases a small huff of laughter. "I guess you'll cry a lot then."

"Will you cry if I tell you I love you back?" I nuzzle my cheek into his hand.

"Maybe. Why don't you give it a try?" The evenness of his voice is an effort.

"I love you."

He doesn't cry, but his eyes soften toward me and love shines through; better than tears in my opinion.

Knox puts the vehicle in gear and heads downtown to the hotel. We get there, but I don't remember the trip. All I know is that I can touch him again, feel him, breathe him in.

That he's mine again…and forever.

Sacked

"I FEEL…DISCOMBOBULATED," I ADMIT AS we wait for the hotel elevator. People stare at us. I suppose we do look a sight. My veil is askew and Knox's jacket drapes over my shoulders.

"I told Matty that's how I felt. Thick headed and muddled. We concluded it's how quarterbacks must feel when they're sacked." He ushers me onto the elevator.

"So we've gotten sacked by love?" I snort. It's corny but sweet, and totally Knox. At the core, he's a romantic. The man saved himself for the *right* girl and somehow, *I'm* her. All my life, I've never been anything but Jack's sister. To Knox, I'm the person he waited for his entire life.

"Yeah, but we're never saying that shit again."

I hide a smile. At least now I have something to torment him and Matty with. Sacked by love! How hilarious. The elevator stops at the fourth floor and Knox leads me to our room.

My humor turns quickly to something else, because the minute the door of the hotel room closes, Knox has me up against the door. His hands shove my jacket off. His mouth fastens to mine. We each toe our shoes off and leave them haphazardly in the entryway. His jacket gets tossed onto the sofa as we pass by it.

He pulls me toward the bedroom, not once lifting his head. We kiss like the world will end tomorrow. Like we haven't seen each other in years. Like he's a soldier returning from an endless deployment.

We kiss like we love each other and don't know how to express it in words, only in touch. His tongue works against mine in ways both fevered and reverent. I can't imagine kissing another man. I don't want to. This taste, this touch, this tenderness is all I will ever want or need.

In the bedroom, we tug at each other's clothes. Our mouths separate so we can get rid of his suit coat.

"Nice." Knox waggles his eyebrows as my skirt comes off with one tug of the bow. We both pull off my sweater and bra until I'm in nothing but a pair of pink panties.

He pushes me onto the bed. "I've missed your hot body," he says before lowering his head to pay homage to one very erect nipple. The other nipple gets plucked and tugged by his left hand while his right makes quick work of the buttons on his shirt.

We both groan when his hand finds its way between my legs.

"I love how wet you get for me," he mutters against my breast. "Wet and hot." He sinks one finger inside me and I nearly expire right there. "Wet and hot and *tight*."

"It's been so long." *Three weeks has been three years*, he'd said. Right on the money.

"Yes," he starts to dip lower, but I grab his shoulders.

"What is it? That time of month?" He looks anguished and I have to stifle a laugh.

"No. I need you inside me. Now. Because it's been so long."

He understands. I see it in his eyes, the way they darken and become hungry. Well, hung*rier*.

He pushes to his feet. As his hands go to his waist, I suck in my lower lip in excitement. He's so beautiful and I pause to take it in. Everything about his frame speaks of power and strength, from the width of his shoulders to the massive span of his arms. But there's vulnerability, too, in the surprisingly narrow waist, accented by the hard obliques, and centered by the slabs of rectangular muscles outlining the dark hair arrowing down to the heavy shaft that bobs eagerly in the air as Knox steps out of his pants. He shrugs off his shirt, removes his socks, and then stands motionless before me.

I run my eyes over every inch of him once, and then do it again. It's hard to believe that all this goodness is mine.

"Like what you see?" he mocks gently.

"Yes, very much so."

"My turn," he says and reaches for me. I lie back and let him remove my panties. He reaches between my legs and strokes me lightly, teasing me even after I told him I could not wait. "You're fucking gorgeous, Ellie. Fucking gorgeous."

He lowers himself between my legs and runs his big hands along my ankles to my knees, then to my inner thighs, until his thumbs meet at my sex.

"You're so pretty down here. Pink and wet." He leans forward and runs the flat of his tongue from my clit to my pucker and back again. "And you taste like a fucking dream."

"Please, Knox." I'm not too proud to beg. "I need you."

His fingers tangle in my curls as he continues to lap between my legs as if I'm not almost dying for the want of him. I dig my fingers into his hair and tug. He pushes his shoulders between my legs, spreading me out in an intensely vulnerable way.

"I want you to come on my tongue, Ellie." His lips move against my skin and even that contact is so erotic I lift my hips to seek out more. "Every night we've been apart, I dreamt of you. I had your taste in my mouth and your scent in my lungs, but it would disappear when I woke. Now that I have you…" He pauses to curl his tongue around that throbbing bit of flesh at the top of my sex. "I want to eat you until I coat my throat with you."

Above him, I shudder in full surrender. His words are nearly as erotic as his touch. I give myself to him, to his clever fingers and his adventurous tongue. He works me over for what seems like hours, one languorous caress after another, until I come in a flood, my toes curling into the air and my thighs trembling against his shoulders.

He surges upward then, his mouth glistening with the evidence of my orgasm. Between his legs his shaft hangs heavy, and the tip of it is wet with his own excitement.

I reach for him and wrap my fingers around that stiff cock. He allows me to guide him to my center. My release has left me swollen, and despite the wetness he coaxed from me, I'm tight around his generous girth.

His lips pull back in a hiss as I suck him in slowly. He lets me set the pace this time, and I treat him with the same studied deliberateness he inflicted on me.

"Aww, fuck, baby," he rasps out. "You feel so good. So good."

He falls forward, bracing both arms next to my head. The languid slide of his body against mine is exquisite. And because I'm not afraid this is the last time I'll ever have him, I take my time reacquainting myself with his very perfect physique.

Each push forward and each retreat is slow and deliberate so that every tiny movement of his shaft inside me registers. The head drags against the softest, most sensitive tissue, eking out more pleasure than I think possible.

I rub my heels against his calves, the wiry hair scratching against the soles of my feet. His shoulders tense under my hands and his biceps flex with each measured thrust inside my body.

"I love you." I turn and press my mouth against one of those flexing muscles. "I love you," I repeat. I say the words again and again, punctuated by kisses. He growls above me, the cage of his arms shaking with his effort to stave off his own orgasm.

But he's a world-class athlete, and he uses whatever mind over matter voodoo that lets him forget pain during a game to hold off the fire that licks over his body. He employs his strength and unmatchable endurance to work me into an utterly mindless frenzy, where all I know is sensation, pleasure, and never-ending joy.

His head dips to sip at my mouth. His tongue tastes my happiness and swallows my moans of delight. With hardly a break in rhythm, he pulls out and turns me over until I rest on my knees.

When he slides back in, a harsh groan breaks the silence, punctuated only by our wracked and uneven breathing.

His hand curves over my bottom, lifting me off my knees until all my weight rests on my elbows. He takes me then, with furious strokes. His need has overwhelmed him, to my great enjoyment. I push back with all the strength I have in me, but his hands clamp on my hips, holding me still as he hammers inside me.

I give myself over to his dominance. His wildness feeds my own until I barely know where he ends and I begin. We are one, infused with the same euphoria, possessed by the same need, bound together by the same love.

He releases one hip and dips between my legs to pluck at my clit until I explode around him.

"Yes, that's it." His voice cracks, loaded down by his hunger. "Come for me."

I do. I convulse around him, hugging his shaft with tiny tremors until I feel his release inside me, filling me, completing me. I give myself to feeling and let it carry me away until all I know is him.

I barely register Knox pulling out, the warm wet of him on my thighs. He covers me with a blanket and then pads lightly to the bathroom. I hear a toilet flushing and then running water. I should clean up, but I'm too exhausted, too replete.

He returns and does it for me. My eyes flick open to see him running a dampened towel between my legs. He gives me a tender smile and leans down to kiss the freshly washed skin. From a suitcase that I didn't notice before resting against the wall, he pulls out a new pair of panties and slides it up my legs. I raise my butt.

"You kept all my T-shirts?" he asks with a sly grin. He must have helped pack my things.

"Of course." If I had energy, I'd roll my eyes.

He chuckles low and I hug myself at the happy sound. Knox pulls back the covers and climbs in, taking up the position against the wall. I burrow into him, pushing my butt into his groin and laying my head on his biceps.

"Hammer's submitting an article to an online woman's magazine about how sperm is good for a woman's body. Think it'll be accepted?" His hand strokes leisurely down my side.

"I'm scared for womankind," I answer sleepily.

"But kind of curious?" He presses a kiss against the crown of my head.

"Scared." But yeah, kind of curious. I drift off to sleep, full of contentment.

37

KNOX

THE ATMOSPHERE IN THE LOCKER room consists of subdued hope. We're one game away from ending the season with only one loss. We win today and we're in the conference championships which is one step closer to our goal of a National Championship.

Coach has called reporters, analysts, and other coaches, making the case that we belong in the playoffs. The selection committee isn't bound by the polls that have us ranked seven. They make their own decisions. Today we give the selection committee every reason to place us in the top four.

Beneath the dry fit T-shirt, the pads, and the jersey, my heart beats double time.

I get up on a bench and wait for Matty to pull his headphones out. For Hammer to stop texting. For Ace to gather up the offense.

When the room falls silent, I raise my helmet above my head. "We started this season with one goal—for a chance to play for a title. That goal still exists. For some, this is the last home game we play."

Somewhere in the crowd I hear a gasp. Not everyone knows I planned to declare. It'll be out there soon enough, but what's said in the locker room stays here.

"We'll never again step foot on Union Field wearing the Warrior's uniform. Our locker will hold someone else's uniform. Our time here will become a memory." I tap my helmet against my head.

The team looks at me with rapt attention.

I don't say anything for a few moments because I need to take one—one last time. Even if we win today, this might be the last time I wear the gold and blue. It's been a crazy, exhilarating, mind blowing, heart aching, unforgettable three years. I'm not leaving without a fight. I'm ready to lay everything I have out on that field.

"Every second on that field, we have a choice. We can play together as one unit, one machine, one heart. If we do that, no matter the outcome, we will have met our goal. Today I plan to play as if I will never get to play again. If I am still standing at the end of the game, I have not tried hard enough. Men!" I call sharply. "This is my heart. My will. My desire."

I thump my hand across my chest twice in rapid succession. Matty follows. So does Hammer, then Ace, and then the entire locker room fills with the percussive beat of joined will. To that beat, I shout: "No one can defeat us if we believe. You have the heart of a Warrior?"

"Yes!"

"The pride of a Warrior?"

"Yes!"

Matty quickens the pace. The rest follow.

"The will of a Warrior?"

"Yes!"

The din of our fists against our hearts is overwhelming. I have to scream to be heard. "Then we will fight as Warriors. We will bleed as Warriors. We will win as Warriors."

I jump down and grab Ace. We put our heads together and the team of ninety plus men gather at our backs. We move as one. One giant mass of flesh, muscle, and desire.

"Fight! Bleed! Win! Fight! Bleed! Win! Fight! Bleed! Win!" The team roars its promise. Someone opens the doors to the tunnel and we burst out, running like we're chased by bulls. No, we're chasing the bulls. We're the meanest, nastiest, toughest fucks on the planet, and today is our time.

The Lions win the coin toss and elect to receive. They want their number-two-ranked offense in the country on the field first. Fine. I jam my helmet down. I want to introduce Mr. Heisman to the turf as soon as possible. He'll learn the only thing he'll see today will be my number in his face.

It goes our way from the beginning. We win the snap and defer. The Lions start off on the twenty. I line up across from the left guard.

"You might want to kneel down now, because you're about to spend a lot of time on your back," I inform the NFL-bound offensive lineman.

He snorts. "Sure, I am, jack wagon. You'll be using your towel to dry those tears after we light you up."

"Not this year."

I hit him hard, pushing him aside, and run hard after the quarter-back. He must feel my footsteps because he releases early and the pass is incomplete. I slap him lightly on the helmet before helping him to his feet.

"I hope you ate your Wheaties today, because you're about to have a workout."

The Heisman trophy candidate glares at me as I run back to my side of the field.

I jaw all day. To the nose tackle, I ask, "Did you dress more than three deep at the tackle position? Because I'm going to wear you and your backup down to nubs by the end of the first quarter."

"You should stay down, Marshall," I tell the strong side linebacker. "It'll save you some pain."

In the fourth quarter, I feel like I haven't played a down. I slap Hammer's ass hard. "We making good television today, Hammer?"

He laughs like a hyena.

At the end of the game, after the press has left, I'm drenched in Gatorade and sweat, standing on top of the bench. The faces around me are wreathed with unadulterated joy.

It wasn't perfect, but it was enough. We'd beaten the number five ranked team in the country. That means we should take their place in the rankings tomorrow. One short of what we'd need to make the playoffs.

I stand for a moment and look into the stands shrouded in royal blue Warrior gear. Others do the same—seniors who won't go to the next level. Guys who played for four years, but will move on to be businessmen, doctors, lawyers. No matter where they go in their lives, they'll always be able to say that they played for one of the best college teams in the country. I have no doubt that if you asked every one of them if their broken fingers, black eyes, bruised bodies were worth it, they'd snap out a yes faster than you could blink.

Because there is nothing like this game. What had Ellie said? The temple built to the reverence of physical perfection? She's right and she's wrong. It's a place that celebrates sacrifice as much as it celebrates winning.

Ellie's sacrificed so much for the game. For her brother. For us. I wish she could be here. I tilt my head and pretend she's sitting in the very top.

Best seats in the house.

"Miss you, baby," I say into the cool afternoon air. I kiss my helmet and raise it up for her. And then turn to walk toward the tunnel.

A print journalist from the local paper catches me before I can make my way off the field. "There are rumors that you plan to declare. Is this your last home game?"

Behind the journalist stands the team PR lady. She glares at me as if she knows I'd rather run away than do this.

I muster up a smile and bend down to reach the microphone. "This is the last home game this year," I answer carefully, not letting on that this is a bittersweet win. "Being a Warrior is a special opportunity and I'm grateful to be part of the team."

"Do you deserve the playoffs despite the one loss earlier in the season?"

"Yes, we deserve the playoffs." That's reckless, shit talking, bulletin board type of language, that will probably get mangled into something like Knox Masters guarantees a win and will be blasted all over social media. But I believe it 100%.

"Are you saying you're better than the five other teams in front of you?"

"I'm saying we belong in the playoffs. That's all."

"There are rumors of locker room problems. Did that distract you?"

"Did it look like I was distracted today?" I look over her head at Coach, who gives me a nod that I can go. I trot out the lines that we players practice as a joke. "I'm glad I can be part of the Warriors and have the opportunity to play for a national title with the best guys in the world."

I raise my helmet in the air and holler. The guys holler back, and soon it's too loud for questions.

We run off the field, into the locker room where there's more press, more boosters, family members. I hug everyone. Slap a dozen asses. Take a bath in even more Gatorade.

There's no Ellie, but I call her. I pick up my phone and head straight for the showers.

"You played so great, babe!" she squeals. "I particularly liked the first quarter sack. You stood over the quarterback for a while. What did you say?"

I told him he should get used to the turf. "I complimented him on how pretty he looked lying down."

She snorts. "Jesus. You're asking for it."

"I can't wait to come home, wife."

She giggles. "I can't wait to celebrate."

Well, hot damn.

I make her do all the work because my poor body feels sore even after the ice bath. Then we get up and watch the rest of the games. Jack, Riley, me, and Ellie sit in her living room, glued to the television.

We watch in growing elation as the number-two-ranked team in the country falls apart before our eyes. The quarterback loses a fumble on the twenty. On the ensuing punt, the tight end gets a personal foul and the opposing team starts on the forty five.

The twenty point underdogs march down the field, punch the ball in, and the score is fourteen-zero. The phone rings.

"You watching this?" Matty yells. I can hear cheers of jubilation in the background.

"It's the first quarter, bro." I try to play the voice of reason. Jack and I exchange guardedly hopeful looks. Neither of us say anything out loud because we don't want to jinx it.

The second quarter goes about as well for the favored team as the first quarter, and they go in losing twenty-one zero at the half. By the fourth quarter, the team tries to make a run, but it's too little, too late.

"What does it mean?" Riley cries. My phone is blowing up, but Ellie answers for me.

"A selection committee of sorts decides who is in the playoffs. Ever since the loss four weeks ago, the Warriors have dominated. Today, the top ranked team lost to an unranked one, and by a big margin." She gestures toward the television. "The rest of top-rated teams looked hamstrung and confused today."

"When will we know?" Riley leans forward eagerly.

"Tomorrow," Ellie answers. "The slate will be set tomorrow."

I'm glad that this is the one day of the season they don't make us wait until Tuesday for the rankings. Ellie's correct. The final four BCS teams will be announced on Sunday, just one day away.

I don't know if Riley or Jack sleep at all. I can't. I keep waking Ellie for sex because I've got so much nervous energy. Around dawn, she kicks me out.

"Go run. I cannot have your dick inside me one more time."

"I could lick you," I say hopefully.

She slams a pillow over her head. "Seriously, I think another orgasm would feel painful."

Reluctantly, I leave her and go run. I'm not even tired after ten miles, so I go to the weight room. I'm not the only one there. Matty's doing deadlifts. I go over to spot him.

"The wait is fucking excruciating."

"I know it."

Grimly, he gestures for me to put another plate on the bar. "I'm hoping to lift myself into a stupor. Don't stop me until the news comes out."

I go to the bench press and hope I can do the same. After a couple of hours, the strength coach makes us leave. Matty and I go back to the house and play Madden with the boys. If I go home to Ellie, I'm afraid I'll attack her, and then I'll be divorced before the playoffs start.

Around supper time, the phone rings again.

"You gonna answer it?" Matty demands.

Part of me doesn't want to. As long as I don't know there's still hope. But then I give myself a head slap and pick up my phone.

"I sent you a text. Read it," Coach says and hangs up.

I pull up the messages. It's a message from the BCS committee. I scan it. Then read it again. Then read it for a third time. I get up, walk into the kitchen, and put my phone in the far corner. Everyone goes silent. Matty's hand freezes halfway between the Dorito bag and his mouth.

"You have to stop eating that shit food, Matty boy, because the Western State Warriors are fucking fourth seed."

His hand opens and chips spill onto the floor. I couldn't care less.

"You're shitting me?"

"No."

"Fuck, yes!" He punches the air. Someone else flips the coffee table over. In less than five minutes, chips, beer, soda, and furniture are all strewn about the apartment as the guys hug, back slap, and throw shit around in unrestrained rapture. My smile stretches wide as a football field.

We are in.

ELLIE

POST GAME: WARRIORS 13-1

AT THE KNOCK ON THE door, I smooth back my hair back and straighten Knox's home jersey. The Warriors were the away team at tonight's playoff game. They had easily won their conference title and with the win tonight stood only one game away from the National Championship Title. I check the peephole and a good-looking face—minus the close-set eyes and slightly crooked jaw—grins at me.

"Really?" I drawl as I swing the door open. "You think wearing his tie will confuse me."

Ty self-consciously adjusts said tie. "Are you going to let me in?"

"Fine." I leave the door open and walk back to the television, where the commentators talk about Western State's national championship opponent. Ty doesn't come over and sit with me on the sofa.

He closes the door and then stands by it, staring at me.

"You're making me uncomfortable, Ty." I make a face at him. "Do I have eye liner on my nose or something?"

"You really can tell us apart, can't you."

It's not so much a question as a strange lament. He sounds almost mournful that I can see through his little games and tricks.

"Yes."

"How?"

"It's obvious." I don't tell him he's not as attractive as his brother because these boys have big, but tender egos.

"I came too early, didn't I? None of the team came back, so you knew it was me."

If that makes you feel better. Actually, no, I'm not letting him off the hook. "Jack came by twenty minutes ago." I point to the clock. "I figured Knox got cornered in the lobby by some enthusiastic booster."

Ty gets up and begins to pace. "Is it the way I talk? My time in the South has given me an accent, that it?"

"I think the time in the southern sun has baked your brain silly," I say. "Why does it matter? Isn't it a good thing?"

"Not for me." He frowns.

From the stories Knox has shared about the times they've pranked people, from their parents and teachers to girlfriends and coaches, I feel almost relieved I can tell them apart.

It'd be incredibly stressful figuring out who is who. Ty should feel grateful I'm not asking one of them to get a facial tattoo so it's easier for me to distinguish between the two of them.

"What's the deal with your names?" I ask, since Ty can't seem to wrap his head around the fact the two of them look completely different to me.

"What has Knox said?"

"Nothing. Although I've never asked. His is somewhat different. Yours is very unusual."

A dull flush spreads across his cheekbones. "Since you're part of the family, I'll tell you, but only if you swear on Knox's Achilles's tendon you won't tell another soul."

"That's your vow? On your brother's Achilles's tendon?" I roll my eyes. These two…it's a wonder their beautiful mother isn't completely gray by now.

"Do you swear it?" Ty presses.

I hold up my hand, palm out. "I, Eliot Anne Campbell, do solemnly swear never to reveal the origins of your names, even on threat of death, or else the Achilles's tendon of my beloved will be desecrated."

Ty nods in approval. "Nice vow, but you're Eliot Anne Masters now." Whoops. That's still so new I forgot. He threads his fingers together and then stretches his arms fully in front of him, pushing his palms outward, cracking about five knuckles in the process. "So my mom loves romances, specifically Scottish highlander historical ones. I may have even glimpsed a scene with my father wearing a kilt I didn't know he owned and my mother—" He shudders. "Let's not speak of it. I'm still traumatized."

I press my lips together to keep from busting out a laugh at Ty's wide-eyed horror. "You're named after authors? Places?"

He mumbles something into his hand.

"What was that? Shmeroes?" *Shmeroes? Is that even a word?*

"Heroes," he says. "Heroes. We're named after brawny fake highlanders that my mom read about before she met my father. Or after. Shit if I know."

I try not to laugh, but it's impossible. I fold over and end up falling off the sofa onto the floor, holding my stomach and roaring with glee. I can imagine the locker room talk if *that* choice tidbit got out.

"I wish you would have put that in your *SI* profile," I gasp out. Ty throws a pillow at my head.

I'm only partially composed when another sharp rap against the door rings out. I open it before looking through the peephole, figuring it's Jack or Knox's parents.

Instead, it's Knox wearing his blue wool suit and white shirt with a red and white tie draped around his neck, looking mouthwateringly beautiful.

"Why are you wearing your brother's tie?"

Knox gives me a slightly abashed look. "It was Ty's idea." He holds up his phone as if to show me texting proof Ty initiated this. "He said it'd make me feel good."

Exasperated, I place my hands on my hips. "And does it?"

He smiles and looks past me into the room where Ty stands. "Yeah, sorry. It really does."

I throw up my hands and stalk back into the room. I don't get far before Knox gathers me against him to bury his face in my neck. "God, I'm glad to see you. I thought you weren't coming."

"Your parents convinced me. Called it their late Christmas present to both of us." The ban remains in existence, so I can't go to the game. But I can stay in a hotel in the same city as the playoff game and if it just so happens to be the same hotel where the Western State football players are staying? Well, oops.

"Merry Christmas to me," he says in a low, throaty voice and turns me around.

"It's New Year's Eve," I remind him.

He ignores this and places a hot, open mouthed kiss against my neck. I shudder as his lips skate against my skin. His mouth crashes against mine and we forget where we are. That we aren't alone. That the door to the hallway is still open.

Ty's coughing and banging of doors has us reluctantly separating.

"Hate to break up this love fest, but Mom and Dad expected us about twenty minutes ago."

Knox's face is a portrait of disappointment.

I stroke his cheek. "I'm sorry. They wanted to see you tonight, too."

"They did," he complains. "They were outside the locker room. I already hugged them both." He slides a leg between mine. "Please say we don't have to go."

I swallow a tiny moan at the delicious friction, and for a second, my desire to haul Knox to bed swamps my good manners. Sense prevails at the last minute and I manage to peel myself off of him. "No, we have to go. It's the least we can do."

"Fine." He crosses his arms, clearly unhappy. "You wearing my jersey downstairs?"

"Nope. That was to give you good luck during the game."

I tug the large sack of fabric over my head, revealing a skintight black dress I found at a thrift store and that Riley tailored to fit my body. It's a gorgeous piece of real silk, formerly about three sizes too big. I had my doubts, but Riley insisted and the results look stunning.

Knox's mouth falls halfway open and even Ty's eyes have a glazed look to them.

"That's a real nice dress, baby," Knox croaks out as I waltz by him to pick up my clutch—also a thrift store find.

"Thanks." I pat his cheek, thrilled at the possessive, hungry way his eyes eat me up.

Dinner is excruciating. Every touch drives me crazy and it's the same for Knox. We can't keep our hands off each other, and yet the only way to make it through the dinner is to stay apart. I nearly cling to his mother while he stands awkwardly by his brother, eating me up with his eyes.

There are dozens of well-wishers here.

Ty's agent comes by, a brusque, bald man shorter than me. He's a lawyer, Knox tells me, hard-nosed and no-nonsense. There's not a whiff of scandal around him.

After what seems like hours later, we escape back to the hotel. We race each other to the bedroom. He sweeps my hair to the side and runs a broad hand down my back.

"Where's the zipper in this damn thing?" he growls against my neck.

"Side zipper." I lift my arm and show him the pull.

He tugs it down, running two warm fingers along the skin exposed as the zipper lowers. I don't quell the shiver that skates across the surface of my body, because I don't care if he knows how easily I'm seduced by him and his touch.

We have no more secrets between us.

In the crook of my neck, he buries his nose. His chest heaves against me as he inhales. "I started my life the day I met you. Everything before then was practice."

I clutch him closer. Words are easy for me to write, but so much harder to say. He's making it easier by loving me so freely.

"I never knew I could feel so happy until you came along. I never knew what it meant to belong…" I swallow hard because I don't want to cry. This is a time for celebration. I press my head down against his.

"I know, baby." His lips curve against the tender spot where the shoulder and neck meet. He loves it when I get emotional. "We didn't fall for each other. We fell into each other, and now we're carrying each other forward into our perfect future. I can't wait to spend every to-morrow with you." As if he knows that I've hit my limit, he pulls back and throws me on the bed. "But right now I can't wait until I'm inside of you."

Hairpins, ties, underwear go a million different directions until it's just Knox and me, skin to skin, mouth to mouth, heart to heart.

"I love you," he whispers as he moves above me.

His hands roam over my shoulders. The rough pads of his fingers scrape along my collarbone, over the rise of my breasts, pausing to cir-cle my hard nipples. Each touch feels more loving than the last.

"You're so beautiful," he says with reverence. "Beautiful and mine."

I push up against him, ready to be filled. He doesn't hurry, though. We have all the time in the world. Our whole future lies ahead of us.

He settles between my legs and his big frame pushes my legs farther apart until I'm completely exposed to his look, his touch, his caress. I lick my lips when he takes himself in his hand and positions himself at my entrance.

I curve around him, fitting my body against his in the perfect way we learned suits us best. Into his hard edges, I rub my soft parts. He strokes me with a firm and knowing grip, finding that little spongy flesh that makes my toes curl and elicits a sharp, reedy sound from the back of my throat.

"I know you'll win next week," I tell him with a tired and happy smile.

"Doesn't matter." He cups my chin tenderly. "I've already won the most important game of my life."

EPILOGUE

ELLIE

EVE OF DRAFT

"SO MY AGENT SAYS I'LL be drafted by the New York Cobras." Knox gets off the phone and happily lays it on the table. He's not at all perturbed that he'll be the third pick in the draft instead of the first. "He should be here in about ten minutes."

Knox's agent arranged for us to have a dinner together with the family before the draft tomorrow. Knox and I arrived early for once. Usually we're late because we're too busy being newlyweds. Secretly I think his agent may have lied about the time we needed to be at dinner.

If it has to do with football, Knox is on time. With any other obligation, he's more interested in keeping me in bed with him.

"That's so wrong. You should be number one." I'm upset on his behalf. He's the best player in college football despite being a junior, and despite not being a quarterback or left tackle.

He shrugs, clearly not disappointed. "I'm happy. I'm playing with a contender. They have Oliver Graham and he's got a rocket for an arm. If he can get his interception ratio down, the team will have a real chance at a title." He rubs his hands together. "Besides, the difference in signing bonus for the first and third picks is barely a million. Seventeen versus sixteen. I'm really not broken up about that."

"I don't care about the money," I tell him. "I just think you deserve first."

"As long as I'm first to you, baby." He winks. "There's a shit ton of good schools in New York City. Like Columbia. If you move with me, we can set up residency, and you'd get in-state tuition to SUNY if you still insist on paying your own way."

This last bit comes out a little disgruntled. We've had some arguments about money. Even though we're married, I want to work and pay my way through college. I only have a year and a half left, and I know I can do it.

"So I should move with you to New York?" I raise an eyebrow.

"Yes."

"All right." I pick up my wine glass and take a hefty swallow.

"But if you don't—wait. What?" He tilts his head as if not quite sure he's heard me.

"I'll move."

"You will?"

After we'd gotten married, I told Knox I planned to stay in school, but as the semester wore on, with me waiting tables while Knox cooled his heels in classes and worked out every spare minute, I realized I didn't want to be separated from him.

"I don't want to live without you. And I think flying to all your games would be impossible, so I'm willing to move to New York. I'm sure I can get a job somewhere, and I'll save more money given the higher wages. Granted, that will be easier because I'm living with you." His mouth hangs slightly open. I frown. "You going to say anything?"

In a slightly peevish tone he replies, "I've been working on my argument and you've kind of ruined it."

Laughing, I lean over and kiss him on the cheek. "You can fill me in later at the hotel room, and I'll be in the proper position to say yes."

"What's that position?" His voice deepens.

"Whichever one you'd like," I reply saucily and squeeze my legs together at the thought of which positions he likes best.

"Do we have to finish this dinner?" he whines.

"Yes." I smooth my napkin over my lap. "Your agent is coming, along with your parents and Ty."

Knox drums his fingers against the white tablecloth. "No, I don't think I can wait." He takes my hand and places it between his legs. My fingers curl reflexively around the quickly thickening shaft. He groans. "You know what's on my list? Bathroom sex."

"We've had that," I respond primly but I don't remove my hand. It feels too good around his hard length. "We did it in the second floor bathroom in Walker Hall and the basement bathroom in Carter along with the nightclub in Miami that your agent took us to."

"Mmm." He looks upward. "That was a good night. Real good."

I blush because it's actually one of my favorite memories, too. Knox and I clung to each other on the dance floor of this incredibly posh nightclub and then found out the bathrooms in the VIP section were individual rooms. Knox made good use of that privacy. He pushed me over the sink, ripped my panties down, and hammered into me so hard I worried the sink would break off. That is, I worried until I couldn't focus on anything but his hard cock driving into my—

"Stop thinking about that night," he growls in my ear. I jolt to attention.

"How do you know what I'm thinking?"

He grunts. "Your eyes are all glazed and your cheeks flushed. Your hand is glued to my dick. It's like you want me to throw you down on the table."

I don't want that…do I? I look at the table and then at the surrounding patrons. It's very crowded but the pulse between my legs begins to throb uncomfortably.

"Ahem."

Knox and I look up to see Ty rolling his eyes. I pull my hand off Knox's dick. Knox and I look at Ty and then at each other.

"Ty, you look very nice in your suit," I say and pull the napkin off my lap to set it on the table.

His eyes narrow. "Um, thanks."

Knox and I stand as one.

"So, here's the deal," Knox says. "I need to go back to the hotel. Ellie's not feeling well."

I place a limp, maidenly wrist to my forehead and moan in what I hope is a sickly, not sexy, way.

"Right," Ty snorts.

Knox thrusts his napkin against Ty's chest. "You're me tonight. Don't sign anything and text me if the deal gets close."

"Bye!" I wave to Ty as Knox drags me away.

Not even the entrance of his parents or his agent slows him.

"Knox is back at the table. Ellie's not feeling well, so I, Ty, am taking her home," he announces to his parents. "Nice to see you again, Randolph."

Knox, pretending to be Ty, shakes Randolph's hand. His agent has no idea that he's greeting the wrong brother, but Knox's mom's eyes drop immediately to his left hand. Knox shoves it into his pants pocket to hide the ring.

His parents watch with suspicious eyes as Knox drags me outside. They might not tell the twins apart all the time, but they know their boys well enough to recognize shenanigans when they see it.

Outside Knox throws money at the valet. "We need a cab, please. My wife—" I jab him in the waist—"My brother's wife," he inserts awkwardly, "isn't feeling well."

"Sure, no problem. Aren't you Knox Masters?" the attendant asks.

"No. His brother. I play at MU."

"Tell your brother congrats and that we're rooting for him to go high."

"I will."

A cab pulls to a stop and Knox nearly shoves me inside. He clambers in. "The Warwick. At Fifty Fourth and—" He looks at me.

"Sixth Avenue," I finish.

He gives me a grateful wink and then reaches for me. I bat his hand away. "No."

"What?" He reaches for me again.

"You're Ty," I hiss in an undertone. I can see the cab driver watching us in the rear view mirror.

Knox rears back. "I'm who?"

"I mean you're pretending to be Ty so you can't touch me. What if someone sees us and they think I'm cheating on you?"

"But you're not," he argues.

"You told the valet you were Ty. He could tell some gossip rag that he saw you, Ty, get into a cab with Knox's wife."

"You want me to die don't you?" He runs a hand down the front of his pants.

I force myself to look out the window.

The cab ride takes forever.

I force him to stand at the other side of the elevator. He sticks his hands in his pockets and stares at the ceiling. I shift uncomfortably from one foot to the other, growing wetter by the second.

We nearly run from the elevator car to our hotel room. Knox must really have been dying because he has me bent over the sofa in the suite before the door behind us fully latches. My panties drop to my ankles before I can take a full breath. Before I can take another, he's shoving himself inside me. The expensive dress he insisted on buying me gets crumpled between us as he takes me relentlessly, with one merciless thrust after another.

The wool of his pants abrades the backs of my thighs. He tangles a hand in my hair and roughly pulls my head back so he can kiss me.

I love it.

I wouldn't have it any other way.

"You feel so fucking good right now." He bites my ear. "If we'd have stayed in that restaurant, swear to God, I would have bent you over the table and taken you in front of all those people."

"You have untreated exhibitionist fantasies," I gasp.

He shifts his hips and effortlessly lifts me higher so he can drive into me even harder. "No, I just want you 24/7."

His fingers dig into my butt and I know I'll have bruises there tomorrow. Bruises that he'll kiss and smile evilly about later when we're waiting for his name to be called by the commissioner.

And then he shuts up, because neither of us is in any condition to talk. I plead for him to take me harder and he tells me he's going to fuck me into the next room.

I come so hard I see stars.

"You have to carry me," I tell him when I come down off my high.

"Yes, ma'am."

He picks me up as if I weigh nothing and carts me over to the bed. His erection brushes against my butt.

"Already?" I ask.

"I know. Even I'm amazed at my greatness sometimes," he says smugly. Then he throws me on the bed for round two.

Loved SACKED*? Don't miss* USA Today
bestselling author Jen Frederick's fabulous
New Adult series...

UNDECLARED

For four years, Grace Sullivan wrote to a Marine she never met, and fell in love. But when his deployment ended, so did the letters. Ever since that day, Grace has been coasting, academically and emotionally. The one thing she's decided? No way is Noah Jackson — or any man — ever going to break her heart again.

Noah has always known exactly what he wants out of life. Success. Stability. Control. That's why he joined the Marines and that's why he's fighting his way -- literally -- through college. Now that he's got the rest of his life on track, he has one last conquest: Grace Sullivan. But since he was the one who stopped writing, he knows that winning her back will be his biggest battle yet.

ISBN 978-0989247917 • Available in Print and Ebook

UNSPOKEN

Whore. Slut. Typhoid Mary. I've been called all these at Central College. One drunken night, one act of irresponsible behavior, and my reputation was ruined. Guys labeled me as easy and girls shied away. To cope, I stayed away from Central social life and away from Central men, so why is it that my new biology lab partner is so irresistible to me? A former Marine involved in illegal fighting with a quick trigger temper and an easy smile for all the women. He's sliding his way into my heart and I'm afraid that he's going to be the one to break me.

ISBN 978-0989247955 • Available in Print and Ebook

UNRAVELED

Twenty-five-year-old Sgt. Gray Phillips is at a crossroads in his life: stay in the Marine Corps or get out and learn to be a civilian? He's got forty-five days of leave to make up his mind but the people in his life aren't making the decision any easier. His dad wants him to get out; his grandfather wants him to stay in. And his growing feelings for Sam Anderson are wreaking havoc with his heart…and his mind. He believes relationships get ruined when a Marine goes on deployment. So now he's got an even harder decision to make: take a chance on Sam or leave love behind and give his all to the Marines.

ISBN 978-0991426713 • Available in Print and Ebook

UNREQUITED

Winter Donovan loves two things: her sister and her sister's ex boyfriend. She's spent her whole life doing the right thing except that one time, that night when Finn O'Malley looked hollowed out by his father's death. Then she did something very wrong that felt terribly right....Finn can't stop thinking about Winter and the night and he'll do anything to make her a permanent part of his life, even if it means separating Winter from the only family she has...Their love was supposed to be unrequited but one grief stricken guy and one girl with too big of a heart results in disastrous consequences

ISBN 978-1511721349 • Available in Print and Ebook

THE CHARLOTTE CHRONICLES

Charlotte Randolph believed in fairytale endings...And when she's diagnosed with a rare brain tumor at age fifteen, she decides to pursue exactly what she wants. And she wants Nathan Jackson. Her best friend, her neighbor, and her fiercest defender....Charlotte believes their new relationship can withstand anything, even as miles separate them due to her treatment and Nathan's enlistment in the Navy SEALs....Until Nathan abandons their happy ever after.

ISBN 978-1505480269 • Available in Print and Ebook

When a dangerous killer falls for a sheltered innocent, he'll cross every line just to have her...

NEW YORK TIMES BESTSELLING AUTHOR
JESSICA CLARE

USA TODAY BESTSELLING AUTHOR
JEN FREDERICK

LAST HIT

NIKOLAI

I have been a contract killer since I was a boy. For years I savored the fear caused by my name, the trembling at the sight of my tattoos. The stars on my knees, the marks on my fingers, the dagger in my neck, all bespoke of danger. If you saw my eyes, it was the last vision you'd have. I have ever been the hunter, never the prey. With her, I am the mark and I am ready to lie down and let her capture me. Opening my small scarred heart to her brings out my enemies. I will carry out one last hit, but if they hurt her, I will bring the world down around their ears.

DAISY

I've been sheltered from the outside world all my life. Homeschooled and farm-raised, I'm so naive that my best friend calls me Pollyanna. I like to believe the best in people. Nikolai is part of this new life, and he's terrifying to me. Not because his eyes are cold or my friend warns me away from him, but because he's the only man that has ever seen the real me beneath the awkwardness. With him, my heart is at risk..and also, my life.

When a dangerous killer falls for a sheltered innocent, he'll cross every line just to have her...

NEW YORK TIMES BESTSELLING AUTHOR
JESSICA CLARE

USA TODAY BESTSELLING AUTHOR
JEN FREDERICK

LAST HIT

NIKOLAI

I have been a contract killer since I was a boy. For years I savored the fear caused by my name, the trembling at the sight of my tattoos. The stars on my knees, the marks on my fingers, the dagger in my neck, all bespoke of danger. If you saw my eyes, it was the last vision you'd have. I have ever been the hunter, never the prey. With her, I am the mark and I am ready to lie down and let her capture me. Opening my small scarred heart to her brings out my enemies. I will carry out one last hit, but if they hurt her, I will bring the world down around their ears.

DAISY

I've been sheltered from the outside world all my life. Homeschooled and farm-raised, I'm so naive that my best friend calls me Pollyanna. I like to believe the best in people. Nikolai is part of this new life, and he's terrifying to me. Not because his eyes are cold or my friend warns me away from him, but because he's the only man that has ever seen the real me beneath the awkwardness. With him, my heart is at risk..and also, my life.

About the Author

Jen Frederick lives with her husband, child, and one rambunctious dog. She's been reading stories all her life but never imagined writing one of her own. Jen loves to hear from readers, so drop her a line at jen@jenfrederick.com, or visit her website at www.jenfrederick.com.

Facebook: AuthorJenFrederick   Twitter: @JenSFred

Made in the USA
San Bernardino, CA
19 November 2016